RED
FLAGS

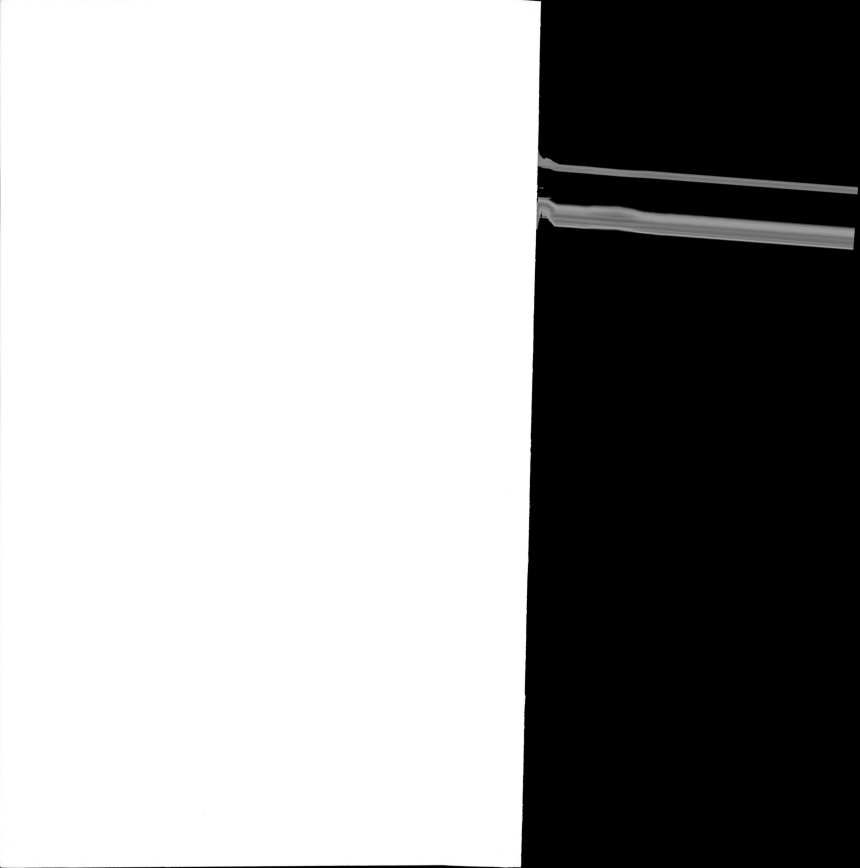

For Mary.

You started this. Now you have to read it.

PUBLISHED BY WORDS AND WOOD
Wilmington, NC
WWW.WORDSANDWOOD.COM

ISBN-13: 978-1517131029
ISBN-10: 1517131022

RED FLAGS

PROLOGUE

On your first trip, there are plastic buckets and shovels, beach balls, and flimsy umbrellas for shade. Then, sandcastles and bigger creations but the water always takes them away. There are rafts, boogie boards, and dad lifting you over the big waves. Then he takes you out where it gets deep—so deep that you yell back to shore and wave for mom to look at you.

There are new friends and sand is thrown by the fistfuls at the boys, then at the girls—who you run away from, then you turn around and chase. Paddle ball, the arcade on the pier, and getting away from mom and dad. They wave for you to come back but you walk away with a group of boys—the girls join too.

Then there is one girl and another chase begins. You catch her, but you run again because you are scared—*that* is what the beach is, what it becomes. Simple marvels; holes that miraculously fill with water, caving in upon themselves no matter how much sand you pull out; sandbars, shells, ghost crabs, piers to walk to, dunes to climb—everything is magic and pure. You are on vacation. The beach lures you with the unknown. The ordinary is left at home—back in another state or town where it is always a few degrees colder.

You grow older and wish for those memories again. You go back to the beach but it isn't the same; you can't leave that other state or town completely. There's a job you hate and a boss you want to throw sand at. There is less pleasure in digging a hole—only frustration because you have learned that life always fills it with more than you can manage. There were friends that disappeared when you needed them; teachers and parents who were human; girls that didn't love you as much as you loved them. The hole always fills back in.

I wasn't on vacation during the summer of 1993. I didn't hate the hum of fluorescent lights then or appreciate the lonely satisfaction of a strong cup of coffee in a quiet cubicle. When I drift back to this beach I catch myself and shake it out of my head. It's just a daydream now for all but this one week.

That was the summer the beach became something else—something more than a vacation. I am once again consumed by it all—so engrossed by the simplicity of sitting on the beach of my youth, at this moment in my life, that I don't hear the girl screaming for help.

A mother sees her child and starts the alarm. She runs to the edge of the water and calls out. Cresting waves absorb her voice and block her view. Past them, a current pulls the little girl away from the shore. The mother stands still, hands covering her terrified expression. With each flushing wave her feet sink into the sand. The water in front of her boils, swirls, and dances with the continuous wash.

The little girl's hair wraps around her face like black seaweed. She has only enough energy to fight for air between waves—not enough to call out or wipe the hair away from her eyes. Her tiny arms are nearly lost in the middle of a large patch of seafoam.

The beach is a statue garden. I stand powerless and confused. Reality hits me when the woman drops to her knees. Her hands wilt and fall from her face. A man stands up in front of me. We never take our eyes off of the child. I drop my book, toss my sunglasses—the other man leaves his on—and we sprint to the water. I beat him by a few steps and when I pass the mother, I hear her cry with a faint breath, "Help."

I lose sight of the girl until a wave breaks in front of me. When I see her again she is ten yards farther out. The waves beat the shore in thunderous lines. I high-step through the water until it gets knee-deep. A large set wave forms in front of me. I prepare to dive through the face but stumble when I hit a hole and my right leg buckles. My entire body twists and I fall to my knees. The cold wall of water smacks me on the side of the head—knocking me flat. The sky and water mix into a blur of blue and tepid green.

The onslaught of waves continues one after another. I push myself up but the sea grabs me. There is a flash of red in front of me. It joins the other colors swirling around my head. My chin hits the ground, causing my teeth to snap together. My face scrapes against the sandy bottom. I am being pulled, but all sense of direction escapes me. I steal quick breaths when I can.

The red is gone as fast as it appeared, but air is my only concern. My hand grabs onto the sand. It gathers in my fists, but I keep being pulled. I claw and kick but my feet slip on the sand.

Then it's over.

The set subsides and I manage to crawl to the beach. The water drains from my eyes and shapes come into focus. Waves suck out as I move against them. The sand is dry now and it gathers in the corner of my mouth. I roll onto my back, expecting to see red.

"Hey, buddy."

An upside down figure looms over me, the shade he

casts allows a partial view of his face after my eyes adjust. He wears dark sunglasses and I recognize him as the man I beat to the water.

"You okay?" He reaches down and offers to help me up. I extend my arm and feel his large hands wrap around my wrist. He pulls, but I only manage to sit up. Water drains out of my nose. My forehead burns where I hit the ground but my fingers run across it and produce no blood. I touch my swollen lip—the side without sand—again, no blood. Then I remember the girl.

The mother is still on her knees. Water passes around her like she's a permanent fixture.

"The girl?"

The man, facing the ocean, points. His hand drifts down the beach with the lateral current. "There."

I scan the water and see where he is pointing. A blaze-orange buoy splashes against the incoming waves. Its brightness a stark contrast to the wash of soft greens, blues, and creams. It bounces and dances its way over and through the aggressive surf as if propelled by a motor.

The line on the buoy goes slack and then tightens as a wave approaches. I see the swimmer on the other end of the rope when the wave passes. From this distance all I can make out are his rhythmic strokes. He uses the current in his race to the little girl.

Spectators silently cheer. The mother sinks farther in the sand. She can't see over the head-high shore-break. The man with the sunglasses tries to comfort her with it'll-be-okays but she doesn't hear it.

She lost her daughter.

On vacation.

She will drive home with an empty seat in the minivan—a long trip north to Ohio or Pennsylvania. Back to an empty bedroom. Her daughter's friends will not understand when they come looking for her.

She's still at the beach.

I don't know what the girl is thinking during the last

moments before the sea swallows her. I can't see her face from here. My own breath is gone—caught in the same rip current. I hear nothing above the surf and it'll-be-okays.

Then the swimmer calls to the little girl and we all hear it clearly. It's the only thing the wind carries back to us. The mother stands up.

There's a mechanical rumble behind me. A calm voice speaks, but not to me. I turn to see a boy —no more than twenty years old—sitting on a four-wheeler within arm's reach of me. His blonde hair is pushed back and tucked behind red ears. The skin on the top of his nose is pink and raw from peeling. Black sunglasses wrap around his face like a shield. His feet are bare. He is toned from his legs to his chest. He rises from the seat of his four-wheeler, stands on the footrests, and looks out over the water. The V of his abdomen plunges into red shorts.

He cups his hands around a radio and I hear him say, "705, 10-23. Lifeguard has reached victim."

I look at the water and see the swimmer and the little girl drifting south with the current. The swimmer raises his arm and bends it down, touching his head and forming a crude circle.

The boy looks to his right. "Lifeguard and victim are 10-4. Victim is in-tow. Cancel all other response."

Down the beach a few hundred yards, red flashing lights zigzag from the dune to the water's edge and back up again. The boy sits down again and past him I see the lights go off. The truck settles into ruts in the sand and makes its way toward us slow and straight.

The boy looks down at me from his four-wheeler. He is assessing me—passing judgment on an old fool who tried to do something he has long outgrown. He smiles and it kills me—perfect teeth, controlled arrogance, youth; I want it all. I want to confide in him that I was once a lifeguard here—that this was *my* beach a lifetime ago; but I know it is a stupid thing to say.

"Hard part's over now." His voice is deep, but I hear

years of change to come.

I long for the power—for the authority to do no wrong. It was handed to us each morning with our whistle and stand assignment. For a split second, I am the one standing tall, knowing everything is in control.

The swimmer has the girl in waist-deep water. I recognize the red that flashed before me while I got tossed around like a broken shell. The color is wrapped around a solid body from the shoulders to the waist and I marvel at the package it contains. She—not he—holds the girl with one arm and the orange buoy with the other.

"*No fucking girl will ever work here.*" I hear Rick's voice from two decades earlier—like water I can never shake from my head.

This girl, probably in college, walks out of the water with the same confidence as the boy standing next to me. He doesn't move to help her; he only smiles. She returns it between catching her breath and making small talk with the child. I used to ask if they had pets. Children rarely cry when they talk about their pets.

The little girl walks with her head up—searching the beach for her mother. The sandy chains loosen their grip and send the mother running to her child. Only when she grabs the little girl does the lifeguard let go.

I walk away from the scene, back to my chair and my book. I pick up my sunglasses. The sand crunches in my teeth and I spit a few times—quietly. A red truck pulls up, sirens off, but lights still spin around, doing little more than reflecting the sun. The driver doesn't get out but the lost eighteen-year-old in me recognizes him. He doesn't see me and I am relieved. He looks at the lifeguards, nods, turns off the lights, and continues down the beach.

"Lifeguards for Life" was our motto. It was written on the back of our T-shirts, stamped on the training manuals, and embroidered on our jackets. We said it with a mocking teenage tone that speaks of being proud and too cool at the same time. I think about the stories and try to understand how boys—trying to become men—were failed by trust. The salt water still burns my eyes when I think about the night he died here on the beach.

CHAPTER 1

"Don't come home with a tattoo." My father stood with one arm around my mother in the driveway. He called across the yard and lifted his hand. "Use rubbers!"

She nodded and waved. With the Jeep in reverse, I looked through the windshield and waved back.

"She's scared I won't go to school when the season's over." I looked over my shoulder to the road and cut the wheel."

"Yeah, I can see that." Harry nodded along with the radio.

"Well, I can't break the hundred year tradition," I said with a derisive tone. I habitually mocked my private school upbringing in an effort to distance myself from the trust-fund preps I graduated with. We waved until the house was out of sight.

"Is it a hundred years of students getting accepted to college, or actually *going* to college?" Harry read my mind.

"I don't know. Who cares?"

"Exactly." Harry used his fingers as drum sticks on the dash and then smacked the visor. "Let's go to the beach!"

It was years before the expressway from Virginia Beach aided the flood of northern tourists in their annual summer migration. Harry and I took back roads past forgotten farms and crossroad towns. The road straightened out when we hit the North Carolina line and ran under a canopy of old-growth cypress along the Dismal Swamp.

"I always thought the Dismal Swamp was make-believe." Harry watched the ancient trees pass overhead.

"I thought it was in Florida."

The smell of brackish water grew strong long before we came to the curve on Highway 158 before the bridge. The bay water was choppy and slapped us with a chilly welcome that we weren't prepared for in our topless Jeep.

"Isn't it supposed to be hot at the beach?" Harry buttoned his letterman jacket to the top.

"It's only May." I turned on the heater. "There's plenty of time for it to warm up."

The excitement of reaching our destination kept me from pulling over and raising the top. The bridge, low in the center, rose slowly to a hump over the channel—high enough for a normal boat to pass under. My hands on the steering wheel stung from the cold wind but I couldn't wipe the smile off my face. The tires clicked and hummed as they left the concrete bridge and rolled onto the smooth asphalt of our home for the next four months.

Beautiful waterfront houses greeted us on the left. The homes, set between loblolly pines and knobby cedars, were more rugged than mainland buildings. Built to withstand hurricanes and coastal storms, they had a whimsy that lured everyone who saw them to dream of packing it all up and moving to the beach for the rest of their lives.

On the right, there was a mini-golf course with real grass and unnatural blue ponds. Just past it, a car dealership sprawled along the highway and seemed unnatural in this setting. Why, I thought to myself, would anyone drive here to buy a car?

My eyes drifted to the sexy hood of a silver Corvette peeking out from a long line of station wagons and sedans.

"Cop!" Harry pointed at the Vette, a late seventies model with a silver star painted on the side.

"Shit. Why don't you just wave at him?" I looked at my speedometer; sixty-two.

We couldn't help but stare at the cop sitting in the driver's seat of Corvette as we passed. He watched us drive by and lowered his radar gun.

"What a sneaky bastard."

"What's the speed limit?"

"Fifty-five, I think."

It took no time for the Vette to catch up to our Jeep and chirp his siren.

I pulled to the side, rolling to a stop directly in front of a black and white sign that read, "Speed Limit, 50."

"You've got to be kidding me."

The officer took his time getting out of his car. He looked young for a cop, but his high and tight haircut assured me that I was screwed.

"Driver's license and registration, please."

I reached across Harry and fumbled around in the glove box. Two years worth of gas station receipts fell to the floor pan and swirled around in the wind. A few blew out and landed on the ground. I looked up at the officer. He raised an eyebrow and looked at them.

"Man, get those." I pointed past Harry.

He unbuckled his seat belt and stepped out of the Jeep. I turned back to the hand the officer my information.

"In a rush to get your summer started?"

"Yeah, sorry. I didn't realize the speed limit dropped when you get off the bridge."

"You were going sixty-two. That's speeding even on the bridge." He turned to go back to his car. "Be right back."

I saved money throughout my senior year; a birthday

check from my great grandmother, graduation checks from random family members, squirreled away lunch money I didn't use. I couldn't afford any kind of ticket. Harry and I barely covered the deposit for the house we rented.

"Think I got 'em all." Harry climbed back into his seat. He looked over his shoulder at the cop sitting in his car. "Think you're gonna get a ticket?"

"I've got a Virginia license and tags, probably."

"Sorry about pointing."

"Don't worry about it. He had me as soon as I came off the bridge." I looked in the rear-view mirror. "Here he comes."

The officer handed me my paperwork.

"Where're y'all working?"

"North Dare Watersports."

"Well, slow down." He actually smiled. "Old Grandy won't care if you're a little late to work as long as you get there."

"Oh, you know Mr. Grandy?"

"It's a small beach Mr. Brooks." He looked at the paper in his hands.

"I guess so." I smiled and hoped that was a good thing.

"This is a written warning. It won't affect your record."

"Thank you officer," I glanced at his nameplate, "Laverman."

"Have a good summer, boys." He started to walk back to his car. "Stay out of trouble."

Harry leaned toward my side and called out, "Is it always this cold in May?"

"If you don't like the weather, wait five minutes." Laverman lifted his hand and continued to his car without looking back.

I looked at Harry and shrugged. What a welcome. We didn't talk for the last few miles. The wind howled through the Jeep. I was pretty sure it would blow us off the road if I had the top on.

My family vacationed on the Outer Banks for as long as I could remember. I was comfortable with the layout of the beach and it gave me a feeling of ownership. I wasn't like all of the other tourists; I grew up here, albeit a week at a time.

Harry vacationed with me the summer after our junior year. He had a break from summer football practices and it was that vacation when we hatched the idea to move to the beach the day after graduation. We collected pamphlets for restaurants, surf shops, Jet Ski rental businesses, and hotels. Over the course of the school year we arranged for a place to live, without a clue what it looked like. I convinced the owner of North Dare Watersports, Mr. Grandy, that I was practically an expert at fixing small boat engines.

Harry got a job working at an all-you-can-eat seafood buffet called George's Junction, a short walk from the house. He didn't have a car for the first couple weeks. His older brother, stationed in Norfolk, was shipping out and leaving his car for Harry.

I turned left from the four-lane bypass onto Neptune Street.

"That's it, 102." Harry pointed ahead.

"There's no way." I looked at the number on the directions and again at the house. It matched.

The cottage was perched ten feet high on old creosote treated telephone poles. It was built sometime in the sixties, after a destructive storm forced the building regulations to change, calling for all new houses to be up on stilts. The porch on the front ran the width of the house. The red paint on the railing was dark and peeling. There were no shutters on the windows. The screen door hung crooked and slightly open.

Harry couldn't hide his excitement. He hopped out of the Jeep before I cut off the engine and ran up the stairs. He spread his hands out wide and then looked toward the ocean.

"You can see the water from here." He pointed and rose up on his toes to see over the sand dunes a short block away. I smiled and shook my head. It was perfect.

The rumble of the motor gave way to the sound of crashing waves. Then I heard voices coming from under the house near a back storage closet. I looked hard to try and figure out where exactly they were coming from.

I walked under the porch and heard running water. There was an outdoor shower behind the storage closet with steam rising above the plywood walls and four feet visible below them.

I retreated back to the front of the house to make sure, once again, that it was the right place. The front door was wide open and I couldn't see Harry anywhere. It was the right house so I went back toward the shower.

"Hello?"

The feet shuffled around and then froze. The water cut off and I heard the squeaking knobs turn to a stop. I took a step back again to avoid looking into the stall. The door opened. A naked man walked out and retrieved a brown towel from a nail on one of the poles.

He wiped his face dry and only then covered himself up by wrapping the towel around his waist. He slicked his long hair back and tied it up with a rubber band from his wrist. A large wave tattoo stretched across his chest and peaked at the base of his neck. It was the most impressive tattoo I had ever seen in person but I did my best not to stare.

"You live here?" He gave me a quick once over and took a towel off a different nail. He reached into the stall and the towel disappeared.

"Yeah." I looked up at the rafters and all around to hide my uneasiness. "Well, we're moving in today." I pointed up, just in case it wasn't clear.

"I'm Lucas. That's Liz." He nodded toward the shower. A hand reached over the side of the stall and waved in my direction. "We live next door."

"I'm Wesley." I looked at the house to the right of ours.

The exterior was a sprawling patchwork of closed in porches and concrete landings. The complex was more like several little cottages stacked on top of each other, all with different siding and various shades of cream colored paint. There were at least five different doors leading into the place and each had a letter above it.

"Are those apartments?"

"Shit-hole cell blocks." Lucas slipped his sandals on. "That's why we shower over here. Ours doesn't have any pressure. You don't mind, do you?"

"Um, no." I didn't feel like I could stop Lucas either way. "I don't think that's a problem. I'll tell my roommate."

"Thanks." He looked at me and it was clear that the conversation was over.

"All right, well, I'm gonna get my stuff upstairs."

Lucas nodded, but didn't say anything. I walked back to the Jeep and leaned into the back for one of my bags. As I gathered my stuff I looked over my shoulder and, through the windshield, saw Liz step out of the shower stall. She had jet black hair that tapered to a wet point between her shoulder blades. She held her towel closed in front of her, letting it hang loose in the back. I didn't see any tattoos and decided she was pretty based on the quick glance.

I backed out of the Jeep and heard Lucas call out, "Hey, you surf?"

"No. But I want to learn."

They both smiled. I was right about Liz. She had sharp eyes and I could tell from her face that she was much younger than Lucas. It was easy to call her sexy.

"We've got a couple old boards lying around. I'll grab you the next time I paddle out."

"That'd be great."

"Least I can do for letting us use the shower and

all." He raised his hand and they walked toward their place. Liz skipped through the cold air, hopping from one patch of sand to the next to avoid sand spurs and cacti.

I retrieved a few boxes from the small back seat of the Jeep and made my way upstairs. The house was furnished with crate-style chairs and couches and worn down everything else. A rental property for years, it was stocked with random dishes and linens. The faux wood walls were adorned with the requisite nautical themed pictures and a fishnet collage. Two ceiling fans hung from vaulted rafters in the living room and one over the table in the dining area.

Harry called from down the hallway, "I'm gonna take this bedroom if you don't mind. It's got a shitter in it."

"That's fine." I put a box of groceries on the kitchen counter—spoils from a quick raid of my parent's pantry before I left home. "This place smells like a thrift store." I flipped light switches until the ceiling fans came on and wrestled with the kitchen window to get some fresh air inside.

"Is water included in the rent?" I waited for a response from Harry, but he was already taking advantage of the convenient facilities in his room.

Harry was the youngest of three siblings. With two older sisters, he developed a way of charming girls with his unassuming smile and blue eyes. He was the definition of non-threatening and he used it to his advantage every chance he got.

I unpacked some clothes and took stock of my new room. The queen-sized bed faced a sliding glass door leading out to a back deck. I shook my head again at my good fortune.

"Not a bad view." Harry leaned against the doorframe behind me.

He was right. There was nothing between our house and the beach road but empty lots filled with sea oats and a few timeless cottages.

"I was hoping for oceanfront, but I guess this'll work."

Harry laughed. "You wanna go check out the beach?"

"Let's do it."

The temperature dropped with each step we took toward the ocean. We walked over the dunes and it plummeted ten degrees. The damp air smelled of seaweed, dune grass, and wet sand. The wind howled out of the northeast and the water pushed all the way to the stairs of the beach access—the normally wide stretch of beach was reduced to about fifteen yards.

A couple walked hand in hand but they were too far away to be sure of their age—they could have been fifteen or fifty. A lifeguard was there too. No one was swimming or even considering it, but the guard sat up in his stand, huddled under a tilted umbrella—a makeshift windscreen—bundled from head to toe. I stood near the stand in my bathing suit and sandals while he hunched over and adjusted the collar on his red jacket. He wore socks, sweatpants, and a knit hat. He looked like he was riding a chair lift on a ski slope.

The faded chalkboard on the side of his stand read, "Lifeguard - Ed; Water Temperature - 58; Advisories - Look out for Rips."

I looked down at my bathing suit and inspected it for any tears that might be embarrassing. He turned his head and nodded at me. He wore dark sunglasses even though it was overcast and looked at me for an extra second, probably trying to figure out my swimming intentions. The sloppy surf and cool air cured any desire I had to even touch the water. I looked up and down the beach once more and turned back to the steps of the access. Harry hadn't even gone down the stairs to the sand. Ed slouched in his chair and returned his stare to the water.

CHAPTER 2

The steady wind that welcomed us on our drive in lasted for two weeks. I'd never heard the term nor'easter—rather I'd never paid enough attention, but I quickly learned that the unforgiving wind was as much a resident of the beaches as the tides. Everything outside of the house was coated in a grimy film of salt spray from the onshore blow. We hadn't ventured to the beach since the first day. From our deck I could see the water churned up with mustard colored foam whipping around what sand was visible.

I got up early each day and called the sailing center to see if it would be open. The water on the bay side was warmer and calmer but the sporadic rain and cold gusts coming from the ocean side made renting kayaks and small boats undesirable at best. Despite the terrible conditions, the tourists still showed up on the dock. The fanny-pack wearing, all-you-can-eat buffet fools were determined to get their hard earned money's worth. I looked at them through narrowed eyes when they pointed at the Jet Skis and said, "How fast do those things go?"

"It's pretty cold once you get out there." I'd pause before turning over the keys and give them one last chance to back out. It never worked.

If all I had to do was watch the people zip back and forth from the gazebo I wouldn't have cared. Unfortunately, each time a Jet Ski went out for an hour, someone had to be out there with them, sitting and freezing.

When there weren't any customers we sat around the gazebo and I listened to my co-workers tell stories from summers past. Their attitudes were contagious and we bonded over the fact that we weren't tourists anymore. Most of us were transplants that had the same dream of moving to the beach. True locals grew up around tourists. They moved amongst the northern invaders without really seeing them unless it was to take their money or their food order. The natives' was an existence just below the surface of this beautiful place. They led real lives with mortgages, kids in school, and worries of saving enough money to make it through the winters.

The Outer Banks had long been a safe haven for people from all over the East Coast. Shipwrecked sailors washed up on the beaches and some never left. Hunters from New York set up lodges that became family homes. Even the oldest fishermen on the piers were from Pennsylvania or Ohio.

On a map, the Outer Banks are the northeastern most sliver of North Carolina. The location, however, had no bearing on the customs and mannerisms. There was hardly a trace of true "Eastern North Carolina"—that blue-collar, tobacco stained, pulled-pork way of life that made people wave in passing just for the sake of it.

Brett, a thirty-year-old manager who was raised just across the bridge in Currituck County, told us the story of a family that rented a catamaran a few years before. He started by shaking his head and pointing out to one of the twin-hulled boats tied near the shore and covered in bird shit.

"We're all sitting here waiting for Grandy to tell us to go home. Shit was blowing thirty knots and we hadn't rented anything all day. This family comes up and you could tell the two kids wanted nothing to do with it. The mother was pushing the two girls but she didn't want to go out either. We told them, 'Y'all come back tomorrow,' but they were checking out the next day and the father was determined to show everyone what a sailor he was. I called Grandy in the office and he said to let them go—I couldn't believe it."

Brett looked up at the second-story office above the dockside and continued, "I gave them their safety speech and about a hundred opportunities to change their minds. Then I got in the water and started going over the boat. The guy blew me off. So, I said, fuck it, and pushed them off the mooring. Dude sheets out and takes off like a rocket. The kids roll back and just about fall off the tramp. I went straight to the patrol boat. Before I even cranked the motor I looked out and see the jackass try to jibe—full blow at his back. It was all over. The mast hit the water so hard it snapped at the base and sheared the cotter pin completely. The current had them halfway to the bridge by the time we got to them."

I looked south across the Currituck Sound. The bridge was miles away and barely visible through the cold gray skies.

"The girls were crying and the mother was cursing like she was the sailor. It was a bad scene. Someone in a waterfront condo saw it happen and called nine-one-one so the fire department, Ocean Rescue, and an ambulance responded. We called in on the radio that no one was hurt but they were still hanging around by the time we dragged everything back to the dock.

Grandy was standing there with the man's damage deposit slip. The guy put up a little fight about the money but he knew he'd fucked up and gave in." Brett shook his head and laughed. "That's a long drive home."

He looked over to the empty parking lot and waved his hand.

"Y'all go home. Nothing to do here today. Call in the morning."

Harry and I sat at the kitchen counter hovering over our plates.

"Thank God you get to take food home." I scooped fried shrimp from a Styrofoam container and piled them on top of some baked flounder. Harry's job was the only thing keeping me fed. My paycheck for the first two weeks, after taxes, was under a hundred dollars.

"I'm already sick of the smell of that place." Harry leaned back and looked at the food like it was covered in mold. "You don't even want to know what happens in that kitchen."

"Don't tell me. I don't care. Anything's better than Spaghetti-Os."

"Yeah, I guess." He rolled his head back and stared at the ceiling.

"When are you gonna bring one of those waitresses home with dinner?" I didn't look up from my food.

"Shoot, you really don't want to know what they do back in the kitchen. I'd rather take my chances with the crabs on the buffet."

I wrinkled my nose and kept eating. "There's not much more to choose from at the sailing center. I thought I'd be up to my ears in bikinis. All I get to see are one-pieces, life jackets, and aqua-socks."

Harry laughed and shook his head. "The hottest girl I've seen was the one bagging groceries the other day."

"Well, there you go."

I knew he wanted to go back to Virginia. This wasn't what Harry had signed up for.

"Man, as soon as this weather breaks, things will pick up." I spit out a pin bone from the flounder.

"Hope so."

That weekend—the second in June—the wind shifted to the southwest, the water warmed to seventy-eight degrees on the sound side, and the sun burned off the standing water on the porch. The Currituck Sound—a shallow portion of the Intracoastal Waterway warms faster than the ocean and is considerably calmer. On those days, when the ocean temperature still hovered around sixty degrees, the tourists flocked to the sailing center. They crowded the gazebo and yelled across the desk for prices on everything from parasailing to windsurfing. The chaos and the grating accents made me glad to be hip-deep in the mud-brown water.

My job was motor boats. They were pretty simple really—two rigid-hull inflatable boats, no more than fourteen feet in length. One, we rented out. The other, we used to retrieve broken-down Jet Skis or capsized sailboats. There were a few jet boats—the first on the market— nothing more than undersized and underpowered ski- boats.

And then there were the Jet Skis, or wave runners, as they were starting to be called. They were new the year before but showed the signs of a season's worth of use. The sailing center marked off an area with red buoys— roughly a mile wide and across—where the riders did their thing. In theory, they were to observe every Coast Guard regulation. We gave them a safety talk, made them sign their lives away, and then turned them loose.

Everyone was supposed to have a driver's license. Since I didn't do any paperwork, and because I started driving boats when I was ten, I didn't worry too much about the age requirements unless someone was obviously incapable of operating the boat. Even then, it wasn't my place to second-guess the manager. Basically, we'd rent anything to anyone and at five bucks an hour, I stayed out of the way.

My responsibilities when I was on "patrol" were simple: keep the hot-doggers away from each other, corral the wayward drivers, and tow in anything that broke down. For the most part, I sat with my feet up and watched the lemmings zip around, charging full throttle from one boundary line to the other.

We had all types of drivers out there. Inevitably, any Jet Ski with a passenger ended up with one person in the water. I'd hear the screams, the motor would quiet, and then I'd watch the white spray as the passenger skipped across the surface like a tossed stone. Each driver wore a wrist lanyard hooked to a kill-switch to prevent the ski from running away.

It takes some skill to sit on a Jet Ski when it is stopped in the water. The awkward balance requires the driver to maintain at least a slow speed to prevent tipping over. "Momentum," I would say, "is your friend."

When people fell off, even in shallow water, the process of climbing back on could be trying, if not impossible. Sometimes customers spent more of their rented time trying to get back on the ski than driving it.

There was a weight limit per ski—about three hundred and fifty pounds. This allowed two, sometimes three, people to ride around with ease. Some couples—the ones who kept Harry busy at the buffet—pushed the weight limits. But I knew better than to ask a woman what she weighed or tell a man that he and his wife were better suited on the pontoon boat.

It was a clear day and most of the skis were out. I was on patrol and for the most part people did what they were supposed to do. I enforced the boundary rules here and there, but two girls were playing chicken and I pretty much looked the other way. They were cute from where I sat, probably sixteen or seventeen years old. They watched me go after someone who strayed past the buoys and decided it would be amusing to see how far I'd let them go.

I played along. One girl made a big loop around a boundary buoy and I intercepted her when she came back into the course.

"Did I go too far?" She smiled, giving herself away. The other girl pulled up on the other side of my boat, forcing me to turn my head as I spoke.

"You see these red markers?" I pointed nowhere in particular. Both girls nodded, the second one giggling. "Do me a favor and try to stay inside them."

"Yes sir." The second girl pushed forward on the thumb throttle and sped off, weaving in between the markers.

I looked at the first girl. "Did she just call me 'sir'?"

"That's my little sister." She shrugged. "Well, how old are you?"

She wasn't as cute as she looked from fifty yards away. Her face was too small for her forehead—which is a terrible thing to say, but with her hair wet and pulled back, I couldn't help but notice. Her eyebrows were bushy and her shoulders much broader than mine were.

"I'm eighteen." I wanted to go back to my patrol.

"Yeah, I guess that's not that old. She's only thirteen."

I tried to hide my surprise.

"Well, can y'all just stay inside the buoys please?" I could tell she wanted me to stay and talk but I motored up and drove to the far buoy, tied up to it, and resumed my hard work after a careful application of sunscreen. I reached overboard with the least amount of effort possible and rinsed my hands in the brackish water. I was content. The pay was nothing, but so was the job. There were minor inconveniences, but I couldn't really complain.

A Jet Ski puttered out from the rental gazebo. The

wind was light—a nice change. Some small sailboats passed the ski as it pushed its way to the corral. I looked through binoculars and understood the situation.

A large man was driving—at least three hundred pounds. He had bright red hair, white skin, and neon everything else. His lifejacket looked like a bad joke—buckled and stretched so tight that the foam squeezed from between every nylon strap. His sunglasses—bright green with mirrored lenses barely hid the concerned look on his face. To top it all off, he wore aqua-socks.

His lips moved and I realized that there was a second person on the slow ride. They got closer to the patrol boat and I lowered the binoculars. The passenger had a death grip on his lifejacket. She wasn't large by any means but it was still too much weight for the small vessel. She was painfully dressed in a matching outfit and I couldn't help but laugh.

They passed my boat and the man got brave. I assume, by the horrible sound that the ski made, that he was full throttle. The bow lifted and the back dropped. He cut the handlebars sharply and the woman dropped off into the water. He didn't know she was gone. The man made another clumsy cutback and saw her terrified face about thirty yards in front of him. He let off the throttle, which immediately took away his steering ability. In a desperate effort, he moved the handlebars back and forth violently but the ski maintained a forward course. Fortunately, the man's weight bogged down the boat enough to slow it without hitting the woman; but it was close. She grabbed onto the bow and, with some hesitation, made her way around to the side.

The worst part of the whole situation is that I knew exactly what was going to happen—and I let it. The man reached down to pull her back onto the ski as if he were helping her up onto a horse. When she grabbed his hand the ski rolled and dumped him into the water. He held on until the vessel was upside down. At that point I started the boat and made my way over to them. When I got closer I could see that she was crying. The man's face was bright red and his glasses were gone. He squinted and breathed heavily while he tried to push the ski over from the side.

I didn't want to get in the water. That would mean dropping the anchor and being wet for the next hour. This wasn't really an emergency—not to me. The man's efforts were getting him nowhere; they certainly weren't making the woman any happier.

I leaned over the side of my boat and pointed to the ski. "Go around to the back of the ski and turn it clockwise. It should pop back over."

He nodded and looked at the shore. I knew he wanted to be on dry land. He made his way to the back of the ski and turned it like a large steering wheel. It rolled easily.

"Now, we need to get you on from the back. If you go from the side you'll just tip it over." I said it as though I hadn't seen them capsize the first time.

He nodded like it was common knowledge—his chubby face shining in the bright afternoon sun. But he couldn't pull himself up. He tried three times, each effort ending in a pathetic splash back into the water. The woman tried to hold the ski but her slight weight did nothing to help the situation.

There was little I could do either—whether I was in the water or not. I'd never had anyone that couldn't get back on before.

"Why don't we get you onboard with me and then we'll worry about the Jet Ski?"

"Okay." He took a deep breath.

The patrol boat sat high out of the water—the top of the inflatable pontoons were almost two feet above the water line. I reached down and grabbed his arms but they slipped right through my sunscreen covered hands. I wiped them off on a rag and tried again but it was hopeless. Brett saw the situation from the gazebo and came out in a small dinghy. The lower profile of his boat might give us a better chance of getting the guy back to shore.

Brett looked confused when he got to us. I tried to make up in sensitivity what I lacked in prevention.

"We're having a little trouble getting things going again." I gestured to the ski as though it was the problem. Brett nodded. He looked at the two in the water and then at me. I shrugged as if being new excused me for having no answer to the problem.

"Wesley, go ahead and tie that ski up, you can tow it in." He looked at the man. "Let's see if we can get you on here with me." Brett tapped the side of his little boat.

A short frayed line hung on the port side of Brett's dinghy. The rubber pontoons were slippery and there were no footholds for the man to hoist himself up onto. He pulled on the line and the starboard side of the boat lifted out of the water. Brett's arms flew into the air with exaggerated circles. He grabbed the motor to regain his balance.

"Whoa, hold on a second or I'm gonna be in the water with you." He sat on the opposite pontoon to distribute the weight evenly and the man tried again.

We'd drifted about twenty yards closer to shore but not close enough to wade in. The water was only four feet deep but the bottom of the sound was pure muck. The woman lifted her legs one at a time, shifting her weight to avoid getting stuck. She moved over to help push the man up, and in doing so, sank up to her shins.

The walkie-talkie on Brett's console crackled with static and Mr. Grandy's voice. "Everything okay out there?" He watched us from the gazebo.

Brett and I looked at each other. The man was out of breath and no closer to getting in the boat than when he fell. The woman twisted her skinny arms like she was dancing—her hair flung around and stuck to her face.

The man tried to get onto Brett's boat one more time and he managed to pull up far enough to drape his arms over the side, but that was as far as he made it. He hung on and looked up at Brett.

"Just go. Just drag me in." The defeated look on his face wasn't anything to argue with but Brett couldn't start the boat with the man hanging onto the side. If he slipped the propeller would chew him up.

Again, Grandy's static voice, "Brett, tell me what's going on out there. Do I need to call the ambulance?" Brett looked at the man but didn't say anything.

The man turned his head back to where the woman continued to wiggle in an effort to get out of the muck. The color in his face was gone—like it had been washed away. He looked up but not directly at Brett.

"I can't do it again." His chest heaved in and out. He laid his head on the rubber pontoon.

Brett picked up the walkie-talkie and clicked the button, "Yeah, you might want to do that."

He pointed at the woman. "Wesley, toss me your anchor line and help her."

I untied the anchor and threw him the line. Then I moved my boat around to the woman and pulled her up with both of my hands. Her feet were bare and clean, but her shins were caked with black muck. Her aqua socks were gone. She didn't notice and I didn't say anything. I could barely look her in the eye.

Brett jumped in the water. He was careful not to get stuck as he tied the line around the man's waist. He passed it through the life jacket a few times and under the man's arms. He tied a quick bowline knot just before the man let go—dropping to the water with a splash. When he collected himself the man rubbed his left arm.

"Damn thing's gone to sleep from holding on so long." He took a deep breath and let it out almost comically—his cheeks puffed out like a trumpet player. "Please get me back in."

Brett climbed aboard with ease and looped the bitter end of the line to a cleat. He stood for a moment, looking at the man, who floated on his back about fifteen feet behind the engine. I could see his pale face from my boat. He waved with his right hand to the woman. She covered her mouth when she saw how Brett rigged him up to be towed. She tried to smile but turned away and took a seat on the port pontoon.

Brett slowly made his way toward the gazebo. The man's mouth opened enough to take in air without letting the splashing water in. We crept along at such a slow pace that we had nothing but time to stare at him. The lifejacket rode up and made it difficult for him to turn his head sideways so he was forced to stare back at us. I lifted my head up like I was looking ahead but behind my sunglasses I could only watch him.

"So, where are y'all from?" I sounded like a cab driver. I didn't look back at the woman when I spoke. I just drove the boat.

"Virginia." Her voice was faint—drowned out by my motor and no desire for my mindless chatting. "Fairfax."

"Oh, yeah? I moved here from Virginia." I paused. She said nothing. My voice trailed off as I said, "Norfolk area." and the conversation ended.

She saw the color escaping from him as clearly as I did. His white, then red face was stark white again. We were still a hundred yards away from the dock. I could see the flashing lights of an ambulance and then more lights behind it. The man looked at me, then at her. From me he wanted a sign that we were close. I offered nothing but the nervous stare of an eighteen-year-old. He looked at her and put his thumb high in the air.

She started crying. Brett kept looking back. He wanted to go faster but he couldn't. We saw the medics standing at the end of the dock with the crowd that gathered in the gazebo.

I was ashamed at my helplessness. I couldn't even console the woman because I was imagining how the man was going to die—tied up like some fish that was too big to bring aboard and dragged back to the marina to be weighed. I watched him fade away at idle speed.

The crowd at the dock was thick when we pulled up. Firemen, medics, and two lifeguards with "Ocean Rescue" embroidered on the back of their jackets stood with a cache of bags and machines. One of them, a tall man with short dark hair, grabbed Brett's bow line and tied it off. The other lifeguard took off his jacket and jumped in the water. He untied the knots and unbuckled the man's lifejacket. He looked up at the other guard. His sunglasses were mirrored but I could tell he was making a silent reference to our crude method of pulling the man in.

There was a short ladder that led to a docking platform. The man tried to climb up on his own but didn't have the energy. He slipped and the lifeguard caught him. The firemen grabbed his wrists and pulled him up on the platform. He rolled to his back—his skin pasty white and shining in the afternoon sun.

I tied up my boat and helped the woman off. A medic wrapped a towel around her and retrieved a metal clipboard from his bag. I stood next to her for a moment because it felt like the right thing to do.

"JJ. Joseph James O'Neill." She nodded and watched the medic spell it. "I don't know our phone number here—it's my mother in law's place." She pointed at the form, "Two Ls." She shook her head and cried.

The lifeguard in the water pulled himself up onto the dock and stepped around me. I felt like I should be doing something but I was just in the way. The other lifeguard, the taller one, stood a few feet from Mr. O'Neill and talked into a hand-held radio. He looked at me. His polarized sunglasses did nothing to block what he was thinking. He turned away but I heard him speak into his radio. His voice was deep and he spoke fast in a code. Then he stopped talking in code and turned back to look at me.

"Yeah, tied 'em up like a dead whale." He shook his

head and smirked. He looked down at his feet where the medics worked on Mr. O'Neill. "We've got him on O₂." There was a pause like in a phone conversation. I only heard static and more abbreviated codes. "They're hooking it up now."

The shorter lifeguard passed a medic two white stickers with wires coming out of them. One of the medics cut Mr. O'Neill's shirt down the middle, exposing his chest, which was even whiter than his arms. They dried him off with a towel, peeled the back off of the white pads, and stuck them on his chest. The medic plugged the other end into a briefcase-sized machine.

I did my best to ignore the crowd, of which I was now one more helpless member. The sisters from earlier pulled up on their Jet Skis but no one helped them tie up so they floated around the pilings looking up and craning their necks to see what was going on.

The younger sister looked confused and asked out loud, "Are they gonna shock him?"

Mr. O'Neill heard her and, for the first time, there was noticeable concern on his face. The closest medic looked him in the eyes and shook his head.

"It's just for monitoring. You're looking good."

He didn't look good at all. His mouth was covered with a clear plastic mask that fogged up each time he breathed out. A web of green straps and tubing wrapped around his face and disappeared into green nylon bags. His eyes darted back and forth each time someone crouched down next to him. He nodded his way through a series of simple questions. The medics and lifeguards worked together in near silence. Only when they stepped away to talk on their radio could I hear anything. They were calm— seemingly numb to the urgency of situation.

The tall lifeguard asked Mr. O'Neill if he could lift up enough to get onto a stretcher. They lowered it to the ground, he nodded, and with the help of three firemen, pulled his way onto it. The men surrounded the stretcher and simultaneously lifted. Their teamwork was swift. Their professionalism added to my embarrassment.

No one ever asked me what happened.

I sat alone on our porch that night. The wind had switched again and so had my mood—from embarrassment to bitterness. The porch faced north. All of the furniture was grayed by sea spray and rain. The big Adirondack chairs, with their cool planks, soothed my sunburned back. I slipped gently along the weathered boards, careful not to catch a protruding screw or splinter. Water rings from countless beer cans and glasses of sweet tea adorned the arms. Not using a coaster was a comfortable relief.

Two chicken breasts grilled over not enough charcoal on a cheap table-top grill. They cooked slowly, but I wasn't in a rush to eat. I flipped the breasts over every few minutes—ignoring my father's time honored cooking method of only turning meat once.

I flipped and stared and thought about Mr. O'Neill. Just before the medics loaded him into the ambulance there was a lot of commotion. The lifeguards and firemen ran around the stretcher, pointing and grabbing at bags. One stood in the back of the ambulance and waved his hand for them to stop. "Do it here, don't load him."

Two long seconds passed and everyone's hands went in the air. Through a break in the crowd I saw Mr. O'Neill's body shudder once, then again. After the third shock they loaded him into the van and sped away with lights blazing and sirens chirping.

I sat on a ski, retying a frayed lanyard. Brett called it "beating the dog" when we did something to kill time. It was a crude expression but I kept repeating it to myself as I wove the red string in and out of the metal lanyard loop. He and Grandy stood in the gazebo.

"Wesley, go find something to do for a while." Brett didn't look at me when he spoke. I felt no more welcome there than I did on the docks when the lifeguards stared at me with such disdain.

As I watched the pink and white chicken turn brown, I realized that Brett must have felt inadequate too. He hadn't trained me at all—certainly not in rescuing someone. Regardless, I resented him and Grandy all the same. That poor guy probably would have had his heart attack later in the week—dipping his crab legs in a bowl of butter—but I was left feeling like what happened was more my fault than anyone else.

I didn't want to go back to work the next day, but I did. I didn't want to give them anything else to say. I felt like they were cowards for shunning me in that moment. I guess they needed someone to point to when people asked what happened. A few days later someone did exactly that.

"Wesley, can you come down and have a seat with us for a moment?" Mr. Grandy, a pseudo-escapist with a scraggily beard and pieces-of-eight necklace who wished he was in Key West, always spoke to me like an uncle who thought he knew me better than he did. "You remember Mr. O'Neill, from last week? He was the gentleman you helped with the Jet Ski."

I stared at Grandy and nodded.

"This is Mr. Harper, his attorney. He has a few questions he wants to ask you." He put his hand on my shoulder. I was taller than him and it felt awkward. "You're not in trouble, son. Just answer the questions truthfully."

My clinched teeth barely contained a week's worth of pent up bitterness.

"Of course. Is he okay?"

Mr. Harper nodded. "He's going to recover. Thank you for asking."

I answered Mr. Harper's questions under Grandy's watchful eye. It was simple stuff really; what I said to the O'Neills and what I saw.

I didn't want to cause any further drama but when I thought about Mr. O'Neill and his thumb up in the air and engine exhaust swirling around his head, I considered exposing the sailing center's blatant disregard for safety.

I wanted to tell about how they'd rent a ski to anyone or how the sailboats constantly tipped over from lack of proper instruction. I wasn't a spiteful person but as the lawyer rambled on about Coast Guard regulations that he'd obviously read for the first time that morning, I thought about the time Mr. Grandy told me to clean the bird shit off of the catamaran.

"Looks like the ducks had a little party out there last night." He nodded his stupid head out to the shallow water.

The sailboat was covered with shit. I was down-current, waist-deep, and throwing buckets of brackish water on the canvas—hoping to wash it off without actually climbing on. I had the bucket—a cheap plastic one that a child left behind—and a scrub brush.

Grandy watched from the dock and yelled to me, "Gonna have to climb on and give it a good wipe down."

I stood and stared at the boat, the shit, and four ducks sitting along the shoreline. I climbed on the port transom. "I hate sailboats," I looked at the birds, "hate you too."

This is what went through my head when Harper—who was dressed in a flowered shirt and pleated khaki shorts, like he was in Bermuda or something—asked me what safety instruction I received when I was hired. Mr. Grandy tried to answer for me. He pushed a stack of paper at the lawyer—talking about company training policies.

Harper waited for me to speak.

I didn't know Grandy that well. He carried himself like he knew everything that people say behind his back and he couldn't care less. He acted like he was the god of water sports in North Carolina. His office had pictures of racing yachts and posters from regattas. A half-dozen red hats hung neatly on another wall. They were faded to various shades of pink and they all said just about the same thing: Mount Gay Rum Race Week - Key West and then the years dating back, in succession, to 1987. On sunny days, when he taught a lesson on one of the sixteen-foot sailboats, he wore the newest hat, along with his sunglasses on a cord around his neck. He said the hats were very rare and that he had a friend who got him one each year— payment for Grandy teaching him how to sail.

Grandy wore 1991 and waited for me to answer the lawyer.

"Yeah, we are taught how to recognize an emergency and what to do if something goes wrong—nine-one-one and all that." I nodded as I spoke but I looked down and away from the table. "We go over all of the Coast Guard manuals."

Grandy leaned back in his chair.

The lawyer looked at me for a moment. I had an honest face—he trusted it. He picked up the manual and stuffed his yellow pad and all of the papers into a leather case.

"One more thing." He snapped his case shut and looked at me.

I raised my eyebrows. Grandy leaned forward.

"Whose idea was it to tow my client in with a rope?"

I thought about it long enough for the lawyer to know that I needed to think about it. I squinted and looked up to the right. "He said, 'just drag me in.'" I considered my wording. "So, I guess he sort of asked us to."

He nodded once and stood up. "Thank you, gentlemen."

The lawyer walked away. Grandy stood up and stared at me. He knew he owed me and I actually thought for a moment that he'd make good on it.

"You handled yourself very well." The brim of his hat was completely flat and I thought about how ridiculous he looked. "You almost made up for giving that guy a heart attack."

He raised an eyebrow at me and I wanted to punch

his bearded face.

"Go back to the gazebo and see what they need you to do." He walked toward the storage shed and then stopped. "Actually, that catamaran needs some cleaning." He pointed to the water. "Can you take care of that?"

I looked at the ducks near the sailboat. Every square inch of the deck was covered. He waited for me to answer.

"Sure."

"Good boy," he yelled back to me as he walked away.

Brett and I were the last two at the sailing center that night. Grandy left early for a Jimmy Buffet concert in Virginia Beach and the two of us barely spoke while we shut things down. I gathered the lifejackets off of the railing and brought them to the storage area in the gazebo. Brett finished the paperwork and started to sort the cash drawer. I heard the bell of the register ding a few times and then he cursed to himself.

"Wesley, can you do me a favor?"

I dumped a handful of jackets on the bench next to him.

"What do you need?"

"Run up to the office and grab me a roll of register tape." He unclipped the keys from his belt loop and singled out the one I needed. "There should be a box on one of the book cases."

I walked down the long wooden pier. I knew my time at the sailing center was done right about the time I reached the gumball machines full of duck food. I climbed the steps to the office, flipped on the lights, and looked around for the box.

I grabbed two rolls, locked the door knob from the inside, and started to leave but before I closed it all the way I noticed the row of red hats. I stopped and stared at them.

"How can a hat be rare?" I said out loud.

1991 was gone. I looked through the window at

Brett in the gazebo and grabbed 1992 from its hook. I felt a
rush of adrenaline and quickly stuffed the hat under my
shirt. I pulled the door shut and when I got to the bottom
of the steps I walked straight to my Jeep. I stashed the hat
under the front seat, looked around, and made my way
back to the gazebo.

"You find it?" Brett didn't look up from the cash in
his hand.

I placed the rolls on the counter.

"I won't be here tomorrow."

Brett stopped counting. He stared at me for a
moment. Then he nodded slightly.

"What happened with that guy on the Jet Ski wasn't
your fault."

"I know that."

"You can't let Grandy get to you. I know he's
arrogant but he's just covering his ass."

"I don't care about it." I looked away and he knew I
was lying.

"I can see you've already made up your mind."

"I have." I raised my head and did my best to look
confident in my decision.

"Who's gonna clean all the duck shit off the boats?"

I stared at him.

He stared back and then he smiled.

I laughed and shook my head.

"Can you do me a favor?" I looked Brett in the eye.

"What's that?"

"Give Grandy my best."

"Will do." He laughed again. "Go ahead and take
off. I'll get the rest."

I grabbed my bag and walked down the dock one
last time, cursing the ducks as I passed. I pulled out of the
parking lot and headed home.

I was searching for something to eat when Harry
appeared from the hallway.

"New hat?" Harry sat on a stool and picked up the result of my spontaneous rebellion from the kitchen counter.

"I took it from my boss' office today just before I quit."

"What? That's a really random thing to do." He looked at it again. "Mount Gay Rum?" He smirked. "That sounds,"

"Gay?"

"Well, yeah. It's not like you can wear this."

"I've got a plan."

"What are you going to do, take a shit in it?"

"No. Come with me. I need to run an errand." I grabbed my keys and the hat from the counter.

"Is this errand illegal?" Harry jumped from his stool.

"Yes." I walked out the front door. "Grab any quarters you have and meet me in the Jeep.

We pulled into the sailing center just before the sun was completely down. Brett was long gone and the gazebo was closed up.

"What are we doing here?" Harry looked around the parking lot.

"Just a little payback."

"Okay man, I really don't want to get into trouble."

"Relax, I just have to return the hat, that's all. I wouldn't get you in trouble."

Harry looked relieved.

"Good, you had me worried."

"Quarters?" I reached out one hand and dug through the ash tray with the other for more change. Harry gave me three and I found two more. "Thanks, stay here." I retrieved the hat from under the seat and walked to the dock.

I quickly plugged each coin into the duck food machine and with each twist of the handle watched as the hat filled up with brown pellets. When I was done, I walked down to the sandy beach, waded out to a catamaran, placed the hat next to the mast, scattered some of the pellets around the boat, and smiled at the best dollar twenty-five I had ever spent.

CHAPTER 3

I decided to take a few days to enjoy myself before I got another job or packed up my things and headed home. I shuffled through the newspaper on the dining room table, picked out the classified section, and walked to the beach with a chair and cooler. I settled into a spot in the sand just above the high tide line.

Two girls, maybe my age, were laid out a dozen or so yards to the right of me. The same lifeguard, Ed, walked by me and both of the girls' heads follow him. This time Ed only wore red shorts. He wasn't in nearly the same shape as the other guards I saw at the sailing center but he walked with confidence. He didn't appear to notice the girls when he passed by them. He walked to the edge of the water and let a small wave roll up the sand to his feet. He looked at his watch and then up the beach. The girls weren't the only people watching Ed. An elderly couple, two young boys, and a little girl near the water all kept their eyes on what he was doing—which, of course, was nothing.

He turned around, his back to the water, and made his way to the stand. On the way he smiled at the girls and lifted the walkie-talkie in his hand like it was too important for him to let go of and wave. When he passed by me I heard the girls giggle. I was jealous as hell. I didn't expect the girls to notice me but when I saw how they watched him I wanted the same attention. Aside from his tan, there was nothing impressive about his physique. I looked just as fit.

When I was seven years old my parents made me join the community swim team. I learned, from swallowing half of the pool, that I was not a natural swimming star. It was a way, they said, for me to meet kids my own age in a new neighborhood. I discovered the backstroke and the amount of water I swallowed decreased significantly. By the end of the summer, the combination of early morning swim meets each weekend and the parents who ran up and down the pool yelling each time their child took a breath kept my mother from signing me up the next year. Ten years later, I could still do the backstroke, but no one on the Olympic team was in danger of losing a spot on my account.

I had a friend in high school that went to college to swim. He tried to teach me the butterfly once. I splashed around the pool like I was trying to punish the water. He asked me to stop when people started pointing. Needless to say, I never went the route of pool lifeguard as a summer job while I was in high school. The idea of having to test water regularly in order to swim in it bothered me. I never took any interest when we talked about CPR or first aid in health class. Nine-one-one was simple enough for me, so the thought of being a beach lifeguard was pretty far-fetched.

The girls in front of me packed up their things—a pile of magazines, towels, tanning oil, and a cooler—and walked toward Ed's stand. They stopped in front of him and danced around on the hot sand. One girl reached up and handed him a piece of paper. He nodded and they waved as they giggled their way up the access stairs.

"Excuse me." I looked up at Ed, sitting in a folding chair on his stand. "What kind of certification do you need to be a lifeguard here?" I felt stupid asking him the question. It was like riding a bicycle to a Mercedes dealer and asking about a trade-in.

"Was it the girls that sold you?" He looked down at me over the top of his sunglasses.

"Oh, yeah, I guess I saw them."

"How could you miss them? Too bad they'd still be illegal if you added their ages together."

"Really?" I looked over the dunes but they were long gone.

"Probably." Ed scanned his water. "How old are you, buddy?"

"Eighteen."

"Ha! You'd be okay then. You really want to be a guard?"

"I need to do something."

"That's the spirit."

"No, I mean, I want a good job. I just really need to pay rent."

"Relax. I'm not the one interviewing you. The truth is, there's really not that much to it. I've been doing it for three years." From his little perch, he looked down and shook his head. He laughed a little like he was letting me in on a secret.

"Honestly, all you really need to do is go apply. You look like you're in good enough shape and I'm sure Rick's still hiring." He grinned and scanned the water again, prompting me to take a step toward the access for fear of distracting him.

"It's the best job around here. You can't beat the perks." He lifted his hand and I recognized the scrap of paper in it. "If you can put up with all the little bullshit between the guys, it's not so bad. You ever guard anywhere before?"

I shook my head, fearing he was going to take the keys away before my test drive.

"Doesn't matter. Go put in an application." Ed scanned the water again and I took it as a cue to end the conversation.

"Thanks." I nodded and started up the steps.

"Just go over to the office. It's on Wright Street—a block back from the beach road. Good luck."

The directions Ed gave me led to two buildings on a side street roughly a hundred yards from the beach. They weren't exactly what I expected to find. There was an unusually large parking lot for the two relatively small buildings. One was simply a single-wide trailer with "Office" stenciled on the metal siding. The other, a larger garage-like building just steps away. Through a sliding glass door I could see two couches, a desk, and a sink with a mirror above it. There was a sign above the door that read, "The Shack".

The attached garage bay had room enough to fit two cars bumper to bumper. The space was cluttered on the sides with yellowed surfboards, siren speakers hanging from the rafters, and torn flags attached to metal conduit and buoys. There was more stuff piled in the back of the garage but I caught myself standing in front of the door feeling like a trespasser. I walked over to the office and stopped at the tinted door window.

Guarding the door—or perhaps stranded in front of it—a decrepit old white sheep dog sat; his frosty eyes stared at a greenish-brown tennis ball. He didn't move when I approached—just stayed on the landing and looked at the ball. His head was lowered as if he expected it to bounce away on its own and that it was only a matter of time before it did so. His mouth drooped around the edges showing bits of pink and speckles of brown decay on his teeth. I leaned over the dog—still no movement—and knocked on the door.

When my knuckle hit the glass the dog came to life and let loose a ferocious bark. I nearly fell off the bottom step but I found my balance against the window. I pushed away, leaving my handprint on the glass and the feeling of intrusion instantly returned. The dog only barked once and continued staring down. I kicked at the tennis ball and watched a circular spray of slobber spin as the beast rose up and gave chase.

I was concerned when the dog drifted off course and over shot the ball. His tail stuck out to the right at a ninety-degree angle like a defunct rudder—throwing off his balance more than steering him. It was hard to watch the dog waddle—both back legs swung in unison while the front ones pulled and lurched in a determined pursuit of the fuzzless slimy ball.

"That's Otis." The deep voice came from behind me. I turned to see a tall tan man standing near the garage. "Pathetic old fuck isn't he?" He twisted an oily rag around his hands. Wearing red swim shorts and tennis shoes, I recognized him as one of the lifeguards from the sailing center and I nodded. It was a shy nod—both to acknowledge his presence and his comment about the dog.

I walked toward the garage and lifted a hand.

"Hi, I'm looking for Rick."

He didn't move and I thought maybe he recognized me. He raised his head slowly.

"Oh, are you Rick?" I was sweating naiveté from every pore and he laughed.

"Shoot me right now if I am." He spit into the gravel lot—a dark brown string that didn't want to let go of his lips. He lifted his rag and pointed at the office with it. "He's on the beach. You need to look for his truck." He spit again, this time the chaw landed in the middle of a zero painted on a paved section of the driveway. The numbers 7-0-0 stretched a truck's width across the space. "If you see a white Bronco parked there, he's in his office. Shouldn't be more than a half hour or so. What do you want?"

"I was wondering if he's hiring."

He stared at me and a creepy smirk appeared at the corner of his mouth.

"Look for his truck."

He walked around the back of the garage and disappeared behind a line of worn down wooden boxes. Each box was the size of a car and overflowed with broken beach chairs and splintered umbrella handles. A flat sheet of plywood with dozens of rusted nails sticking through it leaned against one of the wooden boxes.

"Thanks." I raised a hand. He didn't hear me. The dog was staring again. I kicked the ball, sending Otis waddling and I walked to my car.

I needed to kill some time and reconsider my career direction. I escaped the early afternoon sun in the air-conditioned Shipwreck convenience store, just a few blocks from the lifeguard office. The once small deli had grown to keep up with the demand of the flocking tourists. The owner was expanding the building to incorporate a "Beach Supplies" section filled with all of the standard junk: rafts, boogie boards, sun block, and long foam noodles—the newest trend on the beach that year.

I bought a sandwich from the deli at the back of the store and bypassed the endless shelves of souvenirs on my way to the picnic table out front. I watched the traffic moving north and south on Virginia Dare Trail—more commonly referred to as the beach road. A steady line of mini-vans with out-of-state tags and lifted pickups, some with confederate flags waving behind them cruised by.

An older compact car pulled into the space in front of the picnic table. I saw a hurricane re-entry sticker on the front bumper—the easiest way to identify a local. Two girls got out, both wearing bikinis and appearing to be around my age—I wasn't really sure, but at least one of them was driving. She had bleach-blonde hair and bare feet and ran around the front of the car like the asphalt was burning her. She quickly disappeared into the store. The other girl, a brunette with long hair pulled into a pony tail, laughed and took her time walking to the front door. She wore flimsy blue sandals and a blue and white striped bikini. I couldn't take my eyes off of her.

Her slower step gave her a few seconds to notice me—something the first girl clearly didn't do. Of course, I sat alone with orange fingers from my cheese puffs, a pile of bread crust in front of me, and a bottle of chocolate milk in my hand. Her laugh continued but she tried to hide it. It was enough for me to feel like she actually took notice before she too disappeared through the door.

I thought about going back into the store when I finished my milk—maybe look at the sunglasses, but just before I stood up the door flew open and the driver—in the same manner as she entered—ran out of the store, bag in hand and yelling like she was walking on embers.

She looked back. "Come on, this shit's gonna melt before we even get it back to the beach." Her voice was deep and again, she didn't notice me sitting there.

The brunette didn't say anything. She shook her head and laughed again. Then, out of nowhere, she looked at me. She smiled apologetically for her friend like it was a habit and I returned it as if I cared about her friend's behavior. She got in the passenger's seat and the blonde threw the little car in reverse before the other girl even shut her door. She stopped to shift into drive and I could tell the brunette said something. The driver looked through the open window. I was still sitting at the picnic table— entranced by the show they were putting on. She lowered her sunglasses, like a movie star from the fifties, looked past her friend and pointed at me.

"Hey, you're cute." She yelled it out the window like she was ordering a burger at a drive in. My eyes got wide. Then she turned to her friend. "Yeah Lilly, he's cute." she said in the same voice. Lilly, the brunette slid down in her seat and covered her face. Once again, the blonde turned to me. "Bye, cutie!" She laughed and the car chirped as they headed south on the beach road.

I watched them drive away and waited for the taillights to glow but they didn't. All I could see was Lilly's dark arm hanging out of the window and her fingers tapping on the door.

Rick's white Bronco was spotless. The truck sat high on large tires. Decals covered the hatch and wrapped from the rear bumper to the front: *OCEAN RESCUE, For Emergency Dial 9-1-1, Diver's Alert Network, AED, 0_2 on Board, Swim Near a Lifeguard, USLA Advanced Agency, Move to the Right for Lights and Sirens,* and the number *700* in at least a half-dozen places. The truck read like a résumé.

I didn't know what the abbreviations meant—just that I was over my head and a split second from turning around. Then the tall guard appeared from the garage.

"Go on in." He stood there and waited for me to move. He was still wiping grease off of his hands from the four-wheeler he'd been working on. A Grinch-like smile crept across his face.

I nodded and stepped up to the office door. I knocked on the wood frame and waited. I could hear someone talking inside but it wasn't directed at me, so I just stood there. I looked to see if the guard was still there but he was gone. I tapped on the glass and took a step back at the same time. I didn't see Otis anywhere. I stared into the mirrored window and tried to avoid my own eye contact. My hand print from earlier was gone.

"Come in." The deep voice was quick and crisp. I'd already formed a picture in my head of what I expected Rick to look like. It was a combination of the guard from outside—aged ten years—and despite my best efforts to avoid the stereotype, David Hasselhof.

The office was dark and something blocked the door so it didn't open completely. I squeezed through to see

Otis on the floor in front of it. Stepping over him and looking around I saw a fit but pale man sitting in a black chair behind what looked like a door that had been converted into a desk. He was completely bald or had shaved his head to finish what nature started. He talked into the air and wore a funny headset. With his hand he motioned for me to come in. He stared directly at me as I walked into the small office, then he held up one finger and pointed it at the chair next to me. I sat down and watched him nod along to the conversation he was having.

"Ah … ah … I don't want blue, I want white! Yes. Yes. That'll be fine." He looked at me over the top of his thick bifocal glasses as if I were the person on the other end of the phone. "I'll send my nephew over to pick them up tomorrow. Thank you."

He spun in his swivel chair and hung the headset on a little silver hook behind his desk. He shuffled some papers and opened a few drawers without retrieving anything. I sat quietly and looked around the small office at the pictures and plaques on the wall. He turned back to face me. I started to stand up.

"So, why the fuck do you want to be a lifeguard?"

Those were the first words Rick ever said to me and I'll never forget them.

My eyes got big and at the same time I searched the room for an answer written somewhere on the wall or perhaps on his desk. He leaned forward and I saw his jaw muscles tighten in anticipation of my response. I did my best not to stutter or appear visibly shaken but really—I nearly shit myself.

"Well, my father was a lifeguard and he always said what a great job it was."

It was a lie. My father was a lifeguard in 1962 and told me a story of the fat lady he pulled in one time. Her top fell off in a wave and her husband never even got out of his chair. That was as glorious as he made the job sound. He spoke of boring days renting chairs and umbrellas on the Myrtle Beach Strand and the old crook he worked for who ripped off everyone that guarded for him by paying only commission for the rentals.

"I also want a respectable job that I can be proud of and do something to help the community." I hoped to at least land on my ass when he threw me out of the office.

His forehead relaxed and his head tilted to one side.

"So, you're a smart one, huh? Good answer, good answer." A smile appeared from under his thick blonde mustache and he stood up to shake my hand. I found relief in my own bullshit and even more in his apparent good nature.

"What's your name?" He was at least six inches taller than me but slightly stooped over. His skin was almost translucent. He shook my hand hard and held on.

"Wesley Brooks."

"Wesley? What the hell kind of name is that?" He spoke fast—like he was from somewhere north of the Mason-Dixon Line.

I shrugged a little and resisted the urge to explain the English lineage. "It's just a name," I said with no confidence.

"I'm Rick Carroll. I own the service. You met Buck?" He let go of my hand.

"Yeah." I looked out the window and nodded reluctantly.

"What'd you think?"

"We didn't really meet; he just told me when to come by. He seems nice though."

"Nice?" Rick waited for me to change my mind. I didn't say anything. "Buck's a dickhead." He reached across his desk and pressed a green button on a small TV screen. I could see Buck on the monitor. When he heard the click he pulled his feet off the desk in the shack.

"Isn't that right Buck?"

"What's that?"

"Aren't you the biggest dickhead we've got?"

"The biggest one on the beach." He put his feet back up on the desk and picked up a magazine.

Rick laughed, I didn't. He lifted his finger from the button.

"Damn good lifeguard though. Can you swim?"

"Yes. Pretty good."

He waited a few seconds.

"We'll see." He looked at the TV again and then back at me. "Are you wearing a bathing suit?"

I looked down at the blue suit and thought about the turkey sandwich and chocolate milk sitting in my stomach.

"Well, yeah but I just—"

He pressed the intercom again. "Buck, get your ass in here."

Buck walked out of the shack. It took him a few seconds to get to the office and in the meantime Rick just looked at me—like he was trying to figure me out. When Buck walked in he blocked most of the sun and looked like a tan hit man. He wasn't smiling and I felt bad for disturbing his reading.

"Buck, take Lesley here down to the beach. Have him swim to the marker and drag you back."

"Yes sir."

Rick looked at me. "Go with him. He'll let me know how you do."

I nodded and followed Buck out the door.

We walked through the gravel lot toward the shack.

I tried to break the ice a bit and asked, "Are you from here?"

"No. Do you have a towel?" Buck didn't look at me as he walked into the garage.

"I think I have one in my car."

He mounted his red four-wheeler and drove to where I parked. He handed me an orange rescue buoy.

"I'll meet you over on the beach."

Buck drove away and at that point I thought about hopping in my car and going to see about a job at the miniature-golf course. I knew Rick could see me through his window so I quit hesitating, threw the towel over my shoulder, and walked toward the beach access.

Buck zipped across the beach road, through the parking access, and over the sand dune. I stood on the side of the road waiting for a break in the line of traffic. From the rumble of vehicles I heard a whooping like groupies at a concert and turned in time to see a car full of girls blurring by. The only word I could understand from the yelling was "lifeguard." I felt a little fraudulent but enjoyed the moment nonetheless.

I climbed the wooden walkway over the dunes and saw Buck talking to the guard stationed there. A round yellow buoy, bright against the flat green water, bobbed a hundred yards out. It really didn't look too far and I felt a little relief.

My shoes were in the car and the sand was hot as hell. I did my best not to look uncomfortable as I approached the stand. A girl lay on her stomach next to the stand. Her top was untied and she perched herself up on her elbows while talking to Buck and the other lifeguard. I got closer and became clear that she wasn't shy. She wore a black thong bikini bottom and her breasts barely rested on the towel. The only thing keeping her covered was her bleached hair draped over her shoulders.

"Shit's hot isn't it?" The guard in the stand looked at my bare feet.

"Yeah, just a little." I shifted my weight back and forth until I found some cool sand in the shade of the stand.

Buck looked up, "Grey, this is Lesley. He's gonna swim the buoy."

"Good to meet you." Grey reached down to shake my hand from his high seat.

"You too. Actually, my name's Wesley. Rick got a little confused."

Grey laughed.

"And that's Sandy." He looked at the girl who had lowered herself down on the towel. She raised her hand and barely looked my way. I thought he was joking about her name but didn't say anything.

"Okay, I'm gonna swim out to that yellow buoy and raise my arm. You swim out, stop about five feet from me, and hand me the can. Got it?"

I hesitated.

"Hand me the buoy." Buck pointed at my hand and seemed agitated.

I nodded and he walked down toward the water line. He got about halfway and turned around.

"One other thing, keep your head out of the water as you swim. You always need to see the victim. And don't try to tie me up like a fish when you get out there." He looked up at Grey with the same smirk I saw on the dock. While it didn't calm any of my anxiety, I was relieved that he finally acknowledged our prior meeting.

"What a dick." Grey shook his head and settled back into his chair.

Buck ran into the water. When he was knee-deep he threw his arms out and jumped over a small wave like he was diving off of a cliff. It was as close to flying as I'd ever seen. He slipped into the water just behind the next wave and came to the surface in the middle of a perfect stroke.

Grey spoke again, but I didn't look up at him, "Don't worry man, it's not as far as it looks."

Sandy smiled but never looked away from her book. I walked out of the shade and made my way down to the water. Everyone on the beach watched me—just like I watched Ed earlier. The buoy in my hand might as well have been a flashing light.

"Hey!"

I heard a familiar voice on my right and turned to see a large group of people.

"Lilly, look. It's the cute boy from Shipwreck!" The blonde leaned against a guy next to her. "We just saw him when we got lunch." The guy looked at me and nodded with no expression. The others in the group were equally unimpressed but Lilly smiled.

"So, you're a lifeguard?" It was the first time I heard her speak. Her voice was softer than her friend's—less aggressive, but not shy.

"Actually, I'm…" I saw Grey in the corner of my eye. He waved at me with both arms like he was swatting flies. I looked out at the buoy. Buck had his hand straight up in the air.

I turned to Lilly, "Be right back." I said it like a superhero that needed to stop a runaway train.

Remembering Buck's takeoff and trying my best to imitate it, I sprinted into the surf and dove through the first wave. The salt water shot up my nose and sent a sharp sting to the front of my head. My hands and stomach scraped the bottom. I was in about two feet of water. I stood up and realized I was still holding the buoy. The strap hung loose across my skinny frame. I let go and pushed my way through the next wave. Abandoning grace for survival, I tried to dive again but I was too deep to get a good push off.

When I got to the surface, I saw nothing distinguishable—only a blistering collage of blue. Through the water in my eyes I could make out the horizon and nothing else. The back of my throat burned from a salty flush. The friendly ocean slapped me in the face and all I could do was grab for the space in front of me and hope that it pulled me closer to Buck—the last person I wanted as my goal.

I wiped my eyes and, keeping my head in the air, continued toward the buoy. I swam the best I could but looked more like that seven-year-old at a swim meet than any future lifeguard. The orange buoy jerked behind me awkwardly with every stroke.

I could see Buck—one arm splashing while the other worked with his legs to keep him floating. I had to focus to make my legs and arms function together. I tried to keep my head straight, but it dipped. With each stroke I tasted more and more salt. My stomach cramped up. I wanted to stop. I wanted to catch my breath. I wanted to sink to the bottom and stay there until the beach emptied—or at least until the girls left.

Then a thought washed through my sloshy head; if I didn't make it—if I quit—I might as well ask Buck for a ride back in and go straight to my room to pack up my things. I looked back to the shore. I was out far enough that faces were unreadable.

Everyone's watching you—a pitiful attempt at motivational self-guilt. Joining the salt-water sting, the sour taste of bile burned the middle of my throat. My muscles screamed. The water muffled every noise except one and when I heard it I stopped mid-stroke.

"Come on Wesley … you can do it … let's go … yeah … not much farther, man … come on you can do it."

It was Buck. The shock of his encouraging voice was enough to snap me back from the watery wasteland that I'd slipped into. I lifted my head once more like I was supposed to. I thought about Grey's encouragement; Buck's arrogance; Sandy's ass.

I spit a few times—trying to clear the burn. My legs felt like they knew what the rest of my body was trying to do and kicked a little stronger. My hands—which dragged through water like they were made of chicken wire—pulled like oars.

Buck, the biggest dickhead on the beach, was my beacon. When I got to him I remembered to stop five feet away and push him the buoy. I smiled like a goofball—thrilled that I didn't let him down.

"What the fuck took you so long?" Buck stared at me like a drill sergeant. The puke taste returned.

"I had a little trouble wi—"

"Shit, I was waving forever before you even started. Weren't you watching?"

"Sorry." I rolled to my side and kicked. This made us face each other. I could tell he was kicking too. I pulled with one arm and held on to the buoy strap with the other.

"You can take your time getting back in."

I looked at him to see if he was testing me. I wanted to tell him to quit living up to his reputation, but the first wave knocked off my balls. They were floating around somewhere in the shore break.

And then the son-of-a-bitch laughed.

"I thought you were gonna drown, man."

It was the first time Buck was close to personable. It didn't matter that my pride was the icebreaker between us. "You really hit that first wave pretty hard."

From my sideways position I saw the scrapes on my stomach where I dove too shallow. I shook my head and looked at him. I had to laugh too. The dickhead was right.

We reach a point where we could stand. Buck let go of the buoy and swam to the beach.

"Dry off and go back to Rick's office." He walked out of the water and made his way to the four-wheeler. I stood near the water line and wrapped the strap around the buoy, trying not to make eye contact with anyone. He paused when he passed the girls and smiled at Lilly. She turned her head and pretended to be talking to someone else. Buck took a few more steps, looked up at Grey, discreetly pointed at the girls, and shook his head. Grey smiled.

"Longer than it looks, huh?" Lilly's blonde friend tried not to laugh and I appreciated the half-hearted interest but all I wanted to do was crawl up to the soft sand and pass out. The guys chuckled—a brief round of man-giggles that felt like lemon juice on my scraped up stomach.

Lilly didn't laugh. She didn't really do anything. She looked at her friend and allowed me to pass without further humiliation. I wanted to think it was a courtesy but it was the most embarrassing part of the day.

"Good job, man." Grey's words swirled around with

the water in my head. I was dizzy and weak in the legs. The dunes moved like waves while the sea oats swayed with the wind and blurred my efforts to focus on something stationary. When Buck drove over the dunes, I leaned against the walkway and threw up everything I swallowed during the swim and lunch. I looked around. Grey stared at the water. Sandy was asleep. The girls were talking. I kicked some sand on my mess and carried myself back to the parking lot.

I found relief against the shady side of my car. Buck was in the office but I got the feeling that they were watching me through the window. I did the best I could to catch my breath and settle my stomach while drying off. There was a paper cup from a fast-food meal the night before in the cup holder. The ice had long melted and mixed with whatever soda was left, giving the watery mixture a cola-brown tint. The idea of drinking something other than salt water was enough to make me ignore the temperature. I downed it with two gulps—the diluted sweetness lingered in my mouth. I walked to the office and knocked on the door. Buck came out. He didn't say anything. He just kind of raised his head at me and walked to the garage.

"Come on in here, Lesley."

I stood in the doorway with my towel wrapped around my waist.

"It's Wesley." I tried to smile when I said it for fear of offending him.

"Oh yeah, Wesley. Have a seat."

"Uh … I'm kind of wet."

"Of course you're wet, you're a lifeguard." He leaned on his desk like before. "How does it feel?"

It felt like I'd been tortured, dragged across sandpaper, and put on public display.

"Great."

And it did. I expected Rick to tell me, at the least, to work on my swim and try again. It wouldn't have surprised me if he told me that I wasn't cut out for the job.

"Buck said you need a little work on your swim. We'll take care of that."

"I don't have any certifications." He hadn't asked me about it earlier. I never really thought it would go this far.

"Don't worry about certifications. We'll take care of that too. We do everything in-house. Do you want the job?"

"Yeah."

"Yes sir." His expression was flat when he corrected me.

"Yes sir."

"I guess we'll have to work on your manners too."

Again, he shuffled papers on his desk without really doing anything.

"I'll have you saying sir and ma'am all fuckin' day." He stood up and stuck his hand out. "I'll see you here on Monday at nine. We'll start your training then."

CHAPTER 4

I don't know if it was the chance he took on me—a skinny kid that couldn't swim—but something about Rick made me want to impress him. The confidence in the air of his office and the shack were intoxicating.

The parking lot was full of cars and trucks that Monday morning but no one was around. I knocked on the office door. No one answered. The door to the shack was open so I went in and sat on one of the couches. The building felt like a museum. Nearly every inch of wall space was covered with some sort of memento. Newspapers with headlines reading, *Lifeguard Hero Pulls Four*, and *Rips Terrify Tourists* were entrancing. The certificates, plaques, letters of commendation, antique buoys, and tattered red flags, all hung simply—but with a sort of deceptive modesty. "Lifeguard of the Year"; a hard-bodied guy, maybe twenty or so, knelt in the sand and holding a trophy. Another plaque hung just below it; "Outer Banks Lifeguard Olympics–First Place, 1992." The most impressive was the wall of group photos from years past.

There was Buck—skinny and smiling in 1989; Grey in '90 with long blonde hair. I recognized Ed from the year before. All of the pictures, except for 1991, had one thing in common—no girls. In that one, there was a thin girl with dark hair. She stood on the end of the back row, taller than most of the guys.

An article from the local newspaper caught my eye. It read, *"Private Ocean Rescue Service Investigated."* It was dated July 15th, 1990 and explained some of Rick's background. The article was almost cryptic about some things but went into great detail about others.

He made his living selling insurance but the article didn't say why he stopped. He bought Ocean Rescue Service in 1971. It was also the year he moved to the Outer Banks from New York. ORS made its income from the town of Kitty Hawk, which contracted Rick to provide lifeguard service to its four miles of beaches. He also had sole concession rights to rent chairs and umbrellas.

> *Mr. Carroll's service has been under scrutiny after a claim that the service's lifeguards had not received proper training and certification. These claims have been investigated and cleared by the USLA, the governing organization that oversees all professional lifeguard agencies in the country.*

There were a few more paragraphs in the article but I was distracted by a shuffling noise in the connected garage. It was about ten minutes to nine when a dripping wet guard burst through the side door of the shack. His hair was slicked back and he shook water off his hands frantically. He noticed me on the couch and raised his head in an unimpressive gesture of acknowledgement. He looked like every stereotype of a surfer in the early nineties. Everything about him was exaggerated; his bright white teeth; his tanned face and sunburned nose; his hair—long on the top and shaved on the sides. His body was sculpted in a way that instantly made me feel under-developed.

"I'm Fig." He looked at me quickly, like he had

already formed his impression, and spun around on his heel to a large chalkboard. Then, with deliberation he slid across the vinyl floor to the desk. He shook his hands again and grabbed an assortment of pens and index cards from a drawer and threw them on the counter next to the desk. One of the pens fell to the floor providing a quick percussion in the quiet room. I sat motionless and acutely aware of the silence. The pen was an opportunity to help Fig and remind him that I was there.

I picked it up and placed it with the others. Fig lifted the phone handset, looked at me standing there, and nodded with a brief smile that suggested I return to the couch and wait for him to finish his oddly choreographed routine.

He stared at the chalkboard and tucked the receiver between his ear and shoulder. He unfolded a piece of paper that looked like crib notes.

"Good morning, can you please tell me the water temperature?" He used his finger to read the chart in his hand. "Thank you, have a..." I could tell the person hung up before Fig finished. He looked at the phone like it was the face of the person he called.

"Fucker." He picked up a nub of chalk from the ledge and wrote "65" next to the space for water temperature. "85" was already drawn in the space marked "Air" and he left it there. He filled in the low and high tide spaces, "11:34" and "5:28", respectively. Under "Weather Conditions" he wrote, "West wind, watch inflatables. Drink plenty of water and stay under your hoods."

Fig grabbed a bottle of lotion from the sink area and looked around. "Where are those fuckers?" In the same manner that he entered, he slid out of the shack.

I heard a rumble like Buck's four-wheeler but it sounded louder—like there was more than one; then a loud screech. The door flew open and Fig ran back in. He landed in the swivel desk chair and howled with laughter. Another guard walked into the shack—his hands palm up in an overstated expression of disbelief.

"Jesus Christ Fig, you little..." The dark-skinned guy looked at me and reserved his comment. He had sun block all over his face and chest—obviously the result of a well coordinated sneak attack. He muttered to himself and wiped off the lotion with a towel. Then he looked at me. "You the new guy?"

"Yeah, I'm Wesley."

"I'm Preston." He was skinnier than Fig, but carried himself with more confidence. "You meet the funny guy here?"

I nodded like we'd been properly introduced. Preston moved closer to the chair where Fig sat in a defensive position. He spun the chair around, nearly sending Fig to the ground.

"Watch your ass around this pretty boy. We're not too sure about him."

"Your mother was pretty sure about this last night." Fig pointed to his crotch.

A shrill noise buzzed above my head and Rick's static voice spread throughout the shack from a small speaker in the corner.

"*Fig. Watch your fucking mouth about my sister.*"

Fig laughed and covered his face.

"*You two ready in there?*"

"Yes sir." Preston flicked the last of the lotion at Fig.

Voices outside grew louder. I stayed on the couch, looking around and wondering what exactly Fig and Preston were getting ready for. The sliding door opened. Four guys walked in—all of them wet, barefoot, and shirtless. Three more behind them pushed their way in. I recognized Ed and sat up a little on the couch. He lifted his head like the others and actually spoke.

"Hey man. Heard you did the swim." He smiled and fell in line behind the others.

"Yeah, I tried." I didn't know what he heard about my episode with Buck so I kept it short.

"You puked?" He waited for me to answer. Several guys, Preston and Fig included, looked at me. I thought about denying it.

"Just a little water…went down the wrong way."

Ed laughed, "It isn't supposed to go down at all, man." A few other guys in line laughed.

"Ed, you pussy, you threw up at every PT your first week." Preston shook his head like he was disgusted.

Fig sprung from his chair in an animated way that made everyone turn back to the counter. "Alright you fuckers, get your shit and get to your stand. I'll run-swim every one of you if you're a second late."

Somebody, I didn't notice who, muttered, "Sit down, 7-0-bitch."

"What? Who said it?" Fig put both hands on the counter and lifted himself up.

Four more guys walked in, Grey among them. All of them talked to each other or someone in the shack. There was a hurried feeling in the room but obviously a method to the chaotic atmosphere. Moving from right to left, each guard grabbed a walkie-talkie that rested in battery chargers on the side of the counter. Then Fig handed each guy a metal box and a whistle from a large wooden grid of cubby holes on the wall. At that point some guards turned around and went through the side door. Some slid down to Preston who handed them a small gray zip-up bank bag.

By nine o'clock everyone was out of the shack except for Fig, Preston, and me. Tires scratched at the gravel outside as guards sped off to their respective stands.

"Everyone make it in?"

Fig and Preston looked at the cubby holes. There was still one box and whistle.

"Who's sitting at Mullet Street today?" Fig shuffled through some papers as he asked the question out loud. "I knew it. Fucking Stanley."

Preston walked to the glass door, slid it open, looked out in the parking lot, and yelled, "Stanley! Get your ass in here." He closed the door and went back to the desk. He looked up at the camera above the desk and spoke into the air; "He's here, Uncle Rick."

"*Thanks.*" There were two clicks. "*Fig, get your feet off the desk.*" Fig dropped his feet to the ground and at the same time a short wiry guy ran to the glass door. He had a shirt on but not tucked in. He grabbed the handle and pulled. His fingers slipped off and he lost his balance, catching himself against the window just before he hit the ground. His hand left a wet arching streak on the glass door. Fig and Preston burst out laughing.

The little guy stood up and pressed both of his middle fingers to the door. "Very funny, Preston." He pulled at the handle again, which was obviously locked. "You are a-a-assholes."

Preston and Fig were almost on the floor with laughter. I couldn't help but laugh a little too. His voice had an obvious lisp and it was instantly apparent that he was the butt of similar lowbrow gags. Preston nodded at me and I unlocked the door.

Stanley stormed past me with no greeting, only a less-than-intimidating threat for the two behind the counter. "If I'm late to my stand, it's your fault."

"Shut-up, Mullet Street. Take your box." Fig pointed at the equipment.

He grabbed it and turned around. He took two steps and turned back to Fig.

"Can I have my whistle?"

Fig extended his arm and opened his hand. The whistle dropped out and hung from its lanyard. Stanley reached for it but Fig pulled back.

"You were the last one out of the water at PT this morning. Do you want to sit Mullet Street for the rest of the summer?" Fig reminded me of a parent holding a bad report card.

"If it m-m-means not having to see your ugly f-f-face, then it's fine wi—"

"Spit it out Stanley, you stuttering fuck."

"Cool it, Fig." Preston shot Fig a harsh look—eyes wide and jaw clenched. I couldn't tell if he stopped the banter on my account or because of the intercom. Fig dropped the whistle on the counter and walked toward the garage. "Get to your stand, Stanley."

"He's a d-d-dick." He walked back to the glass door and checked the lock. He pulled it open easily and disappeared into the parking lot.

Preston turned to me. "Sorry about that, there's some stuff between them. Don't worry about it. Fig's harmless."

A truck pulled up next to the glass door. It had decals similar to Rick's Bronco but there was a stand-up Jet Ski in the rear bed and 701 stenciled on the door. Buck stepped out and spit on the pavement before walking into the shack.

He passed by me and the counter, disappearing into what I had assumed was a closet. There was a pile of lifejackets and bags near the doorframe but no door.

"Damn, Buck." Preston rolled his head and eyes at the same time. "Can't you wait 'til we're done here?"

From the hole in the wall I heard Buck's deep voice. There was a noticeable rasp that hadn't been there at our other meeting. "Go get the door out of your uncle's office and quit your bitchin'." I remembered Rick's desk and smiled.

Preston hitched his thumb toward the back wall and, without speaking, mouthed the word, "asshole."

Outside of the emergency services circle, the lifeguarding responsibilities on the Outer Banks could have appeared incongruous. Duties were dispersed in response to different needs, personal agendas, and varying budgets. In the early nineties, the beach town of Nags Head was the only municipality large enough to have its own services operated by its fire department. Because of the growth of the area and the demand for guarded beaches, all of the neighboring towns needed to be covered as well. This created the opportunity for Nags Head's agency and private contractors to provide lifeguard services to Southern Shores, Kitty Hawk, Duck, and Kill Devil Hills. This resulted in overlapping responsibilities, lifeguarding styles, and more volatile than anything else—egos.

ORS employed about twenty guards to cover its four miles of beaches and contracted areas in Kitty Hawk and Southern Shores. Each public access, all twelve of them, had lifeguard stands, which were manned from 9:30 am to 5:30 pm by one guard. The guard was responsible for taking enough water and food to last the whole shift. There were no lunch breaks. In some places the stands were as close as two hundred yards. The north end of the town, the least populated, had the biggest gaps.

Byrd Street and Chicahauk Street, more than a mile apart, was the largest span without a stand. The Kitty Hawk Pier was the dividing line in the middle and had a stand once, but the rowdy crowd there made a habit of tipping it over nightly or throwing the stand completely into the water. One morning, the guard on duty showed up to find a pile of charred wood where the stand had been the evening before. He had to sit in the sand under his umbrella for the whole day.

Preston showed me how to check in, where to put things, where not to go in the shack and what time I was expected to be where. It was all second nature to him but he was patient and I appreciated his insight. He told me the stories of how everyone came to be there, partly for entertainment, but mostly to show me that, despite the bravado and profanity, everyone started in nearly the same situation: unqualified, nervous, and hesitant.

"The guys who come in with guns blazing," he explained, "are the ones that don't last a week. They talk tough until the first red flag day and freak out when they get into head-high swells." He shook his head like it was nothing for me to worry about and of course, that's all I did.

"But you'll do fine, just remember a few things." He looked at me to make sure I was paying attention, which I was—not wanting to miss any of the things.

"It's simple, really. Always take your buoy with you on a rescue. It's your best friend. If you have your buoy strapped to you, you can't drown. Always make sure someone knows you're going in the water. We have radios." He pointed to the bank of chargers. "We call them radios, not walkie-talkies or CBs. Uncle Rick owns the frequency, but people still listen to us. All of the cops, medics, and firemen have our channel on their scanners so be careful what you say."

I looked at the little hand-held radio like it was a bullhorn—ready to broadcast any blunder I made to the whole county.

"When you call a supervisor on the radio use our numbers. Rick is 700, Buck's 701, I'm 702, and Fig is 703." Then he whispers, "Or 7-0-bitch. But don't say that on the radio." He laughed and, again, I appreciated him letting me in on the jokes.

"Why do you call him Fig?"

"His real name is Jim Figeraro. There were already a few Jims when he got hired."

"And Buck? Is that his real name?"

"Buck could only be his real name. Nothing else would suit him." Preston rolled his eyes. "And last, if you find yourself in a shitty situation, you have to relax. No sense in making things worse by freaking out."

Preston used the phrase "freaking out" about as much as Fig said "fucker" and it concerned me. The pressure increased as Preston talked. I didn't want to be another story that he told the next new guy about.

"No one here has seen it all." Preston pointed at the camera discretely. In a hushed tone that carried more sarcasm than sincerity he added, "'cept for him." He smiled and I nodded, my face was serious.

"Last summer a boy in Duck got smooshed by a huge pier piling that floated down from Virginia Beach."

"Smooshed?" I tried to imagine it, but couldn't figure out the logistics.

"The damn thing was rolling around in the surf— twenty feet long at least. The little boy was playing near it and a wave picked the whole piling up." He raised one hand in the air. It hovered for a long second—longer than a wave takes to break. He snapped his hands together in a crisp smack that bounced around the quiet room. "You never know what's gonna happen out there."

There was a fiery look in Preston's eyes when he told me war stories. But each time he got to the climax of a story—a point where it was obvious that he'd seen the gory details—his voice wavered, cracking sweetly, and he chose a word like "smooshed".

"Rick says you need to work on your stroke?"

"Yeah, I could use a little practice." I was careful about opening up too much to Preston despite my instant admiration.

"Don't worry about it, just focus on it at PT." He read my confusion and continued. "We do physical Training every Monday, Wednesday, and Friday. That's where we were this morning. You can also get with Adrian. He swims most days after work."

I met with Preston for the next two days. We covered the ORS Handbook, I went over radio codes, watched training videos, and went to the pool to practice tows and escape moves. Most guards went through two weeks of training before the season started. My crash course offered me almost too much information to retain but the overwhelming feeling receded as I got more comfortable in the water.

"Just get the basics—most of it you'll pick up as you

go." Each time Preston explained a technique or offered some advice he paused and looked at me to see if the idea was getting through.

I nodded a lot.

"You'll figure it out."

It would have been easy to mistake Preston's hurried attitude for neglect had he not been exactly right. Teaching lifeguarding in a classroom is like trying to explain a recipe to someone who's never boiled water—you just have to turn on the stove and let him work it out. You have to sit on the stand, get in the water, listen to the stories—figure it out for yourself. I memorized the ten-codes and the street locations but until I clicked the button on the radio for the first time, I wasn't prepared.

"Be here tomorrow at seven forty-five." Preston handed me my uniform—red shorts, a white T-shirt, and a blue hat. "Just hang in there. The first PT is always the hardest. You'll know what to expect after that."

I was the first one in the parking lot the next morning. I checked each arriving car for a familiar face. Grey pulled in and parked next to me. I followed him into the garage and he handed me a buoy.

"Gonna try to break ya." Grey grinned as we climbed the wooden steps of the walkway. "He doesn't like to quit until someone pukes—then he uses that as an excuse for us to do more so that we can handle it. Backward ass motherfucker."

"What's his deal?" The low sun reflecting off the water hit me in the face when I reached the top step.

"He picked it all up in the Navy, before he quit." Grey paused, I assumed to see if I'd heard the story already. I hadn't. "Make sense to you?"

"Fuck no."

My grandfather used to say that people who cursed were just proving that they had a limited vocabulary—something that rang out each time I tried to fit in by throwing out an arbitrary profanity.

PT started with stretching—basically an opportunity for everyone to catch up on the previous night's tales and to account for periods of alcohol-induced amnesia. There were some rules of course. The guards—not necessarily the supervisors—had to be clean-shaven and mostly sober.

We finished our calisthenics—a torturous way to begin the day, but necessary. The results were hard to ignore when looking around at the collectively toned body of guards. I didn't feel unnatural about noticing another guy's body. It was something used to sort out the placement in the pecking order. Primal at best, but it was clear who the alphas were—they all had the chiseled abs and broad chests to prove it.

We lined up and started running. Buck kept the pace on his four-wheeler. He yelled out commands and we did our best to appear as enthusiastic participants in his little military fantasy.

"UP!"

We raised our orange rescue buoys high above our heads like they were M16s while maintaining our lines and moderate pace. Stanley drifted from the pack—peeling off from his spot in front of me and taking a position in the back of the line. It didn't go unnoticed by Buck.

"Stanley, you fucking genius! You've just picked the next drill."

I looked around for some sort of hint but there was only contempt, not for the prisoner, but the executioner.

"But first we need to do some flutter kicks!" There was a collective groan and everyone formed a single line—shoulder to shoulder, facing the dunes.

"You wish," Buck pointed to the water. "Turn around."

We did an about-face and felt the icy tingle on our feet—the product of a steady offshore wind blowing the top layer of warm water out to sea.

"Lock your elbows and lie down."

We did and he maintained his drill sergeant voice. "Six inches," he barked.

Our heels rose from their sandy resting place. We were flat on our backs with our heads raised as high as our feet and our arms locked tight with the person on either side like some demented line dance. Our buoys were strapped across our chests and lay at our sides. A wave washed up and teased us but didn't reach high enough to lash us with its cold shock.

"Ready, begin."

Twelve pairs of legs scissor-kicked mostly in unison. Our toes pointed out to sea and stomachs strained to keep the whole thing going. Buck stepped down from his perch and from his military frame of mind. He stood at the end of our line laughing and pointing at the surf like we didn't see the set of waves forming up near the sand bar. He continued to count out the repetitions—once for every four kicks. His evil grin motivated all of us to do the exercise correctly for fear of starting over.

On number fourteen he stopped counting, but no one, not even Stanley dropped his feet to the sand. Someone down the line grumbled, "Count you bastard."

Buck just watched the water.

"fiffffff...teeeeen".

My lower body burned—radiating down my thighs and up to my chest. I winced and next to me Grey turned his head, "Keep 'em up, man. He's waiting for you to drop so he can start over."

Ed stared straight up and joined the conversation. "The hell he is. He's waiting for a big set."

I heard the crash of water and the yelling from the guys on the right side of the line before the wave hit me. It pushed into us, sending legs flailing around in the air and tossing buoys around like orange missiles. Above the chaos, Buck watched and waited for someone's feet to touch down.

"Control your buoys." He leaned over with his

hands on his knees—like a football coach on the sideline at the end of a close game. "Keep kicking." He didn't yell, just stood and stared. "Sixteen."

The backwash swept our bodies with it and carried the line closer to the crash zone. The next wave hit and the chain of linked arms broke, sending both groups in opposite directions and rolling people on top of each other—but no one stopped kicking no matter what position they ended up in.

"Seventeen."

The last wave hit me broadside and I lifted my head as high as I could to get air before it washed over my face. The silence was a welcome break from Buck's barking. He counted to eighteen while I was underwater. I kept kicking.

"Nineteen."

Some guys were yelling, not caring what they sounded like, just wanting to finish. I took a deep breath and kicked until I heard, "Twenty."

A collective sigh and splash rang out as all legs dropped to the cold water and sand. Most guys lifted their arms over their heads and stretched. Grey had a satisfied smile on his face.

Tourists out for their morning walk gathered. They smiled and some took pictures. We looked like a band of refugees caked in sand from head to toe.

Buck pointed and yelled, "Y'all look like a bunch of cat turds." He seemed genuinely disappointed that nobody dropped their feet. "Get back in line. Stanley, in the rear."

We jogged at a slow pace past a bright yellow guard stand. Behind it a boardwalk led to a public bathhouse. Four seedy looking guys with cut-off jean shorts and no shirts sat on the railing. Ed pointed at them and lifted his head.

"The queens of the bathhouse are up early." He waved at them. "Good morning ladies." Two of them waved back, one gave us the finger, and the other turned away.

Buck caught up to us on his four-wheeler.

"Stanley, sprint to the front of the line when I say, 'go'. When he gets there, the person at the back start running."

I relaxed, running wasn't an issue. It was the water that terrified me.

"And we'll have some fun with it." Buck pressed the throttle and zipped to the front of the line. "Follow me."

He lurched forward like a sixteen-year-old at a fresh green light—leaving the hard packed sand by the water and driving as close to the dunes as he could without running over the sea oats. The soft sand grabbed at our ankles and forced us to lift our knees like we were running through tires at football practice. My calves felt like they were tearing apart after fifty yards. Ed led the line and stayed as close to the quad as he could without sucking in the exhaust. It bellowed out thick black puffs, prompting Ed to comment with an exaggerated cough.

"When's the last time that bike got serviced?"

Buck didn't turn around, just yelled over his shoulder, "The last time Rick's check cleared."

There was mixed laughter in the group and a few guys shook their heads. Buck made a sharp turn. The bike lifted slightly on one side and kicked a spray of sand out of the back. The line of joggers bent and followed him. He accelerated and the line spread out over thirty yards but stayed in the soft sand.

"GO STANLEY." Buck lifted his legs off of the bike and held onto the handlebars like a cowboy riding a pissed off bull.

There were cheers and hoots as Stanley sprinted by. He ran like he spoke—with an uncontrollable stutter in his step that kept him from running in a straight line. The next guy, Adrain—slightly older than me and from Delaware—sprinted before Stanley got to the front of the line.

We were united in our loathing of Buck and our shared desire to finish the run. Each time someone began their sprint there was a chorus of cheering, not just from the guards, but also from people on the beach. I looked around at the smiles and I realized that I was getting paid for this.

My turn came and I busted from the back of the pack like Buck was riding on my heels. I wasn't introduced when we started the morning but everyone quickly learned my name. Grey and Ed start a rhythmic chant, "WES-LEY, WES-LEY!"

I was surprised at my own speed and from the middle of the pack I heard, "Fuck, that guy can run."

Buck stopped his four-wheeler. He stood on the seat in an unnecessary display of power. We were about half a mile from where we started. He pointed to the water.

"Stay fifty yards out. I'll see you back at Wright Street."

At that command, everyone—except for me and Stanley—sprinted into the water. I tried to catch up when I realized what was going on but most of the group had already settled into their strokes. I ran into the water as far as I could. I took a deep breath when it got too deep to run and pushed off the sandy bottom. After fifty yards or so my body lost its buoyancy. Flashes of my swim test a few days before came to mind and I watched the pack pull away. Stanley came along side of me but didn't pause, just maintained his determined pace. I thought about Fig's chiding and put my head back in the water.

Most of the guys were on the beach by the time I pulled even with the access. All of the supervisors— Preston, Fig, and Buck—were gathered around Rick's truck watching us.

Stanley was still in front of me and I fought my body's desire to stop in an effort to beat him out of the water. My arms felt like they were asleep—stinging with the cold tingle that comes after numbness. I took a long breath and plowed ahead. There was a pause in my momentum and suddenly I was on a watery treadmill—kicking and pulling but not moving. Waves broke on both sides of me and just a few feet away Stanley was experiencing the same thing. He looked back at me and took a few strokes to the side—not toward the shore. I followed him, assuming he knew something I didn't. The current broke.

Then, my feet lifted slightly and I felt a rolling push. I rode the incoming wave past Stanley into knee-high water, gathered myself and my buoy and looked back. He was still twenty yards out. I lifted my legs up and ran out of the water. There was no great fanfare for next to last place—only Grey's sympathetic pat on the back.

"Nice wave. How'd that rip current feel?"

"Is that what that was?" I grabbed at my shorts and looked at the supervisors.

They leaned against Rick's truck with their arms folded. They said nothing until Fig yelled, "See you at Mullet Street." He shook his head as Stanley walked by—head down with his buoy strap dragging in the sand.

Buck joined in. "Pick up your strap or I'll run-swim you all the way to your stand." He spit some chew in the sand near Stanley's feet.

Grey and I walked through the sandy access. Rick pulled up next to us.

"Get with Adrian. He can help you with your stroke."

"Yes sir." I nodded.

That's all Rick said.

When I got back to the shack I rinsed off with the hose and hung up the unmarked buoy I used for PT.

"Wesley," Preston leaned out the sliding door. "grab Wilkins Street's buoy. You're on your own today." He waited for me to nod. "You got everything you need?"

"Yeah. Thanks."

I walked to the end of the long buoy rack and found my first assignment. Adrian saw me holding the buoy.

"Wilkins Street. Nice. It's an easy stand, no rentals.

I'm at Eckner today—to your north."

I remembered the map Preston gave me and nodded.

"If you see me go like this," Adrian held both of his hands over his head and touched his fingers together. "Meet me between our stands."

I balanced my umbrella on one shoulder, picked up my buoy, my equipment box, looped the whistle around my neck, and followed Adrian out of the garage.

"Do I have to call it in on the radio?"

Adrian shook his head. "No man, just meet up with me."

The ocean looked so inviting when the wind blew offshore. There was a postcard quality to everything. The flat water was clear on those days and the air was the kind of warm that no one complained about, but there was a catch. When the wind blew out of the west like it did during my first week, the top layer of water, warmed by the summer sun, blew out to sea. There was an upwelling effect that dropped the temperature fifteen degrees overnight. Swimmers exited the surf with a bluish tint and a confused look.

Preston said those days were easy for us. No one wanted to get into the water. The biggest concerns were heat-related medical emergencies, lost kids, or people digging holes. Ultimately, battling boredom was our biggest challenge.

After a week of west wind and no action I did anything I could to stay awake. The black flies—relentless on ground—didn't bother us too much in our stands. I couldn't help but laugh at the people who made their way out to the beach, set up all of their gear, and spent twenty minutes slapping furiously at themselves and each other before they packed up and went to the pool. Some guards kept count of how many pests they killed in a day with notches on their armrest. The sadists in the group captured flies and subjected them to a death ray, courtesy of a finely focused binocular lens. The unscrewed lens was also good for burning initials into the wooden stands or leaving a message for the next guard.

I feared the nods—the wicked precursor to sleep. I stood up, stretched, walked down to the water, did a pull up or two on the back of my stand, twirled my whistle, splashed water from the cooler in my face, counted the people on the beach and the ones in the water—anything to avoid the nods.

My fear wasn't missing something in the water—like it should have been. The biggest deterrent to falling asleep on the stand was getting caught by a supervisor and the ensuing run-swim.

Run-swims ranged from a hundred yards to a mile long, depending on which supervisor was dishing them out. Buck was obviously the worst. If he caught someone sleeping or not watching the water, or if he just wanted to fuck with someone he thought was a screw-up, he'd make the guard run and swim until he either puked or came close to passing out. Then Buck put him back up in the stand exhausted and humiliated. When he pulled away on his four-wheeler he would yell back, so the entire beach could hear, "Now don't fall asleep again." He didn't care about public perception. It was hard to believe that Rick did either for hiring such a prick.

Adrian and I sat in neighboring stands for my first week. He signaled me from his stand and, with buoy and radio in hand, I walked north at the water's edge.

"It's just not professional." Adrian quickly confided in me his concern about the way Rick operated. We met on the imaginary line that divided our zones. At five o'clock the majority of the beachgoers had left. The supervisors were assuredly at the shack doing nothing.

"I hate to always say it, but back in Delaware, this punishment run-swim shit would never fly."

I listened intently, forming my opinion on the

subject through Adrian's experiences.

"He makes us all look like incompetent idiots when he lets Buck do that shit. I mean, what the hell do the people on the beach think?"

"I just hope he doesn't get on my case." I leaned on my buoy like it was a cane. The orange nose sunk into the wet sand.

This time Adrian nodded along with me. "Just don't give him a reason to."

"Wasn't planning on it." I looked out at the empty ocean.

"Going to the party tonight?"

"That, I was definitely planning on."

"Good, how many girls did you invite?"

I looked around. "My beach was kinda empty."

"No worries, there'll be plenty there."

CHAPTER 5

I put a collared shirt on for the first time that summer and yelled to Harry that I was leaving. He sat on the front porch and jumped up when I came through the front door.

"Where we going?" He looked at my shirt and cocked his head to one side.

I avoided telling him about the party because I didn't want to be the only guard who brought a guy and no girls.

"Just a thing with some guys from work."

"Oh." Harry leaned back against the railing.

"Yeah, it's probably gonna be stupid, but they invited me and I don't wanna be rude." I tried to shrug it off. "Probably just stop by and say hey."

Harry didn't say anything.

"I'll be back in an hour or so and we can go up to the pier and see if anyone's hanging out there."

"Cool." Harry slipped back into the porch chair and I made my way down the steps, feeling like an asshole.

The weathered two-story building at Magnolia Street was a cross between a rundown frat house and a surf shack. The walls were adorned with borrowed objects from the shack: red flags, buoys, surfing posters and random T-shirts pinned to the fake wood panel walls. There was more sand on the floor than there was carpet and the kitchen was stocked from a garage sale in the seventies. Low-hanging asbestos ceiling tiles were adorned with ever-changing water stains from who-knows-what above. The couches were covered with sheets and, despite the obvious state of disrepair, there was a comfortable quality that made me feel like I was hanging out in a friend's basement back at home. As much as I appreciated my spacious house and my own bedroom, I wished I could live at the Magnolia Street lifeguard house just to be closer to it all.

I walked in and found familiar faces in the living room. Ed sat on the arm of a couch next to the front door. He saw me and pointed.

"Rookie!" He grabbed my arm and pulled me toward him, throwing his arm around my shoulders like we were the oldest of friends. With a beer can in his other hand he pointed to the ceiling.

"Doesn't that one look like a pair of tits?" Ed gestured to two large brown circles above the television. Grey was on the couch looking at the stain and twisting his head.

"I think it looks like two balls." He leaned his head the other way and drew a straight line with his hand. "And there's the dick."

We all looked at Grey for a moment. He nodded with confidence and laughter rang out over the music.

"I guess you see what you want to see." Ed guided me by the shoulders toward the kitchen while he talked. "Grey requested the bathhouse stand so he could hang with all of his boyfriends but he didn't get it." He laughed and handed me a beer and I began my second phase of training.

Unlike the few high school parties I had attended, the ratio of girls to guys at the lifeguard function bordered on a dream. Most guys invited several girls—any sitting in their section of the beach. Each guard huddled around a smaller group with the girls he invited.

It was simply a matter of sorting out who would end up with who—a crude system of matching aided by several kegs and cases of wine coolers for the girls—and for Grey, who didn't apologize for enjoying them.

Each guard had his own party personality; the loud alpha males preened shirtless with large mugs of cheap beer. The older guards sat back musing over the whole scene. Adrian was the "laid back surfer" who regaled his audience with tales of crystal clear dawn peaks and being alone among a pod of dolphins—the gentle beasts flashing their white bellies as they passed beneath his board and teaching him lessons about respecting the ocean. He ran his fingers through his curly blonde hair—constantly stiff with salt—and stared out past the walls as though he was floating in the ocean before dusk and calmly admiring the violent hues of a post-storm sunset.

And the girls ate that shit up.

Grey was a little more stealth in his tactics—a remora who fed off of Adrian's leftovers. He acknowledged his homely looks and took a certain pride in them. He was smart and conserved his energy. He offered tidbits for the girls to nibble on in a witlessly choreographed dance. The steps were practiced each week and I enjoyed the show and the improvisational jokers at work. The setup was simple; the hard part was making it appear natural.

In a voice that begged to be overheard, Grey turned to me and asked, "Did you hear about Adrian today?" He looked at me with wide eyes that I recognized as a sign to play along.

"No, I was up north all day." Which was a sneaky little lie meant to add the validity to the con.

A cute young blonde-haired girl sat in the chair next to Grey drinking from a red Solo cup and looking nervous about being alone in the middle of the feeding grounds. I could tell she was listening to us while her equally attractive friend was in the bathroom. I didn't know who they came with but I did witness Ed's failed attempt to strike up a conversation.

Grey leaned back in his chair and continued, "There was this *insane* rip pulling hard just off the drain pipe near Sea Dunes. I'm sitting to his south and we're whistling people out all day. They're killing us down there, man— won't stay out of the water for nothing." He shifted his eyes enough to see that the girl was slowly sipping her beer with little change in her facial expression. "I go 10-7 when I think it's calmed down enough to take a break. While I'm gone, the sandbar where we've been telling people to swim breaks through." Grey spread his hands apart violently.

"Anybody get sucked out?" I knew she was listening at that point.

"Four of 'em." Grey held that many fingers up. "I run back over the dune in time to see Adrian jumping in the rip and going after them. I'm halfway out and the bastard starts pulling *all* of them in. So of course I look around to make sure there's no one else, and there isn't, so I have to swim in without anyone while Superman pulls in a whole family. And he's smiling like it's nothing. Get this, he says to me, 'swim behind me in case I drop one' and the people are laughing about it too."

"Damn, that's crazy."

"Adrian's a hell of a guard. Probably the best."

"Yeah, didn't he get Lifeguard of the Year last summer?"

Grey looked at me and cracked a smile at my creativity. "He should have if he didn't. Fucking Adrian."

We both took sips off of our drinks. Our job was done. The next move was Adrian's. It was my first party but I knew my role. I finished my beer and made my way to the keg in the kitchen. Adrian was talking to Ed who pumped the tap in slow motion for no apparent reason. I pressed the nozzle handle down and looked at Adrian.

"You're up." I motioned to Grey who'd engaged the

girl in some small talk.

Adrian craned his neck to the living room while Ed shook his head and said, "Good luck with that one man, she's a bitch."

Adrian looked at her and at Ed. "You think maybe it's because you call them bitches that they don't fall for your he-man routine?"

"Fuck off." Ed stopped pumping and stared at Adrian. He was joking but the competitive line was obviously drawn. Adrian had a watch-and-see-how-it's-done look on his face. He looked at Grey then at me.

"Did he call me Superman?"

I nodded.

"Damn." He held his cup out for me to fill and grabbed two wine coolers from the refrigerator. Ed and I watched him stroll into the living room where a girl he'd never met already thought of him as a hero—a superhero at that. Her friend returned from the bathroom and the four of them continued the dance.

Ed drained his cup, filled it, and drank half of his new beer. There was more than a sliver of jealousy disguised as intoxication in his red eyes. He looked at me and then around the living room. All of the girls—the ones worth talking to—were matched up with someone. Even Stanley was stuttering his way through a conversation with a girl. She was bigger than him, but they looked like they were having fun and I had to respect him for that.

Ed grunted at him. "Duff."

I didn't know what he was talking about. A chapter in the manual I hadn't read perhaps.

Ed looked at me again, "You been on a ride-along yet?"

I nodded. "Rick let me ride with him yesterday, just to see all the stands and accesses."

He laughed in a way that was instantly embarrassing. Adrian and his new friends looked up from their conversation at us. The blonde shook her head when she looked at Ed.

"Bitch." Ed stared but not for too long. He put his hand on my shoulder. It was clumsy and heavy. "No, Rookie, not a ride with Rick—that's a whole different thing." He paused like I was supposed to get the joke. "Come on."

We walked out the back door to the porch. There were a half dozen guards and as many girls. Ed went down the steps and disappeared into the dark recesses where the floodlights were blocked by the corners of the house. I could hear him pissing so I took my time. From the shadows I heard his voice.

"Rookie, 10-20?"

"10-17." I followed the sound of water hitting the sand.

Magnolia Street looked like a country used car lot; cars parked in the ditch, minivans scattered in dark driveways, and the ORS truck parked in the middle of it all. Two people made out under the carport next door and Ed made an immature kissing sound before crushing his Solo cup with a frustrated crackle.

"Car's over here." I followed Ed with hesitant steps.

"You want me to drive Ed?"

"Only had two. Get in."

"Hey, let's get Stanley to drive. He hasn't had anything."

Ed started his Jeep. It was a soft top CJ-5 and most of the top was frayed. There were straps hanging off the side with nowhere to go and I felt the same way. I stood in the street listening to Ed's Jeep rattling with no good reason to go with him. Through the window I saw Adrian and Grey laughing and in the distance I heard the two in the driveway giggling.

I climbed in.

"Don't worry. I'm okay." Ed turned to me and I could tell he was fine but I wondered what the act was for. "I just get sick of that scene sometimes. Same guys having the same bullshit conversations they had last week but with different girls." He looked at me and shook his head when he saw that I didn't understand. "Don't worry about it. Let's go find some girls that want to have fun."

I put on the seat belt, propped my foot on the doorless frame, and Ed took off. He whipped around the dark corner, through the stop sign and onto Aviation Drive. He took another right and headed to the four-lane bypass road but he stopped short of the sign and took the Jeep out of gear.

Ed raised his hand as though he was taking an oath. "Wesley...what's your last name?"

"Brooks."

"Wesley Brooks, you are an official..." he lifted his hand higher and looked at mine holding onto the roll bar. I raised mine like his. "You are an official deputy in the Kitty Hawk Booty Patrol."

"Okay." I waited for the punch line, but he just looked at the bypass.

Cars zipped by steadily at fifty miles per hour. The stream of traffic was nothing like the midday rush or the standstill lines on check-in day. Ed flipped on his high beams and the cars passed by illuminated for a brief moment before continuing north or south.

Ed looked at me for a long second. In the awkward moment I stared at the road in front of us hoping he'd say something. Ed spoke clearly but his words fell off at the end of his each sentence as though he had to stop to hear them himself. His head rocked back and forth a little but it was only noticeable in the stopped Jeep. He wasn't drunk but boredom and intoxication were bedfellows to Ed.

"You're gonna have more girls then you can keep track of."

"That'd be nice." I had nothing to offer to the conversation at that point so I continued staring, half-expecting Ed to change his mind and kick me out of the Jeep.

"Now we wait."

We didn't wait long and I knew before we peeled out what the Booty Patrol's assignment was. Ed pulled the high-beam switch back, slapped the dashboard, made a siren sound, and pushed the gear stick up. We slid around on the sand-covered asphalt before finding traction and starting our chase.

"You see that one, Rookie? Four girls in that car." He shifted and made up some ground. "College girls." He pointed to the rear windshield at a decal. *Virginia Tech.* "Ooh boy, gonna get us some Hokies tonight."

I grabbed on to the roll bar and brought my foot back into the Jeep. Ed weaved in and out of traffic— sometimes using the center turn lane to pass. We were doing at least sixty-five—Ed's speedometer bounced around wildly. I gave my seatbelt a tug and Ed let out a ferocious yell. The girls were in the left lane and Ed maneuvered along side of them as we slowed for a traffic light. Just before we pulled even with them he turned down the music.

"Let them look first, okay?"

I nodded.

"Then, when I say so, you look over there casually. You're the scout. If they look good you say so, okay?"

"Got it." All I could do was go along with it.

He pulled the Jeep up to the line. My heart was pounding and I thought it might burst if I screwed up. Until that point the girls had been oblivious to us. They didn't see our two-mile pursuit. Ed looked at the light as though we were late for something and it couldn't change fast enough.

"Go ahead and look...slowly."

I glanced down at the cup holder between the seats and then past Ed's steering wheel through the girls' open window and then back to the road ahead.

I whispered and tried not to move my lips when I spoke.

"They're looking."

"Of course they are. Do they look good?"

"The passenger is hot, I think. I can't see the others."

"Good enough for me." Ed looked over and the girls quickly turned their heads away from the Jeep. "Excuse me." Ed smiled—his aggressive driving face completely gone.

They looked.

"Y'all wanna go to a party?"

The girls looked at each other, shrugged, then giggled. The passenger leaned out the window and yelled, "Okay."

"Follow us." Ed flipped on his right turn signal. When the light turned to green he drove to the empty post office parking lot and pulled in. The girls' car rolled in cautiously. Fortunately, Ed waved them to his side of the car. My head slowly nodded to the muted radio in an attempt to appear distracted or unaffected by the girls' presence. Ed quickly involved me in his game.

"My buddy and I are on our way to a party. Y'all wanna go?"

Damn, it was too simple to work. No girl in her right mind was going to follow us to—

"Sure, where is it?"

Ed tried to get a good look at the driver while he reeled in his catch.

"Back that way a bit. We're on our way to get some drinks. You wanna just follow us?"

"Isn't the grocery store back that way too?" The passenger made a suspicious expression like she'd busted our undercover effort but Ed didn't even balk.

"Gotta run by the bank machine first." He pointed to the opposite side of the road at the maroon sign. I could see two heads turn in the back seat but the tinting of the rear windows and the dark parking lot made it impossible to see what they looked like—only silhouettes.

"What kinda party is it?" The passenger had raccoon eyes—red cheeks and white sunglass marks. I could only see her white shirt, Polo, and a strand of pearls around her pink neck. It was Tuesday—Magnolia Street parties were always on Tuesdays—and the girl was showing the effects of two full days in the sun before her new tan had a chance to turn.

"Bunch of guys we work with get together every now and then."

"You mean, you *live* here?"

It was a funny thing to see people's reaction when they realized that someone actually lived, worked, and went to school where they chose to take their vacation.

"Yeah, we live here. For the summer." Ed tapped his foot on the edge of the doorframe—he wanted the small talk to take place somewhere other than the post office parking lot. It was exciting to hear Ed include me, even if it was only to advance the conversation.

The chase, the girls, and this wild-eyed sort-of-sober guy next to me were more than my adrenaline could keep up with. My prudence was still coughing at the stop sign and I was in a new place. I was instantly older and cooler. The girls followed us, first to the ATM for a gratuitous withdrawal and then north to the grocery store.

They stayed in their car and I could tell they were still a little unsure about Ed and me. We got a few cases— enough for us and four girls—and filled the back seat of the Jeep. The girls never got out. Ed waved for them to follow us.

"So you like the passenger huh?" Ed turned to me with an approving expression that lay somewhere between curiosity and confidence.

I shrugged—not wanting to appear too eager.

"She's all yours, man."

I looked at him to see if there was any more locker room wisdom to follow.

"Yeah, you get her and I'll take the other three.

Deal?"

I laughed and shook my head. It still sounded like a good deal to me.

"Why didn't you tell them we're lifeguards?" I figured it would put girls' minds at ease and they might be more interested than scared.

"No point, they were going to come anyway." He reached back, pulled a beer out of the cardboard case, opened it, and held the can between his knees as we led the two-car parade down the bypass for a short trip to Magnolia Street. "They'll figure it out soon enough. They'll see the rescue truck or something. If you say it right away it puts them on the defensive—like you're using it."

Which, of course, we were but I saw Ed's strategy and I understood it when we stepped out of the car.

The driver got out and asked, "Are you guys lifeguards?" Ed looked back at me and I thought he was going to wink or something but he just nodded and grabbed two cases, leaving me one.

The passenger opened her door and I saw her long blonde hair. It fell just below her shoulders and led my eyes down to her waist. She stepped into the orange glow of one lone street lamp and I turned away quickly. Ed closed the rear gate of the Jeep with his hip and *then* he winked at me.

I whispered an exasperated, "Fuck."

Ed spoke from the corner of his mouth, "What's the matter, Rookie? Thought you liked your girls big in the bottom?"

I looked back at the girl, hoping what I saw was an illusion created by the dim street-light. The two girls from the back crawled out from the front seats. There hadn't been a mistake. These girls obviously read somewhere that black was slimming; each of them wore tight black pants. Their faces were pretty but I couldn't see past the figures.

Being around tight tanned bodies and seeing throngs of bikini-clad girls on the beach had distorted my perception of reality. It was easier to go with the consensus—especially concerning a girl's attractiveness—then to step aside and argue against it. Stanley was the exception. Along with the constant competition for the best stand, the most rentals, and secretly the best rescue, there was an obvious desire to leave the party with the best looking girl. It was gross and immature and selfishly pleasing but there was no end to it and everyone got swept up in the challenge.

The excitement of walking in with the four girls quickly turned to a nervous feeling of guilt. It was all a part of Ed's game. I was just as responsible for the awkward silence that consumed the room when we opened the front door and for the painful whispers from the less tactful guards. I felt a need to involve the girls in the party but Ed had other plans.

"We're gonna go throw these in the cooler." Ed lifted the cases like they were buckets filled to the brim with impudence. He nodded at me and I passed the shameless gesture on to the passenger who stood just inside the doorway with the three other girls. They moved to the middle of the living room, surrounded by cute little girls—most still in high school or recently graduated—their faces were canvases painted with discomfort and self-consciousness.

I followed Ed to the kitchen where he methodically emptied the cases of beer into the fridge as though the rhythm and placement of the cans were a lost art that he was determined to perfect. He took the case I held and emptied it in impressive fashion, leaving two beers out. He handed me one and motioned to the back door.

"Come on."

"What? You aren't gonna take those girls any beers?"

"The Booty Patrol rides again." Ed opened the back door.

I couldn't believe his nerve. Leaving like that felt criminal. The girls stood together for protection. Two guards walked up to the group and the girls smiled. There was a moment of relief—as though I had done them a *favor* by bringing them to the party. Then the passenger leaned around the guy in front of her and pointed at Ed and me. She waved at me and Ed grabbed my arm. He pulled me onto the porch and shut the door.

"Are you serious?" I marveled at Ed's audacity.

"What? You wanna hang with those girls?"

"Not really." I didn't know what I wanted. "It's just a little fucked up leaving them in there."

"That girl would have crushed you."

I laughed—the way guys laugh at something that they'd shy away from if girls were within earshot. But I laughed and it felt good to be that way—to not care.

"You see the way that girl was looking at you?"

"Which one?" I knew he was talking about the passenger but I played dumb to see what his theory was.

"Your girl, the one with the ass."

"The *one* with the ass?"

He laughed with me.

"She was crazy." He spun his finger around near his ear.

"How do you know?"

"Could tell by the way she was looking at you. She would have fallen in love before the week was over—go home all crying and shit."

"No way. I didn't even talk to her."

"Doesn't matter. I've seen it before. You're too nice and she would have fallen in love with you and you would have been too nice to dissuade her and she would get all psycho on you."

"Psycho?"

"Yeah, man. You gotta be careful. You get with the wrong girl and she'll be showing up at your stand the next day, driving down from Virginia after she's left, calling you, wanting to know why you don't call her back and shit. Psycho. When Saturday comes, send her home and look for the next one. Life's too short to hang with psycho chicks, man."

We climbed back into Ed's Jeep and I buckled up. This philosophy caught me off guard—not so much for his fear of attracting clingy girls but for his perception of me and his obvious trepidation when it came to the topic of love.

Ed and I made three more "Booty Runs" delivering a dozen girls to a party that already had too many girls. I found a friend in the last place I expected to. We bonded over an unspoken desire to find a special girl. But in our literal hunt we camouflaged ourselves as insensitive guys that were simply playing a game to see who could score the most.

To that point in my short romantic life I'd treated girls like they were always out of reach; pushing the pedestal so high that I was forced to admire them from a distance. Ed, in the course of an hour, brought them into my grasp and showed me how to toss them aside like they were nothing more than a bruised apple at the grocery store.

I realized Ed enjoyed the attention from the other guards almost as much as from the girls when we brought two gorgeous girls to the party. We pulled them over near the Dairy Queen, asked them if they'd like to join us, and went back to Magnolia Street as proud as we could be.

We walked through the front door like it was the first time that night. Each guard in the room greeted us with the same look or comment from just a half-hour before. The party was the same as when we left except for one addition. Down the hallway I saw a new but familiar face waiting to use the bathroom. Ed saw her at the same time and I noticed a pause in his step when she lifted her hand in polite acknowledgement of our arrival. It was the first time I'd seen Lilly since my swim test.

She looked at Ed and me and then down to the floor. I stopped and waited for her to look up. She didn't.

"Come on, Deputy." Ed called from the kitchen.

The other girls we'd collected through the night watched us walk in but quickly returned to their conversations. I was sure Ed wasn't going to let these two new girls be alone for too long but he opened the door, pointed to the refrigerator and said, "Those two are for you and Grey. Let me know how it works out for you tomorrow."

He shut the door before I could say anything. I turned back to the living room where Grey sat alone on the couch. I pulled out three beers and a wine cooler and motioned for Grey to join me. He looked at the two girls. They were by the door talking to each other—standing very close together.

"Ed left."

"So which one do you want?"

"I don't know; let's just see how it works out." I handed Grey a Bartles and James and one of the cans of beer.

"Cool. What's your plan?"

"Give them a beer and talk to them."

"It's your game." Grey started toward the living room.

"Where's Adrian?"

"He drove those other two girls home."

"You didn't want to go?"

"No point—they had to be home by twelve. They're staying with their family. We might go out with them tomorrow. What's the story here?"

"Christine on the right, Julie on the left. Pennsylvania."

"Lead the way."

Three of the first girls we pulled over talked with each other on the couch. The passenger was no where to be seen. They look pissed and bored and ready to go.

I smiled at Julie and Christine and felt the daggers coming from the couch. I could sense the perversion of the situation but it didn't bother me too much. I was more concerned with impressing the two trophies.

"Thank you." Christine took the can I offered her and Julie took Grey's.

"You like wine coolers?" Julie was interested rather than judgmental. Grey nodded. "Me too."

And the hard part was over. Grey and Julie went to the kitchen, swapped her beer for a bottle and disappeared through the back door out to the porch, leaving Christine and me smiling at each other—hardly able to disguise our nervousness.

"So, Pennsylvania?"

"Yeah."

"Where about?"

"Clarion. It's near Pittsburgh."

"Oh, the *other* side of Pennsylvania."

Christine looked confused.

I tried to explain. "My uncle lives outside of Philadelphia in Doylestown."

Her face came back to life. "Oh I see." She giggled—more at the situation than the comment.

"Where are you staying?"

"In Duck with my family." She pointed at the front door which faced north.

I nodded.

"Where do you live?"

"On Neptune Street." I pointed south to the back door.

She shook her head. She obviously didn't know where Neptune Street was. I looked at the door to the porch, hoping Grey would walk through it and save me. I saw him through the window but he made no movement toward the door. I glanced around. Lilly was no longer in the hallway. Everyone in the living room was deep in conversation. It was easy to gauge the progress by how close the couple sat to each other. Stanley was actually sitting in his girl's lap.

I was about to give up when Christine grabbed my

hand.

"Do you want to go for a walk?" I looked at her like she was an old friend who was thinking the same thing and we'd realized it at the same time.

"Of course I want to go for a walk." My voice relaxed and I was normal again—not nervous and fake. She pulled me through the door and the thickness of the night hit me. I hadn't escaped out the back door for once and there was freshness in the salt filled breeze that made the night feel new again. Ed and the "Booty Patrol" were gone. The musical chairs and pseudo attention of the party were gone. There was just Christine and me standing under a streetlight away from the couple that continued to make out in the dark driveway and giggle randomly.

"What about Julie, won't she worry?"

As soon as the words came out of my mouth I heard Ed's voice screaming with his primal tone, *"Shut the fuck up and take her to the beach, you pussy."*

"She won't even know I'm gone. Come on. That party was creepy. I had to get out of there."

"Yeah, it gets kinda old." I nodded and turned toward the beach.

"Do you do this a lot? These parties?" She let go of my hand when we got to the next driveway and I was like a kid in elementary school who'd been holding hands with the pretty girl at recess and it ended when the bell rang.

"Well, no, not really. I just started working last week."

"So are you like the rest of those guys?"

We walked an arm's length away from each other and the awkwardness returned.

"How do you mean?"

"You know how lifeguards are."

I leaned to the side and, in an exaggerated attempt to take in the whole of her comment, looked at her. "How are we?"

"You spend all day looking at girls on the beach.

Then you throw parties at night and drive around looking for more girls."

Fuck.

"We were on our way to the store."

"Well, are you like that?" She stopped and waited as though my answer determined whether or not we crossed the beach road and went over the access.

"Like I said, I've only worked here for like a week. This is my first party." My hands were out to my side, palms turned up.

"Well, I'll give you the benefit of the doubt." She squinted and looked at me through the side of her eyes.

"I appreciate it." This time I took her hand and pulled her across the empty road to the sandy lot.

The waves were small and slow—creeping against the shore and sneaking up the beach to our bare feet. We both wore jeans and T-shirts—the air crisp but not uncomfortable. Christine rolled her pants tight with the cuffs up as high as they'd go against her dark legs. She looked like Mary-Anne but I didn't say anything. Then she looked at my rolled pants and called me Gilligan and I nearly fell in love with her right there.

She pointed to the pier, "I want to go there."

I laughed and shook my head. "It's a mile and a half away."

"How do you know that?"

I pointed north, "The pier is at milepost one." Then I pointed at the sand at our feet, "We're at two and a half." I shrugged my shoulders, "I'm not a mathematician, but..."

"You got somewhere else to be?" She cocked her head to one side and said it like she couldn't believe my nerve.

There was an air about Christine—like she might turn at any minute and go pick any other guy she wanted and lead him off into the night. She leaned her head the other way and asked, "When do you work tomorrow?"

"I have to be on the beach at seven-thirty for PT."

"PT? Is that some lifeguard code?"

"Physical training."

"I see. Well, consider our walk a warm up for tomorrow."

I bowed my head and lifted my hands in an exaggerated expression of defeat.

"Lead the way."

We passed by the Maynard Street lifeguard stand. Two people sat on the bench. Lights from the beach road cast their shadows down to the water.

"Do you like lifeguarding?"

"I love it. I get paid to sit on the beach."

"Have you had to save anyone?" She crinkled her forehead a bit and looked at the lake-like water.

I felt pressure to defend the profession. "It's calm tonight, but the water gets pretty rough. People get in trouble every day." I shrugged my shoulders and acted disinterested about all of the rescues I had never made.

She looked out at the water. "Is it scary?"

I shook my head. "Not really scary. It can be stressful. But there are so many guys to back me up. I don't really worry about it." I dragged my foot in the sand and looked back at the line it left. "It's more of the stuff that happens before rescues that keeps us busy."

"Like making sure the girls all have enough tanning lotion on?" Her teasing was accusatory in tone and I played along—no longer fearing that she'd turn around.

"Do you think I'm like that?"

"I'm just seeing if you are."

"Well, what will it take to prove to you that I'm not?" It was a bold move but something about the moment made it easy to forget my inhibitions.

Christine shrugged. Despite her lack of response, the way she looked at me said more than she had all night. Her eyes whispered, "Be a summer fantasy—someone to brag to my friends about when I go home; be amazing and cordial and sweet and sensitive; be everything I think you are."

That's what her eyes said but I could hardly ignore the rest of her body. Those things she wanted—the fantasies that made girls simply complex—sounded like they'd make me weak as a hunter. I tried to find a line somewhere between her desires and the stereotypical lifeguard that I secretly want to be. It was a blend of manners and respect that lacked the honesty of the gestures.

We walked the mile or so toward the pier, past the crumbling foundation of the Seahorse Motel—a four-story relic devoured by each storm and high tide. We passed by two more lifeguard stands—both were empty but at the Byrd Street access she took my hand again. By the time we got to the pier we'd talked about things that all teenagers knew—school, friends, things that annoyed us, things that we hid from our parents. The conversation was exciting— not so much for the content—but because it moved along without the awkward moments from earlier.

We made it to the pier but didn't walk under. She led me to the edge of the water where we stood in the second light out from the pier house. Her hand squeezed mine tight when the cold water ran over her feet and splashed against her smooth legs.

Our fluid conversation stopped.

She faced the water and I stepped behind her. She put my hand on her hip and wrapped the other one around her waist like we were posing for a prom picture. Her shoulders eased and settled against my chest. Her hair— brown in the light of the pier—lifted in the relaxed wind and dropped just as softly. She let go of my hand and ran hers through one side of her hair and behind her ear. In the shadow of the pier light I followed a thin gold necklace from her neck down to the V of her shirt where it disappeared. She looked back and caught me staring down at her. I moved my hips away from her back to avoid appearing too eager.

She turned her back to the water and filled the gap between the two of us. She looked up at me for a moment and then stepped away. She didn't let go; she spun me around so that my back was to the water.

"You're too tall." She moved up the sloping beach so that she was eye-level with me. "That's better."

The light from the Kitty Hawk Pier parking lot made it hard for me to see her face. She leaned forward and I closed my eyes.

I heard a cry from above followed by an unmistakable southern drawl, "Yeah boy…you go ahead and kiss that girl!"

We looked up to see three fishermen, poles in hand, standing along the railing peering down at us and smiling as big as the fish that got away.

I lifted my hand and lowered my head. She turned her head south and laughed. We slid under the pier and glanced up and around. No one was in sight so I wrapped one arm around her waist and pulled her to me with the grace of a movie kiss. Once again I found myself trying to keep up with Christine. Her pace was more than I could handle.

She pulled back after the cinematic embrace and shook her head. "I thought you were different." There was no hurt or disappointment in her tone. Her comment was a challenge.

"Didn't you want to?"

"Of course I did, but I thought you were innocent."

"I am."

I pulled her back to me, kissing her again to show her that her conflicting philosophy and actions wouldn't dissuade me. I lifted her waist against mine and she rose up on her toes. We sunk into the sand and I reached back to find one of the pier's pilings. I'd known the girl for about an hour. I didn't know her last name and I didn't even want to. I ran my hand up her back between the blades of her shoulders and back down to her waist. She reached back and pushed it farther down onto her jeans. I gave up on hiding my excitement. My other hand followed the first until it met on her back pockets.

She pressed against me—the piling behind me acted as a wall. Her left hand ran up my neck and gently grabbed at a tuft of longer hair and locked on. Her right hand moved easily down my flat chest and past the waist of my jeans.

The rhythm of my kissing stuttered when she ran her hand against the inside of my leg and then up the other side. I moved my hands around to her front to match her moves but when they reached her pockets she stepped back, put both hands on my chest, and pushed away with a playful force that told me not to move.

"You're not innocent." She looked down at my jeans and took another step back. "You're all the same." In what was becoming her trademark, she looked at me with challenging eyes that begged to be proven wrong.

I'd run out of breath and comebacks. I matched her retreat with a step of my own and she raised her hand.

"We should get back." She started walking and didn't look back until she reached the second light again.

My mouth was still open. The kiss—so abruptly ended— waited to be finished. I leaned my head back against the piling. "What the hell?" The pigeons in the rafters above cooed back in a language that made more sense at the moment then Christine did.

I ran my hands down my face like I was washing it of the moment's confusion, let out a sigh, and adjusted my jeans. I reluctantly walked out into the light and looked up to see if our audience was still enjoying the show. The only things that lingered were the smell of recently cleaned fish and the mile and a half walk back. I remembered telling Harry we'd go to the pier. It was almost 2 a.m. and a warm wave of guilt came over me.

Christine was twenty yards ahead of me and I

thought about walking over to the beach road to avoid following her. She turned around, walked backward, and skipped in and out of the street light that crept down from the gaps between cottages.

"Can't you keep up?" She lifted her hands to her mouth like she was calling from across the ocean itself.

"Do you want me to?"

"Oh, don't be so dramatic." This time she waved her hands at me. "You're the lifeguard—try to catch me." She took off in a full sprint down the beach.

"She's crazy." I yelled it to no one. I abandoned my ego and laid chase.

I followed her footsteps for a few yards and then moved down to the hard packed wet sand by the water's edge. I could hear Ed's voice chiding me for subjecting myself to a girl he would call a tease. I caught up with her in the shadows of the blue house next to the Byrd Street access.

I grabbed the back of her jeans and ran a few more steps so she knew I could keep going.

"What are you... some track star?" I slowed her down and tried to catch my breath.

"Yep."

"Really?" I cocked my head to the side.

"Full scholarship to Penn State."

"Okay, then I don't feel so bad for needing a half mile to catch you."

"You should. I don't run on sand for a living."

I kept a hold on the waist of her jeans but slipped my hand around to the front of them. I took a few deep breaths and tried to catch her eyes again but there wasn't as much light as under the pier so I drew her closer. This time I made no apologies and I pulled her against me with just enough force to make me think—even for that fleeting moment—that I had an ounce of control.

"So what's your plan?" Christine got close enough for me to kiss her.

"Plan?"

"Yeah, your plan. You gonna lie me down in the waves and let them wash all over us while we make love under the starry sky?" She pointed up into the cloudy night and I let go of her jeans. "Or you just gonna screw me in the lifeguard stand so you can tell everyone about it tomorrow?" She stepped back.

The playful look was gone and for the first time that evening we were two real people not caricatures. She really did want to know what my intentions were and I genuinely didn't know.

"I'm sorry you feel that way about me." I glanced down and kicked some sand from one foot to the other. "I thought we were having a good time...and honestly I hadn't planned on doing anything like that." I looked at her and felt like I was apologizing for someone else. "I might have gotten carried away under the pier but I was just going with it."

She stared at me.

"Sorry." I hooked my thumbs through my own belt loops and looked down the beach. "Let's head on back. I'm sure Julie is wondering where you are."

She said nothing and we walked together again. There was no chasing, no witty banter, and no eye contact. When we passed the Seahorse she took my hand.

"What's your last name?" She looked at the sandbags and the stumps that remained from a deck long washed away.

"Brooks."

"Wesley Brooks. Promise me you won't be like those other guys?"

I laughed and smiled because it felt like the right thing to do for her and because all I wanted was to be like those other guys.

Julie and Grey were hugging near her car when we got back to Magnolia Street.

"What are you doing tomorrow?" It was the logical thing to ask. But in the moment, surrounded by beer cans and scattered cars, it came out politely forced. I leaned against the passenger's side door of Julie's Honda Civic.

"Just going to the beach." Christine shrugged and avoided eye contact.

"I'm working at Wilkins Street tomorrow if you're bored." I cringed internally when I thought about Ed's "psycho" warning, but the feeling passed quickly.

"I don't know where that is."

"Less than a mile that way." I pointed in the opposite direction.

"I'll see what Julie wants to do tomorrow." We looked at Julie and Grey and quickly rolled our eyes away when we caught their goodnight kiss.

I rubbed the top of Christine's hand with my thumb. The other couple joined us and I stepped away from the car.

"Okay, y'all drive safe." I opened the door for Christine and waved through the cab at Julie. Grey and I stood apart when the girls drove away. He walked over to me with an eager smile on his face.

"How'd you do?"

"What do you mean?"

"You two were down on the beach for a while." Grey paused and waited for something to be proud of. "You make some sand-angels?"

"No." I waited for an explanation but he just smiled. I realized what it would take to make such a creation and I continued without asking. "Well, you know..." I paused, and tried to figure out how to put to words something I didn't exactly understand. "We had a good time." I smiled and looked at Grey and he nodded once. "We walked down to the pier."

"Really?" Grey did the math in his head. "That's a good walk."

"How'd you do?" I knew—based on the short

goodnight kiss—that the night left something to be desired for Grey.

"I couldn't get her off the porch. I tried to get her to the beach but she wasn't going for it. I think she has a boyfriend."

"But you kissed her, right? Maybe she doesn't."

Grey put his hand on my shoulder and shook his head. "She's got something going on back home. I can tell." I felt like an apprentice. "But when these girls come on vacation they're all single. They all want a little summer fling." He squeezed my shoulder and let go. "You just got to get over that little speed bump."

Grey amused me and it must have shown. He ran his hand in a flat line in front of me and then passed it over an imaginary hump. "Speed bumps man—that's all boyfriends are down here. Once you get over them—it's all downhill. Wouldn't be surprised if your girl's got one at home."

"I don't know."

"A girl that hot's got someone thinking about her somewhere."

I shrugged—the thought had crossed my mind.

"So what's your plan?"

I laughed at his question since I didn't have any better answer for him than I did for Christine. I just shook my head and kept walking.

"You want to see her again don't you?"

"I guess. I'm not sure what she wants." I walked a few steps ahead of Grey.

"They'll probably want to hang out tomorrow."

"So we'll figure something out. I told Christine to come by my stand."

"Yeah, Julie said they would."

"So, we'll see how it goes tomorrow." I stopped next to the car with the Virginia Tech sticker on it.

The front door of the house opened. Three of the girls—the ones sulking on the couch—walked out. They smiled at us but there was no sincerity in their expressions.

They acted like we tricked them. I didn't see the passenger but I heard them talking about her.

"I can't believe she went with him. He's not even cute." The girls lowered their voices as they approached the car.

We stepped aside and tried to continue our conversation in hopes of avoiding the awkward situation but the driver said one more thing before they shut the doors; "Bunch of conceited assholes…."

There was silence again.

Grey heard the comment and made a face while he mocked her voice. "We're just too fat to get any." He continued with the face while I laughed into my hand.

Halfway through my drive home that night I convinced myself that I did Harry a favor by not taking him to the party. He would have been out of place and probably just sat alone on a couch watching TV. We were friends from high school. That didn't mean I had to do everything with him. I'd be quiet when I got home and leave before he was up. At best, I was going to get four hours of sleep; there was no need to make an issue of it.

Cars lined both sides of Neptune Street when I turned off of the bypass. People were in the street and I had to idle through them to avoid a collision. There were at least fifty strangers around, under, and in my house. The porch was packed. I looped around the block looking for a parking space and ended up pulling into the beach access.

A bottle fell from the railing and shattered in the driveway as I walked up the steps. Harry was nowhere in sight and I scanned the crowd for a familiar face. Liz was in the kitchen making drinks. She saw me and raised her glass.

"Our host has arrived!" Her eyes squinted at me then quickly looked around. No one else in the room paid any attention to my arrival.

"Liz, what the hell's going on? Where's Harry?"

She covered her mouth and shook her head like she

had a secret she couldn't tell. She looked down the hallway and back at me. It was the longest conversation I'd had with her and somehow the least productive.

"How did this happen?"

Liz threw the cup back and slammed it on the counter.

"It's a party, you prude."

"Where's Lucas?"

"Night surfing."

"There aren't any waves."

"You're an idiot. He's getting high on the beach."

"Awesome." I looked around. "Who are these people?"

"They're people." She pointed to the couch. "There's Taco Bell guy. There's his girlfriend," She paused and looked confused, "Taco Bell girl." She reached for the bottle of rum behind her and I threw my hands up.

I walked to the stereo and turned the music down.

"Everyone's gotta go. Party's over."

Again, no one reacted and I continued down the hallway to Harry's room. I could hear a girl's voice but I didn't care. I knocked and took a step back.

"No one's here!" There was laughter followed by a loud, "*shush.*"

"Harry, it's Wesley, I'm coming in."

"Hold on!"

The door opened enough for me to see Harry's sweaty face and four legs still in the bed. I lifted up on my toes to see over his head. He moved out of the way and I saw two girls curled up on his bed.

"We'll talk tomorrow?" He looked at me and smiled.

"Yeah." It took a moment for me to gather my thoughts and switch from pissed off to proud. "I'm going to clear everyone out of the house." I craned my neck for another look.

"Have fun." He shut the door quickly and the laughter returned. I stood there and stared.

Liz was gone when I made it back to the kitchen. I took a flashlight from the junk drawer and opened the fuse panel. Flipping off every circuit breaker but the bedrooms' caused groans from the porch and I eventually heard people walking down the steps into the dark driveway.

The glowing hands on my watch showed it was two forty-five. The flashlight guided me back to my room. I double checked that the alarm clock was still functioning before I landed face first on the bed.

CHAPTER 6

The buzzer went off before I could find my way to a dream. It was six forty-five and the sun already filled my room.

"Turn it off."

I snapped up onto my elbows and saw Liz rolling over on my extra pillow.

"Holy shit!" I sprung backward and landed against my dresser.

"Turn off the fucking light." She covered her head with the pillow.

I looked down and saw her jeans on the floor. Her lace underwear and bra were piled on top. I still had the clothes I wore to bed on and that was the only thing keeping me from total panic. I didn't have time to find Lucas and I didn't really want to. I couldn't be late for PT or my day would only get worse.

I got dressed in the bathroom and collected my thoughts. The house was quiet. Taco Bell guy and girl were still on the couch. I didn't care at that point. I flipped the breakers back on, made my lunch, and ate some cereal.

"Got any coffee?"

I looked up from my bowl and saw Liz at the end of

the hallway. She wore one of my shirts and when she lifted her arms to stretch it was clear that her underwear was still on the floor. She didn't wait for me to answer before disappearing into the bathroom. I quickly threw my bowl in the sink and grabbed my cooler. I was out the door and down the steps when I heard the pipes rush under the house.

The sandy yard was littered with bottles and cans. I stepped over it all and was glad I parked so far away when I saw the broken glass in the driveway. My quick exit made me the first one to the shack so I collapsed on one of the couches and closed my eyes.

"Late night, Rookie?"

I felt a tap on my foot. Buck stood with crossed arms. Before I could answer a shower of ice cold water came down on my head. My mouth opened wide to catch my breath. Laughter rang out and I realized the room was full of guards. Fig pointed and howled with the empty bucket in his hand.

Physical training was the necessary evil of being a lifeguard on the beach. No one ever questioned the reason for doing it. There was a constant debate however, over the manner in which it was run. Supervisors were in charge of the exercises with Rick making an occasional appearance to offer us encouragement over his truck's public address system. We all stepped up our efforts a little when he was around. It wasn't to avoid his disparaging remarks—those were inevitable. It went back to a need for assurance. *"Great job this morning,"* was what we all wanted to hear.

Depending on which supervisor had the mildest hangover, PT could be as simple as a long run or as draining as ins-and-outs for thirty minutes. The first real test of a new guard was how well he did at PT. It was literally sink or swim. I was evidence that a decent showing would keep me off the shit list. My swim improved. I was making it out of the water in the middle of the pack with some pointers from Adrian.

With damp shorts from my ice bucket alarm, I happily turned over the title of "new guy" to a pale chubby boy named Doug. Taller than me, he could have been a lineman on any high school football team. Rather than put him through the training with Preston, he was thrown to the wolves at PT.

He walked out to the beach wearing his own bathing suit and carrying a junior buoy—shorter and lighter than the regular ones. He also wore a bright red rash guard. The nylon shirt, worn by surfers to prevent wax irritation, was stretched tight over his belly. He tried to suck it in to no avail—the shirt's collar squeezed tight around the loose skin of his neck. His bleached hair made his skin look pink. Buck wasted no time in addressing the fashion blunder.

"What the fuck's with the rash guard?"

Doug, caught a bit off guard, looked around at the group. "I thought it might be cold."

The rest of us kept stretching—touching our toes and twisting our backs so that our faces didn't show the smirks.

"Take it off." Buck leaned against his four-wheeler with a wad of chew against his gums and a brownish-green Mountain Dew bottle in one hand. He looked like a disheveled drill sergeant feeling the effects of too many drinks the night before. He wasn't in the mood to deal with a stupid rookie in a red rash guard.

"You look like a used tampon."

A chorus of laughter bounced around the scattered group—most came from Fig, who sat like a parrot on the back of Buck's four-wheeler and giggled in a high pitched mocking tone. Doug, to his credit, even showed some interest in the joke when he removed the red shirt. He held it by the tag as though it was what Buck suggested.

With a smile on his face he held it near his nose and then flung it at Buck's feet.

"If it's a tampon then it must be yours—it smells like piss and stale beer." His smile turned flat and his face lost its color immediately. He stared at Buck.

Doug's boldness quieted the group and instantly turned us into an audience. At some point every guard wanted to tell Buck to shove it, but he held some power of intimidation that had gone unnoticed by this plump boy. Doug was probably the target of bullies before and chose this opportunity to confront one. Unfortunately, he picked Buck on a hangover day.

Grey leaned toward me while trying to touch his toes and whispered, "Dude's got some brass balls."

Buck spit in his bottle, never taking his eyes off Doug. He stepped toward him. We all straightened up, not wanting to miss any of the action, although we knew what to expect. I'd already seen a couple of arguments. They were usually a continuation of some prior dispute that ended with crude expletives—maybe a push or two—subsiding with cooler heads stepping in and breaking it up before it became something bigger.

The difference in this case is that no one knew Doug or his limits. On the flip side, we knew how Buck worked. He was a classic bully, thriving on someone else's insecurities. Doug stood in the midst of toned, tanned bodies—but he stood tall.

Buck was an arm's length from Doug staring through puffy eyes. He reached out and grabbed Doug at the waist. Stunned, Doug froze.

With his hand full of flesh Buck growled, "You think you'll ever be a lifeguard, you fat fuck?" He held tight and jiggled Doug's gut. A smirk crept across his dip-laden lips. He turned to look at Fig but his face met Doug's fist midway.

The punch was solid. Tobacco sprayed across the sand and dripped down Buck's chin. There was an audible crunch—a combination of knuckle and nose; the fleeting moment drawn out by Buck's continued grip on Doug's stomach. When he finally let go, a pink handprint appeared on Doug's belly. Buck dropped to a knee and held his free hand over his nose. He let go of the bottle and tried to stand up. By that time Fig was between the two—as shocked as the rest of us.

Buck got to his feet with considerable effort. Doug stood unfazed—his hands spread open like he had no desire to continue the fight. Buck wiped at the dip on his face with the back of his hand, only smearing it and mixing it with blood dribbling from his nose. There was a discernable lack of rage in his expression—embarrassment and confusion took its place. He must have swallowed all of the dip that didn't end up on the sand. As quickly as the punch was thrown Buck leaned over and grabbed his knees. He vomited all over his own feet.

Fig and Doug stepped back and grimaced at the sight. Buck continued until he was dry heaving.

Fig, with a rare suggestion to Buck, spoke up, "Man, why don't you go wash off."

Buck looked at him, then Doug, and around the silent circle of red shorts—his green face awash with hazy confusion. He took a step toward the water and heaved again.

"Everybody over here." Fig snapped into crowd control mode—treating us all like tourists watching an emergency. He pointed to a spot fifty yards away. "Leave your cans and bring your fins."

We left an orange circle of buoys in the sand and jogged down to Fig; the whole time looking at each other in disbelief. Doug picked up his rash guard and shook it off. He walked toward the access and never looked back. Buck stood at the edge of the water with one hand on his hip and the other squeezing his nose while he tilted his head back.

Fig was clearly distracted. He looked back toward Buck and then to us. "We're going to do some Olympics training. Grey, set up for beach flags." Fig pointed south.

Grey collected a fin from each guard and walked thirty or so yards farther down the beach. I moved next to Adrian and gave him a *what the hell are we doing* look.

"It's easy, just like musical chairs. When they say 'Go', get up, run down there, and grab a fin." He pointed to Grey, who stabbed at the ground with each fin, leaving it standing erect in the soft sand. "It's called beach flags—it's one of the events in the Lifeguard Olympics next month. Just follow me."

I lined up shoulder to shoulder with the other guards—Fig included. We faced north, our backs to the line of fins thirty yards away. Grey walked back to the line but didn't join us. He looked at the area between our line and the "flags" and picked up jagged shells and some trash. He tossed a handful of oyster shells and bottle caps up into the dunes and walked around the line of us.

"Okay, everyone down."

Adrian dropped to the sand like he was about to do a push up and then bent his arms in front of his face, resting his head on his overlapping hands. I followed his lead. Grey looked at the line and pointed at my feet.

"Wesley slide back so you're even with everyone." He looked to the end of the line. "Stanley, you fucking cheater, move up."

I looked down the line and watched Stanley crawl like a soldier to even up with everyone else.

"Okay, feet together."

Adrian's ankles pressed together and I did the same.

"Chin on hands." He paused and checked everyone. "Heads up." Twelve heads rose in unison. Grey's tone didn't change. "Heads down." We dropped our heads back to our hands. "Go."

I did a clumsy push up and spun around, bumping into Adrian, and slipping in the soft sand. I fell to my hands as quickly as I stood up and saw everyone's backs running away from the starting line. I scrambled to my feet and ran through the spraying sand from two dozen heels.

The pack was tight. I had no room or time to squeeze through. There was another explosion of sand as bodies piled up around the planted swim fins. A few guards lifted the fins into the air and some rested on their knees clutching the molded rubber like it was made of gold. The last three of us came to a slow stop. Stanley stood on my right, scanning the pile like a kid looking for the last Easter egg.

From my left I heard a sudden call. "FLAG, FLAG." Adrian pointed to one more fin next to him that had gone untouched.

Stanley and I dove together. My longer arms got to the fin first and I pulled it into me like a recovered fumble. Stanley landed in Ed's lap. Ed looked down and shook his head as Stanley rolled off and walked back to the starting line. He and the other guard without a flag sat down in the sand near the dunes.

"Stick them back in but leave two out." Grey called from the starting line but made no movement toward us. I pushed my fin back into the sand and walked back to the starting line. Adrian lined up next to me again.

"It's all in the start. Just stay low and try to be as quick off the line as you can. No need to stand all the way up before you start running."

We lined back up and lay down, feet toward the flags. I looked back over my shoulder and saw that Buck's four-wheeler was gone.

"Wesley, eyes forward. No cheating." Grey looked at the line and continued. "Feet together. Chin on hands. Heads up. Heads down. Go."

This time I stayed low to the ground. My feet grabbed at the sand instead of slipping on it. Adrian got a step on me but I didn't fall behind the rest of the pack. I was half a step behind Adrian and I knew he could feel me on his hip. In the middle of his stride he pointed to the right. "Go for that one."

There was no one on my right and with three steps

to go I dove for the flag he pointed to. The ground shuddered as bodies fell all around me. The fin in my hand felt like a trophy. I smiled and looked up at Adrian.

"You've got it. Now it gets fun."

Grey yelled down to us. "Stick 'em back in and leave three out again."

We followed his instructions and walked back. There were four guards off to the side sitting with Stanley. The remaining eight of us lined back up. Fig was on my left this time and Adrian was still on my right as we turned our backs to the flags. When we lay down Fig quickly pushed a pile of sand in front of his face with his hands and at the same time dug a shallow hole with his knees. I watched but said nothing. My body was flat while his looked like he was riding a fast motorcycle—his hands propped up on the mound like handle bars and his ass in the air.

When Grey called "Go" Fig spun around, planted his foot in the hole and was off before I turned to face the flags. I made up for his fast start with my speed in the open area. Adrian and I were even and we pulled next to Fig. Without a word Adrian pointed at the flag in front of Fig. I took an angle on it and Fig pushed me in the back just as I started to dive. The extra force sent my hands in search of a safe landing rather than the flag. They landed two feet past the fin which stuck me in the stomach just below my ribs. I coiled up at the sudden shot of pain and squeezed my eyes shut to avoid the incoming wave of sand from other runners. When I opened them I saw Adrian planting his fin back into the sand, on my other side Fig was doing the same. I took a deep breath, pulled the fin out from my fetal clutch and jabbed it into the ground next to my feet.

I looked at Adrian as I walked back but said nothing. There was already a red line across my torso. He saw it and shrugged. "Part of the game." He looked at Fig. "If you can do it and get away with it."

Fig heard him and shrugged.

We took our spots in the sand again. Grey walked

behind us looking at our feet. He kicked mine lightly and I slid up even with Fig, who had once again burrowed into the sand. "Feet together. Chin on hands. Heads up. Heads down. Go."

With fewer guards, there was more space for the remaining racers to work. I came up with the flag easily as the pack drifted to my right, leaving the entire left side open for Adrian and me to choose from.

The next round was similar. With only four guys I saw that strategy was as important as speed in getting a flag. Fig made his mound. Adrian found me and lay down on my right. Ed was on the far end for each heat, picking up his flags easily each time. The group on the sidelines grew and I realize I'd beaten more of them than not. I got a sudden rush when I hit the sand.

Grey's calls were steady and consistent. I tried to time his call to get another half-second jump. Grey called, "Go."

We pushed up and spun around in perfect unison. The pack was spread and Ed was a full step ahead of everyone. From his position on the far right he took an angle and cut all the way from one end to the other. He grabbed the flag in front of Adrian who stepped behind him and came up short when I dove for the flag in front of me. Fig took the last flag.

Ed stood up and dropped his fin. I held on to mine and looked at Adrian, waiting for him to tell me what to do.

"Good luck, Rookie."

I dropped my flag. Adrian tossed one fin off to the side and picked up the remaining two. He waved me over.

"Now you're going to have to draw straws for position. If you're in the middle, they're going to try to pinch you off. If you start on the outside they'll try to cut in front of you and slow you up.

"So what do I do?"

"Get a good start and just go straight ahead."

Adrian waited until I turned around and walked back to the line before placing the fins.

"Okay, eyes forward. Don't look back at the flags or you're disqualified." Grey held his hand out in a closed fist—three dried up reeds sprouted from the middle of his grip. "Pick a straw—short one gets the middle."

Ed and Fig picked first, each pulling out similar length sticks. Grey opened his hand before I reach for it, exposing a short nub of a straw.

"Wesley in the middle."

I lay down and thought about Adrian's instructions. Good start and go straight. Fig dug his hole and made his mound. Ed did the same. I spread the sand flat in front of me for no other reason than to be doing something.

"Feet together. Chin on hands. Heads up. Heads Down. Go."

Fig and Ed both spun toward me leaving no room for a quick start. They got off so quick they were running shoulder to shoulder before I even found my footing. My straight shot was gone. I drifted to the right just behind Fig. He was a half step behind Ed and had his arm cocked up like a chicken wing trying to block me from coming through them—unaware that I was directly behind him. He looked over his left shoulder to see where I was and I took the opportunity to push him from his blind side. His ankles got caught in Ed's and given the awkward position of his arm he lost his balance and fell in one spinning motion— landing on his back five feet short of the flags.

Ed and I slowed down and stood over the two fins. We bent down in no hurry and picked them up together, then dropped each one after a second. I walked over to Fig and offered him my hand. He laughed and took it.

"You learn quick. But don't make a habit of doing that in the real competition. They'll DQ you in a heartbeat."

"Okay."

"Good luck with Ed. He wins every year." Fig

brushed his chest off and joined Adrian on the end line.

Ed and I walked back to the start. He looked over at me and smiled.

"Not a good day for supervisors, huh?"

I shrugged my shoulders. Rick's truck was in the access and I could see Buck sitting in the passenger's seat. Preston was on his four-wheeler next to the stand.

Grey held one hand behind his back. With the other he pointed at me. "Pick a number—one or two."

"Two."

He pulled out one finger and pointed it at Ed. "Your choice."

Ed settled into his hole from the sprint before. Grey pointed at a spot for me to lie down in and when I did he waved to Fig.

"Alright guys." Grey turned to the group of guards on the sideline. "Pick your horse."

With that, everybody stood up and walked in front of me and Ed. Grey pointed at a spot in the sand next to Ed.

"Ed's side." Six guards walked to that side. "And Wesley's." He pointed to my right side and I watched Stanley and three other guards move to my side.

Fig called down from where he'd placed the final flag. "Loser's group does a run-swim."

I heard the rumble of a four-wheeler and saw Preston pull up to my side. He cut the motor and lifted his feet to the handlebar—leaning back against the first aid kit on the back.

Grey leaned over so that only the two of us could hear him. "Ed, are you gonna let the rookie you brought in beat you?"

"I'd be honored to hand over my crown." Ed looked at me but I stared straight ahead.

"I'm sure." Grey stood up. He pointed to the final flag. Adrian joined Stanley, Preston, and the rest of my supporters. "Fig you ready?"

Fig held a hand up, grabbed the flag and moved it ten feet to his right, making the distance Ed had to run greater than mine. He kicked some sand on the fin to make it stand up. "All set."

"Feet together. Chin on hands. Heads up. Heads down. Go."

Both starts were clean and when we spun to face the flag I heard Ed grumble, "Bullshit."

He started his angle right away but I stayed with him. Shoulder to shoulder we sprinted with matching strides. At ten feet we both dove. I went high as Ed dropped under me. I landed on top of him and never even felt the flag. When I slid off of him to the right, Ed rolled the other way and lay on his back, the fin tucked securely against his sand covered chest.

"Stay low, Rookie." He sat up and went to one knee. I was still lying on my side, catching my breath and trying to understand how he snuck under me to get the fin.

I looked at the starting line where my group was forming a line.

"Better go join them." Ed pointed to my dejected supporters. "You don't have to, but you should."

"Yeah."

I popped up quickly and joined the line next to Adrian. Preston started running and set the pace. We maintained a quick jog and hit the water a hundred yards south of the access. Preston stayed out in front and I made a mental note to beat Stanley if no one else. I got out of the water behind Preston, Adrian, and Roy—ahead of Stanley and two others.

The other guards did push ups and sit ups on their own while we ran—a few body surfed when we got back to the Wright Street access.

Rick's truck was gone.

After PT, we had forty-five minutes to get to our stand. Some guards sat around the shack or went home to shower. Grey and Adrian packed gear in their cars and I did the same.

Adrian backed his station wagon to the middle of the gravel lot and called out the window, "Hey, Wesley. Meet us at the B-hole."

The confusion on my face was obvious.

"The Buccaneer." He pointed north and said, "Milepost two."

I looked at Grey who smiled and patted his round stomach.

There were only five real parking spaces at the Buccaneer. People had to get creative. The area surrounding the restaurant was full of crookedly parked cars and trucks in the morning and around lunchtime. The confusion in the lot was nothing compared to the building itself. Originally a house when it was built in the fifties, it became a restaurant during the beach boom of the seventies. The addition of a sunroom and expanded kitchen area gave it a sprawling appearance. The low roofline was outlined by thousands of Christmas lights everyday of the year.

The Buccaneer was an interior designer's nightmare—a lesson in unrefined tackiness. Life-sized pirate statues stood at the doorway. Their features blended into the knotty wood they were carved from. The sashes and bandanas were real. Their faces a fearsome reminder of the harsh and brutal life lived on the beach hundreds of years earlier. A rusted lantern dangled from one hand—like those used to lure ships onto treacherous shoals. In the other he held a sign that read: *Please wait to be seated.*

Low doorways and dark wood walls made even the shortest person duck while passing from room to room. The walls were decorated with various nautical themed prints that only belonged in a place like the Buccaneer. Fishnets with plastic starfish divided the smoking and non-smoking section.

I followed Grey and Adrian to the bar area where there were three open stools. The other seats were filled with lifeguards waiting for their post-PT breakfast.

"We get a discount here, so most of us come once or twice a week." Adrian looked at Grey. "Some come more than that."

"Suck it, Adrian." Grey grabbed himself before sliding his stool out.

"Who's sucking what?" A woman appeared from another doorway with arms full of oval shaped platter plates overflowing with stark yellow eggs, thin opaque grits, and thick crusted toast. She passed them out to the other guards at the bar and they in turn switched them around until each person was happy with the plate in front of them. She made no apologies for mixing them up and simply proceeded to where we sat. She pointed at Grey and he didn't miss a beat.

"Fried, home fries, wheat."

She pointed at Adrian.

"The same with white."

She looked at me and cocked her head. "What do you want?"

"Can I see a menu?"

"No."

Grey laughed, she didn't.

"You'll have the special." Her voice sounded like a diesel engine. "How do you want your eggs?"

"Scrambled."

"Home fries or grits?"

"Grits."

"Homemade white, wheat, raisin, or store-bought white toast?"

"Homemade."

She turned around and pointed back over her shoulder with her pen. "Menu," she shook her head, "rookie," and disappeared through the doorway.

"Who was that?"

"That's Jan." Grey tapped on the bar, eager for his breakfast.

"She's a ray of sunshine, huh?" I looked at Adrian.

"She's being nice this morning." Adrian laughed and looked around.

Jan reappeared at the other end of the bar. She pulled out a pack of cigarettes and mumbled something to the closest guards while she lit a Marlboro Red.

Ed sat next to Grey. He held up his empty coffee cup and looked at Jan.

"Boy, if you think for one second holding that cup up in the air is going to get it filled, I might as well stick my ass in the air and wait for you all to kiss it." She waved a pointed finger around the bar.

Ed made a kissy face at her and swiveled around on his stool. He walked around Jan, poured himself some coffee and topped off two other cups at the bar.

"What's her story?" I whispered to Grey—careful not to let Jan hear.

"She's cool. She's just messing with us. She loves the lifeguards—hates Rick, but loves the guards."

"Why does she hate Rick?"

"I don't know. Conflicting personalities I guess."

Jan delivered our plates—in the right order.

"Hear about Buck yet?" Grey didn't look up at Jan while he smeared his toast with jelly and then used the knife to scrape the last bit of ketchup onto his potatoes.

"Puked all over his feet, huh?"

"You'd'a loved it, Jan."

"I'd'a loved it if it had been Rick on the other end of that punch." She turned her head and blew a cloud of smoke at the bottles along the wall. "But I guess Buck's just as good."

"He's had it coming for a while." Grey emptied three creamers into his coffee mug.

"Speaking of the partners in crime." Jan nodded at the open back door.

Rick strolled through, followed closely by Fig, Buck, and Preston. They sat at one of the thick wooden tables near the kitchen door. Preston waved at Jan, who returned it with a big smile.

"How's a sweet boy like Preston related to that idiot?" She tapped her cigarette on the edge of a glass ashtray.

Buck sat with his back to the guards at the bar, shielding himself from the not-so-subtle glances at his swollen nose.

I approached the conversations drifting around me with the same blissful naïveté as I had the job to that point. I'd been cast into this fraternity in the middle of the semester. There were histories—some old and complicated, some simply born from different personalities. In this little microcosm of former all-state quarterbacks, bullies, valedictorians, high school drop-outs, graduate students, military vets, wannabes, and surfers there were potential clashes with every joke made, every click of the radio, every girl who fell into view of two different pairs of binoculars.

I kept my mouth shut and listened.

I spent most of that day counting the flies I'd killed and discretely tossing pennies in front of old men with metal detectors. Two black birds pecked at the uneaten sunflower seeds I'd scattered around my stand. They came and went for hours and I enjoyed the company. The stretch of beach where I was stationed fell in between the busy Balchen access and Eckner Street. Every two hours, I was supposed to count the number of people on my section of beach.

"Just estimate. Count groups of five or so when it's really busy. Rick just wants the numbers so he can report them to the town and the USLA." Preston pointed to the beach count section of my daily report during my training.

"And if you forget to count just make sure there's a number there before you give the card to Buck."

At noon I counted everyone on my beach. There were twenty-six people. At two o'clock, most of the same people were still there. The final total after my four o'clock count was sixty-eight.

I put my report in my bag, scanned the dozen people on my beach, only three were in the water, and looked down to Grey's stand at Eckner. I saw two figures in front of his stand. He'd taken a seat on the ledge to talk to them. I found my binoculars, screwed the lenses back into place, and looked north.

Christine and Julie shielded their eyes from the late afternoon sun at Grey's back. Both wore bikinis but had their bottoms covered in floral sarongs. Grey pointed to my stand and they both turned south. Through the binoculars I could see their faces and I lifted my hand slightly but they didn't see me clearly from that distance. I watched them walk around Grey's stand and wave back to him before disappearing behind the dunes.

The radio clicked and then Grey's voice. *"Eckner to Wilkins Street."*

"Go ahead Eckner Street." I looked to his stand when I answered him.

"Signal 8s are 10-17."

"10-4." I laid the radio back on the armrest and waited for the girls.

One long shadow spread across the sand and when I looked down I saw Christine standing alone.

"Hey there." I sat up in my chair and she raised her hand to her eyes again. My beach was empty, so I climbed down and leaned against my ladder. "There's some shade over here." I pointed to the shadow cast by my umbrella.

"Aren't you the gentleman?"

"Southern hospitality." I shrugged.

She looked out at the water for a second and then to the ground.

"Sorry I gave you such a hard time last night. I've just had sort of a bad time with guys lately. A lot of those comments had nothing to do with you."

There was a noticeable gap between us. Despite the unexpected apology I felt like I was still on trial.

"Don't worry about it. I only cried for an hour or so before I fell asleep."

She pushed me on the shoulder. I smiled at her and the moment was instantly more comfortable.

"Where's Julie?"

She looked back toward the parking lot. "In the car. We just wanted to see what you were doing tonight."

"What did Grey say?"

"He said we could go to dinner or go up to the big sand dunes."

"Jockey's Ridge?"

"Yeah, whatever you call it. The place where they do the hang-gliding."

"Why don't we pick you up at seven-thirty?"

"We're staying in Duck. We could meet you somewhere."

"How about the parking lot of the kite store. You know where that is?"

She nodded.

"So we'll see you there at seven-thirty?"

"Seven-thirty." She pushed me again, smiled, and walked around the stand. I watched her shadow retreat across the valleys of her footprints.

Grey's friend Jon worked at the kite store so we went in to say hello while we waited for the girls. We made our way through the toys and airplane paraphernalia and found him on the second floor.

"Grey." Jon, a part-time hang gliding instructor, reached into a cardboard box and pulled out a handful of plastic-wrapped shirts. "What are you up to?"

"Jon, this is my friend Wesley. We're meeting some

girls."

"Nice." Jon nodded but didn't look up from the box of shirts. "What are you going to do with them?"

I looked at Grey and realized our plans were still up in the air. He shrugged.

"Don't know, I guess we'll go across the street and watch the sunset up on the ridge or something."

"Don't waste your time walking all the way over there. Just go upstairs. It'll keep the sand out of your shoes." Jon pointed to a side door of the kite shop. It led to a wooden deck and he explained how to get to the spiral staircase leading up to the observation platform.

"Sounds good to me. I've had all the PT I want today." Grey feigned a stretch.

"10-4," I chimed in.

Grey laughed and Jon nodded. I saw the girls pull into the parking lot and pointed them out to Grey.

"Signal 8's, 10-23."

"What does that mean?" Jon continued to unpack the box.

"It means the girls are here." Grey turned to the door and I followed after thanking Jon for the tip.

The door led out to the second floor and from the top of the stairs Grey pointed into the parking lot.

"Oh, fuck that." He grabbed the railing and stopped.

"What?" I looked over and saw Christine and Julie talking to two guys next to a yellow and white pick up truck.

"Fucking Nags Head guards."

"You know them?"

"One of them." Grey pointed at the other guys.

"What's the problem?" I asked.

"They are. Come on."

The two guys leaned against a truck with the town of Nags Head's logo on the door. They wore blue shorts with the same logo where our ORS logo would be on our red shorts. They were both larger and in better shape than

Grey and I were.

Grey barely acknowledged the girls when he got to the bottom step. He stared straight at the guys with his head lifted up.

"Hey Regal, did you leave your shirt at the bathhouse again?" He didn't stop walking until he was between Julie and the Nags Head guard.

"No Grey, Rick gave me a hundred bucks for it—said he wanted to feel like a real lifeguard for once." He laughed and turned to his friend who stood in front of Christine.

The other guy smiled and said, "I hope he didn't write you a check." His dark hair was short and the area around his eyes glowed white. He had a pair of sunglasses matching his awkward raccoon eyes hanging from a braided cord around his thick neck.

"Don't you guys work together?" Julie looked around at the four of us.

I felt like I was in the middle of a *Grease* standoff. Grey stepped back and looked at her.

"No, we don't work together." He took another step back but didn't turn around. "See you in a few weeks Regal."

"You doing beach flags this year, Grey?" Both guys laughed and looked at Grey's stomach.

"I don't need to."

"You gonna rely on Ed again?"

"Nope. We got a ringer this year." He turned his back to Regal, looked at me, and called over his shoulder, "Wesley Brooks is gonna smoke you this year."

"Who the fuck is Wesley Brooks?"

I lifted my hand. They both grinned. Regal folded his arms and the other guy—whose name I never heard—lifted his arm to the edge of the truck bed. Regal nodded at me and I turned around.

I caught up to Grey at the staircase. The girls walked in front of him.

"Thanks for that." I spoke out of the corner of my mouth but my wide eyes said as much as anything.

"You'll be fine." Grey kept walking.

When we got to the first landing Christine grabbed my hand and whispered in my ear. "What was all of that about?"

"I honestly don't know."

"Why didn't you guys just whip 'em out and measure?" She made a flopping motion with her hand.

I laughed and whispered, "I guess there's some history there."

"You think?" She shook her head.

Grey was agitated. He walked along the porch of the large building toward The Wright Scoop ice cream store. The sign above the door read, "Take Flight with the Finest!" He looked up and shook his head.

"That doesn't even make sense." He pointed to the sign, but it didn't slow him from opening the door.

The thick sugary blast of conditioned air rolled out the door but Christine held me back.

"And what's the *flag* thing about?" Her sharp northern voice jabbed at each word.

"The Lifeguard Olympics is in a few weeks."

She barely suppressed her laughter. "Lifeguard Olympics?"

It did sound funny coming out of a Division-I track star's mouth but I held my ground in defense.

"It's a pretty big deal around here. We've been training for it. I guess Grey thinks I'm going to run in the beach flags event."

"Beach flags? Is that like ribbon dancing?"

"Yes." I tried to be serious. "I'm wearing a speedo and twirling a pink ribbon to the 'Beaches' soundtrack. You really should come see it."

"I wouldn't miss it for anything."

I smiled and wished she would be there all summer.

"It's kind of like musical chairs with sprinting."

She nodded like she understood and I knew she didn't.

"Are we getting ice cream?" she asked.

A thick rope handrail twisted up the spiral staircase from the second floor of the kite shop to the observation platform. Worn gray and frayed on the top, it stretched tight across a contorted ladder of pressure-treated balusters. The wedge shaped treads had the same aged look. As we got closer to the top, the number of cracks in each step increased. There were a variety of different flavored stains dripped all over the observation deck. The cone in my hand dribbled vanilla from the hole in the bottom.

The wind took the evening off. It faded from a steady ten miles an hour to slack. A giant cow windsock hung motionless from a swivel clasp looped through its nose on a pole above us. From forty feet in the air, the ocean had a completely new quality to it. For the first time that I could remember the water was one shade of blue. There were no ripples, whitecaps, or cloud shadows.

The view to the west was most unnatural. Along the eastern edges of North Carolina—where hurricanes find no resistance as they make landfall—in the funny little sliver of land near milepost twelve lies one of the most breathtaking natural sights on the East Coast.

Jockey's Ridge rises and runs with its sandy crests and twisting faces from one edge of Nags Head Woods to another stretch of ancient maritime forest. From our perch high above the rushing traffic of the bypass, we saw the silhouettes of a hundred people lined up on the main ridge to watch the sunset.

Grey and Julie managed to find a private corner on the small observation platform. They leaned against the railing of the hexagonal deck together—his hand wrapped around her waist and her head leaned back against his chest. If I was just another tourist I would assume they'd been together for years rather than hours.

I didn't feel as comfortable inventing a relationship so I leaned on my elbows against the handrail. Christine followed my lead and her shoulder touched mine when she did. It was comfortable and in the silent moment just before the blushing sun dropped behind the ridge I leaned against her and she leaned back with a playful nudge. She turned her head over her shoulder—the one still touching mine—and whispered, more to herself but obviously in my ear, "What is she doing?"

I turned the other way and Grey lifted his head when we make eye contact. Julie's eyes were closed. Christine and I looked back to the dunes.

"What's the matter? Looks like they're hitting it off."

"She has a boyfriend." She squinted her eyes a little and stared off to the far ridge.

I said nothing. I wasn't surprised and I wondered if Grey knew. I wanted to ask Christine if she did too but I was afraid it would spoil the moment if she said yes. I was really enjoying the moment—even more so than the kissing and the chasing of the night before. There was a relief in getting those things out of the way.

"This is weird." Christine sighed and shook her head.

"What is?"

"This—you and me, Julie and Grey, all pretending to know each other." She waved her hand around like she was casting an exposing light upon everyone. "It would never happen like this at home."

"Isn't that what makes it fun?" I completely understood her but I was fighting to hold on to the charade.

"I guess—it's just so unnatural."

"You talk too much." I said it with a straight face. When I felt her glare I smiled.

"You know I'm right." She nudged me again.

"I know."

Christine and I finished our ice cream in near silence. I took the napkin away from my cone and a steady stream of yellow cream fell from my hand. The door below opened and we watched the melted mess land on a man's shoulder as he left the store. He looked around and we retreated from the edge of the railing. My guilty face was frozen somewhere between shock and laughter. Christine grabbed my free hand and looked at Julie.

"Let's go before that guy realizes a bird didn't poop on him." She pulled me to the steps. Grey and Julie followed close behind—unaware of the emergency. We got to the landing, threw our trash away, and ran back into the store. Jon nodded as we made our way down the other steps and out the front door. The man was gone and I couldn't help but laugh out loud at our escape.

"What the hell was that all about?" Grey was obviously out of breath from our rapid decent.

"Wesley dripped his ice cream on a man's head."

"It was his shoulder and I don't think he even noticed."

"Damn, I thought you spit on someone's kid or something. For all that running you should have tossed a brick at Regal's truck from up there."

"I thought you guys had to be in good shape to be lifeguards." Julie looked at Grey; his hands were pressed against his hips and she was not impressed.

He laughed and put his arm around her. "I may not be able to run for miles but I make up for it in other places."

I shook my head and cringed a little. Grey and I climbed into my Jeep.

"They're gonna follow us back to your house." He looked back at the girls as they walked to their car.

"What the hell are we gonna do at my house?"

"You got any beer?"

"Doubt it." I shook my head. "Harry and the rest of

my neighborhood got into whatever was left last night."

"We can stop and pick up something at Food Lion."

"Wine coolers?"

"Probably."

"So lame."

"Shit, I know I'm going to take care of my business tonight. Are you?" Grey looked at me and waited for an answer.

"Don't worry about me." I started the Jeep and shifted into reverse.

"Okay, Rookie."

"That Rookie shit is getting old." I said it with enough conviction to keep Grey from laughing. He did anyway. The girls pulled behind me and I waited for a break in the traffic before turning north on the bypass.

"Christine told me that Julie has a boyfriend."

"Yep, she told me." Grey made his imaginary speed bump with his hand and smiled. I laughed at his indifference.

"It doesn't ever bother you?"

"Never." He leaned back against the headrest and sighed. "They all have boyfriends. But you gotta figure there's something missing if they wanna hang out and fool around with a guy while they're on vacation."

"True." Once again, I found my own prudence conflicting with the views of my new friends. "Does it ever come back around?"

"What? You mean a jealous boyfriend coming down?" Grey's head rolled back and forth as my Jeep cruised down the bypass. "Nah man, not that I've heard of." He lifted his hand and pointed his finger to the sky. "I take that back. There was this one guard—I couldn't tell you who or how long ago it was—but this guy got busted in a hot tub with some guy's wife at Neptune Street."

"That couldn't have been good."

"Well, the funny thing is, the guard just hopped the fence and ran down the beach until he got to Pelican's

Roost. You know where the Roost is, right?"

I nodded and pictured the dilapidated cottages a half-mile north of Wright Street. The lingering stench from keg parties often blew down from the old plywood buildings when we jogged by during PT.

"Yeah, so this guy runs back to the Roost naked. But the fucked up part is that he met the chick at Neptune Street and had to sit the stand the next day."

"It wasn't Ed was it?"

"No, this was way before Ed. But I wouldn't put that shit past him. One time he had these two girls at Magnolia Street by himself—hold on, I'll tell you that one later." Grey laughed and tapped the side of my Jeep. "Too many fuckin' stories, man."

"So, the guy's wife?"

"Yeah, the next day I guess the husband recognizes him or something but he doesn't say anything."

"Where was the wife?"

"Don't know, doesn't really matter. But the day *after that* the guard's on his way to the stand—I'm sure he's freaking out about the whole thing and what the husband might do. So, when he gets to his stand he looks around and drops his stuff in front of his ladder while he writes on his chalkboard. He had one of those nylon coolers for his lunch and when he went to put it up in his stand there was water running out the bottom through a bunch of holes. He pushed the sand away and found a piece of plywood about two feet by two feet with like fifty nails hammered up through it. The husband thought he'd jump on it.

"That's what that is? I saw it over by the equipment boxes."

"Yeah, Rick kept it as evidence."

"Evidence?"

"I guess Rick was going to press charges or something. I don't know what ever happened from it. Can you imagine? Jumping off your stand and landing on that shit? "

- 131 -

I turned toward the beach and into my driveway. The girls pulled in behind my Jeep but stayed in their car. Christine rolled down her window and leaned out when I walked over.

"We're gonna keep going tonight." She looked at me and I knew her mind was made up.

They had talked about it in the car and I didn't feel like pushing her. Grey was on the other side leaning into the car trying to convince Julie to stay, but she pointed at Christine and said they needed to get back.

"I'm sorry, Wesley. I just need to go. I enjoyed the sunset with you." She placed her hand on mine and smiled.

"I did too." I nodded and stepped away from the car, my hand slipping from under hers. "Maybe I'll see you tomorrow?"

Christine smiled but said nothing. Grey and I watched the car pull away.

"What the fuck?" Grey stared as they pulled out onto the bypass.

"I think it was something with Christine."

"It's cool. I got something else going on. Remember those two girls Adrian took home?" Grey reached into his pocket and pulled out a folded piece of paper. "Can I use your phone?"

I pointed to the stairs.

CHAPTER 7

"You're at Sea Dunes today."

Buck's words hung in front of me for a few seconds before I took the whistle and first aid kit. Grey turned around when he heard.

"It's Roy's day off. Just follow the rental map he left you and you'll be fine." Buck showed me a piece of paper with circles and names of customers and how many chairs and umbrellas each got. "Watch the rips around the drain pipe and north to Neptune Street."

There was a tangible difference in Buck's tone—almost mistakable for sincerity. I guessed the punch to the face took away a bit of his bravado. Either way, I appreciated the advice and took note.

Roy McDonald was the Lifeguard of the Year two summers earlier and had made the Sea Dunes condos his stand of choice. It was coveted for its lucrative rental commission, clean restrooms, and snack machines in the lobby. In the hierarchy of the twelve stands Sea Dunes was just behind the Atlantic Club—with Mullet and Wilkins Street at the bottom of the list.

The perks came at a price. Rentals were not easy, nor were the clientele that patronized Sea Dunes. The uppity couples and the weekenders from Virginia treated the guard like a cabana boy. Occasionally, our patience was tested.

Adrian was always collected in his approach. He smiled in the face of every difficult person and kept an even demeanor about him. He didn't kiss ass but he didn't offend either. At the end of the discussion or confrontation there was often a handshake or a similar exchange. The person walked away feeling content and Adrian got back to his job with nothing lost but a few minutes. He was quick to downplay his authority and put the decision in the hands of the other person—with guidance.

"It's really up to you," he would say, "so let me know if there's anything else I can help you with." He always removed his sunglasses when he talked to a patron.

If Adrian was the poster child for conflict resolution, Rick was the exact opposite. His abuse of power was, at times, overwhelming. There was no hiding it. Rick put it right out there for everyone to see. His authority was announced every time he drove down the beach—over his truck's loudspeaker.

My first day at Sea Dunes was nerve racking, exhausting, and completely uneventful. I placed the chairs and umbrellas exactly where Roy's note described and waited for the rip currents to open up at low tide. They never did and I spent the last hour of the day packing the rentals into the wooden equipment boxes and waiting for five-thirty to roll around.

The last few moments of the shift were my favorite time of day. Most of the beachgoers—the families and the groups of kids—retreated to their rented cottages or weathered ancestral homes. The bikinis and swim trunks of the day were traded for lightweight long sleeve shirts and casual shorts.

I leaned against my stand—there was no need for me to be up in it at five twenty-five. The sand next to me was cold and wet from my dumped out water cooler. My bag was packed, the equipment box locked, the umbrella wrapped up and tucked under my arm, as was my buoy. The black swim fins were looped around my wrists and I knew from afar I resembled the begrudged father who toted all of the beach toys back and forth each day only to watch his children play with a piece of found driftwood and seagull feathers.

My hat was loose on the top of my head and the straps from my bag pulled tight across my bare chest. The load was a pound of feathers compared to the dozens of chairs and umbrellas I'd shuffled from the high water mark to the dunes in the previous hour.

The sunlight at that time was a photographer's dream—a low angled amber slice that cast a rich sharpness across everything left on the wide beach. The white of my stand burst against the blue of the sky—still two hours from fading to pink.

To the north, Ed enjoyed the same show. My radio buzzed with Rick's voice and I watched Ed walk around his stand and over the access. I scanned my water once more and did the same.

The wind howled from the west the next day. Roy was still off and I was back at Sea Dunes. The cool water temperature kept people on the shore while those who could handle the biting black flies read, fished—which was pointless—or played on the beach. It was two weeks since my first day on the stand and I'd yet to have a real rescue.

I helped a six-year-old boy swim in from the sand bar a few days earlier at Wilkins Street. His raft blew out and, because of the cold water, he waited too long to try to come back in. The offshore wind forced him to abandon his float—a signal to help whether it was an emergency or not. I was already by the water's edge. I watched the wind catch him and knew—before he did—that he wasn't going to make it in on his own. He was in good spirits and when Preston arrived on his four-wheeler he said I did well.

After listening to the story he put his clipboard away.

"Sounds good, Wesley. Don't worry about filing anything for it though."

I toweled off and felt good about the incident even though they called it an assist rather than a rescue.

"Don't worry, man." Preston zipped his bike around to face north. "When that wind switches around you'll get a chance to pop your cherry."

I never saw Christine again. I called her to make plans but she politely declined.

"My parents want me to spend time with the rest of my family up here in Duck."

I challenged her to another race on the beach and she laughed. She asked for my address and promised to write.

"Maybe I can go see one of your track meets in the fall," I said before she hung up the phone.

"That would be nice."

A group of tourists roughly fifty yards from my stand had, over the course of the morning, constructed quite an impressive sandcastle. The water was too cold to swim so they created a multi-level complex with requisite moat and flag. Upon seeing this, another man nearby walked over to his cottage and returned with a large shovel. His young son joined him in digging a hole near the family's set up.

I thought back to a family vacation in Duck when I was eight years old. There is a picture somewhere in time of me squatting down in a deep hole that we dug because the water was too rough to swim. The red flags were up that day and the rumor on the beach was that a man drowned because of the strong "rip tide". We dug the deepest hole on the beach as far as I was concerned, using two plastic buckets. My father sat on the edge, using a toy shovel that was funny and useless in his large hands. We were persistent and by the end of the day I heard my mother come from the cottage and exclaim, "Where's Wesley?" in the way that parents do when they know exactly where you are.

I proudly sprung from the sandy pit and yelled, "Here I am, Mom! You couldn't see me could you?" She shook her head and snapped the picture while I grinned from ear to ear—a noticeable gap where my two front teeth were growing in.

The thought occurred to me that this man, with his big shovel, was cheating. Like a lot of father-son ventures, the child lost interest. I felt sorry for the kid but his father was determined and he dug for the better part of an hour until all I could see from my stand were his shoulders and head. He tossed out a few more loads of wet sand and I scanned the empty water.

Rick's truck was parked three stands to the north. It stayed there for a while and I wished he would keep driving. I always anticipated Rick's drive-bys with boyish nervousness. The opportunity to talk to anyone was always welcome but when Rick stopped I felt more important— reassured that I was doing a good job. When he drove by with little or no acknowledgement I was always disappointed.

I scanned the water from right to left and saw a woman running toward my stand. Her hands flapped around in circles while she ran. She screamed nothing discernable but I knew it was serious. I picked up my radio and jumped off the stand exactly like Rick told us not to do.

"If you break your damn ankle jumping off your stand, don't expect me to pay for it," he said once at a morning meeting.

But I did it anyway and it was all so dramatic. I lifted a hand to acknowledge that I saw the woman. She stopped several yards from me and pointed to the spot where she came from.

"My husband." She wasn't out of breath. She turned and ran back.

I looked to the water and saw nothing. I started to panic. Had I missed someone swimming? I followed her in order to see what I needed to say over the radio. I turned around and I blew my whistle three times at Ed but I didn't wait to see if he heard me.

The husband wasn't in the water, he was in the hole. A half-dozen people were gathered around looking at the shallow crater. The father's head was in the middle. He twisted back and forth spastically. His mouth opened and closed with exaggerated gestures but no sound came out. He looked like a carnival clown whose mouth waited to be filled with water from a squirt-gun. His eyes were wild and looked nowhere in particular.

People dropped to their knees around him, scooped at the sand, and threw it behind them; some passed it between their legs like dogs. I clicked the radio and tried to remember my ten-codes. I spoke too quickly, cutting myself off. All that went out was, "...Dunes, 10-18, I'm gonna need help."

I dropped the radio and joined the crowd trying to get the man out. There were so many people around the hole that for each scoop that came out, twice as much filled in—dangerously close to the man's mouth. Someone from outside the frenzied circle yelled, "Keep him calm. Tell him to breathe."

The radio buzzed behind me and I heard Ed's voice say, *"That's gonna be Sea Dunes. It's a caved in hole. Look's deep. Roll EMS."*

The four-wheelers arrived within seconds from the north and south. Preston pulled people back and Fig grabbed a green bag from his bike. He dropped it behind the man's head and I watched him lean as close to the man's ear as he could get without pushing more sand on him. He whispered something and the man's eyes came into focus. Fig dug through the bag and pulled out a metal canister.

"Get it on him and open it up." Preston pulled one more person away and looked at the situation. I was on my knees, fruitlessly pulling sand with both arms. A man came forward with the shovel and posed like he was about to start digging. Preston grabbed it just before the metal blade landed in the sand near the man's right shoulder. He calmly pulled it from the bystander's hand.

"You'll chop his arm off."

I was breathing heavily and still trying to move as much sand as I could when Preston placed his hand on my shoulder. "Step back, Wesley."

I retreated and sat back in the sand.

Preston looked at the man and asked, "Are you straight up and down?" The man nodded. Preston lifted the shovel a few inches and with no great speed, but obvious power, pushed the blade down with his bare foot. "Nod your head if you feel the sand move near your hand.

Fig slipped a clear mask over the man's face and cranked the knob on the oxygen regulator until it stopped. Air hissed from the canister and the green mask fogged up. A plastic bag underneath the mask expanded but didn't fill.

Someone in the crowd pointed this out and Fig, without looking up, said, "It's not supposed to."

Rick pulled up and yelled at the crowd.

"Everyone back, goddammit." He looked at the man and then at Preston. "Wesley, get the tow rope out of the back of the truck and tie it on to the hitch."

I stood up and ran over to the truck. Flashes of Mr. O'Neill came and went. The man in the hole nodded furiously. Then he stopped. His head dropped back and the fog disappeared from the mask.

Rick ran back to his truck and jumped into the driver's seat. I barely finished tying the knot on the hitch and Rick took off, spraying sand and sliding the rear of the Bronco sideways. He stopped it ten yards from the hole and pointed the Bronco south. I grabbed the loose end of the rope and ran it over to Fig. He took the rope and looked at it like I had just handed him a bouquet of flowers.

"What the hell am I supposed to..." he looked at Preston—on his knees pulling sand away from the man's exposed arm. The hand was lifeless. The man stared straight up at the bright sun with the oxygen tank still hissing behind his head.

Fig whispered to Preston, "It'll rip his fuckin' arm off, man."

Preston looked at the man, "He's not gonna feel it. The pressure of the sand's already collapsed his lungs. Let's do it while he still has a pulse."

The man's wife held their son nearby. They stared at him like they were simply watching a show on television— both strangely calm—like they didn't believe the man could die in such a way. It would be something to laugh about later as they sat on the porch eating dinner.

People on vacation are complacent. Escaping from their cubicles and hour-long commutes affords them some unearned immortality. They don't consider the consequences of their actions in the same manner as they would in their hometown. I'm sure that man—maybe a doctor or lawyer back home—wouldn't dig a six-foot deep hole in his front yard and jump in. But it's vacation.

Preston took the rope, tied it around the man's hand, and stepped back. He signaled to his uncle to accelerate. Rick's tires spun for a half second until they grabbed at the sand and lurched forward. The slack rope snapped taut and Preston's hand shot into the air. He rechecked the knot. For the first time since he arrived on the scene, he yelled.

"Slow!"

His tone was compassionate; like he was shielding the family and the onlookers from the reality of the moment. Everyone could see that the man wasn't breathing.

The Bronco moved deliberately. Fig stayed close to the father while supporting the mask and oxygen tank. The man's head rested on his outstretched arm and I watched his shoulders emerge like a baby being born. When his other arm was visible, Preston reached in and pulled both while the truck continued. Rick's head was out of the window looking back. Fig held a different mask with a balloon-like bag on it. He pulled the first mask off and plugged the tubing into the new one. He pressed the mask to the man's face and squeezed on the ballooned plastic bag. The man's chest was exposed. It rose and fell at the same rate that Fig squeezed the bag. Preston lifted his hand when the man's waist was visible. The Bronco kept pulling.

"Stop!" Preston let go of the tied up hand and raised his own. Rick kept driving.

"Stop!" Several other people joined in to amplify Preston's command.

Several medics came down the stairs of the access along with two firemen. I couldn't see Rick anymore and with a violent jerk the rope—which had been frozen and steady—popped and lashed around like a downed power line in a strong wind. Everything that was in control quickly wasn't. Preston fell back on his ass; Fig lost control of the man's head sending it flopping around and landing sideways in the hot sand. The oxygen tubes hissed and blew around like snakes being held down by their tails. People in the crowd gasped audibly.

The truck stopped.

Preston, Fig, and I scrambled to brush off the equipment and regain some sort of order. I looked around for something to do but I was reluctant to touch the man. I picked up the broken end of rope and held it off of the sand. Fig looked at the rope and at me and I felt stupid.

The medics and firemen rushed in and formed a tight circle. Most dropped to a knee while the others moved around and passed equipment.

A medic led the mother and son away from the scene. Preston followed with a metal clipboard. Fig neatly wrapped up the two pieces of tow line and stowed them in the back of the Bronco. I looked around for trash from the medical supplies.

Rick held a gray case in one hand—no bigger than a lunch box. He pushed his way into the circle. The methodical rhythm of the medics was jolted by Rick's intrusion.

"Ah...hook him up." Rick cracked the case open. Two wires were connected to a machine that looked like a toy radio I had when I was six. "Hook him up to this AED."

"We're already monitoring him on a twelve-lead." A medic in a blue shirt shielded a green computer screen from the bright afternoon sun. "His pulse is steady and his O$_2$ sat is coming back up."

"If he's on this beach he's gonna be on this defibrillator." Rick looked out over his glasses but the medic didn't acknowledge him.

A fireman who'd been running Velcro straps through the backboard looked up and said, "Rick there's really no need." He pressed the strap down and tucked the man's arms through them so they were no longer in the sand.

"I want the stats for my report."

"There's no point." The fireman—Lt. J. Jones was the name embroidered on his shirt—had one hand on the backboard. His chest was thick and filled out his light gray T-shirt; his arms were thicker than my legs. An orange mustache—full and trimmed—completed the firefighter look.

"Jackson, take that strap off so I can put these pads on." Rick held the two wires in his hand and the accompanying sticker pads.

Lieutenant Jones didn't let go of the board.

"Rick, I don't give a shit how much you paid for that

machine, I'm not holding anything up so you can get some worthless numbers for your report."

Rick shook his head and mumbled. With one hand he peeled the paper backing from a pad; his other hand pulled the board strap back.

Lieutenant Jones grabbed Rick's wrist. "I'm about to put that sticker over your mouth, Rick. Let go of the board." Lieutenant Jones repositioned the strap and stepped in front of Rick, pushing him out of the circle of medics. He nodded to the firefighter nearest the head of the patient and called out, "On three; one, two, three."

The men lifted the backboard in one fluid motion and walked toward the access. Preston, Fig, and I looked around the scene for any trash or items left behind. We avoided eye contact with Rick who packed his AED back into its case. His face was red and his upper lip so contorted that his mustache looked fake and poorly placed. He shook his head as he walked to his truck, took one quick look around, and climbed into the Bronco.

He made wide tracks and sprayed sand all over the beach when he turned sharp into the access. I walked back to my stand while looking at the water and taking deep breaths.

Preston and Fig finished the report with two bystanders. The family followed the man on the stretcher. I climbed into my stand and sunk into the chair with an overwhelming sense of relief that the whole incident was over. Preston drove over, cut his bike off, and climbed up to join me. He sat on the edge of the stand and scanned the water.

"Crazy shit, huh?"

"Yeah." I stared at the ocean.

"You all right?" Preston looked back at me.

"Yeah, I'm just glad the guy's alive."

"He'll be fine." He looked back to the water. "You haven't had any first aid training have you?"

"No, nothing like that stuff."

"No, of course not like that. That doesn't happen too often."

"You mean it's happened before?"

"Yeah." Preston and I scanned the water—which was completely empty. The calm water was soothing to look at after all of the chaos. "It's mostly broken legs or ankles from holes, but there was a guy in Hatteras last summer that died in one. All the crazy shit happens in Hatteras—lightning, sharks; two years ago a guy jumped from the lighthouse."

"Jumped?"

"Yeah, he'd just gotten married the day before and I guess he realized what he'd done and jumped from the observation deck. His whole family saw him hit the ground."

"That's insane."

"People down here are."

"I'm learning that."

"I don't know if this place attracts crazy people or if they go crazy once they get here."

The image of Rick trying to put the AED stickers on the man came to mind. I ignored it.

"So, a guy died in a hole?"

"Yeah, I guess it was a west wind day like this—or a red flag day so he couldn't go in the water. His whole family was there—I heard this all from the National Park ranger who saw it. The guy dug a hole so deep and wide that he had enough room to put a beach chair down in it. He was sitting in there reading a book—"

"He was reading a book in a hole?"

"Yep, reading a book and his kid came to look in. When the little boy got to the edge of the hole it started caving in. I guess the kid slipped in and the father held him up and tried to push him out but the kid was clawing at everything and basically buried his father alive."

Preston paused to let that sink in.

"Those beaches aren't patrolled regularly so there's

no one down there to do anything. I guess he stayed buried for an hour before they could get a backhoe down there to dig him out."

"And they all had to stand there knowing he was under the sand?" I couldn't believe it.

"Yeah, I'd hate to see that kid's therapy bill." Preston let out a half-laugh and shook his head.

"No shit." I shook my head too and understood why he was telling me the story.

He slipped down the rungs of the stand ladder. When he got to the bottom, before he climbed on his four-wheeler, he looked back up at me. "You did good. You didn't freak out."

I nodded and raised a hand as he pulled away.

CHAPTER 8

Every other Friday, Rick bought a keg or a few cases of beer for everyone. He drove out on the beach at Wright Street with pizza boxes stacked high in the bed of the 701 truck. After the hole incident that afternoon we all needed a release. Fig rode in the back of the truck with one hand holding onto the bed rail and the other keeping the pizzas from spilling out onto the sand. The trucks were ready to respond to an after-hours call, but for the most part, they just collected all of the empty beer cups.

During business hours, we told surfers to wear leashes on their boards to prevent the fiberglass torpedoes from impaling swimmers and we spent the evenings surfing without them ourselves. We ordered dog owners to take their pets off the beach and called the animal control officer when someone wouldn't comply. Then we let Otis, Riley, and Titus run as wild as their canine hearts desired.

Then it got dark and girls appeared by the light of our illegal bonfires. Some wore their bikinis to rival our skimpy red shorts. The girls' swim suit fashion of choice that summer was a blue and white striped two-piece sold in every surf shop. The stripe ran at an angle like a nautical flag. Each fresh crop of tourists thought they were on the cutting edge—buying up the latest beach trend like we hadn't seen the same bikini all summer long.

Fire Chief Moorland looked the other way for us. Rick campaigned for him when the county Fire Inspector position opened up. Moorland didn't win but he remained one of Rick's few allies on the bureaucratic side of the town. Similarly, the Police Chief didn't give us too hard of a time. Most of us weren't legal to drink—the girls rarely were—but as long as we kept things to a dull roar and didn't catch anything on fire we were allowed certain freedoms.

Those Fridays always coincided with payday. Some of us—those paying rent and bills—made a mad dash to the bank after checking in our equipment and picking up our paychecks. Most of the guys could wait though—the lure of free beer and dinner was enough to keep them around Wright Street.

Fun Friday—a sarcastic nickname imposed by veteran guards like Buck and Fig, was as curious and simple a form of male display as I've encountered. The alphas stood out. They hooted and hollered and surfed on the biggest waves. They wrestled on the beach just to prove they could. Wright Street was the favored breeding ground of the chisel-chested red-short nut grabber.

The rest watched from the smaller waves. There were advantages to being the quieter ones among the pack. While Fig and Buck made the most noise, Grey and I scanned the beach for the girls that weren't looking for an explosion of testosterone. It was the best of both worlds— a symbiosis of aggression and laid-back fortitude.

The sun was an hour away from dipping behind the beachfront houses. I saw a blue bikini—that's how we described new girls—*"Did you see that black thong; that flowered bikini; that red one piece?"*

The blue bikini walked up the beach from a small motel just south of Wright Street. Because it was impossible to miss a dozen lifeguards in the water, it was funny to watch a girl act like she didn't see us. Some girls pretended we weren't there for fear of appearing too curious—but not the blonde in the blue bikini. She stopped by the water's edge—hands on her hips waiting to see who was going to catch the next wave.

The longshore current spread our pack of riders over a hundred yards. The weaker paddlers like me and Grey drifted away from the main break. We were doing fine by ourselves—selectively riding waves in our size range. I caught two for every one Grey did. He cursed at each one he missed, letting out a "fuck you wave" for the wasted effort.

The boards we rode were exaggerated longboards—about ten feet of thick foam with no fiberglass. Rick bought them as rescue paddleboards but they were nothing more than toys. They were wide and stable; barely a difference between standing on them in the water and on dry land. The hardest part was getting the lumbering planks moving.

Grey and I paddled for a waist-high set wave. The rest of the pack already rode the peak section—the scraps left for us. Normal surfing etiquette was ignored after work. There were no concerns about dinging boards or snaking waves. The priority on those evenings was providing a show. We both caught the wave.

I, being closer to the peak, had a little more control over where I went so I pulled along side Grey. He squatted low on the board. His stance fell somewhere between a baseball catcher and someone shitting in the woods.

He had no idea that I was right behind him. I reached out to grab his shoulders, hoping to pull him off of his board and pass him but the backwash from an earlier wave caused my board to lurch and slow down. The beach got closer—the wave dying with each half second. I shuffled to the front of my board—Grey continued to crouch on his—I stepped on the back of his board. The sudden shift in balance brought Grey upright to compensate. I grabbed his arm and for one long second we both rode the wave.

As spectacular as our stunt felt to me, the ending was probably more enjoyable to everyone else. The momentum of the wave paid no attention to our sudden weight change. The surfboard slowed while we continued with the speed of the wave, toppling over each other and rolling off the front of the board.

"Man, what the fuck?" Grey stood in the knee-deep water. He pressed one side of his nose and blew water out of the other. "That was my best wave. You totally snaked me."

I was laughing too hard to pay attention to his whining. He joined in and pushed me on the shoulder. I fell on my ass—still laughing.

My board washed up at the feet of the blue bikini. Tall and slender with dark legs from the week of tanning, her blonde hair reached down past her shoulders. She bent over to pick up the board and I watched her strain at the unexpected weight. She looked up at me and smiled.

"It's heavier than I thought." It slipped from her fingers back to the wet sand. I stepped out of the wash and walked up to her.

"Yeah, these things are like giant sponges."

"Is it hard?" She lowered her head and looked at me from the top of her eyes. The late afternoon southeast wind blew her hair back and showed all of her features. Her blue eyes were sharp like the angle of her jaw; her lips thick but not soft. They looked like no careless word had ever passed through them. There wasn't an ounce of body fat on her.

"Surfing? No, not really." I looked at the board. Then I looked at her. "You've never tried?"

She lifted her hand to the bare gap on her chest between the triangles of her bikini top, lightly touching herself in a *who me?* gesture. She shook her head.

"Do you want to?"

She cocked her head to one side. "Are you going to knock me off?" She looked at Grey who struggled to make his way back through the waves. He tried to paddle over a knee-high wave at an angle. The little bump threw off his balance and sent him to the water again.

"I promise I won't." I raised my hand like I was in court and then extended it to her. "My name's Wesley."

"Jessica." Her hand was thin like the rest of her. Her long fingers slid along my palm when she let go.

"Where're you from?" I picked up the board under my arm and turned it back to the surf.

"Pennsylvania."

I laughed. "Of course you are."

She nodded like my inference was something she hadn't heard before. She said nothing.

"Where're you staying?"

"Down there at Wilbur's Motel. But I'm leaving tomorrow."

"That's too bad."

"Yeah, I've wanted to try surfing all week, but…" She shrugged, suggesting she hadn't had the opportunity.

"Well, no sense waiting any longer."

"Okay." She smiled and stared at me.

"Let me run up there and grab something real quick." I turned around and jogged up to a large pile of towels, shirts, and swim fins. Grey usually brought his rash guard to the beach but he rarely wore it. I found it near his bag and shook the sand off.

Buck walked out of the water and grabbed a towel—not his own.

"Surf lesson?" He looked at Jessica.

"I guess." I offered as little as possible.

"Wouldn't it be better if you actually knew how to surf?" He didn't even smile when he said it.

"Just gonna push her into some waves."

"Yeah, have fun." He wiped his face, then his ass,

and dropped the towel on top of someone else's stuff.

Jessica watched me walk back. I resisted the urge to shake my head but I did mutter "dickhead" under my breath.

"Here, you might wanna put this on." I handed her the rash guard. She looked at it like the red clashed too much with her blue suit to justify the protection of the thin polyester. "It'll keep everything," I waved my hand around my own chest, "where it needs to be."

She raised her head slowly in acknowledgement. "Thanks."

She put the shirt between her knees and pulled her hair back into a ponytail using a rubber band from her wrist. When she did, her shoulders went back too. Through her bikini I clearly saw every line of her chest. She put her arms through the shirt first.

"Don't want to give the *whole* beach a show." She slipped her head through the neck hole and peeled the shirt down around her.

"So what do I need to do? You gonna make me practice on the beach like in *Point Break*?"

"*Point Break*? No, but I'm impressed."

"You should be."

"Confident aren't we?"

"Well, I'm not going to hurt myself am I?" She looked down at her feet. Her toes drew circles in the wet sand.

"No." I waited for her to look up. "You won't hurt yourself. Falling in water isn't so bad." We both smiled and she reached out to touch the board.

"It's huge." She looked at it from tail to nose.

I ignored the obvious innuendos, "Trust me, it's easier to learn on a longer board." I raised one corner of my mouth, smiled quickly, and continued my efforts to play it cool.

"There's a lot of people out there." Her hesitation surprised me.

"Well, you could wait 'til tomorrow." I raised an eyebrow. She smiled sarcastically and I continued. "Don't worry. Half of 'em can't surf that good anyway." I pointed to Grey just as he tried to stand up. He got to his knees and plopped over into the whitewater, arms flying and feet tumbling.

Grey let out a timely, "Fuck you wave," and she laughed.

"Besides, we're gonna go down the beach so they don't get in our way." I wanted to get away from the guards. They were sharks that would feed on us if we drifted too close.

"Are you sure you have time?"

I looked at my watch like it mattered.

"Yeah."

"Good." She started walking down the beach. "Come on. We don't want to run out of sunlight."

I showed her the basics; paddling, pushing up, and standing.

"Just remember, when you pop up, you have to keep your feet spread apart for balance."

She nodded, laying flat on the board with her head up like I told her. I hung onto the side, treading water and trying not to get caught staring.

"And bend your knees too."

"Is that all? No problem." She looked back for a wave. I turned the board and pointed it toward the shore.

"Alright, this wave has your name on it."

She looked back and nodded.

"When I say so, start paddling. And keep your head up."

"But how do I know when to stand up?" She spoke quickly so she wouldn't miss the wave.

"You'll know when." I held the back of the board. "Start paddling ... go go go!" I pulled myself up in the water with one arm stroke and with the other I pushed her along with the slow rolling two-foot high wave. She rode it laying down for a while and then stood up—her hands out like a bird's wings, legs straight, and feet together. She didn't stay up long—just enough for her to come up from the water with a huge smile on her face. I swam in to get the board and made sure she was okay.

"Nice ride." I was genuinely impressed.

"I wanna do it again."

"I figured."

So we did it again—for about a half an hour—just like that; I pushed, she stood, and then she fell. But she always said, "I wanna do it again."

Grey watched her ride one wave almost to the shore. I could read his mind. Anybody, he was thinking, can surf with someone pushing her into the wave.

Rick sat in his Bronco watching the group of guys about fifty yards north of us. Buck joined him and sat in the passenger's seat with binoculars to his eyes. He passed them to Rick and pointed out at us. From the water I could see his hand through the windshield.

"Shit." I muttered through clinched teeth. Jessica sat upright on the board.

"What?" She looked down and pulled her legs out of the water. "What's down there?" She hugged her knees like the water had turned to acid. "Is it a shark?"

I laughed and shook my head. "I sure hope not." When I looked around with no urgency, she relaxed. I pointed at the moving Bronco.

"It's my boss."

"Oh, am I not allowed to be on the board?"

"You're fine." I took a deep breath. "He's just kind of a …"

Whenever Rick used his public address system, the microphone produced an audible click just before he spoke. It was the tingling feeling before a lightning strike and it froze most of us in place. When I heard the click bounce out over the water I sunk down a few inches and hid behind the thick surfboard.

"*Lesley, is that you out there?*" The light breeze blew his static voice all around. All of the guards and the people on the beach turned to look at the truck. Then, like his voice was a giant pointing finger, they focused on Jessica and me.

I lifted a hand reluctantly.

Rick tripped over his words at first, improvising as he stuttered, "*Your...um...I just wanted to tell you that your wife called the office.*" The PA clicked off and then back on. "*She said she needs you to pick up the kids at the babysitter when you're done out there.*"

Rick wasn't that creative so I knew Buck was prompting him.

I floated for a moment. The sigh I let out made bubbles against the side of the board. I looked up at Jessica sitting on the board. She tried not to look surprised.

"Kids?"

I dipped my head under and back up slowly, spitting water out of my mouth like a clogged fountain.

"I'm eighteen...he's joking."

She looked at the truck and smiled. Laughter rang out over the intercom and across the water from the group of guards. I raised my hand again, this time behind Jessica's back where she couldn't see. I gave what we affectionately call the "Wright Street Salute."

"Can you get up here too?" She looked down at me in the water.

"On the board?"

She nodded.

"I can try." I pulled my way to the front of the board and lifted myself onto the nose. We faced each other like we were riding a seesaw. She scooted back a bit, distributing our weight for balance but stayed within reach of me.

"You're pretty good for never doing this before." I smiled and tried to ignore Rick's eyes.

"I had a good teacher." She touched my hand. "Very

patient."

I knew I was blushing and despite my attempt to maintain a level of bravado, my hormones were no match for her overt seduction.

"You wanna give them something to talk about?" She looked at the truck where Buck's binoculars were still trained on us.

"Always." It was a lie. I didn't want to give Buck anything to talk about.

She leaned in and I took her cue. I shuffled a few inches on the board to get closer. Her eyes closed but until I was sure we wouldn't fall over I watched her. She kissed like she talked—deliberately and confident—challenging me to keep up with whatever pattern her wild tongue made.

I lifted my left hand off of the board to her neck, attempting the same move that drove Christine crazy. She grabbed my shoulders with both hands and pulled herself onto my lap. My hand dropped to the board quickly to catch myself but she kept moving forward until my head landed on the nose of the long board.

I was thirty yards out to sea, flat on my back, eyes wide open, a girl straddling me, the entire beach watching, and trying my best not to topple into the water. Jessica slowed her kissing to a normal rate and then to a stop but she didn't pull away. Her teeth found my bottom lip hanging in disbelief and she bit down lightly. She laughed from her chest and I knew she was amused at my state of arousal. She rocked on my lap twice, still biting my lip and as quickly as she started, she slid back to the end of the board.

Her eyebrows rose. I was instantly aware of my condition—the little red shorts left nothing to anyone's imagination. I could feel the binoculars on my back as I sat straight up and then rolled into the water. When I surfaced she smiled.

"Thanks for the lesson." Jessica stretched out on the

board and paddled toward shore.

I gathered myself, allowing the cool water to do its job and swam along side of her.

She hopped off in waist-deep water and let the board go. It washed up on the beach near Rick's empty tire tracks. She looked back at me and splashed a half-handful of water at me. It did nothing more than tell me the lesson was a success.

"What are you doing now?" She stepped up the ledge and sat on the nose with her legs stretched out in front of her.

"I gotta get this board back before they close up the shack." I sat down next to her and wiped at the sandy water on the blue foam.

"And then?" She crossed her ankles and scratched at some old wax on the top of the board with a fingernail.

"And then I'm going to go home and take a shower." I ran my hand through my tangled hair. She nodded slowly and looked out at the empty break. I leaned up against her shoulder and nudged her a bit. "And then I'm going to pick you up and take you to dinner. Maybe come back down for the bonfire later."

"You are, huh?"

"Yes, I am."

"Well, that's cute of you to say so, but I'm going to have to decline." She shrugged her thin shoulders. "It's my last night and I'm going to dinner with my parents."

"Gotcha." I rolled off the board and stepped away. I nodded like I wasn't surprised.

"So you're going to have to wait for me to finish dinner and then come get me." She lifted her hand and waited for me to help her up.

I laughed and pulled her up and close to me.

"How will I know when you're finished?"

"Call the motel and ask for room number six. If I'm not there leave your number. I might be out on the beach." She turned away from me and took an exaggerated step over the board. "It's a good thing you know how to surf, because you don't know much about girls do you?"

I lifted my chin a bit. She shook her head and smiled then reached out and patted me on the cheek.

"Just stick to being cute." With that she walked down the beach. She occasionally looked out at the water but never back at me. I was already imagining weekend trips to Pennsylvania and long distance phone bills.

The parking lot at the station was empty except for the rescue trucks. I rinsed off the board with the hose outside the shack and returned it to the rack in the garage. Buck walked out of the side door and stopped before getting into his truck.

"Don't keep those boards out so long. They aren't yours to fuck around with all night."

"Sorry."

"Good luck tonight." He threw his gear bag in the bed of the truck.

"Thanks."

"She looked easy enough. It'd be hard to fuck that up."

"It wasn't that easy."

"Where's she staying?" He opened the driver's side door.

"Wilbur's"

"For how long?"

"Leaving tomorrow."

"Yeah, hard to fuck that up." He put one foot on the running board of the truck—his back to me. "Even for a rookie." He spit out his dip and slid into the seat.

Harry brought home swordfish filets that night. He sautéed the pieces in a mixture of butter, garlic, lemon, and dill and told me how he and his boss took turns getting high in the back room of the restaurant.

"Guess they don't do drug tests." I raised an

eyebrow but didn't look up from my helping of fish.

"No man, they don't." Harry stared at me while holding the frying pan over the sink.

"I'd be out of a job if I even got busted smoking cigarettes."

"Sounds like a shitty job to me."

"Yeah, it sucks sitting on the beach looking at girls all day."

"Oh right. You ever gonna bring one of these girls home?"

"Probably will tonight."

"Oh yeah?" Harry turned his back to me and wiped the counter.

"Met her on the beach after work and gave her a surf lesson. She was practically fucking me on the board in front of the whole beach."

"And you can't get fired for *that*?"

"Hell no, I'll probably get a promotion."

"I'm glad you found your calling in life." Harry dropped the towel on the counter and walked down the hall to his room.

I called Wilbur's Motel and asked for room six. The phone rang for a while, a click, then, "Wilbur's Oceanfront Motel front desk, this is Dawn."

"Hi, can I leave a message for room six please?"

She laughed. "Go ahead."

I left my name and number.

It was about seven-thirty when I took the portable phone into the bathroom so it would be in reach while I showered.

At eight thirty I called Wilbur's again.

"Wilbur's Oceanfront Motel front desk, this is Dawn."

"Room six please." I tried to drop the tone of my voice.

Laughter again then ringing.

A deeper voice answered the phone. "Hello?"

"Is Jessica there, please?"

"No."

I waited for the man to offer some information on when she might be available but he said nothing.

"Okay." I waited. Nothing. "Thank you."

I hung up the phone and stared at it for a moment. She did say she might be on the beach. I could probably just walk over there and find her. It was a bit forward, but she was leaving in the morning. It wasn't like I imagined her eagerness earlier. If she was already on the beach it might be easier to make a move. I picked up a bathing suit off of the floor and grabbed my keys.

Wilbur's was only a few blocks from my house. I parked on the left side of the complex near a boardwalk that led to the beach. There was no moon. The walkway blended into the low shrubs that crept along the worn wood. The breeze was out of the northeast—cool and damp. It amplified the sound of the surf. The small waves from earlier in the evening were building with the onshore wind. Wilbur's single flood-lamp illuminated the jagged peaks of water tumbling and rolling up the beach. Several pairs of flip flops rested where the boardwalk met the sand. Any one of them could be hers.

To the north, about a quarter of a mile up the beach, the glow from the Wright Street bonfire hovered along the dark shoreline. I considered the wind blowing onshore and thought out loud, "They're gonna catch the dunes on fire."

"Excuse me." A man in sweatpants reached back to guide a girl down the dark steps.

"Yeah, sorry." I smiled and nodded at the girl.

They kicked off their shoes and walked south. I hoped they didn't hear me talking to myself. It was close to nine o'clock. Short of walking up and down the beach looking for Jessica, I didn't really know what to do. I didn't want to go home and face Harry.

"Screw this. I'm not desperate."

I looked at the balconies again. I counted over from the end. What I guessed was number six was dark.

Instead of turning left to go home, I drove up to the Wright Street access. The parking lot was full so I pulled into the sand along the road. I wasn't worried about showing up empty handed. Other than Buck, no one knew I made plans to see Jessica after the surf lesson. I climbed over the tall walkway and met voices blowing through the access. From the top of the steps I saw dozens of flickering shadows scattered around the beach. The stand was occupied. There were people leaning against a rescue truck. Someone was running around in the soft sand near the dunes. I couldn't make out any faces but the sounds were familiar.

"Wesley!" Grey called out while raising a clear bottle in the air.

I lifted my hand in a broad wave to the group. My eyes hadn't adjusted but Grey's signature shape and wine cooler made it impossible to mistake him. He sat in the sand and leaned against the front tire of the 701 truck. I reached down and shook his hand. He pulled down with urgency. His eyes, glassy and red in the firelight, were wide.

"Dude." He whispered loudly. "What the fuck?"

I shook my head. "I don't know, man. You tell me."

"Fuck Buck." The smell of Strawberry Breeze blew past me and Grey let go. "You're cool, Brookie."

He dropped his head. The sentiment about Buck wasn't a new one so I paid it little mind. I leaned against the front grill and scanned the beach. Stanley was the one running around by the dunes. He carried a bottle of water in one hand and held the other out to his side for balance. Adrian played his guitar. His mop of blonde hair fell carelessly out of his hooded sweatshirt. The people near him huddled under blankets and I thought how generic it looked. He sang "Fire and Rain" and I laughed to myself.

"It's too early for you to start laughing at us." Ed handed me a red cup.

"I wasn't. It just kind of struck me. You know?"

"Kind of stupid, huh?"

I laughed again and shook my head. "No, I love it." I took a sip of beer. "We could have it a lot worse."

"You think?" He nodded to the back of the truck.

"What?"

Ed looked at me from the corner of his eyes. "The ultimate snake."

"Who is that?"

"Sorry buddy, I thought you saw already." Ed pointed with the same hand that held his cup. "It's Buck and your surf lesson."

The harsh orange din of the bonfire was just enough to throw light on the bed of the truck. Jessica wore a red ORS jacket and Buck had his arm around her. I stared at them like Ed was wrong—that it wasn't her. Buck talked in her ear and she dropped her head in laughter. When she brought it up she turned and faced him. He said something else and she stopped laughing. He took his arm away. She turned and looked straight at me.

She lifted her hand and waved quickly without smiling. It was the first time anything about her looked soft. Her lips curled in and she turned back to face the water.

Buck didn't. He looked at me with that shit-eating, bully-from-grade-school, always-the-other-guy grin.

I hated him. I hated that I couldn't do a fucking thing about it.

"Nice." I looked at Ed. "Real cool."

"He pulled up about an hour ago with her in the truck. No one said anything to him."

I was trapped between wanting to go home and not wanting to show Buck that I was pissed.

"Fuck it. That chick was psycho anyway." I looked down into my cup. "I'm over it."

"Good." Ed looked impressed. "Booty Patrol?"

"Not tonight." I pointed at Adrian and his revelers. "This shit's winding down anyway."

"Yeah, you're right." Ed looked around the dwindling crowd. "Fuckin' Stanley."

I turned my head back up to the dunes. "What the hell is he doing?"

"Spark duty."

Stanley watched the embers float up from the fire and drift toward him. Like an outfielder he followed them until they got within splashing range and he waved the open bottle into the air.

"Is he actually doing anything?"

"Buck told him to do it." He shook his head.

I joined him and watched Stanley dance around like a fool.

"You should get him back for that shit." Ed spoke between sips.

"I'm not worried about that crazy chick." I shrugged it off the best I could. When I glanced back to the tailgate no one was there.

Ed looked up to the dunes. "Yeah, you keep telling me that—not the point. You'd be doing all of us a favor."

"Yeah, but seriously, what am I going to do?"

Ed shrugged. Grey poured sand from two cupped hands into his empty wine cooler bottle with the determination of a brain surgeon. Ed looked down at him.

"Hey Wright Street, you building sand castles down there?" Ed dribbled some of his beer into the moat that formed around the bottle.

"Wright Street to Neptune Street."

Ed smiled, looked at me, then back at Grey. "Go ahead for Neptune."

"10-go fuck yourself."

Ed and I laughed at Grey.

"Wright Street to Rookie."

"Go ahead."

"10—" Grey let out an exasperated sigh and threw the sand left in his hand. "10-fuck Buck."

"10-4." I laughed and reached out to shake Ed's hand. "I'm heading out." I finished my beer and threw the empty cup through the passenger's window of the 701 truck. I imagined Buck driving down to Wilbur's and looking for Jessica. I wasn't sure how he made contact with her but however it happened, it pissed me off the more I looked at his truck. "On second thought." I nodded at Ed.

He made a siren sound and slapped the hood. "Deputies Brooks and Henderson reporting for duty."

"Booty duty!" Grey made a siren sound to match Ed's but it fell off and he slumped down onto the sand.

"Let's drop him off on the way." Ed reached down and lifted Grey up by the elbow. I took the other side.

"Sounds like a plan."

We dropped Grey off at Magnolia Street and drove south for a few miles.

"I think it's a quiet night." Ed looked around while he drove.

"It's cool. I just don't want to go home right now. My roommate's being a baby."

"What's his deal?"

"I think he's pissed that I'm not hanging out with him more. It's nothing."

"You two are friends from home?"

"Yeah, we grew up together but he's into different things."

"Gotcha." Ed tapped on the steering wheel. "You been to the Point yet?"

"No, I'm not twenty-one."

"It's cool."

"How am I going to get past the door guy?"

"I am the door guy."

"Oh. That's convenient."

We parked behind the Point. The out of place two-story log cabin loomed like a stranded ship from a century ago. The large dark timbers a stark contrast to the low shrub brush growing around the sides of the building and the simple beach houses on adjoining lots.

The inside smelled of pine and stale beer. Surfboards hung along the log walls next to vintage lunch boxes and an inexplicable collection of antique bicycles and broken guitars. The bar was surprisingly empty for a Friday night. Ed picked a stool and smiled at the bartender.

"Good evening, Miss Evelyn." He made a grand gesture with his hands.

She leaned against the bar, pointed at me, and looked at him.

"This is Wesley." He turned and put his hand on my shoulder. "He's my twin cousin from Virginia."

Evelyn smiled. Her hair was long and dark. She wore a tight tank top with dark tattoos peaking out from the strap on each shoulder. She looked at me with her striking green eyes.

"If he's your twin, he must be of age, huh?"

Ed slapped the bar. "There you go."

Her smile showed a crooked front tooth that made her more exotic. When she dug out two bottles from the cooler I saw another tattoo on the small of her back. She placed the beers on coasters in front of us and grabbed a pack of cigarettes from under the counter.

"Watch things for me?"

"Do I get anything in return?" Ed grinned at Evelyn.

"You and your cousin get to drink and I won't call your tab tonight."

"Deal." Ed watched her walk down the hallway where she disappeared through the back door. He turned to the bar. "One night with her and I'd swear off every other woman in the world."

"I didn't even know you worked here."

"Only a few nights a week. Fridays and Saturdays are

usually slow. People want to spend time with their families before they leave. I just do it to stay sane and for the open tab." He stared at the bottles lined up along the rail behind the bar. Behind them, a mirror reflected the small dark room. "I need a break from guarding. Too much bullshit."

"If you hate the job so much why do you keep doing it?"

"I don't hate the job. I love lifeguarding. I just hate the drama. You know?

"I'm starting to see. Why don't you just go down to Nags Head."

"Same bullshit, different colored shorts." He thought for a second. "But at least they get paid."

"Okay, what's with that? Why does everyone joke about Rick's checks?"

"He's broke. His financial strategy is to rent as many chairs and umbrellas as he can and win the lottery. If those don't both happen he'll be done by next summer."

"Doesn't the town pay him enough?"

"Sure, but the money goes other places. And just before it runs out he hustles it from somewhere else and the checks come for a little while longer." Ed took a sip from his bottle. "Why do you think he gets us all pizza and beer every Friday?"

I shrugged.

"Come on, Rookie." He waited and I stared at him with a blank expression. "He may spend fifty bucks or so but what he's really doing is keeping us on the beach until the banks close. Then he gets a weekend's worth of cash from rentals to deposit first thing Monday before we can cash our paychecks."

Ed sensed my confusion.

"Look, it's not sinister. Rick's got a good heart. He's just a lousy businessman. I don't hate Rick—he's just a fucking idiot." He turned and pointed at me. "And I'd never go down to Nags Head—bunch of pricks."

"Okay."

"I know I talk a lot of shit about ORS—"

I interrupted, "Well, yeah considering you're the one who told me to apply."

He looked at me again. "Aren't you glad you did?"

"Of course."

"Well, there you go." He rubbed the neck of his bottle with his thumb. His tone changed and his voice rose a bit. "I know I talk shit but I defend us too. Let someone call me a sucker for working for Rick and see what happens."

I watched his gestures and listened carefully. I liked it when Ed got carried away—but he sensed it and pulled back.

"Anyway, you'll figure it out."

We both turned and faced the mirror.

"Yeah, you keep telling me that."

CHAPTER 9

Buck had the weekend off. I made it through the two days with no mention of Jessica. Harry and I avoided each other and I looked forward to the quiet escape of my stand. Fig ran PT from his four-wheeler that Monday morning. He was hung over and told us to run to the pier and back. No one argued and we all took the opportunity to go at our own pace. Adrian and I ran side by side near the front of the group.

"Why aren't there any girls on staff?" I never asked Preston or Fig because the answer might be too obvious and I didn't want to appear naïve.

"I don't know. I tried to get a girl from my college swim team a job—told Rick she was better in the water than me and he still blew me off." Adrian ran closer to the water where the sand was a bit firmer. "I kind of knew he'd say no but I wanted to see what his reason was."

"What did he say?"

"He started mumbling all this bullshit about not having separate facilities for males and females and it was a code issue and that he'd have to carry extra insurance."

"There's no way that's true." I side-stepped a dried up blowfish and yelled a warning the rest of the pack.

"BLOWFISH." Bare feet were no match for the prickly spines.

"I don't know, I guessed if there were girls he'd have to have separate showers and bathrooms and all that." When Adrian defended Rick he always shook his head at the same time.

"You really think so?"

"I don't know. But there's definitely more to it."

"Ed must know something about it." I looked up at the approaching pier.

"He might. I know he and Fig were talking about it a while back at the B-hole because Katie said something about it being a boy's only club."

I slapped one of the pier pilings and we both turned around and ran south.

"Here comes Grey. Ask him"

"Ask me what?" Grey stopped twenty yards short of the pier and joined us.

"Wesley's wondering if Rick wears boxers or briefs and I told him you were the one to ask."

"Fuck off." Grey was already losing steps to Adrian and me. "Has he heard the tighty-whitey story?"

"Not sure I want to." I stepped to the side so Grey could run between us and he made up the difference. "We're wondering why there aren't any girls working here."

"Inadequate facilities." Grey's response was quick.

"Bullshit, that's what Adrian said."

"Hey, that's what Buck told me. Ask Ed."

Ed was a hundred yards ahead of us so I dropped the issue. Adrian and I increased our pace. Grey hung in for a few strides but fell off by the time we reached Maynard Street. Four divers were coming out of the water with spear guns in hand and mesh bags full of triggerfish and sheepshead.

When we got back to the shack for check-in, Buck handed me the Sea Dunes' whistle again without a word. I said nothing either but looked at Grey as I walked by with the kit in hand.

"Moving up the ladder pretty quick, Rookie." Grey raised his eyebrows with knowing approval.

I shrugged. "It's just while Roy's off—not a big deal."

Grey checked in and followed me out to the garage where the buoys hung on their racks. I picked up Sea Dunes' orange buoy and spun it on the palm of my hand like Grey showed me the day before.

"Not bad." Grey again looked as though he was impressed by my quick ascension through the ranks from Wilkins Street rookie to Sea Dunes. I raised the buoy again and spun it.

The handle slipped from my palm and sent the plastic buoy to the concrete floor. The rattling noise bounced around the garage as it danced awkwardly like a dropped football. Buck yelled from inside the shack and I quickly scooped up the buoy before he could open the door to see who was making the noise.

Grey and I walked away without looking back. We stopped at his car on the north end of the parking lot. He loaded his equipment and spoke with a top-secret tone.

"Roy's not coming back." He looked around to make sure no one else could hear.

"What do you mean?"

"Just that. You're Sea Dunes from now on." Grey waited for a response but I let him to continue. "Unless you fuck up, of course. Then your ass'll be permanently attached to Wilkins Street."

"What about Roy?"

"Gone man. Ain't the first, won't be the last. This place is pretty much a revolving door like that."

"Yeah, but why?"

"Plenty of time to figure all that out—if you stick around."

"Man, why does everyone always do that? If this place is as bad as you say, why are you still here?"

He laughed and climbed into his car. "If everyone loved their job you'd have something to worry about. Just watch the rips down by the drain pipe." He looked past me and lowered his voice. "And make sure you turn all of your cash in at the end of the day."

Grey backed up and rolled out of the gravel parking lot slow and deliberate—the same way he ran at PT. I looked down at the money bag in my hands.

Ed sat at Neptune Street like usual. We'd been slow all day on account of the west wind. Most of the radio chatter was about rentals and the supervisors were busy moving equipment around from the stands that had too much to the ones that needed it.

It was nearing four o'clock and I'd packed most of my rentals in the large plywood equipment box. I signaled Ed and we met at my northernmost chair and umbrella.

"Hey, Ed."

"Rookie."

We turned and faced the water with our buoys pressed down in the sand in front of us.

"So, why there aren't any girls on staff. Do you know?"

"Too much bullshit." Ed's voice took on an irreverent tone. "You start hiring girls and all of the sudden you have to schedule around their girl times and they have to sit a stand that's near a bathroom."

I nodded as though that were reason enough to keep the staff all guys.

"Inadequate facilities, huh?"

Ed got the joke and laughed.

"Well, how can you have a lifeguard that can't go in the water for two or three days each month?"

"Why not?" I honestly had no idea.

"Sharks." Ed pointed to his crotch. "Once a month. Get it, Rookie?"

"Are you serious?"

"Not really." He laughed. "Rick says they are too much of a distraction."

"Yeah, I can see that—especially around this group."

"So, that's why he never really liked having girls on staff."

"Who's the girl in the group photo in the shack?"

"You don't miss much do you?"

I shrugged. "She kind of stands out in the picture."

"He did hire a few here and there. The girl in the picture, Jamie Franklin, wanted to work and her father was a town commissioner so Rick pretty much had to suck it up and hire her. It was my first season—the first year Buck was a supervisor."

"Why didn't she just work for Nags Head? They've got half a dozen girls."

"Her father was a Kitty Hawk commissioner—it'd be like the mayor living in another town."

"I guess."

"She was a good guard. She beat half the guys at PT—didn't put up with any of their shit—really held her own. She was almost too good and some of the guys felt threatened—guys like Buck."

"Well at least he's not a discriminating asshole."

"He gave Jamie a harder time at PT than anyone else—rode her ass and pushed her too much. Then he started scheduling himself in her zone and sitting in the stand with her—just making her uncomfortable and shit like that."

"Was she hot?"

"I didn't think she was but I guess Buck did 'cause he started talking big and hitting on her one day."

"Big surprise." I shook my head.

A little boy and girl ran past us and we both looked around for their parents. They were sitting in Ed's zone—not too far away.

"Yeah, but she ignored him and it only pissed him off more. But he was still a first year supervisor and that's when he was dating Lilly so he kept it to himself as much as possible."

"What? Buck dated Lilly?" I turned and stared at Ed. "You've got to be fucking kidding me."

The little girl turned around when she heard me and I immediately felt flushed. I lifted my hand and waved.

"You know Lilly?" Ed looked at me like I'd been holding out on him.

"Not really, but I know who she is. We talked once." I shrugged it off as best I could without being obvious.

"Okay, yeah." Ed turned to me. "That's right. I heard she was on the beach when you did your swim test." He laughed. "Be careful with that."

"It's nothing, I only talked to her once—I'm just surprised. Those two don't seem to match up."

"I guess not, she dumped him that summer."

"How old is she?"

"Twenty, I think. She was in high school then." Ed turned back to the water. "Anyway—about the Commissioner's daughter. We're all at Magnolia Street one night and Buck's shit-faced. Jamie rarely went to the parties because she had a boyfriend but she showed up that night. I was working on some girl on the back porch but apparently Buck waited outside the bathroom for her and when she opened the door he pushed her back in and closed the door. He tried to kiss her and had his hands all over her." Ed laughed. "She practically beat the shit out of him—gave him a black eye and busted his lip."

"Wow, I would have loved to see that."

"It was a sight."

"For a former SEAL he sure gets his ass kicked a lot."

"Could be why he's a *former* SEAL, if he ever was one in the first place."

"True."

"She got her boyfriend and left without saying a word."

"Wait. The boyfriend was at the party too?"

"Yeah, didn't I say that? Whatever, later that night—after she told him what happened—he came back to the house and found Buck passed out in his room. He couldn't wake him up so he tore up the room and started trashing the house. It woke up everyone. Fig, a few other guards, and I jumped him and called the police."

"All over this girl?"

"Yeah, but we didn't know that at the time. He was just some guy in our house tearing shit up. The next day, after we all went to our stands Buck met with Rick, the Police Chief, the Commissioner, and Jamie. They all agreed—except for her—to keep it quiet for the sake of the town and for everyone's personal agendas. There were no charges against the boyfriend in return and Rick agreed to suspend Buck for two weeks with no pay. She never worked again."

"And that was it?"

"Yep. Buck went to Virginia for a couple days and was back to work that same week."

"Figures. But why did the Commissioner drop it so easy?"

"I don't know. I'm sure there's more to it." Ed shrugged and I assumed that he knew how much more there was to it. "It was probably just easier than dealing with the whole public ordeal."

"So, that's why Rick doesn't hire girls?"

"He can't afford the risk. He's actually lucky it was the Commissioner's daughter. I don't think anyone else would have kept it quiet."

"No one outside ORS knows about it?" I really couldn't comprehend it.

"On this beach? People know about it. It's just one of those back page stories."

"Back page?"

"It's a tourist town. People on vacation don't want to read about local scandals the same way they don't want to read about people drowning or shark attacks."

"Drownings? Not in Kitty Hawk though?"

"Back page man." Ed leaned on his buoy and kicked some sand against it.

"Rick said there hasn't been a drowning here in like five years."

"No drownings, but there's been a handful of heart attacks in the water—that way no one has to admit they drowned—easier on the family and the town and everyone that way. People are supposed to have heart attacks—people aren't supposed to drown."

"But there aren't really shark attacks."

"Oh, of course not." Ed's exaggerated sincerity was alarming to me. "But there are a lot of deep lacerations from phantom surfboard fins and unseen submerged objects. We just treat the wounds. We don't admit to seeing a dorsal fin that morning. It's the ocean—it's where they live."

"So, what's the tighty-whitey story?"

Ed turned his head and looked at me. "Where'd you hear that?"

"Grey said something."

He laughed.

"That one's not quite as serious. It's just another stupid-Rick story." He scanned the water and continued. "We had a rookie guard ask Rick how well he could swim. We all listened to hear how Rick would react. I mean, the dude's practically an albino. I don't think I've ever seen him in the water.

Rick told the story about how one winter when he was the only one around to respond to calls he got paged out for two people in distress right up there in front of my access. Lucky for him, the fire department got paged out too and responded right behind him.

So there goes Rick, tearing down the beach, lights and sirens. When he gets to the access he sees two men in the water. According to Rick, they were twice as big as him—which is hard to believe seeing as Rick puts on twenty pounds in the winter—and they're hundreds of yards out but I'm sure they had just stepped off the ledge and gotten stuck in the trough." Ed pointed at the dip between the shore and the sandbar. "I mean, who goes swimming in December?"

Ed scanned the water and continued.

"So, he grabbed a buoy and dove in. He didn't radio in. He didn't set up a tow-line. He just stripped down to his underwear and charged his ass into the water. We called him on breaking procedure but he argued that he didn't have time to put on the wetsuit that was in the back of his truck. The last thing the Fire Chief saw was Rick getting slammed by a wave and nearly losing his Fruit of the Looms. Rick saved the men in his version but Jackson— the fireman that actually pulled all three of them in told me that Rick was 'blue in the face and whining like a bitch.'"

I laughed at the mental image but I was still hung up on the other stories.

"You believe it? I mean all of it—the Buck story, the sharks, Rick."

"Well, yeah. I was there for the Buck thing. Happy it happened. It forced Lilly to dump his ass. The rest of it's probably true, but you can't take any of it seriously."

"But it is serious. It's a life and death job."

Ed let out a sigh and I instantly felt foolish for assuming to know anything.

"It may be deadly sometimes but don't make it your life."

"How many years have you done it?" I didn't mean to imply anything about Ed's choices but I obviously touched a nerve.

"Hey Rookie, as long as I go away at the end of the summer it's not my life. I'm not riding a four-wheeler and I stay away from the bullshit. It's a job. The day I let it get to me is the day I quit. Don't go looking in to it too much. Keep the job simple."

"You mean ignore the obvious?"

"Yep, that's exactly what I mean. Stay low like I told you. It won't go away but at least you can claim ignorance when it goes to shit." Ed wasn't angry. His voice turned soft and trailed off.

"So what's another stupid-Rick story?"

Ed checked his watch and I did the same. It was ten after five and we had enough time for another before check-in.

"Well, Rick suspected that this one guard was screwing around on the radio—making animals noises and mocking Rick, but he couldn't prove it. Buck gave the guard a fucked up radio—one that hummed after the microphone was keyed up. The guy using it couldn't hear it but everyone else could. They switched his radio at check-in and when the guard answered up for role call at nine-thirty we all heard the hum. I was riding along with Rick that day because the water was so high at Luke Street that my beach was empty. I could tell he was just waiting for the guy to fuck up.

He's like, 'We'll get that little fucker now.'

He always gets excited about that kind of shit. He loves busting guards for insubordination.

Around eleven o'clock the humming started as a few clicks and then some pathetic seagull calls—all followed by the hum.

'Click ... *caw caw caw* ... *Come here O-O-O-Otis* ... hum.'

'Got'em,' Rick says.

I could see him turning ten shades of red. He didn't say anything else to me about it but he picked up the radio and told everyone to stay after check-in for a meeting at six o'clock." Ed had his radio in his hand and twirled it by the antenna—something Buck would run-swim him for if he saw it.

A lot of us rode along with Rick on our days off.

Sometimes we got a free lunch at the Buccaneer out of it. Regardless, it was always entertaining. Rick saw me at Shipwreck the week before and asked if I wanted to check out the scenery. People waved at us when we drove by and girls stared. I sat in the passenger's seat trying to look cool. I listened to Rick rant about the drunks on the bulkhead near the pier. He pointed at one in particular and called him Geronimo. Then he raved about the topless woman who regularly lay out at Byrd Street.

"Are they allowed to be topless?"

"Why the fuck not?"

"I just didn't know if there were laws or not. You know—indecent exposure or something?"

"That's indecent." Rick pointed at a woman walking out of the water. Her bathing suit was twisted and practically see-through. Her thick body hardly fit into the bikini and one of her breasts hung out the side of her top.

"I wish I hadn't seen that." I looked out the other window and tried to shake the image from my head.

"What's the matter, Rookie? Don't you like your girls with some meat on their bones?"

"That's just gross Rick. Really, that's gross."

"It's not illegal to be topless. The town doesn't approve but I encourage it." Rick always wore sunglasses but it wasn't to shield his eyes from being caught staring. He wouldn't care if he did. "If someone starts bitching about a topless woman, tell the girl she only needs two Band-Aids and a cork."

Ed continued with his story and I imagined how mad Rick must have been. Not only was the guy screwing around on the radio but he also made fun of Rick.

"We waited until six o'clock or so. Buck was getting pissed and annoyed by everyone being in the shack. We were all sitting on the couches or the floor. A few of us knew what the meeting was about and we couldn't help but watch the guy who was about to get fired."

Ed unscrewed his radio antenna and then screwed it back on before he finished the story.

"Rick came into the shack holding a copy of the handbook and immediately started flipping through it. He said that he wasn't going to put up with people fucking around on the radios.

'This is a professional organization and we're going to fucking run it that way,' he said. Then he looked at us like we were all guilty except for the guy that did it.

Then he said, 'I told you all yesterday that if I found out who was screwing around on the radio, he'd be done at ORS. Well, I know who did it and when I find out who it was, I'm gonna fire him.'

He looked at us all again and walked back to his office.

We sat there looking at each other—trying to figure out what the hell just happened. Fifteen guys and not one clue what the hell he was talking about.

'I know who did it and when I find out who it was, I'm gonna fire him.'

No one said anything. I heard his office door shut and could just imagine him sitting there watching us on the monitor. We went out to our cars and tried not to laugh until we were out of sight.

'I know who did it, and when I find out who it was, I'm gonna fire him.'"

Ed shook his head and laughed a little. "What a fucking idiot."

"Did he ever fire the guy?"

"He couldn't really. We were short-staffed at the time and the guy was already on the schedule for the rest of the week."

"That's ridiculous."

"Welcome to ORS."

Our radios clicked and Rick's voice came on.

"Good job on the beach today. Let's keep it up. Make sure all of the trash is out of your area before you leave."

I rolled my eyes at the idea of picking up trash. Ed looked at a Corona bottle between us and pushed it down into the sand with his foot, burying it out of sight.

"I'll put up with a lot but he doesn't pay me enough to pick up these fuckers' trash." He looked out at the water and lifted his hand to the northeast. "Wind's gonna pull around tonight. Might have to flag it tomorrow." He kicked some sand over a cigarette butt and turned back to his stand. "See you at check-in."

CHAPTER 10

Ed was right about the wind. When I left the house the next morning I was greeted with cool heavy morning air. I made sure I had my sweatpants and drove down to the shack. The chalkboard had the usual information but at the bottom one of the supervisors wrote, 'Outgoing tide all day—Watch out for RIPS!'

I wrote the same warning on my stand information board, replacing RIPS with Rip Currents to avoid any confusion. I was getting used to the people on the beach and felt better about the water but I still welcomed the red flags that morning when Buck and Fig set them out. It stood to reason that the flags made our jobs easier. Surely people knew better than to swim when the flags were up.

I learned quickly. People are idiots.

My beach had roughly three hundred patrons over a quarter mile stretch. I knew where the rips opened up; a hundred yards south at the drain pipe; twenty yards north of my stand; in between Neptune Street's zone and mine. I kept an eye on these areas specifically but treated all of the swimmers like they were the next to be pulled out.

The water wasn't too rough—it didn't really have to be. Rip currents pull hardest at low tide. There's less room for the outgoing water to move over the sandbar, causing the outflow to move fast and with enough power to pull a grown man thirty yards out to sea before he knows what's happening. Low tide was just before one o'clock that day when the beach was full. The flags were up all morning and people started getting brave.

I watched the father of the family in front of my stand walk down to the water. He went in up to his shins and stood with his hands on his hips while looking out at the moderate surf. Then he glanced down at the water swirling around his feet.

His two little boys were covered in sand from their castle creation. They ran toward him. I sat up in my chair. He turned quickly, raised his hands, and bent down at the same time, scooping them both up in one motion. He said something to the boys in his arms and they all looked down. They were about ten yards from the rip near my stand and I knew he felt the pull against his legs. He carried the boys up to dry sand and put them down. He pointed to the water, then to a red flag, then to me. I waved at the boys and went back to scanning.

A quick whistle burst drifted down from the north. Through my binoculars I saw Ed down off his stand pointing. Two swimmers made their way out of the water near the rip between us. My beach was too populated to get down and approach people like that.

Unfortunately, not everyone was as conscientious as the father in front of me. Down by the drain pipe a man was knee deep in the water. Then he went in up to his waist. He turned back to his friends and waved at them to join him. He faced the water again and threw his hands out in front of him, diving through a small choppy wave. His friends grabbed a variety of floats and ran to the water.

I stood up and peeled off my red jacket. I hesitated to pick up my radio because I didn't know exactly what to say. I couldn't go all the way down there and leave the rest of my beach unguarded. Whistling at them would be a waste. A warm wave of panic surged through me. I looked to the north. There were no supervisor four wheelers within sight. To the south I could see Adrian at Sibbern Street standing up and looking through his binoculars at the group.

My radio buzzed and I heard, *"Sibbern to Sea Dunes."*

I stared at the people, hoping they'd feel the pull too and come back in. My pulse raced and again I looked to the north. I saw Ed on his stand looking in my direction.

"Sibbern to Sea Dunes."

I had to respond. "Go ahead for Sea Dunes."

"Do you have a visual on those people at the pipe?"

"10-4." I held my thumb over the radio button, praying the people would turn around. They didn't. Adrian didn't want to say anything else on the radio that might get me in trouble. I still didn't know what to say back. There wasn't a ten-code for swimmers who weren't in trouble. I reached for my manual that I kept in my bag and quickly realized how stupid that was.

"Fuck it. I'll just go down there," I said to myself.

I turned around and reached for the rung of the two by four ladder with my foot—watching the swimmers the whole time.

"I'm right here. I'll take care of it."

I looked around the beach. The front of Buck's truck peeked through the access between my stand and the pipe. I stayed on the ladder, waiting to see what he'd do. The truck slowly rolled down the slope of the beach and settled a few yards above the high tide line.

The PA clicked. *"Swimmers, exit the water immediately."*

Everyone on the beach and in the water turned toward Buck's voice.

"Sea Dunes, get down here."

I hit the sand running and grabbed my buoy and fins from their resting place in front of the stand without breaking stride. I was fifty yards from the truck when Buck lifted his arm through the driver's window and pointed to the first swimmer who went in. He said nothing as I approached—just stared at the swimmer and pointed.

I passed the others who had made it to shore without issue and high stepped through the wash. I knew exactly where the trough began and planted my foot on the lip before it dropped off. The push off sent me flying over the incoming set wave and I threw my hands out in front of me like I had practiced.

I pulled my way though another wave before surfacing and spotted the man while I took in my first breath. I slipped my swim fins on without missing a beat. The waves forced me to climb and drop as much as I swam. Each passing wave pulled my buoy but it didn't slow me. I called out when I made eye contact.

"Hey! Sir!" I never dropped my head and pulled myself within ten yards of the man.

His face was pointed straight to the sky; his body completely vertical below the surface.

"I'm a lifeguard, take this buoy."

I stopped within arm's reach and pulled the line behind me. His hand surfaced just as the buoy whipped around my body. He grabbed a hold and pulled it to his chest.

"What's your name?" I yelled from the adrenaline. It snapped the man's attention away from merely surviving and he took a deep breath.

"Marcus." His voice was clear which told me that he was breathing well enough. I turned toward shore and signaled to Buck that the situation was under control and that the man was okay. Buck leaned against the hood with his arms crossed. When he saw my signal he returned it casually and crossed his arms again.

"What happened?" Marcus wiped the water from his face with one hand while still holding tightly to the buoy.

"You walked into this rip current." I looked around and so did he but there was no reference point. "We're going to swim back in at an angle. Do me a favor and kick as hard as you can."

Marcus nodded and I turned to my side. With his efforts, we had no problem getting back to shore. Before we exited the water completely, Marcus, about thirty years old and in decent shape, dropped the buoy.

"I'm sorry for going out there. I didn't realize it was that strong." His head was down and he fought back tears.

"It's no big deal. That's why we're here. Could have happened to anyone."

I stepped up the lip of the trough and reached back to help him. He didn't let go right away and shook my hand before returning to his waiting friends. Buck approached him with a clipboard in hand. I wrapped the strap around my buoy and scanned the water.

"Get back to your stand." Buck pulled a pen from the top of the clipboard.

I nodded and turned to walk back. As I passed the family in front of my stand, the father looked at me and gave me a thumbs-up. I smiled and lifted my hand in acknowledgment. I settled back into my stand and scanned the water.

"*Sibbern to Sea Dunes.*"

"Go ahead for Sea Dunes." I looked south at Adrian. He stood with an arm in the air.

"*Good job, Rookie.*"

I waved back in acknowledgement.

"*701 to Sibbern. Watch your water.*"

Buck drove toward my stand. I expected him to stop and talk to me about the rescue—my first. He pulled up, parked in front of me, and looked up through the truck window.

"Why did you let them in the water?"

I didn't expect a hug and pat on the back from Buck but I wasn't prepared for blame either.

"I couldn't stop them before they got in."

"Use your whistle next time."

I nodded and chose not to argue.

"If you can't handle this stand, I'll put you back at Wilkins Street."

"I got it." My jaw clenched and I felt my voice start to quiver. If I had to say anything else it might crack.

Buck stared at me like he sensed it as well. He watched me for a few seconds. I scanned the water. Without another word, the truck moved forward and he continued north.

The radio continued to buzz throughout the dropping tide. For the next few hours lifeguards made routine rescues despite the red flags. The lack of an enforceable ordinance made the flags simply a warning and not an unlawful violation. We didn't advertise this loophole, but it didn't take motivated vacationers long to figure it out.

About an hour after my rescue, a man walked up to my stand with his young son right behind him.

"Can we swim?" He pointed to the water.

"No sir, I'm sorry. The rip currents are very strong."

"What about later today?"

"No sir, once the flags are up, they are up for the day."

He thought about that.

"What about tomorrow?"

"I really can't tell. We'll just have to see. It's doubtful." I shook my head.

"Well, can we just go in to our knees?" Again, he pointed to the water.

"No sir, the currents are very strong today."

"How about we just get our feet wet?"

"We're asking that you stay out of the water completely."

"Oh come on, just our feet." He pointed to his feet.

"Sir, we're asking that you stay out of the water for the day."

He looked around and then back up at me.

"I pay a lot of money to be here."

"I know you do, sir. But today the water is off limits."

"Off limits huh? What time do you go home?"

"Five-thirty, sir. But the flags will stay up."

"What beaches don't have lifeguards on them?"

I looked at his kid and felt sorry for the boy.

"They all do, sir."

I had similar conversations over the next few days with the addition of:

"How old are you, anyway?"

"What are you gonna do, hold me out of the water?"

"I'm a police officer back home; I know the law."

"I swam competitively in college."

"Only kids and old people drown."

There were more of course. We each had our favorite. Mine quickly became, "It's okay, I'm a lifeguard too."

"What beach do you guard on?" I always asked what *beach*. The reply was the same, "Oh, not on a beach. I guard at a pool back home in…"

"Please stay out of the water," I'd say with a smile.

Rick's static voice bounced from his speakers. As shrill as the wind, it had the same chilling effect when he made his way down the crowded beach in his Bronco. On calm days, Rick was a welcome diversion to the boredom. On busy days he only added to the tension. His loudspeaker rattled with muffled warnings. The wind made it hard to understand anything he said even when he was coherent.

"Attention folks we … extremely … rip currents. The no …. flags will …. the rest of the day. Stay … water."

At best, people on the beach could pick out key words. Most waved him down and asked him what he was saying. The one thing Rick hated more than dealing with the town bureaucracy was public relations. In his mind, having to stop and explain himself was a waste of his time, so he drove fast and rarely made eye contact with people. He just waved as he passed the stands. People he ignored often made their way up to the guards with questions or complaints.

Three days into the nor'easter, Rick was flying up and down the beach warning people about rips. The crowd forced him to slow down near my stand and he came to a stop just short of a sandcastle and two children. The boy and girl ran to his truck. The Bronco sat so high that they couldn't see in the window. From my stand I watched them reach up and try to peek at Rick. He looked at them through the passenger's window. He said something, rolled the window up, and drove over the sandcastle.

The boy and girl stood still and watched him drive away. I knew what was coming next. As sure as the kids ran to their mother, the woman made her way to my stand with the children closely following.

"Excuse me." The woman stood in front of me with her hands fixed on her waist. I couldn't see her eyes through her dark sunglasses but I imagined they were pretty pissed.

"Yes ma'am." I also noticed what great shape she was in. Her black one-piece bathing suit was trimmed with gold and cut low around her chest. A triangle of freckles led my shielded eyes down her cleavage.

"I'd like to make a report to your supervisor."

"My supervisor?" I had learned the fine art of acting surprised at everything concerning Rick. I played dumb—like I didn't see what he'd done.

"Yes, I'd like to make a complaint about that man in the white truck."

I made a puzzled face and she continued.

"My son and daughter went to ask him what he was saying on the loudspeaker and he told them to get their grubby hands off his truck."

The boy and girl pouted when she repeated what he said.

"And then he ran over their sandcastle. What kind of..." She paused and I could hear the word *asshole* in my head. "Who does that?"

I looked at the childrens' hands for some justification.

"Ma'am, there's no excuse for that and I'll make sure I fill out a report when I get back to the station." I pointed to the flag next to my stand without looking at it. "It's been a rough day for all of us; lots of rescues. Everyone's a little on edge, but again, there's no excuse for that. I'll make sure it's taken care of."

She was content with my bullshit answer. I wrote down her name on my brown lunch bag and offered the children two *Ocean Safety for Kids* coloring books. They were content and in the distance the northeast wind blew Rick's words all over the beach.

I told Grey the story after work and he quickly one-upped me.

"Rick drove by my stand today and there was a family down by the water. I had talked to them earlier and they weren't an issue. The little girl—probably five years old or so was playing in the wash. Rick pulled up, told her over the loud speaker to get out of the water."

"He yelled at a five-year-old over the PA?"

"Yeah, so this little girl with pig tails turned to him and yelled, 'Why?' It was kind of funny. Rick didn't miss a beat, just cued up the mike and yelled, 'Because you're gonna die!'"

I stared at Grey and waited for more. He shook his head and threw up his hands.

"Yeah, I had nothing. I just buried my head in my hands and prayed the family wouldn't say anything to me."

"Did they?"

"Hell yes they did. I thought the father was going to

tip my stand over he was so pissed. Did you hear me call Fig down for assistance with equipment?"

"Yeah."

"I couldn't say what was going on or Rick would've circled around and made it worse."

"Fig made it better?"

"Yeah he took care of it—gave the little girl a coloring book."

"What'll it be tomorrow?" I tossed my bag in the back of the Jeep. I just wanted to go home, eat dinner, and lie down before I went out.

"Same shit, Rookie."

"I had a rescue today. Am I still a rookie?"

"Nice try." Grey tapped the side of my Jeep and got into his car. "Meet me at the Point tonight?"

"Definitely."

The smell of pot hit me when I walked into my living room. Lucas and Harry sat beside each other on the tattered couch and watched me drop my things by the door. Harry let a steady stream of smoke escape from his puckered lips and leaned back against the cushions. I turned on the ceiling fan as I passed through the kitchen and continued down the hallway.

From my room I heard the front door open and close, then footsteps in the hallway. I stood with my towel in hand, ready for a shower but waiting for Harry to be gone. When I didn't hear anything, I opened the door and stepped back at the sight of Lucas standing in front of my room.

"What's up, man?" I turned my shoulders slightly so I wasn't face to face with Lucas.

His expression was flat and it appeared like he didn't know what he wanted to say. His eyes squinted and looked at my bed.

"You fuck my girlfriend the other night?"

"Jesus, no!" I took a step back. "I woke up and she

was in my bed."

"She naked?" He didn't appear angry, just cold and direct.

"Yeah, but I had all of my clothes on from the night before. I swear nothing happened."

He took a step toward me.

"Not what she said."

"What?" I took a step back. "What could she have said?"

"Said she sucked someone off in the shower."

"I had to work the next morning. I was the first one there. I left her in bed and ran out of the room."

"You ran out of your room with a naked girl in the bed?" His eyebrow rose. "You queer?"

"What? No." I didn't know what he was getting at or what he was capable of. Either way I was sick of the accusation. "I've got to take a shower."

"Want me to tell her to meet you in there?"

I shook my head and took a deep breath. "Tell her whatever the fuck you want, man." I pushed my way past him and hit his shoulder with mine as I did. The bathroom was a few steps away and I didn't look back as I went in and shut the door.

Grey waited for me while Ed "checked" my license. He lifted it up to the light and exaggerated his inspection.

"Welcome to the Point, sir." He passed the ID back and turned to the next person in the short line.

"It's nice knowing people, huh?" Grey scanned the room when we walked in.

"Yeah, I don't get into too many bars."

"Well, don't feel too out of place, most of the girls in here are underage too."

"How do they get in if..."

Grey looked at me with a flat expression. I nodded.

"Yeah," he said. "Crazy shit about your neighbor. You need to start locking your door."

"My dumbass roommate invites him over to smoke."

Grey shrugged.

"Isn't that the guy from PT over there—the one that punched Buck?" I looked across the small room. Doug leaned against the wooden wall talking to another guy. Grey followed my stare.

"Definitely is. We need to buy that guy a drink. What was his name?"

"No clue." I followed Grey as he approached the two.

"Hey man, we need to buy you a beer." Grey pointed and grinned.

"Yeah you're our hero for punching Buck," I eagerly added.

Nothing about Doug's face said he was interested in what we had to say.

"I'm good, but thanks." He turned toward the steps and pointed to the area where the pool table was. His friend nodded and followed, leaving Grey and I alone.

"Guess he's still a little bitter." I was surprised.

"Well, not everyone's cut out to be a guard." Grey leaned against the wall where Doug had been. "I'm not seeing a lot of talent here."

"There were a couple of girls over by the bar."

"Nah, man. Those chicks are locals—not big fans of guards." Grey motioned toward the door. We went outside and found two seats on the deck.

"Speaking of Buck, what's the story with him and Lilly?"

"Were we speaking of Buck?"

"You know, how that guy punched him and all." I pointed back to the door.

"Right. Do you know Lilly?" He thought for moment. "Oh yeah, your swim test."

I stared at Grey and wondered if I was ever going to live that down. "I don't really know her—seen her around.

Just curious how anyone could put up with his shit."

"She didn't really. Not much to it. She fell for him the first year he was a supervisor. He pulled some stupid shit..."

"The thing with the Commissioner's daughter?"

"Shit, if you know so much why are you asking me? Yeah. She realized what an ass he is and dumped him. He acts like he hates her but, you know. She's kind of off limits for that reason."

"Off limits? That sounds kind of stupid."

"There's plenty of girls without going down that road. She'd never go out with a guard again anyway."

"Sure would be a fun way to get back at Buck though."

"Yeah, if you were going to do it, that would be the way." He looked at me. "You trying to get him back for snaking your surf lesson?"

"No, nothing specific. He's just such an asshole."

"He's just been around too long. He wasn't always so bad; but think about where he is in life. He got rung out of the SEALs and had to beg Rick for his job back after the drama with Jamie. He's pretty much stuck here."

"Not a bad place to be stuck really." I looked around the deck filled with tan carefree bodies.

"You haven't been here for a winter have you?"

I shook my head.

"Yeah, it's not all it's cracked up to be when everyone goes home. It's cold, the wind never stops, and everyone just stays inside and drinks themselves stupid— kind of a miserable existence really." Grey shook his head. "I couldn't do it. I can't wait to go back to school by the end of the summer."

"I can wait. I was thinking about sticking around— deferring for a year."

"Go to school, man. It's a death sentence here in the winter. It's why all these locals hate us so much. We spend the winter having fun in college, then come down here for the summer, make the money, get the girls, and go back before it gets cold again."

"Still, I'm just not sure I'm ready to go straight to school. I've been going to school for thirteen fucking years. I need some time off."

"Good luck. You can visit me at ECU when you get bored." A grin crept across his face. "Lilly goes to school there."

"Thanks. Is she still off-limits in the fall?"

"Knock yourself out, Rookie." Grey watched a group of people ascend the stairs. "Here we go—four girls and only two guys."

The four girls had varying shades of blonde hair and fresh tans. They wore bright sun dresses and walked straight through the crowded deck without looking around. The two guys stood in front of Ed while he carefully examined their driver's licenses. He passed the IDs back to the first guy and shook his head.

"That's bullshit man. I've been in here all summer."

Another bouncer walked over and stood behind Ed. Muffin—his real name was Tim—crossed his arms and stared at the two guys. At over three hundred pounds, his presence made up for his nickname.

"Yeah, real tough guy with your goon behind you." The guy pointed past Ed but stared right at him.

Muffin moved Ed out of the way. The two guys skipped back and quickly made their way down the steps and out of the back of the parking lot.

Ed looked over his shoulder, "Save one for me." He pointed at the door where the girls disappeared.

"Nice work, Ed." Grey turned to me. "Come on, let's go." He hopped out of his seat and made his way to the door.

We were already late to the bar where the girls had procured four prime seats. Their backs were to the half-dozen guys gathered around them. Like fighter pilots swooping in on a target, each guy tested his ammo.

"Can I by you a drink?" Grey wedged his shoulder in and managed to get a hand on the bar top.

"We're already a few deep, but sure." The girl closest to him pointed to three overturned plastic cups that Evelyn had placed in front of each girl to mark the drinks they had coming.

I pulled on Grey's shirt sleeve. "Dude, they aren't worth the trouble. They're just soaking up free drinks."

One of the girls yelled, "Body shots!"

She climbed up on the wooden bar top. Evelyn rolled her eyes and made room for the girl to lie flat on her back. The girl pulled her spaghetti straps down over her shoulder and completely exposed a pink bra. Her chest was flat but nonetheless enticing. There were no tan lines anywhere I could see. I looked around to see what lucky guy would take the shot. The rest of the crowd was just as curious.

Another girl in the group climbed up on her stool so that her knees rested on the padded top. Evelyn reluctantly set down a shaker of salt and went looking for other customers. The friend sprinkled salt on the first girl's chest and rested a lemon wedge in the middle of her bra. Then she placed the full shot glass in her friend's mouth. She held the glass in her teeth and the collective level of anticipation was enough to take the air out of the room.

The friend leaned over, took the shot glass in her mouth, tipped her head back, let the glass fall to the floor——causing a glare from Evelyn, ran her tongue down to the pink bra, and bit down on the lemon wedge. She squeezed her eyes shut and stuck her hands up in the air to a loud round of applause.

I looked at Grey. "We don't make enough money to keep these girls drinking all night."

"Look." He pointed to the two girls who didn't partake in the body shots. One was drinking a light beer and the other had a mixed drink in front of her. They smiled at their friends but they sat with crossed legs and their purses secured on their laps.

"Gotcha."

We moved around to the other side of the crowd. The first two girls traded places on the bar and set up for another round.

Grey caught Evelyn's eye and held up two fingers. He turned to me and said, "You wanted another beer, right?" He spoke loud and within a couple inches of one girl's ear. By far the most attractive of the group, in her mid-twenties, she turned at the noise and was greeted with Grey's smiling face.

"Would you like something too?" Grey asked, knowing exactly what her response would be.

"No, thank you. We have plenty."

"I'm Grey and this is my good friend Wesley." He reached back and grabbed my shirt to pull me into the conversation.

"Okay." She smiled politely and I knew exactly how interested she was. I hoped Grey got the message.

He didn't.

"What's your name?" Grey took the two beers from Evelyn and passed one back to me.

"I'm married." She smiled politely again.

"Mary? Nice to meet you, Mary."

I didn't know whether he heard her or not but she laughed and it was enough to break the ice. Her other non-horizontal friend turned toward us.

"No, you dummy. I'm *married*." This time she held up her left hand and pointed to her ring finger.

"Oh. Well in that case, congratulations." Grey held up his bottle and she joined in the sarcastic toast. "How long have you been married?"

"Why do you want to know that?" She was amused but hardly impressed by Grey's effort.

"I'm just wondering if you've been married long enough to be bored with it." He leaned on the bar and waited for her to either answer or slap him.

"Grey!" This time I grabbed his shirt.

He held up his hand and I stopped pulling. He kept looking at her and she returned to her forced smile.

"I think you should leave." She swiveled on her stool so that her back was to us.

Grey looked at me and shrugged. I walked straight to the door hoping he'd follow. The deck was empty except for Ed. He looked at me and lifted his hands as if to say, "*Well?*"

I shook my head. Grey joined me at the steps and Ed laughed.

"There's only so much I can do, boys." Ed counted money from the cover charge.

"Fuck off, Ed. They're married." Grey shook his head and waved his hand back in the direction of the door.

"All of them?" He didn't look up from the cash in his hands.

"Enough of them."

"And you let that stop you?"

"Rookie here freaked out." Grey pointed at me and acted disappointed.

"Don't blame that on me. There was no chance of anything happening there. Not on your best day."

"Grey's best day was many years ago." Ed laughed to himself.

Grey made a face and continued, "I'd make her forget her vows in two minutes."

Ed stopped counting and looked up. "You make it too easy, Grey."

Grey hopped back up on the bench seat that surrounded the deck. "Anyway, did you know that Rookie is in love with Lilly?"

Ed leaned back against the railing and smiled at me. "Yeah, everyone knows that."

"Oh, fuck off." I tipped the bottle back and hid behind the amber glass. "I was just curious about her story."

The night continued with a series of crude volleys aimed at my interest in Lilly, Ed's inability to stand up to Buck, and a heated accusation of Grey masturbating in his stand on a rainy day.

It was all a welcome distraction from our long days on the beach. Grey and I stayed until the Point closed. We watched several more rounds of body shots through the window and Grey waved at the group of girls as they stumbled down the steps. Mary didn't wave back.

CHAPTER 11

No one talked about the reason Roy left—not around me at least. I did well at Sea Dunes. I rented all of my equipment most days and often called for more, turning in a lot of cash at the end of each day.

The equipment was shit. The chairs were deteriorated by salt water. The hinges and joints creaked regardless of the WD-40 Preston sprayed on them. As bad as the chairs were, the umbrellas were worse. The "hoods" as we call them, were blue canvas and pretty expensive to replace. Some of the spokes were broken and required a tetanus shot to deal with. Many of the clips that held them open were missing, so we jammed a piece of shell into the slot. I called them my umbrella shells and kept a handful in my bag.

I made rescues—mostly at the drainage pipe, which caused a fairly consistent rip current. I blew my whistle more frequently but still selectively. There was an entire section in our training handbook devoted to prevention— the most important aspect of lifeguarding and unfortunately a mantra lost on most of the guards. Despite the adage that the "best" lifeguard is the one with no rescues, there was always a desire to prove one's self.

In the training manual, a rescue was broken down quite simply:

1. *Recognize victim*
2. *Take action to save victim*
3. *Safely return to shore with victim.*

Prevention, as obligatory as it sounds, was the source of most of my frustration. I drew diagrams in the sand so that kids and adults could understand how a rip current forms and carries water out to sea. I handed out tide charts as a way to break the ice and I advised about the warnings. I wrote on the chalkboard about tides, wind, and other dangers. I walked the beach when I could and pointed out trouble spots. For the most part it worked. Buck told me I was wasting my time and that my patience would wear thin quickly. I chose to be proactive.

The red flag on my stand snapped incessantly. Over a week of northeast wind and the combination of salt spray and glaring sun made cleaning my sunglasses a chore I repeated every twenty minutes. I noticed a child down by the water's edge fifty yards north of my stand. An elderly couple stood within arm's reach of the boy so I paid minimal attention to him as I scanned the beach. A few minutes later the six-year-old was five yards out into the water. I climbed out of my stand and made my way to him. I didn't sprint. The rip was to his left and I didn't want to cause a panic.

"Is he with you?" I spoke to the older man but didn't take my eyes off of the child.

"No, we don't know where his parents are. We've been standing here watching him for five minutes or so."

I brought the whistle to my mouth but before I could give it a quick blow the boy stepped into a hole. He spun around and grabbed at the air. His eyes were wide, ignoring the saltwater splashing in them. I handed the man my radio and sunglasses.

"If you could hold these, sir, I'll be right back." I

dropped my buoy to the sand and ran in. The water was shallow and the boy barely ten yards off the beach. My legs swung over each wave like they were hurdles on a track. The boy climbed an imaginary ladder in front of him, failing to find anything to grab onto. I got to him in what was neck deep water for me. My presence, however, did little to calm him. His eyes went from open, to squeezed shut, to open again. His mouth was frozen in a silent scream. I swam straight to him and grabbed under his arm with one hand while treading water with the other.

My hand around his torso snapped him out of his vacant stare and brought all of his attention and his arms to my face. He climbed onto my head like it was a playground apparatus. I slipped under the water without letting go of his chest. I cursed myself underwater for not bringing my buoy, but found relief that I didn't call the rescue in over the radio. His grip on my head loosened and I immediately reached around him, switching hands but maintaining a firm grip on him.

"Easy…easy…what's your name?"

The boy cried—a good sign. I was anxious to get back to the sand before anyone realized what I had done.

"Okay, you can tell me when we get back to the beach." I looked to the shore and saw a crowd gathering around the spot where I foolishly left my buoy. *Shit*, I thought. The older man passed my things to his wife and was waist deep in the rip current. I waved him back to shore emphatically. I didn't want a multiple victim rescue without a buoy or back up—but more than that, I didn't want any help.

With my free arm I pulled my way to the sandbar and stood up in the waist-deep water. I picked the boy up, let him wrap his arms around my neck—safely this time— and supported him on my hip while I walked out of the water to scattered applause and a general feeling of relief.

Adrian was up on the armrest of his stand signaling me and looking though the binoculars. I returned the okay sign and he waved.

"Look, there's the sand," I whispered into his ear while lowering the boy to the ground. He clung for a few more seconds, enough time for me to smile and drop down on one knee, bringing my eyes level with his.

"Alright big guy, I'm Wesley, what's your name?"

"Michael." He sniffled back a few last tears and wiped at his eyes with the back of his right hand.

"Okay Michael, where are your parents?"

He raised his hand toward the dune line and pointed in a general direction. I smiled again and took him by his left hand.

"Let's go find them." I picked up my buoy and found the woman who had my radio and sunglasses. "Thank you ma'am." We walked up to the softer sand.

Michael had a goldfish named Fluffy.

"Funny name for a fish," I said, smiling.

Crinkling his forehead, he whispered, "No it's not." He pointed toward a man sitting in a lounge chair with his back to the water. The afternoon sun was fading behind the condos and the man had moved with it to better his tan.

"Excuse me, sir." The father looked away from his newspaper and up at me. "Sir, do you know where your son is?" The man turned quickly to see Michael sitting in the shade behind his chair.

"Yeah, he's right there." His response was sharp. "What the hell do you want?"

Normally I wouldn't have pressed the issue. It didn't serve the kid any and the parents were usually in enough distress after seeing their child rescued, but the man was oblivious.

"Sir, do you know where he was a few minutes ago?" My tone was flat—my voice low and confident.

"He's been here with me all day." He twisted in his chair and pulled his feet under him. I was still charged with adrenaline from the rescue and not about to back down. I looked at the water and nodded. Then I looked at him.

"Actually, he was fifty yards out on that sandbar." I paused long enough for him to look at the water. "Then he stepped into a rip current before I pulled him in."

He looked at me for a long moment and had nothing else to say.

"Well sir, I need to get back to watching the water. I'd suggest you pay attention to your child." I stared a few more seconds to reinforce my point.

Eighteen years old. There I was telling a grown man to be a better parent. I scanned the water when I walked away and was oblivious to Michael waving goodbye or the man's enraged expression. I didn't look back until I got to my stand. Through the glare of the late afternoon sun I saw Michael's arms jerking up and down. His father grabbed one of the arms and hit him on the ass enough times to make him cry again. The boy's face looked the same as it had when he stepped off the sandbar. I was frozen in my seat.

I could call the police and report him for neglect or abuse but I realized, as I sat there listening to the boy wailing, that I'd done enough damage with my intrusion. I felt great when I carried Michael out of the water and even better when I told his father off. At that moment though, I regretted the whole damn thing. I faced the water and listened to the boy's cries as his father dragged him off the beach.

It was close to six o'clock that evening and most of the guards had turned in their equipment and hurried off to get ready for the Tuesday night Magnolia Street party. Rick sat on one of the couches in the shack when I checked in. I took my time putting away the equipment and waited for the shack to clear out. When everyone but Buck had left I took a seat and told Rick the story about Michael— omitting the buoy and radio part. The situation bothered me, but there was a fine line in our boy's club between concern and weakness—one I was careful not to cross.

"Did you call it in on the radio?" Buck looked up from a stack of daily reports.

"Oh, no it wasn't worth a report. I barely got wet."

Buck went back to his work, eager to get ready for the party himself and glad that I wasn't adding to his pile of papers.

"The little brat needed an ass whooping, if you ask me." Rick laughed when he said it. "He won't do it again." He looked down his nose, over his glasses, and waited for me to respond. I suspected he knew that it got to me but as my laughter joined his, he rose from the old couch.

"Have fun at the party." He gave me one of his dirty winks that made us all cringe because we knew that Rick still thought like us.

The party that night had a much different tone than the previous weeks. Collectively, we were tired. A few of the guards did their best to liven up the mood—singing loud and pushing drinks. For the most part, we told our stories from the week of rescues and close calls. The crowd was mostly familiar—girlfriends, summer locals, and friends.

Grey and Adrian huddled on the couch with two random girls. I sat at the picnic table in the kitchen with Ed and Sandy. She and Fig had been sleeping together for a couple weeks and it seemed to calm his bravado and antics a bit. Ed avoided talking about his rescues. When Sandy asked, he just waved his hand and for once was sincere in his modesty.

He smacked my leg under the table and nodded at the door.

"Your girl's here." A group of people walked into the living room. I looked up and made eye contact with Lilly. She smiled and turned to her friends.

Sandy looked back and saw Lilly. Then she turned to me and smiled.

"She asked me about you."

I felt warm and instantly under the spotlight.

"I don't think I want to go down that road."

"Why? Because of Buck?" Ed was pointed in his question. "That's all the more reason. Fuck that guy."

"That's not a reason, Ed." Sandy looked at him and he knew better than to continue with that line of thought. "He should talk to her because she's amazing." She turned to me. "She really is. I know she's local, but she's not crazy like the rest of us. She's got a lot going for her."

"What did she say?" I peeked up from my drink to see where Lilly was.

"She just asked about you. Does it matter? Don't worry; she already knows how well you swim." Sandy and Ed both laughed.

I joined in and added, "I've gotten better."

"Right, you're a big boy now, so go talk to her." Sandy shooed me away with one hand and took a sip of beer with the other. "Go on."

I looked to Ed for some help.

"Stay here, Rookie." He stood up and went into the living room.

Lilly stood with her friends. Ed walked up to the small group, ignored everyone else, and took Lilly by the hand without saying a word. He led her into the kitchen and stopped next to the table.

"Join us." Ed waved his hand around the room. "You know Sandy and Wesley."

"Ed, you're an idiot." She looked at him with feigned frustration.

"That is absolutely true and completely irrelevant. Have a seat."

She sat next to Sandy and looked at me.

"Hi." She smiled and dropped her eyes.

"Hey." I smiled and looked up at Ed.

"Lilly," Ed didn't bother sitting down, "you need a drink, let me get that for you." Ed moved toward the back door and motioned for Sandy to join him.

"I'll help you." Sandy popped up and followed Ed to the keg on the porch.

"They're not obvious at all." I looked over my shoulder like I needed to see where they were going.

"Obvious about what?" Lilly leaned her head to the side.

"I mean, it just… I think they might think that you and I might…"

"I'm kidding, Wesley. I know what they're doing." Her voice was soft. She looked around the kitchen and then right at me. "I asked Sandy about you the other day." She looked down at the table. "She likes to play matchmaker."

"She mentioned that." I nodded slowly and looked down at the table too. Every lifeguard for a decade had carved his name in the wood. There were a few smiley faces and lots of penises as well.

Sandy walked back in with a drink and a grin. Lilly looked up at her.

"She did, huh? What did Sandy say?"

"Uh oh, I think Ed needs me." Sandy placed the cup on the table and quickly retreated through the back door.

"They're funny."

"What do you think about her and Fig?" I asked.

"I think it'll be over before he leaves for school. They're not serious about anything."

"Well he's been easier to deal with at work." I shrugged.

"Sex is funny like that." She looked at me and realized how frank she'd been. I laughed and she blushed.

"Oh, this is cute." Buck appeared and joined in the laughter. He leaned against the door jamb. "It's Wesley and Buttercup." He grinned and stared at Lilly. "Can I join you?"

She hid behind her cup and avoided looking at him. "It's your house," she muttered.

I took a deep breath and said nothing.

"Am I making things awkward?" Buck loved it.

"It's what you do." Lilly's wide eyes stared at the bottom of her cup.

"Hey, Rookie. Why'd you make a rescue without your buoy?"

"What are you talking about?" I avoided eye contact too.

"We'll talk about it tomorrow at PT." He stared for a while longer. Lilly and I sipped our drinks and looked at each other over the tops of our plastic cups.

"This is boring." Buck finished his drink and went out to the porch muttering, "Wesley and Princess Buttercup."

"I'm sorry about that." Lilly stared at the door when Buck closed it.

"It's not even the right name."

"What's not?" She looked amused.

"The character is *Westley*. I've been getting shit about that since junior high."

"At least it's a good movie." She smiled and lifted her empty cup in the air.

I joined her in a feigned toast. I set my cup down and asked, "You two dated, right?"

Lilly nodded with hesitation. "I know what you're thinking. He was different then." She shook her head and shrugged. "Or he wasn't and he was just better at hiding it."

I nodded and looked around the dying party.

"You wanna walk down to the beach?" I pointed toward the front door.

She cut her eyes at me.

"Or we can sit here." I retreated. "I just didn't want to deal with him when he comes back in."

She looked at the back door for a moment.

"Okay, let's go."

"Really?"

"Yeah, come on."

We walked through the living room and I avoided all of the knowing eyes. Lilly turned to me when we reached the bottom of the stairs outside.

"How many girls have you taken to the beach this summer?"

"What?" I almost laughed at my own feigned confusion.

"Come on, deputy. I know the game. I saw you and Ed a while back."

Fortunately, the truth was on my side.

"I walked down there with one girl but I never saw her again," I said with a shrug.

"Isn't that the point?" Her teasing was playful.

"Depends on who you ask."

"I'm asking you." She stopped walking and leaned back against the 701 truck in the driveway.

Here we go again, I thought.

Lilly nodded at the house. "I know what the rest of those guys think. I've been around lifeguards a lot longer than you have."

"I think I've had a crush on you since I saw you at Shipwreck and I don't know anything about you other than you dated Buck." I pointed at the truck.

"Great, that's all you know." She looked down and brushed her flip flops against the sandy concrete. "Please don't hold that against me."

"Don't hold it against me that you're not the first girl I walked on the beach with." I smiled and tried to catch her eye.

"Deal." She reached out and offered her hand. I shook it gently.

The dance was over. Everything after that was easy. We didn't walk to the beach that night. Instead, we sat on the tailgate of Buck's truck in the driveway.

"What if he gets a call?" Lilly looked over her shoulder to the front door.

"He can't respond. He's been drinking." I looked back at the front door and secretly hoped Buck was watching me sit with Lilly in his truck. "Preston's on call tonight."

She looked at the truck then at me.

"I think you're a trouble maker."

"I swear I'm not." I leaned back and rested my hands on the ridged bed.

Lilly swung her feet and explained her feelings about the Outer Banks like she was in confessional. "My grades are my ticket out of here."

A year older than I was, she went away to school and came back to a smaller home than the one she left. She studied art at the large state university two hours from the beach. Anyone else might come across petulant in her newfound view of home after living away, but not Lilly.

"This place inspires me, it really does." She turned to me like she was trying to convince me, or maybe herself. "I just think I need to leave to appreciate it. Get some perspective, you know?" She looked at me with so much honesty. How could she be anything but right?

"That makes sense."

"Does it?"

Lilly played with her hair while we talked. She'd pull it all over one shoulder and run her fingers through it like a comb. Then she'd flip it to the other side and braid it loosely before shaking it out and doing it all over again.

"My father moved us here when I was fifteen. It was hard going from a big high school in Virginia to a class of a hundred. It's a different world when the summer's over."

"I'm thinking about staying for a year before I go off to school."

"Why?" She dropped the hair from her hands and looked at me.

"I just don't think I'm ready."

"You'll be ready by September." Her gaze drifted back to the street. "I have a hard time even coming home for holidays. It's miserable out here in the winter—the cold and the wind. If it weren't for my family and friends…" She shrugged. "This isn't home for me. I don't really fit in here."

"Where do you want to be?"

"New York." She didn't miss a beat.

"And you complain about the cold here?"

"It's different. I belong in the city." She looked up at the clear sky like the stars were windows on skyscrapers.

"I understand." I didn't.

"I want to design amazing things and go to museums and shop at Bloomingdales." She giggled at the thought, lost in a world she visited each boring night in her parent's home.

"So, do it." I said it into the night and watched her reaction from the corners of my eyes. She turned to me quickly.

"I will."

"I believe you." I wasn't nearly as confident as I pretended to be.

Lilly smiled and my lip quivered at the thought of kissing her. She was the entire summer sitting in front of me. I took a deep breath and watched the sea mist blow across the streetlight. I spent the whole week breathing in salt spray. Lilly's perfume danced lightly in the thick night air then tapped me on the tip of my nose.

She whispered, "Take me home?"

I nodded without a word.

Lilly's parents lived down a white sand road that meandered through a maritime forest full of water oaks and cedars. My headlights bounced each time I hit a worn root in the tire ruts.

"Cut your lights." She pointed at my dash.

I put the Jeep in neutral, shut off the engine, and pushed the light switch in. We rolled up to the house quietly. It was a large two-story beach house clad in cypress ship-lap siding and decorative scrollwork. An old pickup truck and a new Cadillac sedan took up the two parking spaces.

Lilly peeked through the windshield at the dark windows.

"My parents are asleep." She turned to me. "I'd invite you in but…"

"I understand." I tapped on the steering wheel. The radio was off. "Can I take you to dinner tomorrow?"

"Lifeguards don't take girls to dinner." She laughed and pushed my shoulder. I smiled and waited for her to answer. "Yeah, okay."

"I'll pick you up at seven."

She looked at me. The corner of my lip quivered again.

"Thanks for the ride, Wesley."

"You're welcome. I'd open your door for you, but…" I looked at the frame where the Jeep's door would be.

"Such a gentleman." She swung her legs out and hopped down from the seat.

"Lilly."

"Yes?"

"What's your last name?"

She looked at me suspiciously.

"Grace."

I nodded and smiled at her.

"Goodnight, Lilly Grace."

CHAPTER 12

"Let's hear it, Rookie." Grey plopped down in the sand next to me as I stretched for PT.

"We won't be running with you today on account of the large target on your ass." Adrian stood and stretched his arms.

"I don't care about that. I wanna hear what happened when he took Lilly home." Grey stared at me.

"Nothing happened." I reached forward and grabbed my toes.

"Bullshit." Grey leaned down so his face was an inch from the sand and looked up at me. "I heard she's a naughty one."

"What?" I snapped back.

"You know—the quiet type. But when you get her in bed she's an animal."

I didn't say anything. I just stared at my knees and stretched. I could feel my face getting warm.

"Sorry man, I didn't realize you'd fallen in love with her overnight." Grey sat up and shook his head at Adrian.

Adrian crouched down. "Hey, I was just kidding about the target thing." He looked back at the access just as Buck was pulling through it. "But, you still might want to watch out. Buck was pressing me last night about that rescue you didn't call in."

"What did you tell him?" I stopped stretching.

"Nothing. I said I didn't see anything—that it must have been nothing if you didn't call it in."

"That's all you said?" I looked at the truck. Buck sat in the driver's seat watching us stretch.

"I think he knew more but I just played dumb." Adrian looked at the truck too, then back at me. "He asked me if you took your buoy in."

"Where's he getting this shit?"

Grey chimed in, "They've got eyes all over the beach."

"Don't be surprised if he goes after you this morning. He knows you left with Lilly last night." Adrian sat in the sand and reached for his toes.

"Great." I went back to stretching and imagined the worst.

"Circle up fuckers!" Fig rode into the middle of the group and cut off his four-wheeler. Buck stayed in the truck. Fig ran us through the normal circuit of calisthenics, all with a smile on his face. Despite our fatigue from the week of rescues we were all in mid-season stride and easily knocked out the exercises.

On the last set of leg lifts, Fig crouched next to me. I watched him while I held my feet six inches above the sand. Buck looked over from the driver's seat and nodded to Fig, then drove south toward the town line. Fig didn't say anything until the count was up to fifteen.

"Hey, Rookie," he whispered.

"SIXTEEN," I yelled. "Yeah?" My voice shook from the tight muscles working to keep my feet up.

"I heard you fucked Lilly in the back of Buck's truck last night?"

My feet hit the sand.

"Are you serious?"

Fig yelled to the group, "Everyone start over. Rookie

dropped his feet."

This was met with scattered groans.

"Don't be last out of the water today." He stood up and walked back to his four-wheeler.

When the count finally hit twenty I dropped my head to the sand and pulled my knees up to my chest to reduce the burn. I took a deep breath and wondered how far this was going to spiral. At the very least, I knew I could always beat Stanley.

Fig started his bike and spun around in the sand until he was facing south. He stood up on the foot rests and yelled to the group.

"Leave your fins here. Swim out fifty yards and then down to the town line. Last one out of the water…" He looked at me and smiled. "Well, we'll just see."

"The current's going north." Adrian pointed up the beach in protest. Fig looked out at the water.

"Yep." He pointed south. "Hit the water you fuckers."

We grabbed our buoys and jogged toward the water. Fig blew his whistle and we all stopped in our tracks.

"STANLEY! Go back to the shack and help Preston set out flags."

Stanley didn't hesitate. He spun around, grabbed his gear, and ran over the access. I looked at the group and sprinted to the water in hopes of getting a head start. I cut the corner on swimming out fifty yards but didn't care. The current was strong and I needed all the help I could get.

It took over twenty minutes to get down to Sea Dunes. The line of guards stretched out for a hundred yards. I was dead last. With each breath, I looked up and watched guards on the beach running back toward Wright Street. I lifted my head and saw Buck's truck and the four-wheeler parked at the town line. I accepted my fate and tried to settle back into a rhythm. I would need all the energy I could save for the inevitable punishment.

When I cleared the drain pipe I started to cut the

corner to the beach. Two blasts from the truck's air horn shot out from the beach. I straightened back out and plowed on. My head was foggy by the time I passed Sibbern Street. I turned to the beach and saw two sets of arms swimming in front of me. I thought it was strange for tourists to be out so early. I looked again and saw the arms acting like they were swimming but not making any progress.

I pulled even to the two people and realized it was Ed and Adrian. They looked at me and smiled. I glanced back at an approaching wave, pulled hard, and threw my hands out in front of me. I coasted in on the white water and stumbled on the ledge when I got out. I stood straight up, took a deep breath, and looked back at Ed and Adrian. They were right behind me, shaking their heads and holding their hands high in the air pretending to catch their breath.

I looked up at Buck and Fig. They stared at me from behind their dark sunglasses. Ed and Adrian started jogging and I joined them. Ed slapped my back and looked over his shoulder. Buck pulled behind us and drove so close to our heels that we could hear the crunch of shells under his tires over the pounding surf. We drifted closer to the water where we knew he couldn't follow. The truck sped up and Fig followed him back to Wright Street. They crossed the access and disappeared.

"Thanks." I looked forward but could see Adrian and Ed nodding on either side of me. We jogged back to the access in silence; all wondering what was waiting for us at check-in.

Guards were packing their cars for the day and heading out to the Buccaneer for a quick breakfast when we made it to the parking lot. Adrian, Ed, and I walked into the shack to get our gear.

"It's the Three Amigos." Fig set his feet up on the counter and put his hands behind his head. "Cute stunt."

I scanned the room and was relieved when I didn't

see Buck.

"What did Wesley do to you, Fig?"

"Stay out of it, Ed."

"So, nothing. You're just Buck's little bitch puppet, huh?" Ed stared at Fig.

Adrian and I stayed quiet. Fig dropped his feet, retrieved our boxes and whistles, and threw them down on the counter. He looked past us at the camera mounted in the corner. The intercom clicked and we heard Rick's voice.

"Ed, come into my office."

Ed's jaw clenched and he stared at Fig.

"You're such a little bitch," he whispered without facing the camera.

"Don't be late to your stand." Fig sat back down.

The small victory over Buck and Fig empowered me throughout the day. Regardless, I still felt uneasy each time they drove by. I wondered what Rick had said to Ed. I hoped we'd be able to meet up at the end of the day before check-in. Sometimes I wasn't sure whose battle Ed was fighting.

My impending date with Lilly concerned me more than anything. I was afraid word would get back to her and she'd think I was responsible for people talking about things that didn't happen. I took a bathroom break around noon and called her from the pay phone in the condo lobby.

"I just wanted to touch base and make sure we were still on for tonight."

"Of course, why wouldn't we be?"

"Oh, no reason, just confirming."

"Are you okay?"

"Yeah, just a bunch of the guys saying things this morning about you and me, that's all."

"I see. You know that's going to happen, right?"

"Yeah, I know. I just wasn't expecting it this morning at PT."

"Did Buck give you a hard time?"

"I'll tell you about it tonight. Everything's fine."

"Okay, I'll see you at seven."

"Bye."

The next few hours passed quickly. I had two rescues and found a missing child from Neptune Street. Around four thirty, when things calmed down, I walked to the north end of my zone and signaled to Ed. He looked at me and returned to scanning his beach. I gave it a moment then walked back to my stand and counted the minutes to five thirty.

I waited in the parking lot for Ed after I checked in. He pulled into the space next to my Jeep and nodded when he saw me.

"Sorry I couldn't meet up with you today." Ed gathered his stuff from his Jeep and climbed out.

"Everything alright?"

"Yeah, it's fine. Rick gave me shit this morning so I couldn't get off my stand and give him a reason to come down on me again."

"Was he mad about PT?"

"No, nothing to do with that. I'll tell you later. Grab a drink at the Point with me?"

"Can't, I'm taking Lilly to dinner in an hour."

"Good for you, Wesley. I'm glad that's working out for you."

"Thanks."

"Where are you taking her?"

"I was thinking about Papagayo's."

"No, man. That's a tourist trap. I mean, the food's great, but it's not good for a date. There's a local place down Colington Road—sits right on the creek. Not too expensive either. I can't remember what it's called. Just past the church where the road curves."

"Sounds perfect. Thanks."

"Watch out for her father. He's got a lot of guns."

Ed laughed and walked toward the shack.

I wore my best collared shirt for the date. It hadn't left my bag since I moved in two months earlier so I rubbed it with dryer sheets before I left the house to freshen it up. Harry sat at the counter eating and said nothing when I walked to the front door. I was content to let the silence continue but something stopped me.

"Did Lucas say anything to you about Liz and me?"

Harry didn't look up from his cereal bowl. With a full mouth he said, "No."

"He got in my face and accused me of screwing around with her."

"She was naked in your bed. Not hard to see why he was pissed."

"I didn't have anything to do with it. He said I took a shower with her that morning."

Harry stopped eating and looked up but not at me. "Did he say anything else?"

"She admitted to doing something with someone."

He shrugged and continued eating. Just before I turned to leave Harry looked at me without turning his head and grinned.

"No shit." I walked toward the counter. "I thought Lucas was going to kill me and it was you?" I put my hand on the counter and made eye contact.

"I heard you leave and went to the bathroom. She was in the shower and told me to get in. Who am I to deny her?"

"Were those other two girls still in your room?"

"Yeah." Harry laughed and looked at me. "You got a date?"

"You dirtball!" I punched his shoulder and laughed. "Yeah, I'm taking this girl to dinner."

"Have fun."

With that, things were fine between Harry and I.

I pulled into Lilly's driveway a little before seven. To my relief, the truck's parking space was empty. All of the window blinds were down so I quickly checked my teeth and hair in the rearview mirror before hopping out. In the reflection I saw the old truck rolling up the sand road. The driver lifted his hand to acknowledge me and I returned the polite wave. The truck idled past me into its spot with a grumbling effort.

I didn't want to appear eager so I tapped my back pocket and then looked under the seat as though I'd misplaced my wallet—a desperate effort to stall and make the introduction more natural. The driver sat in the truck without opening the door or even cutting the engine off. I tried not to keep looking at the truck for fear he was watching me.

I took a deep breath, stood up straight, and walked toward the old Ford. The brake lights flickered and the engine died. The door creaked and a booted foot kicked it and held it open. I walked slowly.

"Who are you?" The man leaned against the steering wheel and peered at me without turning his head. He wore a dark brown cowboy hat and a thick mustache. When he spoke, only his jaw moved. His head appeared to be shaved or bald but his eyebrows were wild and thick like his facial hair. A dark flannel shirt draped over his large shoulders. I stopped and raised my hand.

"Hi, I'm Wesley. I'm a friend of Lilly's."

"How old are you, son?"

I hesitated.

"Almost nineteen, sir."

"Nineteen?" He looked straight and tapped the steering wheel with his thumb just once. "I was wading through a rice paddy in Khe Sanh holding a nine pound M16 over my head and hoping I didn't catch a round to the face when I was nineteen. What do you do, son?"

"I'm a lifeguard, sir."

His eyes got wide and both hands grabbed the

steering wheel. His knuckles turned white. I took a step back. The front door of the house flew open and Lilly ran outside. She stopped a few feet from the hood of the truck. She looked at me and quickly yelled.

"Daddy! Stop it!"

Her father cut his eyes but didn't loosen his grip. He turned his head toward me and flared his nostrils. He breathed like a bull about to be released from its pen.

"Wesley, it's okay."

I looked at her. She was shaking her head. I looked back to her father. The scowl changed to a smile and he laughed maniacally. He swung his feet over and looked at his daughter.

"Dammit, Lilly. I had him going." He raised his hands.

"It's not funny anymore, Daddy."

"It was hilarious." He turned to me. "I had you going, right?" His demeanor instantly changed from outlaw to drinking buddy. "I had him going." He held his hand out and walked toward the spot I had retreated to.

I looked at Lilly.

"Sorry, he does this."

I took his hand with caution and shook it with all the confidence I could muster.

"Well, at least I'm not the first." I tried to smile.

"Daddy thinks it's fun to hide at the end of the driveway and creep up on my friends."

"Especially lifeguards." He pointed at me and walked toward the front door. "Almost nineteen." He laughed and waved back at the two of us. "Don't stay out too late."

My expression was still somewhere between fear and confusion. Lilly took my hand and caught my stare. "The doctors said the fresh air at the beach would be good for him."

"Are you serious?"

"No, relax. He just likes jokes." She dropped my

hand and walked toward the passenger side of my Jeep.

"He was waiting for me?"

"Yep. He probably had the truck backed up into the woods." She climbed in and looked at me through the driver's side. "Where are we going for dinner?"

I shook my head and took a deep breath. "A place down Colington Road that Ed told me about." I grabbed the roll bar and pulled myself up to the seat.

"Ed told you, huh?"

"Yeah, you know it?"

"Nilson's? Yeah, it's my favorite."

I turned to her. "Does Ed know that?"

"He does." She nodded.

"Is that a story?" I started the Jeep and put it in reverse.

"Maybe." She smiled. "Do you need to run by your house first?"

"For what?" I stopped before shifting to first.

"To change your shorts." She laughed and instantly covered her mouth. I nodded along and couldn't help but smile.

Nilson's Crabhouse was an actual home at some point. The low ceilings and dark wood-paneled walls embraced Lilly and me when we opened the old screen door and walked into the dining room. I felt like I was visiting a relative I'd only heard stories about. The tables were covered with red and white checkered table cloths and some had baskets filled with small containers of butter spread.

"Do you want to sit out on the porch?" I pointed through a side door but Lilly quickly responded.

"No." She pointed to a booth. "There."

We both looked around the room when we sat down. My back was to the door and I took in the atmosphere while Lilly's eyes bounced from face to face of each customer and server.

"Well, if it isn't little Miss Lilly." A thin woman in her fifties stopped at our booth and propped her hand on her hip. She wore a pink T-shirt and jean shorts pulled up high on her waist.

Lilly slid out of the booth and wrapped her arms around the woman.

"Rebecca, I missed you." Her hug was genuine and it made me smile to see.

"Well, whose fault is that you beautiful thing?" Rebecca held her arms out straight and looked at Lilly. "Bless your heart; I couldn't be mad at you." She turned and looked at me. "Who are you?"

"Rebecca, this is Wesley. Be nice, Daddy already gave him a hard time."

"The truck thing?"

I nodded and smiled.

"Not another lifeguard is he?"

"Rebecca! Hush."

They both looked at me.

"Hi." I lifted my hand.

"You don't want to sit out on the porch?" She looked at Lilly.

"The booth's fine. I want a change of scenery."

"Oh, we got scenery." Rebecca looked at me again. "And the best darn hush puppies this side of the state line. I'll get y'all some menus and—" She pointed at Lilly.

"Sweet tea."

Rebecca pointed at me.

"Two of those, ma'am."

She grinned at Lilly who shooed her away with a smile.

"Have you been here before?" I propped my elbows on the table and rested my chin on my hands.

"Just once." She raised one eyebrow. "Guess I made an impression."

"You tend to do that."

"Do I? What impression did I make on you?" she

asked.

"I'll tell you, if you fill me in on this place."

"Okay, but you first."

I leaned back against the vinyl seat and looked at her.

"The first time I saw you—"

Rebecca walked up behind me and set down a heaping basket of fried hush puppies. She stood for a moment and looked at me. I waited for her to say something but she just stared at me. She made a motion with her hands for me to continue.

"The first time you saw her..."

I looked to Lilly for help but she just lifted her chin, raised her eyes, and waited for me to finish. I laughed and shook my head, then turned to Rebecca.

"The first time I saw her," I raised my hand in Lilly's direction. "I thought she was really pretty."

Rebecca's shoulders slumped and her head tilted. She looked at Lilly and pointed at me with the end of the pen in her hand.

"At least he's cute." Rebecca shook her head. "You gonna have to read the menu to him or do you need two?"

"We'll take two please." Lilly giggled and passed me a laminated sheet of paper.

"The special is two soft-shells with fries for ten dollars. I'll be back with your drinks."

I waited for Rebecca to disappear into the kitchen before saying another word.

"Do I have a kick-me sign on my back?"

"I think you just have a sweet face and people like to tease you. They wouldn't do it if they didn't like you."

"They don't even know me."

"Okay, they wouldn't do it if I didn't like you."

I was more than content with that answer and decided it would be a great time to stop talking. I smiled and broke a hush puppy in half to let it cool.

"Do you know why Ed and Buck don't get along?" Lilly peeled the foil lid off a butter packet scooped at it with her knife.

I shook my head. "I just figured they've worked together too long."

"That's part of it, but a lot has to do with me, I hate to say."

"You?"

"My friends and I used to go to lifeguard parties the first summer I lived here. I was sixteen and clueless. One night, Ed and I spent the whole night talking on the back porch at Magnolia Street. It wasn't anything romantic at all—just two people having a nice conversation. Ever since then, he's acted like a big brother to me."

Lilly and I reached for the same hush puppy and she quickly snagged it from under my hand.

"Ed always made sure I got home, kept the creepy guys away from me, took care of me if I drank too much, that kind of thing. The next summer I started dating Buck and it was really awkward. Buck was jealous and didn't like that Ed and I were friends."

"I can see that being an issue for Buck."

Rebecca brought our drinks and tapped her order pad.

"The special, please." Lilly looked up and smiled.

"The same." I passed Rebecca the menus.

"Two specials." She put her pen behind her ear and walked to the kitchen window.

Lilly continued, "After the whole thing with the Commissioner's daughter I broke up with him. Ed and I spent more time together and it just caused a lot of tension." She looked around the dining room. "Buck and I used to come here once a week—it was kind of our place."

"Why didn't you say something when I told you we were coming here?"

"I like the food." She shrugged and grabbed another hush puppy.

"Why would Ed tell me to bring you here if he knew that?" I already knew the answer but it seemed like it needed to be asked.

"Either he wanted to help you out and suggest a place he knew I liked or he wanted Buck to know I came here with you—or both." She shook her head. "Ed said I was too young for Buck when we dated. I'm not sure that really mattered; he just didn't trust him—for good reason. And that's enough about all that."

"It makes for a good story I guess."

"There are plenty of stories without talking about Buck." She looked around the restaurant then leaned in like she was telling me a secret. "You know Rick's broke, right?"

"I've heard a few things. I don't really understand how that's possible if the town is paying him and he's getting rental income."

"Yeah, no one really knows where the money goes. My mother works in the town manager's office and the rumor is that the Fire Chief and the commissioners want to take over the lifeguards."

I thought for a minute about the resources that would require.

"Wouldn't that be more expensive?"

"Mom says they don't think Rick has been paying his insurance or worker's comp premiums."

"What does that mean?"

"It means he's in violation of his contract."

Rebecca stopped at the table with a pitcher of sweet tea.

"You must be talking about Rick Carroll."

Lilly nodded. "What do you know Rebecca?"

"I don't talk ugly 'bout people. But if I did, that man would make me say some things." She topped off my glass.

"Did he run over your sandcastle?" I looked up at her.

Rebecca set her hand on her hip again and put the pitcher on the table.

"I was on the beach last summer down by Mullet

Street. We go there 'cause no one bothers us when we're having a few drinks. The group of people next to us put up a volleyball net and walked down to John's Drive-In for a milkshake. Rick drove by and asked if the net was ours. We said, no. He said it was blocking emergency vehicles and rather than roll it up and lay it down, he pulled out a knife and cut it right down the middle."

She stared at me like she was waiting for an explanation.

"Was it a red flag day?"

"Nope, like a lake out there."

I just looked at Lilly and shook my head.

"Your food'll be up in a minute."

Lilly finished her thought. "People just don't like the way he does things and are looking for a reason to get rid of him."

"I understand that he's a little rough around the edges."

Lilly looked at me with raised eyebrows.

"Okay, he's unprofessional and out of control but he gets the job done. People on the beach are safe. Sandcastles and volleyball nets aren't safe but people are."

"And kites, fishing poles, tents, blankets, rafts, surfboards, dogs…"

Rebecca appeared with plates in hand.

"Careful sugar, plate's hot." She set one in front of Lilly then me. "These little fellas were swimming not an hour ago. Enjoy."

Lilly wasted no time spearing a crispy leg with her fork. "I'm addicted to these things." She brought the crab to her mouth but stopped when she noticed me looking at her. "What? Is yours okay?"

"It's perfect." I couldn't take my eyes off of her. She had a momentum to her—like everything that occurred in that moment was shaping my life from that point on. It was real and it filled me with awe.

I turned down the sandy road to Lilly's home and slowly rolled across the rough path. I wanted the time with her to last as long as possible.

"Up here before the curve." Lilly pointed to a large live oak tree. "See that clearing to the right?"

"Is your father waiting for us again?" I craned my neck.

"No," she smiled, "take a right there."

I cut the wheel and the path got narrow. Wild wax myrtles and a thick grove of beauty berries gave way to a clearing. The quiet water of the Albemarle Sound lapped at a dark sand beach in front of us. There was a picnic table and room for one car. The loblolly pines on each side of the clearing bent toward the water. The reaching branches created a canopy that let just enough moonlight in for me to cut the headlights and see perfectly once our eyes adjusted.

"This is nice." I stepped out and walked toward the little beach.

"Watch out for sand spurs." Lilly hopped out of the Jeep and joined me.

We looked across the sound at the light cast by the sparse homes of Roanoke Island. In the dark blend of water and land, the flickering amber lights defined the horizon and held our gaze like a dozen lit matches.

"This is my favorite place on the Outer Banks," Lilly spoke as though anything above a whisper might blow out the lights and end the magic of the moment.

I nodded and took her left hand in mine. She stepped in front of me, her back to the water, took my other hand, and pushed down while lifting up on her toes.

On that moonlit shore, surrounded by firewheel flowers, I kissed Lilly the way all first kisses should be—anticipation and hesitation gave way to a melting moment of timeless comfort. When the moment was over, she dropped down from her toes and leaned against my chest, the side of her face pressed just below my chin and my gaze once again drifted out over the water.

CHAPTER 13

The nor'easter settled in and approached the end of its second week. The older guards talked about the summer a few years earlier when the same thing happened. "*Not as bad as this though*," they'd say in agreement.

The strong surf tore up the beach, shifting most of the holes in the usually consistent sandbar. Rip currents pulled out to sea every hundred yards or so. One morning I watched a ten-foot long piece of broken wood from the pier float straight out through the neck of the current, get to the head of the rip where it dissipated, drift down the beach, get washed in by a wave, and start the cycle all over again.

What was left of the Kitty Hawk Pier stretched out above the rough surf like a skeleton finger—crooked and menacing. I asked Preston during training if he'd ever jumped off of it and he looked at me like I was crazy.

"That pier's been knocked down and rebuilt so many times. You're liable to land on an old piling and spear yourself right up the ass or get tangled up in old fishing line. You couldn't pay me to jump off that damn thing. Plus you never know where the sandbar is—break your neck if you land wrong."

Different agencies had different ways of displaying the red flags—some on large poles by the street; ours were on small poles jabbed into the sand all along the beach. However they went up, the message was the same: stay out of the water.

Dissecting the issue became hopeless. The idea that their lives and their children's lives were at risk were lost in their wallets. They fought it every way they could and as much as we tried, diplomacy often gave way to frustration.

I imagined Adrian on my shoulder telling me to relax. I heard him say things like, "Dude, they'll be gone in a few days. They're just pissed because they'll be sitting in a cubicle in Ohio on Monday." I did my best to prove Buck wrong. I didn't want to give him the satisfaction of seeing the pushy tourists get the best of me. If I could put up with that prick at PT, I told myself, than I could handle some minivan-driving bozo.

People stopped waving at me when I walked by. They looked annoyed when I approached them. A teenager gave me the finger when I blew my whistle at him. One man muttered "Fuck off, you *Baywatch* wannabe," after I advised him of the red flag conditions.

Eventually it happened—my attitude fell victim to the nor'easter. I talked to myself in the stand—just to voice my frustrations, even if they were lost in the howling wind.

"Screw it. I'll just let the prick get in trouble. If he doesn't believe me, then let him feel that current pull." I said while watching a man inch his way into the surf. "I'll let him panic a little before I get his ass."

That was it.

On a day in early August, I became a true ORS lifeguard. I had enough power to make that call. Up to that point I second guessed everything I did on the beach. But when I said, "Fuck'em…let them feel it first," I gained all of the power.

Each guard pulled at least five people a day out of

rip currents and heavy surf. We were exhausted and pissed as all hell. Rescues happened so frequently that sometimes we didn't even call them in on the radio. There was no one to hear it; everyone was in the water or out of their trucks.

I had eight rescues one day—for twelve people and that wasn't the most on the beach. Grey pulled in fifteen. People actually walked past me into the water while I was carrying someone else out. I barely had the energy to yell at them to stop. I certainly didn't have enough patience to argue with them. At times, other people on the beach, usually locals, warned them for me.

It was around four o'clock. The winds slacked off but the current showed no sign of weakening. The calls slowed down because the beach was mostly empty. I looked a hundred yards south and watched two men run over the dunes. They dropped their towels near the high tide line and sprinted into the water. All of my patience was lost in the ocean—swirling around out of reach.

I walked down and stood on the large iron drain pipe that routed rainwater from the street to the ocean. I cupped my hands around my whistle and blew until my chest stung. The lateral current swept the two idiots another fifty yards south. One turned and saw me on the large pipe. He yelled at his friend and the two swimmers turned back to shore. The small victory was a thrill on such a long day. One blast of the whistle and the problem was solved.

One of the men tripped on the ledge as he exited the water. I stood next to one of the dozen red flags that dotted my beach.

"Man, don't even start with us." The larger one snarled and stared at me from under a mop of wet black hair.

They both had a few years and a few pounds on me. They breathed heavily and clutched their beach store body boards. Their faces glowed red from their sunburns and they wore matching checkered bathing suits. I was so taken aback by the fatter one's declaration that I didn't say anything at first.

"Yeah, man." The other one stepped closer to me. "Those flags are just an *advisory*. You can't legally keep us out of the water."

They were right.

I didn't want to deal with technicalities at that moment. I had enough of the two assholes.

"You're absolutely right." My shoulders slumped a bit and I took a small step back. My lack of defense caught them off guard. I started to walk away.

"Of course, I'm not *legally* required to go out there and save you when that hundred-yard-long rip current pulls you out." I spoke as I walked—meaning everything I said—not playing games with them. They could fucking drown. The lateral currents would take their bodies down to Nags Head before anyone missed them.

"That's a great attitude to have, man. You have to go out there if we get in trouble."

I turned back and walked up to the fat one. His expression teetered between *"Aren't I right?"* and *"Go fuck yourself."* I got so close to his face that I could see the rubber bands tangled between the braces in the back of his mouth.

"You're right, that is a bad attitude." I squeezed the handle of my buoy. My voice was raspy and the back of my throat rattled when I spoke. "You two go on out there..." I paused, "and when you get in trouble..."

He took a step back, sensing my level of impatience.

"I'll come out and pull you in." I stared at him.

They looked at each other, a bit confused.

I matched his retreat with another step—my face as close to his as I wanted it to be. My bare chest almost pressed against his thin wet white shirt.

That time I didn't pause when I warned them, I just raised my buoy a bit. "You go out there and when I pull you in I'm going to drag you up on the beach and beat the shit out of both of you."

A drop of salt water ran into his eye. He blinked and turned to his friend. He could have crushed me with one swing but the rage he saw in my face was enough to send them on their way.

Blame it on the water, the rescues, exhaustion— anyway you look at it I was abusing a power that I barely had control of. They didn't look back after they picked up their towels, just lowered their heads and dragged their boards by the flimsy blue leashes. I stood there, white knuckled, heart bumping as loud as the crashing surf and stared at them until they disappeared over the dunes.

I wasn't okay. Red flags and white water were in my head.

Lying in bed that night, I heard a chorus of "*I should'a said,*" and "*Did I say that?*" I was alone in the house. Harry went to Virginia for a family reunion. Lilly was out with her friends. She invited me but I knew I'd be a drag. I hadn't had a day off since the nor'easter started and the next day was merely a long blink away.

Twelve solid days of red flags, rescues, and resuscitations. Our suits were never dry. No one knew when the wind was going to switch. Even when it did, there would be a few days of placid water and churning rips to contend with before things were back to normal.

The onshore breeze did allow us to cut off the air conditioning at night. I listened to the pounding surf rage a block away. It crept into my room—the sea, bound by land but ignoring its borders, blew through my windows and made the air sticky with salt spray. It clung to everything in the room; the thick latex paint on the paneled walls, the swirling blades of my box fan, the sheets and pillow cases I rolled around in—trying to find a dry enough spot to fall asleep on. My breathing was deep and each time I drew in the heavy air the thickness rattled around below my throat. The sea filled my chest and squeezed it from the inside.

My inner alarm woke me at seven thirty. When I opened my eyes and rolled over to check the clock I could barely make my body turn up on its side. It took every bit of energy I had and when I read the neon red numbers I let gravity pull me back into the recess of my mattress.

I drifted in and out of sleep for another half hour before I made it out of bed and to the bathroom. I was late for work. I couldn't pull in a full breath and it wore me out to stand up and piss. I leaned against the wall and the water in the bowl spun before I flushed. In the mirror I saw a pale face and drooping eyes. I managed to pull my shorts up before bumping into the doorframe and falling into the living room. I landed between the coffee table and the couch. My head slipped down the side of the cushions to the carpeted floor. Sand pressed on my face. The smell of sleep breath leaked from the corners of my mouth and I drifted into the paisley pattern on the front of the yellow couch.

Occasionally, I dreamed in ten-code. It wasn't complete but it was enough to make the dream feel real when I woke up. I often sat in my stand trying to recall the dreams. When I was bored it was like remembering a movie in my head—something to pass the time.

Passed out on the floor, I dreamed about running down the beach with my radio but no buoy. I was looking for a victim but I didn't know if the person was on the beach or in the water. The noises were all perfect. The sirens, the codes, the voices—Preston's, Rick's, Fig's. There were medic voices—which struck me as odd.

I never made it to the victim.

When I woke, I had a clear tube running down my right arm into a thinner red tube on the top of my hand. The blue plastic curtain on my left was covered with shells and leaping dolphins. I saw shadows speeding by underneath it mixing with the glare off of the shiny tile floor. There was a black clip on one of my fingers. The cord came off of a machine that flashed *70 ... 71 ... 70.* I took a deep breath and felt the plastic nasal-canula above my lip like those on our oxygen tanks at work.

71...72 ...71.

The dolphins and shells slid across the metal rod. A nurse in purple scrubs stood with clipboard in hand, looking at my monitor.

71 ... 72 ... 72.

"Good, your O_2 is coming up. You were at sixty-two when they brought you in."

"Who brought me here, ma'am?" The voice I heard when I spoke sounded like an old man's—weak and full of labored syllables.

"Everyone brought you here." She laughed. "You had quite the escort of emergency vehicles."

"What's wrong?" I looked at the machines surrounding me.

"You've got yourself a nice case of pneumonia."

"Pneumonia?" The word came out like a question and an answer. I was still struggling to speak. "It's the middle of the summer." The paper-covered pillow crackled and slid to the nape of my neck.

"The lifeguards that brought you in said you've been busy."

"Yes ma'am." I looked around the small room. There was nothing of mine there; no shoes, no bag. I had nothing but the shorts that I wore to bed the night before. The nurse realized I was scared before I did. She moved to the side of my bed and put her hand on top of mine.

"When you boys go making all those rescues you get saltwater in your lungs." She tapped the oxygen monitor with the end of her pen, searching for something to add to make me feel better. "We've seen a lot of people these last couple weeks—water in their lungs like you. Probably people you saved."

I stared up at the pock marked ceiling tiles. Preston

told me about it when he trained me. He called it secondary drowning—once salt water entered the chest, it drew water from the rest of the body, slowly filling up the lungs with fluid and eventually causing a "walking drowning". We warned victims and their families to look for the flu-like symptoms after we pulled someone in. It was lip service at best. I didn't really understand it until that moment.

"You're lucky they found you when they did. You've got fluid in both lungs."

I stared at the ceiling again and shivered. The small beach clinic didn't have the facilities to treat me properly. I had full-blown, bilateral, pneumonia. The official diagnosis written in my chart attributed it to *"Inhalation of salt water during multiple rescues."*

Outside the curtain, the radio squawked, *"Central, medic fifty-one, patient transfer, Chesapeake."*

With my chest X-rays laying across my body, the medics loaded me into an ambulance and we drove an hour north to Virginia.

There were no curtains with dolphins at the hospital. The nurses came and went—I never saw the same one twice. There were questions about insurance cards and my medical history and existing conditions.

"These shorts are all I have."

I was put in a dark room—not a real room—more of a storage area. "Overflow One" they call it. The rest was a blur of bedpans and light from a quickly opened and shut door. The voices spoke around, not to me.

A lot of things crossed my mind while I lay in that bed listening to noises I didn't recognize. I was cold and stiff—too sore to lift my head and look for a blanket. I thought about swimming and how I would need to work on my stroke when I got back but that made me feel colder. What guard would sit in my stand while I was gone and would he know where to set up the Anderson's umbrellas and chairs? My guard uniform—how musty and rank it would be when I got back and pulled it out of my bag. Those were the worthless things that distracted me. At one point I jolted myself awake for fear that I'd forgotten my buoy and whistle and the murderous PT that was sure to follow.

I thought about my parents and how my father would be furious if I was still in that room when he got there. My mother would stand next to me while he quizzed the doctor on what drugs they'd given me and why the hell they'd left me alone in that dark room.

I didn't think about dying.

Call it naïveté; call it youthful ignorance. Either way, I never realized that I was a few labored breaths away from my last one. I threw up every antibiotic they gave me. The time they waited between treatments took me closer and closer to the bottom.

I finally got a dose of something that brought me around. A flash of light from the door then a thunderous voice boomed, "Why is he in HERE?"

The room filled with people.

"Insurance?" My father spoke to someone holding a metal clipboard. "You'd better have insurance for yourself if you don't get him into a real room. Where's his doctor?"

I felt a hand on mine. A bile odor poured out of my mouth when I opened it.

"Hey," is all I could manage. My own breath made me nauseated and embarrassed at once. My mother's arms wrapped around mine and her voice covered the room like a blanket.

I was finally warm.

CHAPTER 14

"Don't your parents want you to go home for a little while?" Lilly made the hour-long trip to the hospital twice to visit me. She filled me in on the beach drama and lifeguard stories I was missing.

"There's no point. I'd rather relax and recover on the beach than on their couch in Virginia." I shrugged off the reality that I should take more time.

"But you won't relax if you go straight back, you'll be in a stand the next day." Lilly sat on the edge of my hospital bed.

"The wind switched, right?"

"I guess so." She shrugged.

"Then sitting in the stand will be the perfect place to recover."

"That's stupid and you know it." She tilted her head and looked at me like I was insane.

Harry came with her on the second trip but only stayed in the room for a few moments. He walked in with a to-go box full of fried shrimp and set it on my tray table.

"You look like shit." He opened the box, ate a cold shrimp, and smiled when he walked out of the room. No one else visited. I convinced myself that they were all too busy making rescues. Lilly said they sent their best.

"Fig and Sandy are done." She raised her eyebrows and waited for my response.

"You won that bet." I laughed and lifted my hand for a high five.

"Yep." She smacked it and lifted her arms in victorious fashion.

"What happened?"

"He walked in on her with a Nags Head guard at her house."

"Regal?"

"Oh, God no. She wouldn't stoop that low." A little grin appeared and she continued, "Not again."

I sat up in the bed and listened eagerly to the stories and rumors about Sandy, Fig, Nags Head's lifeguards, and even Rick. Lilly carefully avoided stories about Buck; if he was mentioned it was merely in passing.

She was the only person I met that summer who didn't make me feel like I was two steps behind. When she told me her stories and thoughts about them we became equal observers of the circus. I was her outlet. Her summers before hadn't been as magical as they were routine. Lilly's vacation was just time to pass before rejoining her college friends. At the beach, she enjoyed a quiet ride in the passenger's seat soaking up the stories and rarely revealing her own.

"The summer's almost over." It felt like a question when she said it.

"I wish we had spent more time together." I took her hand.

"You were busy." She patted my hand with her free one.

"I thought y—"

"It's okay, Wesley. I know how it works. It's summer. It's just fun."

I shook my head and looked her in the eye. "No, it's more than that." I sat up in the bed. "I mean, I want it to keep going with you and me."

"How's that going to work?"

The conversation wasn't going the way I had hoped.

"I don't know. I'll visit you at school. I'm going to have time once Rick shuts things down for the fall."

"So you're not going to college?" Her expression flattened and she looked away.

"I have another week to decide if I want to defer." I said it like I hadn't already made up my mind.

"Please go to school." She turned back to me. "Don't fall into the trap. I know you think it's great now but you're going to be miserable."

"You sound like my father." I leaned back against the paper covered pillow.

"Good, you need to hear it." She smiled and kissed my cheek.

I had two priorities when I got out of the hospital: get back to work and be ready for the Lifeguard Olympics. The end-of-summer ritual was looming just a week away and I'd lost a lot of my strength resting in the hospital.

Lilly tried again in vain to convince me not to work while she drove me home from the hospital. I asked her to drop me off at the shack before I went to my house. We pulled into the gravel lot and Lilly put her car in park.

"I don't understand what your rush is. You can't help other people if you're sick."

"I'm not sick anymore. It was like the flu. I'm over it."

"Wesley, you were really sick." She looked down. "They said you could have died."

"Who said that?"

"Ed, my father, a lot of people. I just care about you and don't want to see you hurt yourself because you feel like you have to make Rick happy."

I couldn't look at her. "That's not what it's about," I snapped back. "Thanks for the ride." I stepped out of her car and said, "I'll call you later."

Lilly pulled out of the parking lot without saying anything else. I knew I'd been short and I turned around to apologize but she was gone.

Rick was in his office and called out, "Come in," when I knocked on the door.

"Hey, Rick." I lifted my hand.

"There he is! The living example of how to drown on land." Rick moved from behind his desk and grabbed my shoulders. "We were worried about you. Scared the shit out of everyone." His face looked concerned. "You look terrible. Need to get you back in the sun."

"I'm feeling better every day."

"Good, that's good to hear." He took a seat and pointed to a chair by the desk for me to use.

"How's everything been around here?" I sunk into the folding canvas chair.

"Dammit, Wesley." Rick leaned forward, both elbows on his desk, rubbing his bald head. He looked at me over the thick rims of his glasses. "I'm losing it Wesley. These fuckers from the town are breathing down my neck. Vampires, fucking vampires." He dropped his chin, eyes wide open, and shook his head slowly. It was the first time Rick spoke to me like I wasn't a rookie.

"What are they after you for?"

"Same old bullshit they come up with every year; they're trying to cut funding. One year they decide we need to reduce the number of stands, the next year we need more. And now they're talking about going in-house with the fire department."

"No shit." I matched his shaking head. He didn't say anything so I did. "This might not be the best time but I told my father I'd ask." I looked down at the desk. "I understand if you can't, but is there any way for me to get paid worker's comp for the time I missed?"

Rick stared at me. He didn't look mad, more like he was trying to work through something. His expression didn't change, but he tilted his head and said, "Worker's comp for what exactly? For catching pneumonia?"

I felt challenged and uncomfortable. "Yes sir, because the doctor said it was from making rescues."

"Can the doctor prove that's when the water got in your lungs?"

I balked and tried to back off. "I don't know."

"It's not that I don't want to help you out; I'm just bringing it up because that's what the insurance company is going to ask if I file a claim. You understand?"

"Yes sir." I leaned back in my chair and looked down again.

"It's good to have you back, Wesley." Rick stood up and extended his hand. "You'll have to excuse me. I just drank my lunch and it's running through me like custard."

I hesitated when I shook his hand and made a repulsed face that he didn't see. He quickly moved down the hallway to the bathroom. From behind a closed door I heard him say, "Buck's in the shack. Go tell him that you're back so he can get you on the schedule."

I checked in the next morning and reported to my stand at Sea Dunes. The wooden bench made my back hurt—forcing me to shift every few minutes. Nothing was comfortable. I leaned against my thin towel and took deep breaths. My eyes scanned the water.

The ocean was flat—a stark contrast to the churned wash it was before I got sick. The red flags were still up. It caused some confusion for people who had been kept out of the rough water and now saw a calm sea.

I heard Ed's whistle drift down from the north but I couldn't even bring myself to care what he had going on. The radio hummed.

"Neptune Street, 700."

A few seconds passed and Buck answered for Rick with an annoyed tone.

"Go ahead for 700."

"701, can you contact Animal Control?"

"What do you have, Neptune Street?" I could tell by Buck's voice that he was in the middle of something else—probably eating or taking a shit.

"I have a stray dog running all over people's stuff out here."

"Can you get a hold of the dog?"

"Negative, he's running in and out of the water and people are complaining."

"Did you advise him of the red flag conditions?"

I imagined the smirk on Buck's face and shook my head.

"10-4 701, I gave him a pamphlet. He says he wants to talk to my supervisor."

"Animal control's been contacted, standby."

"10-4."

I rolled my heavy head to the north and saw the dog at Neptune Street. The thin dark animal was in full sprint from the dunes down to the water. It splashed just above the ledge and quickly turned back to the beach. From where I sat it looked like a boxer or some sort of pit bull—lacking the grace of a retriever or natural water dog. It hopped between blankets and umbrellas. A man near Ed's stand pointed at the dog as it kicked up sand and made its way back to the water.

I took a deep breath and tried again to find a soft spot on the bench. *Better him than me,* I thought. He had obviously gotten too many complaints to ignore. Ed would do everything he could to avoid calling for Animal Control on a red flag day.

The tide was almost at dead low. From my heightened elevation I could see every contour of the sea floor. The clear shallow water was tinted emerald green—inviting and deceptive. The receding surge from the last few days caused the water to rush through the holes in the sandbar faster than swimmers expected. I watched a line of brown stingrays cut through the small waves. The juveniles showed off for each other—swimming along the surface, flashing their fins a few inches out of the water, and circling back on themselves.

"*Neptune Street, 701.*"

"*Go ahead.*"

"*Do you have an ETA on Animal Control?*"

"*They're coming from Manteo—it'll be twenty minutes at least.*" Buck's annoyance level was at its peak. "*Neptune Street, limit your radio traffic to emergencies only.*"

I shook my head, imagining Ed's frustration.

"*Neptune Street, 701. I'm going in the water to assist some patrons.*"

I stood up and grabbed for my binoculars.

"*Number of victims?*"

"*The dog is caught in a rip in front of my stand.*"

"You've got to be kidding me," I said out loud.

Ed stood by the water. People gathered around him and tried to coax the dog their way. No one was in the water. Every guard within a mile was up on his stand watching. Preston made his way from Wilkins Street on his four-wheeler. Ed slipped the buoy strap off his shoulders and dropped his can at his feet. He passed his radio to a man behind him and started toward the water.

"*Negative, Neptune Street. Standby for Animal Control.*"

Ed stopped and spun around. He reached for his radio and I watched him raise it to his mouth. Nothing transmitted and he lowered it. The dog splashed wildly just ten yards off the beach but in a serious hole. Several bystanders pointed at the drowning dog.

"*Neptune Street, do you copy? Stay out of the water and standby for Animal Control.*"

Ed looked to the north but Preston was still a half a mile away. The dog spun around and around, oblivious to the direction of the shore. It craned its neck high above the surface and slapped at the water with its paws. The rip current carried the dog another ten yards out. Ed handed off his radio again and high stepped through the shallow water, staying to the south of the dog where the sandbar was solid.

"701, Wright Street."

Grey picked up his radio but didn't respond.

"Wright Street, do you have a visual on Neptune Street?"

Again, Grey ignored Buck for fear of getting Ed in trouble.

Ed dove into the rip when he was a few yards away from the dog. The animal faced the shore and was visibly fatigued; it pawed desperately at the water. Ed dove down and popped up behind the dog to avoid getting clawed. He grabbed the tuft of skin on the back of its neck. The contact ignited the dog into a spasm of splashing and twisting.

"701, Sea Dunes."

"Shit," I whispered.

I looked at my radio but didn't touch it. I wanted to give Ed a chance to get back to shore before I answered up. He pulled his way toward the sandbar with one arm.

"701, Lifeguard Brooks."

My throat clenched when Buck said my name. I couldn't ignore him anymore—but I could stall him until Preston got there.

"Go ahead for Sea Dunes."

I saw Grey's arms fly up in the air at Wright Street in frustration when he heard me click in.

"Do you have a visual?"

"Standby."

"Brooks, do you have a visual?"

I took a breath and watched Ed take a few strokes. He was twenty yards out. "Neptune Street is pulling the dog back in—just a few yards from the beach."

"702, 701, I'm on scene. Standby." Preston was still a quarter of a mile away but he saved me from dealing with Buck.

"10-4."

Preston blew his whistle as he approached. The

crowd stepped back. The front of his four-wheeler dipped down and stopped with so much force that his tires pushed a large pile of sand in front of the bike. He looked out to Ed, gave the okay sign, and waited for it in return. Ed swam but didn't respond.

Preston moved down to the edge of the water with only his radio in hand. Ed made it to waist-deep water and turned his back to the beach. He continued backing up and looked over his shoulder at Preston. He held the dog with one hand; with the other he pointed at the beach. He waved a sweeping hand toward the crowd. Several people in the group walked away, taking children with them. Ed shielded the dog with his body and waited in the shallow water.

"701, 702, what's the status?"

"Everything's 10-4 at Neptune Street."

A woman walked down to Preston and gave him a bright orange towel with yellow stripes. He handed her his radio and waded out to Ed. They took their time covering the dog with the towel.

I scanned my beach.

When I looked back, Ed was walking straight toward the dunes with the covered dog in his arms. Preston gathered his radio and Ed's buoy. He talked with people in the crowd for a few moments. Ed disappeared through the access and Preston soon followed.

I sat down.

Twenty minutes passed. There was no radio traffic and no sign of Preston or Ed. I covered Ed's empty water—Grey did the same from Wright Street.

Eventually, Preston rode back onto the beach. He parked in front of the stand and climbed up. Ed appeared on the wooden walkway. He made his way to the shower, pulled the chain, and lifted his face into the stream of fresh water. He shook his head and stood there for a few more minutes.

He pressed his hair back when he finished and

stepped down into the hot sand. A family of four was leaving the beach through the access. The father stopped near Ed to take a break from pulling a cart full of beach chairs, umbrellas, and toys. The mother and two children continue to the parking lot.

The man said something and reached out to shake Ed's hand. Ed did his best to mask his frustration as he returned the gesture. The father moved on and Ed walked back to the stand.

For the next half hour, Ed went from sitting on his armrest to standing on the top step; from pointing with sharp stabs toward the rip current to crossing his arms and shaking his head. At one point I saw him gesture over the dunes in the direction of the shack. Preston listened, nodded, and absorbed Ed's frustrations.

"700, 702."

"Go ahead."

"Preston, meet me at the shack."

"10-4."

Preston sat for another minute and then climbed down. He drove south toward my stand then cut his wheels and made a wide loop. He drove to Wright Street and waved at people on the beach along the way.

Grey leaned down when Preston stopped in front of his stand. They talked for a moment and Preston drove over the access toward the shack. Ed stood in front of his stand and leaned against the ladder. I felt sorry for him. It was barely three o'clock—he had over two hours to think about the dog and how much he hated Buck.

It didn't take me long to get back to the shack after Rick called us in. I pulled into the gravel lot and parked next to Stanley's car. I gathered my equipment and made my way to the garage. Adrian and Grey were talking across the lot so I make a detour.

"Crazy shit, huh?" I set my umbrella down next to Grey.

"Yep." Grey looked at Adrian like I just proved a point. Adrian just shrugged.

"Did Preston tell you what happened?" I asked.

"Nope." Grey didn't look at me.

"Oh."

Grey continued, "I saw what you saw."

I looked around the parking lot. "Have you seen Ed?"

"I wouldn't go looking for him if I were you, Rookie. You should know better than to sell him out over the radio."

"I tried to stall—"

Grey slammed the rear door of his hatchback and walked away.

I looked to Adrian for some explanation.

"You did the right thing. You couldn't ignore Buck." He nodded at Grey, who disappeared into the garage. "He's just upset because he knows Buck's going to give him a hard time." Adrian gathered his gear from the bed of his truck. "Just turn in your stuff and take off. It'll all blow over by tomorrow."

The unexpected drama had me a little rattled as I walked into the shack. Buck's truck was gone. I was relieved when I entered through the side door and didn't see him behind the counter. Grey handed Fig his first aid equipment and whistle. Fig put the gear back in the corresponding cubbyhole. Then he took Grey's nametag and moved it from Wright Street to the far end of the row of boxes.

Grey gave Preston his daily report but said nothing.

"Rick wants to see you." Preston said it quietly, but nobody in the shack was talking so everyone heard him.

Grey left through the side door. I watched him step up to the office and knock. When he went in I turned back to the counter and passed my stuff across to Fig. I looked down the row of boxes and saw Grey's name at Mullet Street for the next day.

"That's bullshit," I muttered.

"What's that?" Fig whipped around and looked at me.

"Nothing." I handed Preston my slip and stepped into the garage.

Both four-wheelers were parked in the tight space so I turned sideways and slipped by the first one. Before I got past the second bike Buck's truck pulled into the space in front of the garage, partially blocking my way out. I stopped, hoping he'd go to the office or through the sliding door.

Before he got out he dipped his head and looked into his side mirror. He smiled and opened his door but waited. I turned and looked at the rack of surfboards like I was considering paddling out.

Buck stepped out and leaned against the cab without shutting his door. He faced the back of his truck and spit into his Mountain Dew bottle. He never looked at me.

"Rick wants to see you."

I turned and looked at him but he was still facing the parking lot. Ed stepped in front of the garage door holding all of his gear.

"Go fuck yourself."

Buck straightened up and squared off on Ed.

"You wanna say that again?"

Ed stared at him—running through all of the things that he'd imagined saying to Buck for the last few hours.

"Fuck this." There was a slight quiver in Ed's voice. He threw his gear down on the cement floor. "I don't need this shit." He turned and walked away.

Buck shook his head and leaned back against the truck.

"Such a pussy." He spit into his bottle and watched Ed leave. When enough time had passed for Ed to reach his car and drive away, Buck picked up the buoy off the floor and hung it on the rack. He leaned the umbrella against the wall and gathered the rest of Ed's gear. He looked at me, still standing next to the rack of surfboards.

"Got another surf lesson?" He smiled.

"No." I slid between the four-wheelers and escaped from the garage.

"Good thing your radio was working."

"Yeah." I kept walking.

I threw my backpack into the passenger's seat and focused on Adrian's advice to get away from the mess as I turned the key. When I reached over the passenger's seat to back up I saw Ed's Jeep driving straight at mine in reverse. He cut the wheel at the last second and it came to a stop a foot away from mine, pinning me in. There wasn't even enough room for Ed to open his door. I shut my engine off and stepped out.

"Get in." Ed looked straight out his windshield.

"Look, I'm sorry about the radio. He called my name and I didn't know—"

"Get in the fucking car."

That was the last place I wanted to be.

"I'm going home." I pointed toward my house to be clear.

"I'm not mad at you." His tone softened and he turned toward me. "Get in."

Grey walked past the Jeep without looking at me.

"This is some high school bullshit." I walked around to the passenger's side and climbed in.

A chorus of wolf howls and barking echoed through the parking lot. I looked over my shoulder and saw Fig cupping his hands around his mouth while Stanley stood next to him laughing.

"Fucking bastards." Ed looked in the rear-view mirror. "Remind me to kick their asses later." He jabbed at first gear and slid on the gravel. The tires chirped when they hit solid pavement. Like I did every time I rode with Ed, I reached for the roll bar with my right hand and grabbed the steel bar above the glove box with the other.

We took a left on Wright Street and another quick left on Lindbergh. Ed blew through the stop sign at Beacon Drive and whipped the Jeep into the dirt parking lot behind the Point. When we came to a stop I took a deep breath then laughed.

"I'm glad we weren't going to Virginia. I would have shit myself before we made it to the border."

Ed didn't say anything. We climbed the long wooden staircase and Ed jerked at the wrought iron handle. Even though it was locked, the old door popped open. It startled Evelyn who stood behind the bar wiping bottles.

"Hey, Eve."

"What are you doing here so early?" She looked at Ed then at me.

"I need two beers and some quarters?" He put a few singles on the bar.

Evelyn reached into the cooler and passed me the bottles without saying a word. Ed disappeared through what looked like a closet door where a narrow staircase led to the third floor loft space. Evelyn looked at me for an explanation.

"Rough day." I collected the quarters and followed Ed up the stairs.

Ed rolled two crooked cues along the thin green felt while I plunked the quarters into their slots. The percussion of balls dropping bounced around the thick timber-framed walls. Ed waited for me to rack them.

I barely pulled the plastic triangle away when Ed struck the cue ball. Nothing fell but the break spread the balls around.

"Figures." Ed reached for his beer while I lined up my shot.

I had a straight shot on the three-ball and sank it easily. I got lucky and my next shot on the five set up perfectly. Ed said nothing. I dropped the five and the two without moving.

"I swear to God Rookie, if you run this table on

me…"

I smiled and lined up a long shot on the one-ball. It rattled against the corner pocket but stayed on the table.

Ed looked at all of the striped balls. "So, Grey said I was pissed at you?"

"Something like that." I knew Ed wasn't mad at me so I resisted the urge to apologize.

"He's just scared he'll get in trouble."

Ed sank the nine-ball.

"Preston told me he didn't answer up. You did the right thing—I'm not scared of Buck."

"They put him at Mullet Street for tomorrow."

"Big fuckin' deal. I'll go sit Mullet for the rest of the summer." He sank the eleven-ball. "Nothing ever happens up there."

"Yeah, that really sucks about the dog."

"Are you kidding? It's fucking hilarious." Ed waved his hand at the table. "Obviously it sucks that the dog died, but come on."

"Yeah, I guess when you think about it, it's kind of funny." It was a lie and it felt gross coming out of my mouth.

"Here's to the only drowning of the summer." Ed lifted his bottle and I joined him.

"Cheers."

"But the first person that makes a mouth to mouth joke is gonna to get my fist in his face." Ed took a shot on the fifteen but missed.

I took a look at the balls left on the table.

"You just looked pretty pissed on the beach after it happened."

"Yeah, because that cocksucker was sitting on the couch at the shack while we're out there working and I can't do my job because he's on a power trip."

I banked the four-ball off the side rail and it rolled to the opposite pocket.

"Why is he still here?" I moved toward the end of

the table. "I mean, what does he have on Rick?"

"Good question. I don't know, but I wish he would fuck up again."

"He'd probably just get away with it." I missed an easy shot on the one. "He acts like he's invincible."

"He's not." Ed surveyed the table. "He just needs to get caught."

"Yeah, but by someone who will do something about it." I leaned back against the wall.

"He needs to get arrested." Ed leaned over the table and dropped the nine-ball in the corner pocket. "I should call my cop friends when he's got some underage girl drinking at Magnolia Street."

"Remind me not to piss you off." I held up my empty beer.

He lined up the fourteen and missed bad. The green and white striped ball rolled into the eight ball and sent into the side pocket.

"Fuck." Ed rapped his stick on the floor and yelled, "Two more Eve!" He looked at me and smirked. "You wanna go get those?"

I thought about Eve and the look she was undoubtedly giving us.

"No, not really."

Two more turned into too many more. Our last game took thirty minutes to finish before I scratched on the eight ball. Ed came up with a dozen extravagant ways he'd like to see Buck go down.

When I couldn't make the quarters go into the slots I leaned my head against the side of the table and laughed. We made our way downstairs and weaved through the regular Thursday night crowd. The two-story staircase looked like an escalator moving toward me. I gripped the railing and carefully put one foot on the top step.

I got halfway down the steps, still clutching the handrail, and nodded my head at my own impressive progress. I was pretty sure Ed was in front of me when I went outside but I didn't see him at the bottom. The only person at the foot of the steps was Muffin sitting on a stool with his pink mohawk and pierced nose. I laughed but quickly put a hand over my mouth when I realized I was giggling at Muffin.

Someone rushed past, forcing me against the banister.

"What the hell?" My arms swung around and grabbed at the rail cap.

"I'll fucking kill you." Ed jumped from the third step and landed in the parking lot in full stride. Muffin reached out to grab him but missed completely.

Two guys were crouched down behind Ed's Jeep. They took off when they saw him coming. I gathered myself as much as I could and quickly went from happy drunk to concerned drunk. Muffin lumbered and I stumbled toward the unlit back parking lot where Ed disappeared.

I got ahead of the three-hundred-pound bouncer pretty quickly. I could hear Ed off to the right yelling but I only saw one of the guys he chased. When I got to the unfamiliar guy we both looked at each other and took a step back. I looked down in the drainage ditch that ran along the road. Ed held the other guy by the back of the neck. He pressed the guy's face into the slimy muck and pulled it up again.

"Come on man, let him go," his friend pleaded from the road, but Ed heard nothing.

"You think it's funny? Huh?" Ed slammed the guy's face into the muddy water and pulled it out again. "You know what's funny?" The guy swung his arms out behind him to try to get at Ed. "Tomorrow the newspaper's gonna say, 'Nags Head lifeguard drowns in two inches of water'."

I looked at the guy again. He stumbled to get some kind of footing but Ed had him pinned down pretty good. Then I realized who it was.

"Shit." I straightened up.

The friend looked at me and we both jumped into the ditch. I pulled at Ed's arms but he was locked down on Regal's neck.

"Come on Ed, he's not worth it." I got a grip on his hands and after another tug he let go.

Ed and I both leaned back against the side of the ditch. Muffin reached down, grabbed Ed under his arms, and pulled him up to the street. Regal knelt in the water, his hands resting on his thighs. He coughed a few times and then got to his feet. He and his friend climbed out of the ditch and walked away. Ed made a move toward them again but Muffin reached out, putting his hand in the center of Ed's chest. The fight was over.

"What the fuck, Tim?" Ed planted both hands on Muffin's shoulders and pushed. It had no effect. Ed shook his head and turned back toward the parking lot. He took a few steps and looked back. "Didn't you see them?"

"I just got out here." Muffin pointed to the steps. "New guy on the door earlier."

We walked past Ed's Jeep. The hood was covered with dog food and rubber chew toys. Collars and leashes hung from the mirrors, roll bars, and trailer hitch.

"That's fucked up." I shook my head and remembered that I was very drunk. "Ed, wait. Where're you going?"

Ed was giving the new bouncer at the bottom of the steps the third degree. His legs were covered with muck from the drainage ditch but he couldn't care less. Muffin produced a towel from somewhere under the steps and tossed it to Ed who continued to point at his Jeep and yell at the new guy as he wiped himself off.

"Come on Ed. You can crash at my place." I reached out and put my hand on his shoulder.

"I'm good." Ed started up the stairs. My hand dropped clumsily in front of me.

I started to follow him but Muffin stepped in front of me.

"I need to get him." I pointed and looked up the staircase. The swirling in my head returned and I took a step back to catch myself.

"Call it a night, Rookie."

I stared at the pink mohawk for a moment and realized that I needed to carry my underage ass home. I reached out to shake his hand.

"Thanks for helping me back there."

"No problem."

"No, seriously I appreciate it." I stood for a moment staring at and past Muffin. He nodded and sat down on his stool. I walked out the back of the parking lot and turned toward Neptune Street. When I could see my house I dug around in my pockets for my keys.

"Shit." I stopped in the middle of the street and looked up. My car was at the shack.

When I got to the parking lot I was surprised to see Stanley's car still parked next to mine. The light in Rick's office was on but the shack was dark. The door opened and light from the office spilled out into the driveway.

"Thank you again Stanley." Rick's voice was softer than usual but I could hear him clearly.

Stanley made his way down the steps and passed through the single spotlight on the garage.

Rick called out to him as he walked away. "And don't worry about Buck and Fig, I'll have a talk with them."

Stanley waved back and continued toward his car. Rick closed the door and turned off the spotlight.

When he was even with my car he glanced over and was startled to see me.

"W-w-what are you doing here?"

"I left my bag." I lifted my backpack up for him to see. "You?"

"I was tal-tal-talking to Rick." He seemed agitated.

"Everything okay?"

"Yeah." He opened his door. "See you tomorrow." He climbed in, backed up, and left.

I watched him turn onto the beach road. The parking lot was dark and empty. Only Rick's office light was on.

"Weird fucking day." I stuffed things from the Jeep into my backpack and walked the three blocks to my house.

CHAPTER 15

Panic surged through my body. The morning sun was creeping across my bed. It blinded me when I snapped my head to the left and looked at the red numbers of my clock.

7:34.

I forgot to turn my alarm on the night before. PT started at seven forty-five and after the dog incident there was no way I could be late.

The terror of oversleeping took away from my pounding head. At least I was still wearing my red shorts from the night before. I slipped my old tennis shoes on and sprinted through the hall. The clock on the stove read, *7:39.* I looked at my watch.

"It's fast." I swiped my bag from the counter and stiff-armed the screen door. When I got to the bottom of the steps my heart collided with my stomach. My parking space was empty. In my mental fog I'd already forgotten the Jeep was at the shack.

I took off in a full sprint down Lindbergh Drive. It didn't take me long to cover the three blocks. I cut through Rick's side yard, high-stepping through the cactus and dog shit.

7:42.

I threw my bag through the open window of my Jeep and ran into the garage. There were two buoys on the rack—mine and Neptune Street's.

I played Frogger with a line of minivans while crossing the beach road and decided to sprint through the soft sand of the access rather than climb the high steps of the boardwalk. I let out a deep breath of relief when I popped out on the other side of the dunes.

Each guard stretched on his own. Buck, Fig, and Preston were gathered around Rick's Bronco. He sat in the driver's seat talking to the supervisors. I slipped behind the stand, avoiding any eye contact from the group and found Adrian.

"Hey." I planted my buoy in the sand next to him.

"Cutting it close."

"Long night." I wiped the sweat from my forehead.

He didn't say anything, but he nodded.

Buck looked at his watch.

"Everybody drop your shit where you are and gather around." He leaned on the front quarter-panel of the Bronco.

We walked toward the supervisors with a principal's office feeling of dread. Rick stepped out of his truck and looked around the group.

"Come in closer, I don't want to have to yell." He raised his long arms and motioned people in the back to move forward. No one got too close. Grey was off to one side and Ed wasn't there. My mind started racing.

"It's too late in the season for me to be having this conversation." He scanned the group. "When a supervisor tells you to do something, you do it. If he tells you not to do something," His jaw clenched and he looked around at everyone again.

I couldn't tell if he was pausing for effect or if he'd lost his train of thought. Preston was toeing the sand in front of him. Fig stood, arms crossed, trying to look tough.

Buck stared at Grey.

"Just do your job. Watch your water and answer your goddamn radio when someone calls you. We're professionals—not a bunch of fucking cowboys doing whatever we feel like." He turned around climbed up into his Bronco.

He kicked up a rooster tail of sand when he drove away, cutting a deep rut into the beach. Buck pointed to the closest four-wheeler.

"Line up. Leave your buoy and fins."

I realized I'd forgotten my fins and another wave of panic rolled through me, but there was nothing I could do about it. I lined up next to Adrian. No one spoke.

"Ocean Boulevard and back. Go ahead." Buck pointed to the north.

We started the run in two lines but they quickly fell apart. Buck rode next to the main pack for a little while, then sped ahead to Ocean Boulevard. As people turned around and headed south he yelled, "Town line."

I did the math in my head and it came out to four miles. I was relieved that I didn't have to swim with a hangover. Then I saw Grey lumbering toward us and I realized exactly who Buck was punishing.

I kept pace with Adrian on our way to the town line. Buck stopped at Wright Street and sat with Fig and Preston.

"Where's Ed?" It was bugging me the whole run.

Adrian looked over his shoulder to make sure Buck wasn't creeping up on us.

"In jail."

"What? Are you kidding?" I nearly tripped on a tire rut.

"I think Rick's on his way to talk to the Chief or post bail."

"What the hell happened?"

"He had too much to drink last night."

"Oh, shit. Is this about Regal?" I was practically

running sideways.

"Regal? What are you talking about?"

"They got into a fight last night at the Point. We were shooting pool after work and he caught Regal trashing his Jeep when we were about to leave."

"What did he do?"

"Regal?"

"Yeah."

"He and another guy covered the Jeep in dog food and chew toys. They tied leashes and collars all over it."

"That's clever." Adrian rolled his eyes.

"Ed had Regal face down in the drainage ditch and probably would have killed him if we didn't break it up."

"You let him drive?"

"He went back inside but they wouldn't let me in. I walked home."

"Well, that explains why he was so wasted when he got to our house."

We reached the town line and turned around. Grey was a mile behind us, barely to Wright Street. In the distance we watched Buck start his four-wheeler and drive down to the hard sand behind Grey.

"Why did he go to Magnolia Street?"

"He was looking for Buck."

"That's not good."

"No, Buck was sitting out on the porch with some girl. Ed pulled in and started yelling for him to come out into the driveway. It must have scared the girl—they came inside and went into Buck's room. Grey and I tried to calm him down but he came up on the porch and kept trying to get into the house. He was out of control."

"Wow, I knew he was pissed, but he was taking the whole dog thing pretty well. He was even joking about it at the Point."

"Yeah, it's more about Buck than the dog."

"Obviously."

"He started crying and throwing furniture off the

porch. At some point the neighbors called the cops."

"You sure it wasn't Buck that called them?"

"I didn't think about that. But when they got there they gave him every opportunity to settle down. We explained the dog thing and they told us to just take him home."

"Was it Laverman?"

"No, I didn't know any of the cops. He lost it again and threw a plastic chair off the porch. It hit one of the cops—didn't hurt him but they locked him up real quick after that. He put up a little fight but then broke down."

"Jesus." I stared ahead and tried to imagine the scene.

"Keep your head up buddy. Almost done." Adrian looked straight as we passed Grey going the opposite direction. His face was bright red and he stared at the sand as he shuffled along by the water. "Buck put him at Mullet today."

"Yeah, I saw. Pretty messed up."

"Yeah. Well, they charged Ed with assault on an officer, public intoxication, disturbing the peace, resisting, and littering."

"Littering?"

"For the furniture that landed in the street. They were pissed. He was lucky they didn't get him for DWI."

"What a mess."

"Hopefully Rick will be able to get him out of it."

We stopped talking when we approached Wright Street. Fig instructed everybody who finished running to do flutter kicks by the water. We joined the group without a word. Fig barked out different exercises at a steady pace. We went through push-ups, lunges, crunches, mountain climbers, six-inches, arm hollers, and squats. It was clear that we'd be doing it until Grey finished his run.

Fig ran out of ideas and grumbled, "Somebody pick something."

Someone at the end of the line yelled, "Full body

stretch!"

"You lie down and we'll stay here until nine o'clock." Fig looked around. "Adrian, pick something."

Adrian looked to the south where Grey was still chugging along with Buck on his ass.

"I choose running."

Before Fig could say anything Adrian took off in a full sprint. We looked at each other and followed right behind him. Immediately, people started laughing. Someone defiantly yelled, "Fuck Fig!"

Someone else added in, "Fuck Buck!"

We gathered up behind Grey, pinching off Buck's fourwheeler and giving Grey some room to run. Back at Wright Street we watched Fig drive through the access. Buck zipped up to the soft sand and joined him. At least a dozen middle fingers went up in the air.

We slapped hands as we crossed the imaginary line in front of the stand. Some guys rinsed off in the ocean and others body surfed for a few minutes. Stanley passed me without saying a word. He gathered his stuff and walked over to the shack.

"What's the deal with him?" I nodded at Stanley.

"Who?" Adrian scooped up his fins.

"Stanley. I saw him leaving Rick's office last night when I went to get my bag."

"He's an accounting major at Tech. He's trying to help Rick with the books."

I watched Stanley walk through the access by himself.

"Makes sense."

I hurried through check-in so I'd have time to go home and make lunch. I was sorting through the umbrellas in the garage to find the one for Sea Dunes and heard Buck's voice behind me.

"You hear about Ed?"

"Yeah, I heard." I found the umbrella, pulled it out,

and shook the sand from the stake.

"Were you with him last night?"

"For a little while."

I was tired of it all. Literally, I was hung over, exhausted and at my limit with Buck. I had no respect for him. None of his heavy handed tactics mattered. I could handle just about anything he threw at me physically. Mentally, I never wanted to end up like Ed. I looked at Buck and waited for his punch line, just to get it over with.

"We're going to need to bump you up to the first team for Olympics." His expression was neither his trademark smirk nor anger. He was just flat. "We have to rearrange the events to cover for Ed, but all you need to worry about is beach flags and maybe a sprint on the relay. Don't worry; I won't put you in the water unless I have to."

Even with that he didn't smile.

"Okay." I adjusted the umbrella under my arm and waited.

"We're going to practice tonight after work. Be on the beach at six."

Ed never showed up to work. I drove by the Point after I got off the beach that evening. His red Jeep wasn't in the parking lot. I didn't know exactly where he lived and decided to give it some time before I tried to find him.

CHAPTER 16

Preston placed the box for Byrd Street on the counter. I started to point out the mistake but he explained before I could say anything.

"We had to shuffle some things around, with people leaving for the season and all." He pushed the first aid kit toward me.

In other words, Ed was gone and it was throwing everything off. I replaced the Sea Dunes radio and picked out the one for Byrd Street.

"You're going to have a four-wheeler down there today so wait for me to finish checking everyone in and I'll meet you in the garage."

"What about my rentals at Sea Dunes?"

"Draw a map while you're waiting. We'll get them covered."

I took a seat on one of the couches and sketched out where each rented umbrella and chair went. Grey walked in and saw the Byrd Street gear on the floor in front of me.

"Who'd you blow to get that stand?" He didn't wait for me to answer; just took the equipment for Mullet Street and walked out through the side door.

I watched him leave and looked at Preston who just

- 264 -

shook his head.

"He's gotta be mad at someone."

"For what?"

"Forget about it. Let's go look at the four-wheeler."

Preston went into the garage and rolled out a seldom used bike. He explained that it was the reserve and because of the long distance between the pier and the stand at Byrd Street they occasionally used it.

"You shouldn't need it but park it next to your stand just in case. You can ride down to the pier if you need to go to the bathroom." He threw a first aid kit and a few bungee straps on the back rack. "I'll be covering the north zone so don't worry about responding to any calls unless I can't get there before you."

"Okay."

"If you do respond, use your whistle and drive carefully. You've seen us respond to calls. You know how to do it."

"Can I ask you something?"

"Yeah, what's up?"

"Why me? I mean, I'm a rookie."

"You're good on the beach. I've seen you interacting and taking precautions. I know you're not going to take advantage of it."

"Thanks, but won't the other guys be pissed?"

"It's not for them to worry about. I was going to put you at Byrd Street anyway—we need a runner there." He patted the seat of the four-wheeler. "This is here, so we might as well use it."

"I see."

"It's just another tool to use."

"Yeah, okay."

Preston went over the details of operating the bike and fired it up. I hopped on and pulled it up to my Jeep where I loaded my gear and headed out to the beach. I made my way through the access and settled the bike into the ruts up in the soft sand. I sat tall while I rode, careful not to get the bike stuck or hit anyone.

When I passed the stand at Ocean Boulevard the guard looked confused. I waved and kept moving. It happened again at Balchen Street, Eckner, and just about every other stand on the way. I looped the bike around the stand at Byrd Street, parked it, and surveyed the beach.

The people on that beach were different than those at Sea Dunes. Surfers dotted the water from the pier down to the sandbar in front of the stand. Fisherman took advantage of the deep holes formed by the breaks in the bar. A crowd of locals set up camp under the shade of the beachfront home to the north of the access. Even at 9:30 a.m. they had their coolers wide open and music turned up.

I waited until noon to fire up the four-wheeler and ride up to the pier. Several rough looking men and one haggard woman greeted me with a chorus of *boos* as I approached. Each sat along a decrepit wooden bulkhead adjacent to the south side of the pier. The wall spanned the gap from the pier dumpsters to the Surf-O-Rama motel—a relic that had somehow survived the raging surf and decades of storms.

The beach at Kitty Hawk Pier was filthy. Beer cans and cigarette butts littered the sand and the wafting stench of fish floated around. I parked the four-wheeler near the steps to the pier house and took the key with me to the bathroom—a small hot room that made the dumpsters outside smell like an air freshener. I retreated back to my stand as quickly as I could when I was done. The Wall Rats—as Rick called them—waved sarcastically and gave me the finger as I drove off.

I settled back into my stand. The water was flat; the rip currents had finally subsided. I repositioned my umbrella and propped my foot up on the cross rail. The locals were grilling and the smell made me hungry. I scanned the beach and then dug through my lunch bag.

A high pitched tone brought my radio to life. The tone dropped and was immediately followed by the female voice of the county emergency dispatcher. I'd gotten in the habit of quickly turning down the alarms, especially on flat calm days. Typically it was a radio test or call for one of the supervisors to back up EMS on a routine medical call.

With my sandwich in one hand I reached for the volume knob but not before I heard, "Dare Central, Ocean Rescue Service, report of individual fallen off Kitty Hawk Fishing Pier."

I whipped my head to the north and saw a crowd gathered in the middle of the pier.

Preston responded immediately, *"702, copy, 10-17."*

Rick cut himself off when he responded. *"—undred, 10-4."*

I looked to the north. Preston's headlights zigzagged up and down the beach. He was barely to Chicahauk Street.

"702 to Byrd Street, go ahead and respond."

"Byrd Street, 10-4." I jumped from the top rung of my ladder and took one step before mounting the four-wheeler. I flipped the key, pulled back on the throttle, kicked some sand up, and blew my whistle a few times to clear a path. Parents grabbed their children. I leaned forward, and weaved my way through the maze of towels, chairs, and umbrellas until I settled into the ruts near the dunes.

I blew my whistle a few more times and held my radio up to my ear so I could hear any updates. Preston's headlights appeared under the pier. He marked up that he was on scene.

"702, 10-23."

"Whaddaya got down there Preston?" I could hear Rick's sirens coming through the radio and I wanted so badly to beat him to the pier.

"Looks like the guy's trying to swim in. I'm gonna give him a minute. He's making progress."

"10-4."

I hauled ass and even though I knew things were okay, I maintained my speed. To my left, a flash of red light caught my eye and I slammed on the breaks. Rick's truck flew onto the beach from under an elevated home where the dune had a break in it. I barely avoided a collision. Rick never saw me.

Preston's voice came over the radio again. *"Everything's 10-4 here. The, um, victim, is out of the water."*

Rick didn't slow down a bit. I was in third gear and keeping up with him. He cut his sirens when he was about twenty yards from the pier but not before he came to a complete stop. Several children covered their ears. A few parents, who hadn't even seen Preston, stood up and took notice. I rocked my bike into neutral but stayed seated on it.

Preston was talking to a man down by the water's edge. The guy was shorter than Preston—stooped over and red faced despite a patchy beard. He was dressed like the fishermen on the pier who had gathered along the railing to watch the show. The man's green shirt was completely wet, as were his shorts and his brown leather boat shoes. In his right hand was a cooler and tackle box, both of which had a steady stream of water running from the sides and the drain hole. In his other hand he held a fully rigged fishing pole. The hooks were in the eyelets and the weight swung freely as he talked with animated gestures.

I could see that Preston was trying not to laugh when his uncle walked up. Rick looked at the man and then at Preston. He stuttered while he tried to figure out what happened. The man stared back at Rick like he couldn't understand what the fuss was all about.

"Ah...Preston. What...what do we have here?"

Preston pointed to the pier house. "He didn't feel like walking all the way through the crowded building. So, he decided to take a short cut."

The man nodded like Preston explained it perfectly.

Rick got close to the man who, to that point, smiled when he spoke with Preston. The pleasant expression turned to a defensive scowl and the man took a step to match Rick's.

"It's illegal to jump off the pier," Rick growled.

"So arrest me." The man didn't miss a beat.

Rick lifted his radio to his mouth and clicked the talk button. "700, Central."

"Go ahead, 700."

"Dispatch law enforcement to Kitty Hawk Pier."

"Central copy. Reference?"

"10-53, possible 10-56."

"What's all that code for? You callin' me something? Cause if you are just say it." The man looked to Preston for answers.

Rick's energy level hadn't fallen off. He was expecting a scene even if there wasn't one. I got off my four-wheeler. There were five men sitting on the bulkhead next to the truck. Each held an identical brown bag with a dark bottleneck sticking out of the top.

The five men rose from their wooden perch and gathered near the front of the truck, poised to offer assistance to the fisherman, even if it was merely verbal encouragement.

"Leave the man alone, Rick."

I didn't see who spoke but the comment was produced by the courage of the group and the alcohol. They all knew his name—a relationship of mutual hatred. Another man, dark-skinned with long black hair, leaned against the hood. I recognized him as the man Rick called Geronimo.

"He didn't hurt no one," the man barked at Rick. "You albino prick."

Rick took a step back and turned around. He faced the five men. I stood near the rear hatch, far enough away from the group to avoid any conflict. From my safe spot Rick resembled the last kid picked in a playground. He looked around at the wet man, at Preston, at the five drunks, and at me—searching for an answer to a question that no one asked. Rick's ego was the only thing that could make the circumstances worse.

The situation was over. In two minutes a police officer would walk over the access—annoyed that he was getting sand in his patent leather shoes. He'd decide whether or not to take the jumper into custody. And, in turn, spend the rest of his day driving over to the jail in Manteo, twenty miles away, talking to the magistrate, and filling out paperwork for a simple drunk who jumped off of the pier because he was bored, or hot, or lazy, and hit his ass—"bounced" in his own words—on the shallow bottom before wading out of the water to scattered applause from the fishermen and hoots of amusement from the Wall Rats.

That's all that was going to take place and I assumed Rick had resigned himself to the fact until he opened the passenger's side door and leaned over to the console. Despite his height, he couldn't reach without one of his feet coming off the ground. The fact didn't go unnoticed by Geronimo.

"Hey, you need a lift there? Maybe one of these pretty little boys of yours could give you a push from behind?" He looked at me and pointed to Rick's ass. My upper lip twitched and I stared at him.

Rick landed clumsily in the sand and spun around. He stomped up to Geronimo and pushed his Beretta into the man's face—just under his jaw. There was a wave of "*Oh shit*" throughout the crowd and the other drunks retreated to the safety of their bulkhead. I stepped toward Rick but stopped short of the passenger's door. Geronimo was pinned against the front quarter-panel looking down his nose at the black handgun.

"Listen to me you feather-headed fuck." Rick paused.

Preston ran up to his uncle and carefully put his hand on Rick's shoulder.

Rick snarled and pressed the gun into the wedge under Geronimo's jaw. "You light my stand on fire you worthless drunk?" He cocked his head one way, then the other. "Dance around it like a good little Injun? I bet you did."

I couldn't stop staring at the gun. The only thing my eyes could focus on was Rick's finger twitching on the trigger. Preston looked at me and I shook my head like I didn't have an answer.

Rick reached into his pocket with his free hand and produced a pair of silver handcuffs. He held them out but never took his eyes off of Geronimo.

"Preston, take these."

Preston complied and took them as though they were a loaded weapon as well.

"Turn around and put your hands on the hood." Rick leaned in.

Geronimo didn't move. Rick got agitated and his thumbed brushed the safety steadily. My tunnel vision kept me from seeing Officer Laverman come over the access. His voice broke my stare.

"Put the gun down, Rick." There was a controlled firmness in his voice. "Do it now."

Rick held his position for another few seconds and then lowered the gun to his hip, keeping it aimed toward Geronimo.

"Put it away, Rick." Officer Laverman had his hand on his own weapon.

Rick handed me the gun and I nearly dropped it in the sand.

"Brett, it's a good thing you got here when you did." Rick waved his hand around like the gun was still in it.

Laverman nodded.

"This fucker was threatening my lifeguard." He turned to me—my stare still on the Beretta. "Isn't that right, Wesley?"

My glasses hid my wide eyes. I looked at Preston without turning my head and hesitated, but managed to squeeze out a forced, "Yes sir."

Again, Laverman nodded knowingly—fluent in the language of half-truth. Rick looked at me like I'd betrayed him with my pause. Geronimo said nothing. He stood with his head tilted as though the gun was still pressed against his jaw. His solemn lips were sealed tight. Rick stepped back and pointed his hand at the man.

"This feather-head was pressing on my truck and threatening my lifeguard."

I put the gun on the passenger's seat and retreated to my four-wheeler to avoid anymore testimony.

Laverman carefully pulled Geronimo's hands together behind his back. "You want to press charges, Rick?"

"Hell yes, I want to press charges. I'll go after these worthless fucks one at a time if I have to." He pointed at the bulkhead where the Wall Rats were gathered like tin cans on a fence.

At that, Geronimo broke from Laverman's grip and sprung forward, his hands free.

"You want something to press charges about you bastard?" He grabbed Rick's neck with both hands and shook with rage. His face was frozen in an expression pocked with pure malice. Preston went for his right arm and Laverman tried to pry his left hand loose but the man would not let go.

Rick made a gurgling sound and waved his arms around like they were attached to strings conducted by a spastic puppeteer. I sat on my bike, frozen with disbelief. Part of me wanted to see if Rick could defend himself. The guilt of the moment didn't hit me until later and I told no one of the secret pleasure of seeing Rick getting his ass kicked.

He fought for air—not to breathe—but to curse his attacker. "—uckin' feath—", Geronimo squeezed harder and Rick creaked out, "—head."

Laverman pulled an arm loose and pinned it behind the man but Preston wasn't as successful. I snapped out of my trance and ran at Geronimo, wrapped my arms around his waist, and drove through him like I was making an open-field tackle. All five of us fell into a sandy heap.

Rick's neck was free and turning red. Geronimo kicked and twisted but we manage to roll him to his stomach. Laverman shook the sand out of his own hair, knelt on the small of Geronimo's back, and cuffed the wriggling man. My arm was still around his waist and feeling the pressure of the man's complete weight as I lay partially pinned under him. His cutoff T-shirt reeked of cigarettes and cologne. I turned my head away and slid out from under him, rolling a few times to make some space between the man and me.

Rick was on a knee, one hand holding his strawberry-red neck and the other propping himself up. He tried to talk but the words came out more cluttered than usual. "See...charges." He shook his head as though the gesture would alleviate the pain. He managed to stand up and walk past Geronimo who, still lying on the ground, spit a mouthful of sand and phlegm at Rick's feet.

No one spoke. Rick paused.

"Oh God, don't do it," I said out loud.

Geronimo's face begged to be kicked and Rick had that look in his eye. I wished for Rick to do one thing right.

Rick looked at me the same way he did before, like I was in with Geronimo. He looked down at the man, took a half step back, paused and shuffled back to the driver's side of the Bronco. I let out an audible sigh of relief. Laverman hoisted the man up. Preston brushed himself off. I was on my knees trying to take it all in.

Laverman muscled the man toward the access and said something but I could only hear Geronimo's reply; "Nicholas Diaz...Guatemala. *I* want to press charges."

Rick closed the door and backed the Bronco up. He ran over two towels and crushed a Styrofoam cooler. The radio on my bike buzzed, *"700, clear and available, Kitty Hawk Pier."*

"Central, 10-4, 700. Incident number 238."

I told Lilly about the Battle of Little Kitty Hawk that night. Harry was at work and no one was showering under our house. We sat on the front porch. She spit her drink out a little when I told her that Rick pulled a gun on Geronimo.

"How is that legal?" She tried to hide her face while she wiped at her chin.

"I don't really know."

"And you tackled the guy?"

"Not just me, it took all of us to take him down." I shook my head. "It was a real mess."

"Sounds like it. Glad no one got shot." Lilly took a sip of beer. "And the guy jumped off the pier why?"

"He didn't want to walk through the building with his fishing rods."

She nodded like that was a sensible reason.

"I'm not looking forward to sitting there tomorrow. Who knows what I'm going to find on my stand in the morning." I finished my beer and set the empty bottle on the deck. "Have you heard from Ed?"

"No, I tried to call him this afternoon but he didn't answer."

"Do you know where he lives?" I took a sip from my bottle.

"Off Seascape Drive, why? Do you want to go over there?"

"I'd like to. What do you think?"

"Let's go." She nodded then stopped. "Actually, we've both been drinking. Maybe we should wait a little while."

"Yeah, you're right."

The water cut on under the house and Lilly looked at me.

"My neighbors."

"Your neighbors shower here?"

I explained the arrangement, skipping the part about waking up next to Liz and fearing for my life for the better part of a month. Just about the time I finished, the water shut off. There was a thud, like someone smacking the plywood shower walls followed by a soft groan.

Lilly and I stared at each other silently. We didn't move in our chairs. The sounds got louder and quickly passed the point of caring who heard them. Lilly covered her mouth with her hand and turned bright red. I took a deep breath and stared up at the porch ceiling for fear that eye contact with Lilly would make me explode with laughter.

The moans turned into directions. When I heard Liz's voice I couldn't help but remember her standing half naked in the hallway with my shirt not covering her.

"No no no, don't stop." There was a pause. "Dammit, Lucas. Are you serious?" The wood door opened, then closed, and the water eventually turned back on.

Lilly, still with her hand over her mouth, went inside and I followed her through the front door. Not until we were safely in the kitchen did she speak.

"That was interesting."

"That's a first." I shook my head. "That I know of."

"I guarantee that was not the first time that's happened down there." Lilly set her bottle on the counter.

"You're probably right."

"I'm definitely sober now. Let's go check on Ed."

Ed lived in an apartment under another rental house. His Jeep was the only car in the driveway and Lilly parked mine next to it. She tapped on the aluminum screen door and peered into the dark living room.

"Ed, you in there?" She tapped again. "Ed, it's Lilly and Wesley."

The light turned on and Ed appeared at the screen door wearing only his boxer shorts.

"Not a good time Lil." Ed leaned against the frame but didn't open the door.

"We just wanted to check on you, buddy." I stepped in front of the door.

"I'm good."

I heard the toilet flush behind Ed. Sandy stepped out of his room, saw us, backed up, and shut the door. Lilly tilted her head and looked disappointed.

"I don't need you judging me."

Lilly looked at me.

"Come on, he's fine." She took my hand and turned her back to the door.

"Hey Rookie, you need some ORS shit?" He reached to the left of the door and walked out carrying a gym bag full of shirts and shorts.

"You'll need that stuff when you come back to work." I pointed at the bag.

"Yeah, that's not happening."

"Just talk to Rick. You know it'll all blow over."

"Rick's got his own trouble."

We waited for him to continue.

"I heard he almost blew Geronimo's head off today?"

"He wasn't actually going to shoot him. Things just got carried away."

"The DA's gonna go after him for attempted murder."

"What are you talking about? That's not what happened at all." I shook my head and looked around. He dropped the bag at my feet.

"I give up on you, Rookie. Have you listened to anything I've told you this summer?"

"I've heard everything you've said," I raised my hands. "But I don't know what to believe."

Lilly took a step back and added, "You do have a way of letting your emotions cloud your judgment, Ed." She pulled at my hand but I didn't move.

"That's just not what happened." I couldn't understand what Ed was saying.

"Did Rick put a gun to Geronimo's throat?"

I searched for an answer. "Yeah, but he was defending himself."

Ed stared at me. "Would you testify to that?"

The scene replayed in flashes; Rick grabbing the gun then spinning around; the petrified look on Nicholas Diaz's face; Laverman's voice. *Drop the gun, Rick.*

"One of the deputies told me everything. There's a beach full of witnesses. People who want to see him go down regardless of if it's tax evasion, insurance fraud, embezzlement. It doesn't matter, Rick's done."

"Don't look so excited," Lilly snapped.

"The only thing that can make it better is if Buck goes down with him."

"Come on, Wesley. Let's leave Ed to his delusions." Lilly shook her head and stared at Ed. He thought about arguing but knew it was pointless. He'd made his point and his feelings known and Lilly was sick with it.

"Stay low, Rookie." Ed lifted his hand and went back inside.

I drove back to my house. Neither of us spoke for a while. Ed hadn't just left ORS, he'd left me. I'd counted on him to watch my water and back me up when things got carried away—even if he was the one who led me there in the first place.

"What can I do?" I looked straight down the road.

"I was thinking the same thing." Lilly put her hand on my leg and shook her head. "It's not your fight. Listen to him, stay out of it and get through the summer. There's only a couple weeks left."

"I'm going to school when it's done."

"That makes me happy." She nodded but didn't smile.

"I think he's right about Rick. I saw him lose it

today."

We pulled into my driveway and stayed in the Jeep when I shut off the engine.

"This'll blow over, Wesley. These things always do. The summer will end, people will go their separate ways, and next year it will all start over."

I looked up at the porch. The lights were off and my house didn't feel like home. The shower light downstairs was off and everything seemed wrong. I looked at this world I'd been living in and saw only the dark places in it. I glanced at Lilly but didn't turn my head. Her hair hung in front of her face while she looked down at her lap. I couldn't hear the ocean.

"Do you want to take me home?"

"Not really."

"What do you want to do?"

"I don't know."

Lilly looked at me. She undid her seat belt, slid it over her shoulder, and climbed onto my lap. She sat sideways with her legs together, her feet between the two front seats, and her right arm around my shoulders. I leaned my head back against the seat and smiled at her. Her bright eyes filled the dark spaces.

CHAPTER 17

I checked in early the next morning. Preston was the only one in the shack. He was surprised to see me when I walked in at eight thirty.

"Morning, Wesley. What are you doing here so early?"

"I didn't feel like making my lunch this morning, so I wanted to grab my stuff and go to Shipwreck on the way to my stand."

"I see." He reached for my equipment. "You still good to sit up at Byrd Street?"

"Yeah, no problem."

"Let me know if there are any issues when you get to your stand—if it's even there."

I laughed. "I'll prepare myself for the worst."

Preston glanced up at the camera and whispered, "Walk out to the garage with me."

I collected my gear and exited through the side door.

"What's up?" I retrieved my buoy from the rack.

"About yesterday." Preston leaned against the seat of a four-wheeler. "Are you okay?"

I was a little confused. It was obviously a lot to process, but it wasn't my issue.

"Yeah, I'm fine. Just glad no one got hurt or anything."

"Yeah." Preston crossed his arms and looked at the concrete floor. He nodded a bit but didn't say anything else.

"Are you okay?" It felt like a strange thing to ask.

Preston didn't look at me, just kept nodding.

"Like you said, just glad no one got hurt." He pursed his lips and took a deep breath. "Be safe today."

"Will do."

Preston went back in the shack and I pulled my umbrella from the pile.

I was relieved to find my stand in tact and not covered in anything gross. I avoided the pier—swimming out past the breakers to take a piss when I had to. The water was calm and aside from a lost child that we found in five minutes, the day was quiet. I never saw Rick. The crowd on the beach was noticeably thinner; a sign of the waning season. I dreaded the end of summer. I had found my stride on the beach and in less than two weeks it would be over.

The Olympics were two days away. Eager for the experience, I also knew it meant saying goodbye to everyone. Lilly started classes a week before I did. She promised to stay for the competition and wouldn't leave until the following day.

At five thirty, I packed all of my gear onto the four-wheeler and drove south toward Wright Street. When I got to the access Buck was standing by the water with Preston. Several guards were swimming and stretching in preparation for competition training.

Preston waved me over. "Take your gear to the shack and come back. We'll practice your starts for beach flags and go over a few other events."

"Okay, I'll be right back."

Preston nodded and turned back to the water.

I drove through the access and waited for traffic to clear before I crossed the beach road. Two sheriff's deputies slowed and turned west on Wright Street. I crossed and followed them into the shack's parking lot. I lifted a hand to acknowledge them and parked in the garage. The deputies stood outside their cars and talked briefly before looking over their shoulders at two more police cars entering the gravel lot. Rick's truck was gone and Buck's was in its space.

Officer Laverman got out of one of the cars and saw me in the garage.

"Mr. Brooks. Do you know where Rick is?" There was no urgency in his tone. He stood behind his open driver's side door.

"No sir, I haven't seen him today. If his truck isn't here, I'm not sure where he is." The deputies looked at each other and walked back to their cars. I pointed to the access. "Preston's on the beach."

"Thanks, Wesley." Laverman nodded at me.

"Is this about the guy at the pier?"

He took a deep breath and looked off toward the beach access. He waved for his fellow officers to go on then he shut his door and leaned back against the car.

"There's probably a lot about Rick that you don't know, Wesley."

"Like the financial issues?"

"That's where a lot of it starts."

"The Commissioner's daughter?"

"Okay, so you know a few things." He smiled.

"Is he in trouble?"

He took another deep breath and said, "You can't pull a gun on a citizen if you're not a cop. And even then, it's not a great idea unless you've got a good reason."

"But wasn't that guy..." I knew the argument was moot.

"It's not the end of the world." Laverman shook his head. "It's just an issue we have to deal with."

The radio on Laverman's shoulder chirped and a static voice said, "Central to all Kitty Hawk units, be advised, attempted suicide, one subject at Shoal Drive. Standby for address."

Laverman rolled his eyes. "It never ends."

As soon as he said it, the radio on my hip buzzed and we heard Rick's voice come across the lifeguard frequency.

"*-uck, Preston, I need ... I need you down here.*" The voice over the radio was weak and shaky. Not like Rick's. But I knew it was him by the way he cut off Buck's name.

Laverman and I looked at each other and put it all together in a split second. He slipped into his cruiser and flipped on his lights and sirens. I ran to my Jeep. Preston and Buck were on the beach and I wasn't sure if they had their radios within earshot.

"Lifeguard Brooks to 700, what's your location?"

"*Ah ... Wesley, I need you down here ... I'm... oal drive.*"

I drove straight through the empty lot in front of the shack, ignoring curbs and bushes before sliding the Jeep onto the beach road. Laverman got behind me and we raced south.

"10-4 700, advise 10-18?"

"*Yes Wesley... emergency, where's Buck?*"

"*701 to 700, I'm on my way... advise?*" Buck's voice broke up while he spoke and ran.

"*Oh Buck... Buck I've fucked up.*"

I hit the gas and passed a station wagon. My tires slid on a patch of sand. The Jeep lifted as I cut off a pickup truck coming from the south. A caravan of out-of-state tags was going thirty miles an hour in front of me. I pulled up close to the rear bumper of a red minivan and flashed my lights. The driver hit the brakes and I swerved right onto the sandy shoulder to avoid hitting the van.

I cut back onto the road and passed two small cars, this time on the left. I made it to the access going about sixty. Laverman pulled in behind me and screeched to a halt before hitting the sand. I dropped into second gear—the engine growled at the ridiculous downshift and I rumbled toward the soft sand of the ramp. The tires were solid—too inflated to drive in the sand but I didn't have time to let air out. I had enough speed to shift to third, and when I did I got bogged down in the soft sand.

"I just want... I just want to say..." Rick's voice faded as I plowed through the access and looked north; nothing but deep ruts. *"I'm sorry."*

I looked south and saw the flashing lights of his truck. The Bronco faced the water, just above the high tide line. Aside from a few fishermen to the north, the beach was empty. I cut the steering wheel hard and felt the tires shudder until they fell into Rick's tracks. Halfway to the Bronco I hit a patch of loose red sand. I was barely moving and when I dropped into first gear the Jeep stalled.

I started it again, knowing that it probably wouldn't take me any further. I could see Rick from where I stopped. There was no one in the water. The surf was so flat that nothing could have happened in the ocean.

He was in his truck with his left arm on the steering wheel. His head rested on the driver's side window pressed against the glass but from that distance I couldn't see anything else. I reached to the back seat and pulled out my first-aid kit from under the passenger's side. I only took my eyes off of the truck for a split second—not wanting to miss any movement from Rick.

In the rearview mirror I caught a glimpse of Laverman running across the dune. He looked around and clumsily ran south. I took off running too—radio in one hand and bag of useless Band-Aids in the other. I could see Rick's head wasn't moving.

My radio only transmitted our lifeguard frequency on it. I needed to go through Buck to get an ambulance.

"Brooks, 701."

"Go ahead."

"Roll EMS to 300 yards south of Shoal. Stand-by for

further." I was short on breath but my adrenaline made up for it.

"*10-4.*"

I got to the truck and saw Rick with all his weight leaning on the door. Two police officers stood up on a wooden walkover looking down at the truck. One lifted his radio to his mouth but transmitted on a separate frequency. I smacked the window with my open palm, leaving my hand against the glass where his head was. His glasses sat crooked on his nose below closed eyes.

I ran around to the passenger's side and waved for the officers to join me but they didn't move. Laverman was still a couple hundred yards away. I opened the passenger's side door. There was a nearly full cup of water in the console. I saw Rick's nine-millimeter pistol laying on the empty seat, a white box with an open bottle next to it, and pills spilled all over the place. I picked up the gun and looked at his head. There was no blood. The safety was on. I reached outside and placed it carefully on the roof.

"Rick." I leaned over and grabbed his shoulder. "Rick!"

He opened his eyes enough to see me. "Preston...I fucked up." His words were slurred and his eyelids fluttered.

"There's an ambulance on its way, Rick."

"I'm sorry."

I picked up the box and looked at the label. The bottle was twice the size of a normal orange prescription bottle and looked like the ones that line a pharmacist's shelves.

"Rick! How much did you take?"

His eyelids dropped.

I turned off the radios in his truck and took a step back. I cupped my hands around my radio and keyed up the microphone.

"701, advise Central we have a signal one – overdose. Request all available units."

"701, copy."

"We're on our way Wesley." I recognized Adrian's voice.

I took Rick's hand held radio from his console and turned the volume up enough to hear the dispatcher say, *"Central to all EMS, fire, and police units—attempted suicide on the beach at Shoal Drive public beach access—unknown PI, subject is armed, proceed with caution.*

I keyed up the central communications channel, "Lifeguard Brooks to Central, be advised subject is no longer armed—is unconscious and breathing."

The automated external defibrillator was buried under swim fins and sandy rope in the rear. I plugged the cords in while I walked back around to the driver's side. There were only three buttons on the AED: On, Analyze, and Shock. I wasn't going to hook him up until the medics got there. I just wanted to have it ready.

I grabbed Rick's door handle and when it clicked, his weight pushed the door open. I put the AED on the roof and slid one hand inside, lowering him as I opened the door. His head rested against my chest as I pulled him out. The weight was more than I expected. We fell to the sand and I looked around for Laverman.

He was only a few yards away and behind him the red lights of Buck's truck spun bright. The fire trucks and ambulances couldn't make it out in the sand and I knew it would take them a while to get there on foot.

I wiggled out from under Rick and laid him out flat. His head flopped around, resting in a slight indention on the beach. Sand stuck to his mustache and the side of his face. I didn't bother to wipe it off.

Laverman stopped and spoke on his radio but I didn't hear what he said.

I looked at the AED then I looked at Rick. I took a deep breath and stared down at him. His chest rose and fell with no unusual pattern. The color in his face was normal. I bent over and grabbed his wrist hard enough to feel his strong pulse without searching for it. I looked at my watch and counted twelve pulses in ten seconds. Normal. I dropped his hand into the sand, stepped back, and shook my head.

Preston jumped out of Buck's truck before it came to a stop. He sprinted toward his uncle and I stepped in front of him, wrapping my arms around his torso in an effort to slow him down.

"Get off me..." He twisted and leaned away from me. "Uncle Rick!"

"He's okay, man." My grip gave way and Preston collapsed on his knees next to Rick. "His pulse is steady and he's breathing fine."

"Rick!" Preston shook his uncle and looked up at me with tears streaming down his face. "Don't stand there, get the O_2."

Buck ran past me with all the gear they needed. Preston wiped his uncle's face and strapped the oxygen mask on. The clear plastic fogged up with each breath Rick took.

The two police officers came down from the walkway cautiously and stopped when I looked at them. I pointed at the roof of the Bronco.

"His gun's up there."

They were confused by the lack of urgency in my voice.

The fire utility truck pulled up. Adrian, Grey, and two paramedics jumped out of the back. I walked toward them, stopped in front of the medics, and back peddled as I spoke.

"Do you have charcoal?"

"Yeah, we've got some." The first medic asked, "You know what he took?" while looking at Rick.

"Halcion."

"Halcion?" He stopped and looked at me. "Where the hell'd he get that?"

I whispered, "Looks like he got it from a drug store

or something."

"How many did he take?"

"No telling. Half the bottle's spilled out on the passenger's side. But he barely drank any of the water in his cup holder. So, probably just enough to put him to sleep."

The medic knelt down and opened one of Rick's eyes with his thumb. I lifted my hand to tell Adrian and Grey to stay back.

"Is this the only gun in the vehicle?" Laverman held the Beretta in a plastic bag—its magazine separated. Buck nodded.

Both of the medics stood up.

"I don't think we're going to need any charcoal." The first medic looked down and put his hand on Preston's shoulder. "He'll probably just need to sleep it off."

I turned away from the group and walked past the Fire Chief and everyone else who had showed up.

"What's going on?" Adrian was wide-eyed.

I motion for them to follow me and filled them in as we walked toward the water.

"I think he just started taking pills, not enough to do any damage, just enough to knock him out." I kicked a piece of shell into the clear water. "He was sort of conscious when I got here. He thought I was Preston and he just babbled. His fucking gun was sitting right there next to him."

"What did you say to him?" Adrian was still worked up.

"I just told him there was an ambulance on the way and I asked him how many pills he took. But he nodded off."

"Were they just sleeping pills?" Grey was starting to realize the embarrassment that I was feeling—not for us, but for Preston and for ORS.

"Yeah, I guess. I don't know exactly." I searched for an explanation. "The cops were looking for him at the shack. I think he's in a lot of trouble."

"He's such a pussy." Grey cut his eyes and crossed his arms.

The three of us turned and looked at the scene. No one moved with any sense of urgency. Rick still lay in the sand. People circled around and looked down on him. It was more like a chore than an emergency.

Preston paced back and forth, pressing his hair back with his hands and then pointing at his uncle. Buck did his best to lead him back to his truck. When he got Preston in the passenger's seat he slumped down and put his hands over his face. Buck spun the truck around and drove toward us. He rolled to a stop in front of Adrian.

"Will you guys hang out until they're done with the Bronco and bring it back to the shack?"

"Of course." Adrian looked past Buck. "It's gonna be okay, Preston."

Buck drove toward the access, slowly following the utility truck where Rick lay strapped to a stretcher supported by the firemen and medics.

CHAPTER 18

I was overwhelmed when I got to the end of the boardwalk at Ocean Boulevard. There were hundreds of lifeguards and twice as many spectators gathered on the beach. Tourists and family members sat in folding chairs and on towels all along the race course. Music from the PA system flooded the beach and amplified the electric environment. Guards registering for the events and others looking for freebies surrounded a dozen tents for the sponsors and officials.

I made my way along the row of trucks and passed by the guards from other agencies. They watched me walk by without saying anything. I couldn't tell if their coldness was typical for this kind of competition or if they were allowing me to pass without acknowledging the shame of Rick's suicide attempt. Either way it pissed me off.

The ORS contingent was at the end. Several guards jogged and stretched down by the water. Some donned swim caps and goggles for the first event, the Rescue Relay.

"I was not expecting this." I set my bag down and scanned the beach.

"You need to get your number." Adrian grabbed my arm and looked around. "Hey someone find that marker for Wesley."

A black magic marker was tossed from somewhere. Adrian drew a large number one on both of my arms.

"You don't need to worry about anything that's going on around you, okay? There are plenty of people to run this thing so you just concentrate on your events." He tried to write "ORS" on my upper arms but ran out of room for the letters. The "S" wrapped around to my back. "You need to put some meat on you." He laughed and squeezed my shoulder.

"This thing's going to get started pretty quickly." Adrian pointed to the start line for the Run-Swim-Run Relay. Buck stood alone on the start line, swinging his arms back and forth to loosen up.

"You need to be ready for the cheap shots. These guys are going to throw elbows and try to trip you up in every race. You do what you gotta do, but don't retaliate or you'll get disqualified."

"Okay." I nodded and stared at the start line.

"You're fast enough to get out in front of them without worrying too much about it. Just run your race.

"Okay."

"*All racers for the Run-Swim-Run report to the start line.*"

Adrian joined Buck, Preston and Fig at the checkered flags. They lined up, Preston in the front, and got ready for the start. The main race official called out the instructions to the groups.

"Racers, on the start you will run down to the green flag, passing on the high side. Then swim out fifty yards to the yellow marker, around and back to the green flag. The checkered flags are the start and the finish line. Your teammate must wait for you to cross the line before he begins." He stepped off to the side. "Racers take your mark."

He fired the gun and the first leg began. Preston held in the middle of the pack, running controlled and saving energy for the swim. The first racers to round the green flag sprinted straight into the water. The majority of the group followed.

Preston peeled back toward the start line. He entered the water at least twenty yards north of the pack, with only one other racer—a Nags Head guard—right behind him. The strong lateral current pulled the swimmers to the south. Preston shot right to the marker with no extra effort. The first racers into the water struggled against the current and used all of their energy to get back to the yellow buoy. Preston and the Nags Head guard were halfway back before anyone else turned to come in.

Preston caught a wave on the way in, ran out of the water clean, and rounded the green flag on his way to the finish line. When he crossed, Fig took off and used the same strategy to deal with the current. The other teams learned from their mistake but it was too late to catch Fig. Buck and Adrian finished the race well ahead of Nags Head's first team, earning ORS ten points and, more importantly, giving us momentum for the other events.

The last teams crossed the finish line and the official wasted no time calling for the next event.

"All runners in the two-mile race report to the starting line."

Once again, Preston lined up for the start of the run. This time he was alone.

"Let's go Preston." Adrian dried off and got ready for the next event, my first.

The gun went off and the distance runners began their mile out, mile back course.

"Racers for the Sprint Relay report to the starting line."

I took off my sweatshirt and jogged over to the checkered flags.

"Get us a good lead." Buck nodded at me and I returned it.

"Racers, you will sprint around the fifty yard flag, passing on the high side and return. Do not begin your leg until your teammate crosses the line or you will be disqualified. Racers take your mark."

I put my head down, the gun cracked, and I shot off the line. I got a dozen steps and started to panic. I couldn't see or feel anyone on my right or left. I didn't hear anything above the screaming crowd and I feared that I had a false start. Ahead of me I saw the group of ORS guards yelling and clapping. I took a quick look back and realized that I was two full strides ahead of the pack. The green flag came up fast. I dipped my shoulder around it and turned toward the start line, fifty yards away.

The main pack of runners was right in front of me. I went high to the soft sand to avoid a collision. One runner in the rear looked more like he was jogging than sprinting. He moved sideways until he was right in front of me. I remembered what Adrian said and I took a step to the side—he matched it. I didn't have any time to dance around with him so I tucked my chin in and braced for the impact. He lowered his shoulder. Just before we collided I planted my right foot and spun off his left shoulder. The lack of expected contact sent him flying face first into the sand. The crowd erupted and I rode the rush of adrenaline across the line, slapping Fig's hand when I got there. He took off and I dropped to one knee at the back of the line.

"Never seen that before." Adrian looked down at me from the anchor spot.

"Did what I had to do."

I heard Buck laugh just before Fig crossed the line well ahead of anyone else. The ORS contingent cheered from the sidelines as he ran by.

"Go ahead and practice your start for flags." Adrian pointed to the south. "This is taken care of."

The race was over in two minutes. We cruised through the rest of the legs, winning easily. Corolla and Nags Head's first teams finished second and third respectively.

Buck and Adrian wasted no time celebrating. They

retrieved the line reel from the back of the 701 truck and set up for the Line Pull event near the high tide mark. I put my hooded sweatshirt on, grabbed some water, and looked around for a place to be alone. As I walked past the group of ORS guards I got high fives and pats on the back.

A slightly intoxicated Stanley jumped in front of me. He put his hands out to the side, juked left then right, and spun around, crashing into a Nags Head truck. He slid down the side of it and pointed at me.

"I t-t-taught him that shit."

Everyone laughed and I lifted a hand to acknowledge them. I went to the edge of the crowd and saw a clear area south of the access. The cheering got louder as the first Two-mile runner came into view. I craned my neck to see where Preston was. The only racer I could see looked like he came straight from a collegiate track meet. He crossed the line a quarter mile ahead of the next runner and checked his watch as he received congratulations from the other Nags Head guards.

Preston was coming up in second place with a runner for Corolla just behind him. The ORS guards all ran toward the checkered flags screaming for Preston. He looked over his shoulder, saw the other runner, and grimaced. As he neared the finish line the noise level on the beach was deafening. Preston's cheeks puffed in and out with each swing of his arms but the other runner closed the gap—pulling even with just twenty yards to go. Preston squeezed his eyes shut and the pain on his face reminded me of the way he looked when he watched his uncle being loaded on a stretcher.

In the days since, the shack was quiet. Guards checked in and reported to their stands on time. No one screwed around and no one spoke of Rick. When Friday came, we put away our equipment and went home, knowing there would be no pay checks.

We met late in the afternoons between our stands and wondered what would become of ORS. There were rumors of Preston taking over, of an older guard named Larry coming back to run things, but most of us accepted that the town would simply cancel the contract and go in-house. If it weren't for the Olympics, many guards might have just packed up and left but most of us felt the need to finish the summer together.

Preston threw his head back as he approached the finish line, his chest leading him. The other runner tucked his chin and leaned forward. In the final stride the Corolla guard leaned so far that his momentum sent him tumbling across the finish line—just ahead of Preston.

The Corolla contingent erupted and piled on top of their runner. Fig lifted Preston from the sand where he had dropped to his knees. Buck looked at Adrian and continued prepping for the Line Pull.

"Good luck." Lilly's voice drowned out the crowd's celebration.

"Hi." I peeked out from my sweatshirt and smiled.

"Are you about to fight someone?" She raised her fists in a feigned boxing gesture.

"It might come to that. Some of these guys play dirty."

Lilly leaned in and whispered in my ear, "I can play a little dirty too." She pulled at the strings of my hood, synching them tight and quickly skipped back, playfully dancing away and joining her friends but not before looking back and blowing me a kiss.

I practiced my starts in the deep soft sand near the dunes, quietly repeating to myself, "Feet together, chin on hands, heads up, heads down, go."

Grey walked over and nodded. "Want me to call it?"

"Yeah, that'd be great." I returned the nod from my spot in the sand.

We practiced my starts for a few minutes then took a break to watch the Line Pull get started. Teams were spread fifty yards up and down the beach. Each had a corresponding marker out in the water. Fig clipped his buoy to the line and stood at the high tide mark. Buck set the reel in the sand and Adrian pulled about twenty yards of rope off of it, stretching it in neat lines almost to the water. They were methodical in their preparation.

The other teams had their own routines; some of the swimmers started on the beach with their fins on; some teams pulled all of their line out before the start to avoid tangles; the National Park team fed their line out of a mesh bag. Regardless, the goal was the same: swim out to the victim, get him on the buoy, and use the rope to pull both the swimmer and victim back to shore, carrying the victim across the high tide mark for the finish. There was a danger with the strong current and inexperienced teams of lines getting crossed and tangled. The best way to avoid it was get out and in as quick as possible.

Preston swam out to the marker for our team before the official start. He was still recovering from his run so he took his time. As the victim, he simply had to hang on to the rescue buoy when Fig got to him.

The head official used a bullhorn to address the teams. "Race begins on my mark. Using the line, retrieve your victim and rescuer. The race is not over until all members of the team cross the high tide mark. The victim must be carried across." He checked down the long line to make sure everyone was behind the mark and then looked out to the victims. He signaled to another official on a Jet Ski in the water. "Take your mark."

The gun popped and Fig sprinted toward the water. Adrian ran just behind him holding several loops of line in his hand. Buck stood with a foot on the reel to keep it secure in the sand. Fig planted his foot on the ledge and got a good push, diving through the small shore break. He slipped his fins on before coming to the surface without missing a stroke.

Adrian gave him slack while Buck controlled the feed to prevent tangles. Adrian waded out until the water was to his waist and held the rope over his head. He let it slide through his hands as Fig made progress—the elevated rope preventing drag in the water.

Nags Head's second team was to the south so their line wouldn't have any effect. The National Park team was lined up to the north. They used the same technique as Adrian, but they fed too much line out. The current carried their slack close to Fig's line. As long as it didn't cross too much it wouldn't be a problem. There was a slight bow in Fig's line, but nothing to be concerned about. He was well ahead of either team to the left or right and it appeared they'd have no problem coming in first.

Buck watched Fig intently, gauging how much rope to let out. Adrian moved back up to the shallow water, waiting for the signal to start pulling. Buck jogged down to the edge of the water. He gripped the rope and laid it across his shoulder, turning his back to the ocean but watching Fig the whole time. Adrian waited for Buck to start pulling. The signal didn't come.

Adrian looked back and tried to figure out what the problem was. Fig was stuck dead in the water just a few yards from Preston. The official on the Jet Ski sat just outside of the marker watching the whole situation. Fig looked back and yanked on the line but it didn't budge. There was no tangle and plenty of slack in the water. Preston pointed to the problem and Fig started swimming back to shore.

The rescuer for Nags Head's second team was ten yards back, holding Fig's line just below the surface of the water. He saw Fig coming and took a few side strokes to get away. Fig dove under, disappearing completely.

The other swimmer looked around. He back peddled to avoid the fight that was coming to him but all he could see was Fig's buoy drifting a few feet from him. He didn't have to wait long to find out what Fig's plan was. He disappeared under the water, clawing at the surface as Fig pulled him down. Fig wasted little time. I had no idea what happened under water but when they surfaced, Fig sprinted back toward Preston and the Nags Head guard grabbed his own buoy, coughing up a mouthful of water as he recovered.

Fig reached Preston, gave the signal, and held on to the buoy's handles. Buck and Adrian lowered their heads and ran toward the dunes. The slack in the line disappeared quickly. When Adrian reached the soft sand he dropped the line, ran back down to the water, and fell in line a few steps behind Buck. They repeated the circuit several times until Preston and Fig were within reach. Fig screamed for Buck and Adrian to retrieve them.

"Let's go. Come on, get him up there." Fig lifted Preston by his skinny knees while Preston lay across the buoy, holding on to each side handle.

"Those fucking cheaters." Buck grabbed one side of the can, Adrian the other. They carried Preston across the finish line and set him down in the sand. Fifty yards to the north Nags Head's first team celebrated their victory.

Buck found the closest official and made his case. Adrian and Preston cleaned up the reel and sandy rope. Fig waited by the water for the other swimmer. I watched the results go up on the scoreboard as they came in.

Perspective is a difficult thing to have when you're eighteen. Everything is fleeting. There is urgency in each moment because you genuinely don't know what is coming next. Predictability is the death of youth.

I was in a tunnel. Voices around me became a monotone hum. The lights from a dozen trucks shined in on me as I walked toward the start line. I stripped off my sweatshirt and dropped it to the sand, entering the arena as the unexpected hero.

Reporters from the local newspapers set up behind the rubber flags, ready to snap a picture of the winner diving for a piece of cut garden hose. Readers would glance over the picture the next morning, chuckling at the serious expression on my face as I reached out for the prize. On the other side of the dunes, cars and minivans zipped along the beach road, looking for ice cream shops and places to buy three T-shirts for ten dollars.

A hundred miles to the north, Rick rested in a hospital bed. He would come back to the beach quietly a few weeks later. All of the guards would be gone—off to school or already collecting their paychecks from their winter jobs.

I stood near the starting line and watched the other racers stretch and confer with their teammates about strategy. Lilly sat with Harry, Grey, and Adrian. I scanned the back of the crowd, hoping to see Ed. The sun had completely set behind the dunes and darkness crept in from the ocean.

"Wesley."

I turned to see Preston standing at the edge of the crowd that had gathered around the race field.

"Hey."

"You know we need this."

"Yeah, I know." I reached out to shake Preston's hand. He looked down and smiled.

He took my hand and put his other on my shoulder.

"You're the fastest one out here. Don't play their games, just go straight and—"

"Stay low."

Preston nodded and took a step back.

I lined up and got ready. The official announced the rules while I focused on my start. The entire group turned, dropped down, and crossed their hands. The official checked everyone's feet.

"Grab your flag and wait for confirmation that the round is over. Feet together, chin on your hands. Heads up heads down." He paused and I looked up to see what was wrong. "GO!"

Shit. I spun, pushed off, and put my head down as I ran. The flags came up fast and I dropped to my knees in front of one before gripping it tight. On my right, two guards from other agencies dove for one flag. On my left, Regal sat and smiled at me. I stood up, waited for the whistle, and dropped my flag.

I found my starting spot again and stood with my hands on my hips, waiting for the whistle. When I heard it I lay down. The official walked down the line checking feet.

He stopped in front of me and said, "Watch your start. Lift your head like that again and you'll be disqualified."

"Yes sir."

I found my groove as each round passed. The official changed up his cadence each time and left us guessing, but with each grabbed flag, the ORS contingent roared and gave each other high fives. After the fifth round, they chanted, "WES-LEY WES-LEY."

I avoided Regal the best I could but when there were only four racers remaining, the official waved us over to draw straws for our starting position. I drew the first spot, followed by Regal, Nags Head's second team runner, and a guard from Corolla. I knew they'd try to cut me off if they could get a step in front of me and I vowed to myself not to let that happen.

When the official yelled, "Go" we spun and I looked for the flags. There was one right in front of me but Regal was on my hip. The two of us were a full stride in front of the others. I kept even with Regal and felt him pushing against me. He ignored the flag coming up in front of him and set his eyes on mine. Just before we dove, I stutter-stepped and watched him fly by. I had enough time to dive for the flag in front of him—causing the other guards to fight for the remaining one. They both landed on their sides, the flag equally between them and each with two hands holding tight.

They tugged and tried to roll away with the flag. Whistles blew from the officials and they ran in to break up the tie before it came to punches. The racers separated and the official pointed to the starting line.

"Run off."

We all walked back to the line but Regal and I stood aside while the other two set up to race for the third spot. I walked away from the group and knelt in the sand. Regal watched me and followed. I took a deep breath. He stood uncomfortably close to me while the other racers waited for the flag to be placed. I felt him looking at me and I couldn't take it anymore.

"What?" I cut my eyes and was ready for just about anything he said to me.

"Sorry." He reached out his hand and looked me straight in the eye. "For what I did to Ed's car and for what all of you guys are going through with Rick."

My hands were pressed against my knees and I waited for the punch line. He paused for a moment.

"I'm not going to let you win or anything." He dropped his empty hand to his side. "But at the end of the night, we're all out here for the same reason."

I wanted to stay pissed. I needed the motivation. Rick's episode had rippled through the county and embarrassed everyone in red shorts. It didn't even make the back page of the newspaper—it was that shameful.

I stood up, offered my hand to Regal. He took it and I said, "Good luck. I'll tell Ed what you said when I see him."

"Thanks. See you at the finish line."

We joined the other Nags Head guard who won the run off. I drew the middle spot and rolled my eyes. It didn't matter, my start was perfect and I matched Regal's strides all the way to the finish line. The other guard didn't even sprint—conceding halfway through the course. He used the last of his energy during the run-off.

Regal and I dropped the flags without a word. I felt the noise from the crowd closing in as I walked back to the start. The headlights from each rescue truck focused on the finish line. Photographers jockeyed for position behind the last flag. I dropped to my knees and spread the sand in front of me flat.

Strange things happen when you clear your mind. Focus has a way of turning your thoughts to the simplest memory. I stared at the sand. The ground shuddered when Regal dropped to his knees next to me. I took a deep breath and let it out slowly. The crowd got quiet. The official stood with his hands on his knees in front of us.

"Feet together."

I saw footprints in the sand—a long line of them during a morning run.

"Chin on hands."

I saw the pier and my arm reaching out to slap the piling.

"Heads up."

I saw Lilly sitting on her beach towel.

"Heads down."

I saw Rick unconscious in the sand.

"Go!"

There was nothing when I ran—no noise; no feeling beneath my feet; no burn in my chest. I couldn't feel Regal and I didn't look for him. I knew he was there. I timed my dive perfectly—aiming for the base of the flag. *Stay low. Stay low.* There was a bright flash and I once again felt nothing. With my eyes closed, my hand landed on sand and quickly reached for the flag but it was gone.

The roar of the crowd smacked me like a wave. I opened my eyes and saw Regal standing with his arms extended in victory—the flag held securely in his right hand. The Nags Head guards swarmed him. He held them back with his free hand and reached down to help me up. I took his hand, nodded as I stood, and gave in when he embraced me.

"I'll see you next summer, Brooks."

"Yeah." I took a step back. "Congratulations." The crowd filled in around Regal and thinned out everywhere else. I walked toward the area where I'd left my gear in hopes that everyone would be gone by the time I got there.

Trucks backed up and threw light everywhere. ORS guards walked over the access quietly. Lilly stood in the light of the last truck in line. She wore my sweatshirt and held her purse in one hand. With the other she waved—her hand hidden by the long sleeve. She didn't look at me with pity. Her head was tilted and she watched me walk toward her.

Before I could say anything I felt several arms wrap around my shoulder. I spun and tried to keep my feet but the weight of my attackers sent us all to the ground. I wiggled to free myself and looked around. Adrian and Grey laughed and rolled off of me.

"Hell of an effort, Rookie." Grey slapped my back, leaving a sandy hand print.

"You were this close." Adrian held up his fingers and pinched them together. "He just had a longer reach."

"I'll get him next year." I brushed myself off and slapped Grey on his back, hard.

"That's the spirit!" Grey pushed himself up and wiped at the sand. "Come on, we're going to Magnolia Street to celebrate."

"Celebrate second place?"

"Celebrate the end of the most fucked up season yet."

"Cheers to that, but I'm," I looked at Lilly, "gonna have to pass tonight."

"Ah, gotcha." Grey smiled. "Don't be in a hurry to get to the finish line tonight."

"I can hear you, Grey." Lilly shook her head.

I pushed his shoulder. "Get out of here. Maybe we'll stop by Magnolia."

CHAPTER 19

"I'll just be a minute." I held the screen door open while Lilly took a seat in one of the wooden deck chars.

Harry was in the kitchen and raised his head when I walked in.

"That was pretty cool tonight. I didn't realize you were so fast."

"I just wish I'd been one step faster."

"Still pretty cool. I can see why you're so into it."

"Thanks for coming tonight."

"Sure. Maybe you can get me a job next summer?"

"Absolutely." I started down the hallway. "Hey, Lilly and I might stop by the lifeguard house. They're having a low key thing if you want to come with us."

"I'll get ready."

I was greeted at Magnolia Street with handshakes and slaps on the back from the guards who could still see straight. It was barely nine o'clock but the party felt like it was on its last legs. I introduced Harry to a few people and quietly made the rounds. Lilly and I ended up on the back deck with Adrian.

"Back to school tomorrow?" Adrian asked Lilly.

"I'm all packed." She squeezed my hand without looking at me. "My father insists on driving me to Greenville."

"And you?" He looked at me.

"I've got a couple days left, then up to Virginia to see my parents before school starts."

Adrian ran his hand through his hair and looked at me. "Got more than you bargained for this summer, didn't you, Rookie?"

"It was definitely a learning experience." I looked at Lilly. Her lips turned up into a smile but her eyes didn't match.

I hopped off the railing and pumped on the keg. It sputtered and sprayed foam into my cup. I dumped the dregs into the bucket, placed the cup on the handle, and looked through the kitchen window.

"Hey, come here." I looked back at Lilly. "You see this?"

Harry and Sandy sat on one of the living room couches. She had one knee up under her and a hand on his leg. Harry saw us through the window and gave us a silly thumbs-up.

"Oh, no." Lilly put her hand on my shoulder. "Should we warn him?"

"Should we warn her?"

We looked at each other and laughed.

"Let's ditch him," I whispered.

"That's so mean."

"It's not, I promise." I smiled and she knew what I meant.

I took her hand and led her down the back steps. When we reached the driveway she retrieved her keys and asked, "Wanna go to the beach?"

"Why Miss Lilly, how many guys have you taken to the beach this summer?"

"You're hilarious." She stopped and looked at her mother's car. "Shit."

Buck's truck was backed into the driveway and left no room to get around. There were other cars parked on the side but the sand was too deep for the low Cadillac to drive through.

"Guess we'll just have to walk." I started toward the street.

"I don't want to go to the beach right here—too many people. Plus it'll be harder to get the truck moved later tonight."

"I'll go see if I can find him."

Lilly looked at me.

"It's fine. I think he and I are okay now." I ran up the stairs and looked around the living room. I didn't see Buck anywhere. Stanley sat at the picnic table in the kitchen.

"You know where Buck is?"

"Probably his room, why?"

"He's blocking us in."

Stanley shrugged.

"Thanks."

I walked down the hallway to Buck's room. I stopped before knocking and listened at the door. I didn't hear anything. I tapped on the hollow wood door and said his name. There was no answer.

The bathroom door opened behind me and Buck walked out. He wore only his boxer shorts. He squinted when he saw me.

"You say my name?"

"You're blocking me in."

"Oh."

I stepped aside and he opened his door without turning the light on.

"I can move it if you want to give me the keys."

"You can't drive the truck."

"I'll just pull it out and back in."

"You're not on the insurance."

"Buck, there is no insurance, remember?"

He looked at me. His eyes were red and he was barely able to keep them open.

"I got it."

I followed him down the hallway. He walked out the front door in his underwear. Lilly saw him coming and got in the car quickly to avoid any conversation. She started her car and watched us walk by. I joined her while Buck pulled the truck up. We slipped out quickly and Buck backed the rescue truck into place.

"That was almost too easy."

"I think he's over the whole thing." I paused. "Or just too drunk to care."

"Probably the second one. Where are we going?" Lilly looked up and down the beach road.

"Byrd Street is pretty quiet."

We parked in the access lot and walked over to the beach.

"Wanna walk to the pier?" I pointed to the left.

"Not really." A mischievous smile appeared. "I kinda wanna to go for a swim."

"Don't have to ask me twice."

Lilly quickly stripped down to her bra and underwear. She looked around and then darted straight toward the water. I got my shirt off before she made it to the high tide line and was working on my shorts when she splashed through the first small wave. The current still pulled to the south but nothing like it had during the Olympics. Lilly was only a few yards from where she slipped in when I hurdled a wave and dove into the waist-deep water.

When I surfaced, I looked around but didn't see her. The moon was still rising from the east and casting a warm orange glow across the rippling water. I heard Lilly giggle and looked quickly to my right. She sprung from the water and wrapped her arms around my shoulders. She twisted and pulled in an effort to tackle me but I stood tall and straight, laughing at her attempt. She looked at me and growled.

"Just let me win."

"I've lost enough tonight."

"The difference is," her lips were an inch from mine, "now when you lose you still win."

"How's that?"

She slipped her ankle behind mine and pulled with everything she had. At the same time she pushed me square on my chest. My hands flew back in wild circles and I landed with a spectacular splash. The water was shallow enough for me to sit upright with my chest still above the surface. Lilly climbed on my lap and squeezed my sides with her knees. My back was to the small incoming waves. With each one that rolled in she pushed up on my shoulders and then rocked back down on my lap.

"You win." My hands extended behind me, holding both of our weight from tumbling backward. Lilly's hair was pressed back. Her high cheeks framed her bright blue eyes while a stream of water trickled between them and down the side of her nose. When the water reached her lips it bent and took a detour around her smiling mouth. She lifted up and leaned over my face. A drop of saltwater fell from her chin to mine.

"So do you." She kissed me deep and pressed down against me. With one hand she reached down and pulled at the waistband of my boxers. I leaned forward, freeing my own hands and wrapped them around her cool wet back. Our energy was only matched by the incoming waves. They splashed around us and moved on toward the shore.

I dropped my hands to her lace underwear and attempted to peel them off. Her knees were still pressed against my side and it limited how far they'd go. She reached down with her other hand and moved them to the side—working her way into my shorts at the same time.

My closed eyes saw flashes each time her hands moved. I opened them and saw red lights coming over the access.

"What the hell?"

"What?" Lilly bolted upright and stared at me. She saw my eyes looking past her and quickly turned to see Buck's truck making a deep turn by the water's edge.

"Is he looking for us?"

"I don't know. He must have seen your car in the parking lot. He's psychotic."

"Does he see us?" Lilly dropped down in the water in an effort to hide from Buck's headlights.

"I don't think so." I didn't move.

A passenger leaned out of the window and swept a spotlight along the water's edge. The truck continued north toward the pier. We had drifted slightly south of the access and were out of range of the light.

"I don't think this is about us." I watched the truck drive north.

A blue light flashed past the access and flickered in and out of the spaces between the oceanfront homes.

"Something's happening down at the pier." I adjusted my shorts and turned toward the shore.

"So let it happen." Lilly's voice was sharp. "I'm sure they can get along without you."

"Are you sure?" I craned my neck to the north. "Do you remember how drunk Buck was when we left?" I slipped out from under her and stood up.

"Are you kidding me?"

"I have to."

"You're an idiot."

The truck swerved a few times near the dunes as the tires searched for solid ruts. When it got a few yards from the pier the driver cut the wheel and pointed toward the water, shining the headlights through the pilings.

I wasted no time slipping my shorts on and picking up Lilly's clothes. I met her by the water and kept an eye on the lights of the truck. Shadows of at least two people appeared and disappeared quickly against the wooden pilings. Lilly took her clothes and I sprinted north.

The lowered tide offered plenty of room to run. I tried to see what was going on but nothing was making sense. Blue lights rotated in the parking lot and an officer ran up the ramp and into the pier house. He and his flashlight reappeared a few seconds later, stopping every few yards and shining the light down on the calm water below.

When I reached the truck both doors were open. The Jet Ski was gone and there were drag marks from the bed all the way to the water.

I called out, "Buck!" There was no answer. The floodlight shined bright on the floor of the passenger's side. I grabbed it and trained it on the water.

The hull of the capsized Jet Ski lit up when I swept the light from left to right. It was only a few yards from the shore and no one was near it. I ran to down to the edge.

"Hey," A deep voice came from my right.

I whipped the light around and saw Buck wading through waist-deep water just south of the ski.

"What's going on?"

"What are you doing here?"

"I was down at Byrd Street." I pointed to the south. When Buck followed my finger he saw Lilly.

"We got this." Buck waved his hand at us.

"Who's we?"

"Stanley is around here somewhere."

"What happened to the ski?"

"Don't worry about it, Rookie. You two love birds can get the fuck out of here." Buck turned and walked toward the truck.

"Come on Wesley, I told you." Lilly stood a few yards from me with her arms crossed.

Adrian and Grey appeared on the bulkhead next to the Surf-O-Rama. They jumped down and ran toward Lilly and I when they saw us.

"What happened?" Adrian looked at the water and

the overturned ski.

I shook my head. "Not sure, we were down the beach and saw Buck's lights. What was the call?"

"Buck got paged out for a nine-one-one call about someone falling off the pier. Stanley went with him."

"Guess whoever it was made it to shore." Grey looked out at the calm water. "Should we go get the Jet Ski?"

The ski slowly drifted to the south. Someone yelled from the end of the pier and we all turned our heads. The police officer's light was focused on something between the pilings—a hundred yards out. We couldn't understand what he said but there was panic in his voice.

The three of us sprinted toward the pier. Adrian pointed to the steps and called out to Grey, "Go up there and see what he's yelling about." He turned to me as we ran and said, "Grab a buoy off the truck rack."

Buck sat in the truck, unable to hear the officer. I smacked the window with my hand and then went to retrieve a buoy from the holder on the passenger's side. It was missing. I ran behind the truck and grabbed the driver's side buoy and met Adrian at the water in a full sprint.

I put my head down and pulled as hard as I could, checking the pier as a reference with each breath. Adrian cruised along and was yards ahead of me in moments. I lifted my head when I was near the end of the pier and heard Grey screaming.

"He's under the pier! He's tangled!"

Adrian yelled to me, "Come around wide. There are fishing lines everywhere."

I stopped where I was and tried to understand what was going on. The narrow beam of light from the officer was steadily trained from above but danced around when it hit the water. The pier lights glowed stronger and reflected off dozens of broken fishing lines, hooks, and lures left discarded among the barnacle covered pilings.

"STANLEY!" Adrian's voice cracked when he screamed. He allowed the waves to slowly push him under the pier. I swam around to the end, searching for a place that was clear enough to get in. I found a spot and slipped out of the buoy strap to avoid getting it caught. We got to Stanley at the same time.

His only movement came when a wave passed and pushed him against a piling. A large treble hook pierced the skin of his wrist and suspended his entire arm just above the surface. His head was face-down in the water and his buoy bobbed just inches from his neck.

We both screamed his name but he didn't react. I grabbed his buoy to get it away from us but the yellow line that held the strap was wrapped around the piling. When I tugged on it Stanley's head dipped further below the surface. Adrian reached out and grabbed his hair. He pulled back with one arm and tried to roll Stanley onto his back.

He wasn't able to turn him completely because of the hook and whatever else was tangled around Stanley's body. Adrian pulled again on his hair, this time pushing on Stanley's back with his foot. We saw his face.

His eyes stared straight up to the light. His open mouth hung like a ventriloquist's dummy. The yellow line and strap from the buoy wrapped tight around his neck. Adrian pulled himself up with one stroke and landed his own mouth on Stanley's. He attempted to force some air down but it didn't go.

I reached for the line with one hand and tossed the buoy toward the piling that it was wrapped around. I pulled but it didn't budge. I put my foot against the piling for leverage and pulled again. That time the buoy whipped around and sprung free but not before I sliced my foot on the thick layer of barnacles.

I unwrapped the line from Stanley's neck and Adrian tried to get air in again. It didn't work and he looked at me.

"We don't have time for this. We have to get him out of here."

I nodded and tried to push the hook out of Stanley's skin. Two of the three treble hooks were in tight so I pulled on the entire line and it eventually snapped from where it was caught.

We towed Stanley toward the end of the pier and just before we cleared the last piling something pulled back against us. We each had a grip under his arms and pulled harder but he wouldn't budge.

"Something's wrapped around his leg." Adrian pointed but I was already reaching for whatever it was. I felt a thin line cutting into his ankle and tried desperately to unwrap it. I could only go by what my hands could feel. Lead weights rapped my knuckles and snap swivels spun, but I couldn't break his leg free.

"I need help."

"Grab my hand under his back."

I reached down and felt Adrian grab my wrist. Our arms supported Stanley's body while we worked on freeing him. Grey screamed from above.

"The medics are on the way. I'll meet you at the beach." He ran toward the pier house.

We pulled but had no leverage. Each wave threatened to push us back under the pier. We tried to keep tension on the line in hopes of popping it free. Finally, the line snapped and sent Stanley's head back under water.

Adrian and I regrouped, grabbed him under his arms, lifted his head and pulled toward the shore with everything we had left.

"Stanley!"

"Stanley!"

We screamed his name between every breath as we swam. His eyes stayed open the whole way in.

Buck and Grey splashed through the shallows and grabbed his feet. The four of us carried him to the edge of the water and set him down on the hard packed sand. Adrian immediately began chest compressions. Grey ran to the truck and retrieved the O_2 canister that he had already set up.

He placed the bag valve mask on Stanley's face and cranked the regulator. I held the rubber mask gasket to create a tight seal. Adrian settled into his rhythm of compressions and called out to Grey, "Breath!" Grey squeezed the bag and Stanley's chest rose. "It's going in. Again!"

Buck hooked up the AED and peeled the stickers from the monitor pads. He wiped at Stanley's chest and placed the pads. The machine beeped and a mechanical voice said, "*Monitoring.*"

There were two more beeps and the machine's voice said, "*Preparing to shock.*"

We moved back.

"*Delivering shock.*"

Stanley's body quivered.

"*Monitoring.*"

Two beeps.

"*Preparing to shock.*"

We watched.

"*Delivering shock.*"

Stanley shuddered again.

"*Monitoring.*"

Two beeps.

"*Preparing to shock.*"

I heard a faint cry behind me.

"*Delivering shock.*"

I turned to see Lilly holding her hands over her mouth. I stood up and walked toward her. Adrian continued chest compressions. Medics raced past me.

Buck stumbled back when a medic knelt in front of him. He stood and stared down at Stanley. The only noise came from the half dozen radios around us. We watched the medics work knowing the outcome as well as they did. Lilly buried her face into my chest and I turned my head to watch. A medic put his hand on Adrian's shoulder and whispered for him to stop. He wouldn't. The medic tried again but Adrian smacked his hand away and continued pumping until his arms buckled beneath him. He collapsed and rested his forehead on Stanley's chest.

When Buck saw this he erupted.

"NO!" He stepped toward Stanley but was held back. "Keep going!" Buck swung at one of the medics but it was a clumsy effort and was easily avoided. The officer from the pier grabbed Buck's arm and bent it behind his back. He quickly put his handcuffs on the wrist he controlled. Buck felt the steel on his skin and went limp.

The officer reached for the other hand and said, "This is just until you calm down, Buck."

Buck fell to his knees and looked up at the officer. His head dropped and he sat back on his heels.

"Have you been drinking, Buck?"

"What the fuck are you asking me that for?"

"You rolled the Jet Ski and I can smell it."

Buck didn't answer. He watched the medics load Stanley on a backboard and carry him up to the steps. Laverman met them at the top of the stairs and waited for them to pass before making his way to the other officer. They spoke briefly and each looked out to the Jet Ski. It had washed to shore and rocked gently as the waves lapped against the hull. Laverman waved for me to join him.

"Brooks, what did you see?"

I let go of Lilly and gestured with one hand. "We were down the beach and saw the truck come over. When I got here Buck was coming out of the water. Stanley must've swam out to help but," I pointed to the end of the pier and managed to say, "got tangled." Something swelled up in my throat. The pressure built in my head and tears streamed down my face. I tried to talk through them but my mouth wouldn't let the words come out.

"Sorry, Wesley. Now's not the time." Laverman put his hand on my shoulder. He turned me around and pointed me toward Lilly. Then he looked down at Buck. I heard him say, "Right after the nine-one-one call about the pier jumper, we got another call about someone driving the rescue truck under the influence."

Buck's head was still hung; his hands secured behind him. He shrugged without a word. Snot and tears dripped from his nose into the sand.

Adrian sat by the water, holding his knees to his chest. Grey stood next to him. I looked around at the crowd that had gathered. People staying at the Surf-O-Rama watched from their porches. In the moonlight I saw random figures quietly standing everywhere. At the south edge of the motel deck someone leaned against the building's cedar siding. I stopped a few feet away from Lilly.

"What is it?" She wiped her face with the back of her hand and followed my stare. When she turned, the figure stood straight and disappeared behind the motel.

"I know what this is." I craned my neck. "He did this." I took off in a full sprint. I'd forgotten about my cut foot. It stung with each step but didn't slow me.

I turned the corner and saw a man walking under the neighboring house. I called out to him, "Stop!"

The man quickly turned. He was confused but saw the look on my face and took a step toward me.

"Do you need help, son? Is everyone okay down there?"

My shoulders dropped. I didn't recognize him.

"No sir. I'm sorry. I thought you were someone else."

He lifted his hand and turned back to the steps of his cottage.

I scanned the beach through swollen eyes. Lilly ran up to me.

"What are you doing?" She grabbed my arms but I looked past her.

"He's here somewhere."

"Who?" Her voice pleaded for me to make sense.

"Ed." I looked at her. "He did this."

"Oh Wesley, stop." She reached up and wiped my face. "You're upset."

"I know I am, but this is Ed. Don't you see?"

Lilly cried and banged her fist on my chest. "Stop it, Wesley."

"The nine-one-one call with no one there." I pointed at the pier. "He knew Buck would respond." I looked around. "He's here somewhere; he wouldn't miss seeing Buck in handcuffs."

"I can't take this anymore." She threw her hands up, stared at me for a moment, and then turned toward Byrd Street.

She walked back to her car alone.

I sat in the sand with Grey and Adrian. We watched the police investigate the scene and answered their questions. I didn't say anything about Ed until we got back to Magnolia Street. Grey and Adrian listened without argument. We took a few shots of whiskey and walked to his house. His car was gone. Everything was cleared out. There was no note—no cute words of wisdom scribbled on a tide chart. There was nothing.

Word of Stanley's death quickly spread around the beach towns. Guards who had already left for school drove back the moment they heard. As the nights passed we gathered at each other's homes unsure of what to do.

Rick was gone. Buck was released on bail—charged with suspicion of DWI and under investigation for manslaughter. He disappeared and everyone assumed he'd gone to Virginia to be with his family. We speculated about whether he'd come back for the service. He didn't.

EPILOGUE

We scattered his ashes so that Stanley would always be a part of something he treasured and so that we could move past the thing that scared us all—mortality. I was in the middle of the group that morning—swimming to the horizon with him floating around us; but the lens of a newspaper reporter frames my memories of that day. The picture that appeared the next morning on the front page of the Coastal Times had a small article with the headline reading, "Lifeguards remember one of their own."

When sunlight meets the ocean and reflects back upon itself, spreading across the soft North Carolina sand, it's impossible to look away. When twenty boys swim out into that ocean and the silver light of morning provides a backdrop that can't be recreated on film or paper or even the imagination, I accept that there are moments we are never meant to understand and that my feet are forever wet with them.

I left the beach that September. The town of Kitty Hawk came in and seized all of Rick's property. I joined the other freshmen at a small private college in Virginia, unpacking my things in a dorm room no bigger than the kitchen of my house at the beach. I met the nineteen-year-old resident advisor who would guide me through my first semester and help me make the right decisions; decisions far too difficult for a freshman to make—registering for classes and understanding the meal plan. I joined the ranks of the doe-eye students and the boys on the hall eager to start their own life's adventure. They sensed my sour attitude toward the rules and they showed worrisome glances when I scoffed at the curfew. I had become what I despised most—a regular prick.

After a few weeks of alienating myself from those I viewed as kids, I slipped off my high horse and rejoiced in the simplicity of worrying about exams and choosing a date for the Fall Formal. My summer faded and I pushed it away. It was a movie I watched once but didn't want to see again. I felt I had better things to do.

Four years passed and college was over. I had a whole different episode to put on the shelf but I felt nostalgia calling me. I looked at old photos—me in red shorts holding my buoy by my side—my best friend; a shot of Magnolia Street, captured on the back deck with Ed, Grey, and me. I laughed and put the shoebox away, next to the one marked "old letters and family pictures". I ignored the note in the box from Lilly. I'd read it so many times when I got it in the mail that just seeing the envelope made me sad. She asked me to give her time before visiting. I never saw her again.

Now I have my own family and I find myself sitting back at Wilkins Street for my annual vacation; my wife shopping at the outlet mall; my son plugging quarters into a video game on the pier—which has a lifeguard again. I sit here alone on the beach wiping sand from my mouth and catching glimpses of Lilly—rolling over on her beach towel and looking like a movie star so much that it hurts. I hear the radio spitting out ten-codes behind me and other codes that I don't understand but know to be inside jokes, carefully designed to sound official.

I was one of twenty guards at ORS that summer; the next year Kitty Hawk hired even more. As the patches of sand decreased—covered with blankets and towels and fat northern bodies, the number of guards increased. The town of Kill Devil Hills started its own agency. Nags Head had forty guards. Duck, Corolla, and the National park all had agencies bursting with better swimmers, faster runners, and better looking guards—both men and women.

Relics before we were twenty years old—outdated and as useful as the metal buoys that once hung from the rafters in the shack. We huddled together under Rick's umbrella. I may not have thrown chairs off balconies or been busted with two underage girls and a case of beer, but there is forever a sense of guilt by association. While I silently condemned it, I laughed at the jokes, I slapped high fives at the clueless girls, and I waited—oh, God—I *waited* for the poor fools to get in trouble.

We left this place—my beach—but it hasn't changed. We didn't have as much power as we thought. The sand still shifts, the water still swirls and dances, and the wind still blows onshore from the northeast—cutting the sandbars and opening up rip currents that only the trained eye can see. The tourists still ignore the warnings. Not until someone pulls them out of the water—grown men coughing and fighting back tears of embarrassment— do they understand. The pounding surf makes the warnings hard to hear; the sunlight glaring off of the beautiful water makes it hard to see the red flags.